"Great God Almighty," Phelps bawled. He was the first to see the approaching Sioux, and the first to die. He got his hands on his rifle, but as he lifted it to his shoulder, two arrows thunked into his chest. Falling flat on his back, he watched in silent terror as his blood pumped out around the deadly shafts. His comrades were no more fortunate than he. Only Nemo got off a shot, and it slammed into the ground at his feet. It was over in no more than a minute. Some Indians had already caught up the horses, while others sacked saddlebags. There were shouts of glee when they discovered the remaining store of whiskey in the buckboard. In the distant thicket, Christie Beckwith bellied down, trembling. She was unable to take her eyes off the gruesome scene unfolding before her. Some of the Sioux were taking scalps. . . .

NorTH
TO THE
BitterrooT

Ralph Compton

St. Martin's Paperbacks

NORTH TO THE BITTERROOT

Trail map design by L. A. Hensley.

Copyright © 1996 by Ralph Compton.

ISBN: 0-312-95862-5

Printed in the United States of America

St. Martin's Paperbacks edition/October 1996

St. Martin's Paperbacks are published by St. Martin's Press, 175 Fifth Avenue, New York, NY 10010.

10 9 8 7 6 5 4 3 2 1

This work is respectfully dedicated to L. A. Hensley, who shares my appreciation for the old ways, the old days, and trails grown dim.

AUTHOR'S
FOREWORD

❧

*W*estward ho, the wagons!

The trail led west, toward the setting sun, and those who undertook the journey were as diverse as their reasons for going. But the dangers and hardships of the trail were only the beginning. Blizzards, hostile Indians, outlaws, and possible starvation often lay at the end of the trail, where survival became the ultimate test.

Men labored in the diggings in Colorado, Wyoming, Montana and Dakota territories, spending much of their earnings on food. These were the days before the railroads, and all supplies depended on the courage and resourcefulness of men who freighted goods over the treacherous trails. Food, clothing, medicine, ammunition—everything—had to be freighted in on pack mules or in sturdy, mule-drawn wagons.

There was no "easy" trail. Freighting from California involved crossing the formidable Rocky Mountains, where drifted snow often made the way impassable for nine months of the year. The other route, from Independence, Missouri, led westward across lands claimed by the Plains Indians—a distance of more than six hundred miles, to Fort Laramie. From there, the dread Bozeman Trail stretched north to Montana Territory, right through Sioux country, the domain of Chiefs Red Cloud and Crazy Horse.

These men who rode the high boxes of the freight wagons—call them mercenaries or soldiers of fortune—knew the risks and considered themselves equal to the task. Most of them were armed with at least two revolvers, a .50 caliber Sharps or Henry repeating rifle, and a well-honed Bowie knife. True, some of them died, selling their lives for unmarked graves along some lonely, forgotten trail. But most of them were survivors, men with the bark on. So tough, some of them vowed they "wore out their britches from the inside."

With the completion of the Union Pacific Railroad, the government abandoned the forts along the Bozeman Trail in a futile attempt to placate the hostile Sioux. It was a shortsighted move, for the worst was yet to come, as manifest by the Fetterman massacre on December 21, 1866. The trouble with the Sioux would continue for another ten years, until the bloody fight at the Little Big Horn. The Bozeman Trail, unprotected, was still vitally necessary for the freighting of supplies into the diggings in unsettled territories to the north.

But the Indians weren't the only problem. There were outlaws ready to gun down the teamsters and the outriders, stealing their cargo and selling to the highest bidders in the gold and silver camps. The western frontier offered opportunity and riches to men long on courage and quick with a gun, but death was a constant companion. It was a lawless time that brought out the best and the worst in men who rode toward the westering sun, to meet whatever destiny awaited them.

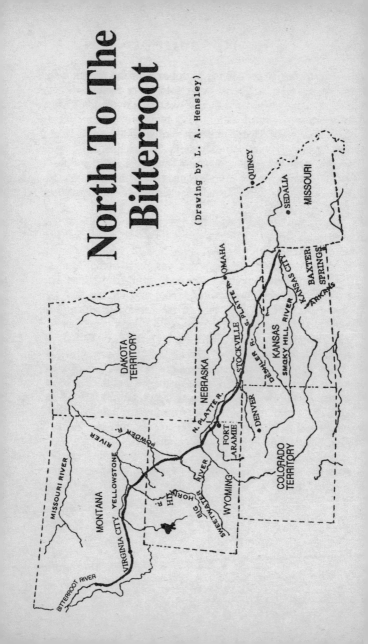

North To The Bitterroot

(Drawing by L. A. Hensley)

PROLOGUE

❧

Kansas City, Missouri. September 3, 1855.

*A*n orphan, sixteen-year-old Dutch Siringo had left Ohio, seeking what he hoped would be a better life in the West. Broke and hungry, he stepped off the steamboat, very much aware of the burly gambler right behind him. The man had taken the last ten dollars Siringo had, in what Dutch had belatedly realized was a crooked game. Dutch had called the gambler a cheat, and the deckhands had separated the two of them just shy of a fight. Now that they had reached the dock, the big man was prepared to continue the argument. Defiantly, Dutch Siringo turned to face his adversary.

"You young pup," the gambler snarled, "you don't get off callin' Sol Bohannon a cheat. I'm goin' to thrash you within an inch of your life."

"When you're ready," said Dutch, his hands on his hips.

Siringo had dark hair, gray eyes, and at sixteen, weighed a hundred and eighty, and not an ounce of it fat. He stood six-four. His opponent, thirty pounds heavier, clearly didn't like Siringo's cocky attitude. He charged, only to fall facedown on the dock, after Dutch tripped him. Most of the passengers from the steamboat were aware of the argument that had taken place on board and had paused to watch.

Bohannon was further enraged by the laughter and crude jokes as he got to his feet. Rough-and-tumble as he appeared to be, he still had the look and dress of a dude, while most of the observers were Westerners. Dutch waited until Bohannon was on his feet, and then brought up a right all the way from his knees. But Bohannon saw it coming and moved his head enough for the blow to miss his jaw and smash into his left ear. He recovered quickly, driving a boot toward Siringo's groin, but Dutch caught the foot and twisted it. Again the gambler went down, groaning.

"Damn you," Bohannon cried, "you've crippled me."

He palmed a sleeve gun, only to have Siringo kick it out of his hand. He scrambled to recover it, but Siringo stomped hard on his hand against the dock's heavy oak planks. The commotion had drawn the attention of a lawman. A deputy sheriff's star was pinned to his vest.

"What's goin' on here?" the deputy demanded.

"Hell, Perkins," said a man who apparently knew the deputy, "the varmint with the sleeve gun done some slick dealin' on the boat. When we docked, he forced a fight. The kid ain't armed."

"Get up," Perkins said, his eyes on Bohannon. "I can't do nothin' about what you done on the boat, but hereabouts, we don't take it kindly, pullin' iron on an unarmed man. You want me to chunk him in the hoosegow, boy?"

"No," said Siringo, "let him go."

Dutch Siringo immediately left the dock, forgetting the incident. He had nothing but the clothes on his back, and his only concern was finding work so that he might feed himself and have a place to sleep. He was pleased to find warehouses strung out along the river, most of them with wagons backed up to loading docks. Thunder rumbled and a chill west wind brought the promise of rain. Siringo quickly discovered that most of the sheds and warehouses along the river were just storage facilities. The freighting offices, livery barns, and wagon yards were located elsewhere. But as he neared the end of the string of warehouses, he found what he was looking for. There was a wagon yard, a livery barn, and a warehouse with loading dock. Next to the loading dock, steps led to an office, and a neatly painted sign above the door read BECKWITH FREIGHT LINES. Siringo climbed the steps and entered the office. There were several filing cabinets, four hard-bottomed oak chairs, and a battered desk. A girl sat behind the desk, and when she looked up, Dutch Siringo forgot how broke and hungry he was. She had dark hair, brown eyes, and Dutch decided she wasn't a day over fifteen, if that. He was struck dumb for a moment, but as her smile faded, he regained his voice.

"Ma'am, I'm needin' work. I'd like to talk to Mr. Beckwith."

"That's my father," she said. "He's in the barn. You're welcome to wait."

"Thanks," said Dutch, taking one of the chairs. He didn't mind the wait, for his eyes were on the girl. She became conscious of his staring, and when she looked up, he could see the irritation on her face.

"I'm sorry, ma'am," Dutch said. "I know it's rude to stare, but you're the prettiest girl I've ever seen."

He had spoken the first thought that had popped into his head, and he felt like a fool. He expected anything but what he got, for she flashed him a smile that dimpled her cheeks, and then she laughed.

"Thank you," she said. "That had an honest sound to it. May I ask your name?"

"Dutch Siringo, ma'am. I'm from Ohio."

"I'm Christie," she said. "Are you a teamster?"

"No," said Siringo. "I've worked some with horses, mules, and oxen, but I couldn't honestly call myself a teamster. I'd like to be, though."

"My father likes men who talk straight, who aren't afraid of hard work, and who leave the whiskey alone. He just fired a hostler who was drunk more than he was sober, and showed up when he felt like it. He's in the barn, mucking out stalls."

"I'd take that job in a minute," said Dutch, "if he'll let me prove myself."

"I like you, Dutch Siringo," she said. "Go on out to the barn and talk to him. Tell him what you've told me."

Dutch didn't waste any time. The barn was larger than it looked. There were horses and mules in separate stalls, while within larger pens, as many as six oxen fed off hay from a common rack. Within one of the empty stalls, a graying man leaned on an eight-tined fork, wiping his brow with a bandanna. He leaned the fork against the wall as Dutch approached.

"Mr. Beckwith," said Dutch, "I'm from Ohio, and I'm needin' work. Chris . . . uh . . . the lady in the office . . . says you're needin' a hostler. I'm Dutch Siringo."

"So you've charmed Christie, have you?"

"Not intentionally, sir," Dutch replied. "I need to work, and I will work. All I'm asking is a chance to prove myself. Christie was kind enough to let me come into the barn to talk to you."

"You would take a job like this, day after day? Could I depend on you?"

"I would," said Dutch, "and you can depend on me."

"I appreciate your honesty, son," Beckwith said. "I reckon you're the first that's ever asked for a mucker's job. The others all want to hire on as teamsters, and not a blamed one with a scrap of experience. The pay's twenty dollars a month, but there's a bunk and blankets in the warehouse. It's up to you to see that nobody comes jackin' around the place at night."

"I understand," said Dutch. "I'll start on the stalls now."

"It's a mite late in the day," Beckwith said, "and to-morrow's Sunday. I don't hold with a man workin' on the Sabbath when he don't have to. You can start Monday. I'll pay you every Saturday. Here's your first week in advance."

"You're a trusting man, Mr. Beckwith," said Dutch.

"Not really," Beckwith said. "I judge a man by how strong he leans on me, how much he asks for, without proving himself. You only asked for a job, although you look broke and hungry. That says a lot for a man. Come on to the office, and I'll have Christie add you to the payroll."

Dutch Siringo lived up to his promise. Within a year, a few days past his seventeenth birthday, Josh Beckwith put him in charge of the livery barn. He bought and sold horses and mules as the need arose, bought hay and grain, and saw to the needs of the livestock upon which Beckwith Freight Lines depended. His earnings increased to fifty dollars a month, and he never tired of listening to the veteran teamsters talk of the trails, of Indian fights, and the increasing threat of outlaws. Dutch bought a secondhand Colt and spent all his free time learning to draw and fire the weapon. Just when it seemed Dutch Siringo's star couldn't rise any higher, it did. Christie Beckwith had taken an interest in him, and the more he lived up to the expectations of Josh Beckwith, the more the girl seemed drawn to him. After four years—when Dutch was twenty-one—he decided it was time to speak to Josh Beckwith about his relationship with Christie, and about his future with Beckwith Freight Lines. Beckwith had taken to inviting Dutch to Sunday dinner, and Dutch picked one of those quiet times to speak to his genial boss. Christie had cleared the table, leaving the men alone, while she retreated to the kitchen.

"Sir," said Dutch, "I need to talk to you. It's about Christie and me."

"If you're askin' my permission," Beckwith said, "you got it. You're the kind of man I'd always hoped she would choose. You have a future on the frontier, son."

"Thanks," said Dutch, "but there's more. Before I . . . we . . . settle down, I feel the need to learn the rest of the freighting business. Mr. Beckwith, I want to ride the trails to the High Plains, to the gold camps, to the boomtowns. Am I being selfish?"

Beckwith laughed. "Not to my thinkin', Dutch. That was my life, until Christie was born. When she wasn't quite two years old, her ma died, and my career on the high box died with her. Christie needed me. But now she's a woman and don't need me, but I'm an old man. All I can do is watch the big wagons roll west, and remember the old days. Was I your age—woman or not—I'd be trailin' west."

"I'm obliged for your encouragement, sir," Dutch said. "I haven't spoken to Christie about . . . riding west."

"Let me talk to her first," said Beckwith. "Somebody's got to run this business when I'm gone, and he needs to know it backward, forward, and upside down."

Dutch Siringo was elated. While he didn't want to think of life without old Josh, just the prospect of taking the reins of Beckwith Freight Lines was staggering. Adding to that the winning of the heart and hand of the beautiful Christie was almost more than he could bear.

A few days after his talk with Dutch, Josh Beckwith took the time to call on Jasper Sneed, his lawyer. Sneed had always seemed capable, and Beckwith had no reason not to trust him. What Beckwith didn't know, was that Sneed— almost twice the age of Christie—had his eye on the girl. As Sneed saw it, he had only to win the girl, and when old Josh cashed in, Beckwith Freight Lines would fall into his hands. Now, as Josh Beckwith spoke, all Sneed's plans came tumbling down in ruins.

"Sneed," said Beckwith, "I want you to draw me up a will. When I'm gone, I want half of Beckwith Freight Lines to go to Christie, my daughter, and the other half to one of my most trusted men, Dutch Siringo."

"Mr. Beckwith," Sneed said, "that strikes me as being rather unusual, taking half of Christie's inheritance and giving it to a stranger."

"I don't care a damn how it strikes you," said Beckwith, "that's how I want it done. If you won't do it, then I'll find somebody else."

"Sorry," Sneed said. "I was out of line. It's your business. I'll take care of it for you."

A week later, when Beckwith returned to Sneed's office, the lawyer handed him the one-page document.

"Read it," said Sneed. "I made two copies, and you'll need to sign both of them."

Beckwith read the copy Sneed had given him, and finding it satisfactory, signed it. He returned it to Sneed, and without reading it, signed the second copy. But the second copy wasn't exactly like the first, and as Sneed placed them in a desk drawer, he sighed with satisfaction. . . .

True to his word, Josh Beckwith had talked to Christie, but she didn't share any of her father's enthusiasm for Dutch Siringo facing the dangers of the western frontier. She wasted no time in conveying her displeasure to Dutch.

"Daddy gave up teamstering because of me," she said bitterly, "and now he's going to relive it all through you. It doesn't matter to you what I want?"

"You know it does," Dutch replied, trying to control his temper, "and stop blaming Josh. This is my idea, damn it. He favors it because I need the experience."

"Sure he does," she said, miffed. "How long am I supposed to wait, while you satisfy your urge to dodge Indian arrows and fight outlaws?"

"I reckon that's entirely up to you," said Dutch.

In the days before Dutch took the trail west, Christie Beckwith spoke to him only when she had to. He feigned indifference, and twice he caught her talking to Jasper Sneed. Dutch, aware that Sneed was Josh Beckwith's lawyer, said nothing, but he hadn't liked Sneed, even before he became overly friendly with Christie. Sneed was always fancied up in dark trousers, boiled shirt, fancy tie, and a black swallowtail coat. The man seemed to go out of his way to further the impression that he believed himself just a little better than anyone else.

"Christie," said Josh, having seen her talking to Jasper Sneed, "what's happened between you and Dutch?"

"He's more concerned with pleasing you than in pleasing me," she said.

"I won't have you cozyin' up to Jasper Sneed," Josh said. "My God, he's twice your age."

"I'm nineteen," she snapped. "I'm old enough to choose my own man, and I don't want one that you've made over in your own image."

"Well, by God," said Josh, "if I have any say, you ain't goin' to have one made up in Sneed's image, either. I aim to tell him to stay away from here."

"I don't care," she said defiantly. "I'll meet him in town, if I want to."

Kansas City, Missouri. April 1, 1860.

The caravan of five big wagons rolled west, and on the box of the fifth wagon rode Dutch Siringo. He had a Colt revolver tied down on his right hip and a .50 caliber Sharps under the seat. The wagons were loaded with everything that the teams of mules could pull, and under certain circumstances—such as heavy rain—they were subject to bogging down. Siringo's companions were all veteran drivers whom he liked, and they liked him. At thirty, Brace Weaver was the oldest, while Jules Swenson was a year younger. Whit Sanderson was just twenty-five, while Rusty Karnes, at twenty-two, was a year older than Dutch.

Months passed, and Dutch Siringo became an experienced teamster, lightning quick with a Colt revolver and a dead shot with a rifle. He became one of the first to own one of the new Henry sixteen-shot repeaters. Each time Dutch returned to Kansas City, try as he might, he got exactly nowhere with Christie Beckwith. She seemed lost to him forever, detracting from the satisfaction he might have enjoyed as a result of Josh Beckwith's pride in him. After the start of the Civil War, the trails became more dangerous than ever, as more and more Union soldiers were drawn into the conflict. The Plains Indians were free to swoop down on wagons, looting, killing, and burning. Beckwith was forced to hire outriders—a mounted man alongside every wagon—for protection. With a loaded wagon in the way, it was virtually impossible for the teamsters to watch their back trail, and it was from this unprotected quarter that most of the Indian attacks came.

Dutch Siringo had been with Beckwith Freight Lines just one day shy of eight years, when the unthinkable happened. Dutch and his four companions had just returned from a run to Denver, arriving in Kansas City on September 2, 1863. After unhitching their teams, they reported to the freight office. There they found Christie Beckwith and Jasper Sneed.

"My father is dead," said Christie. "He left everything to me, and from now on, Jasper—Mr. Sneed—will be in charge."

Dutch and his four companions stood there in shocked silence, and Sneed spoke.

"There'll be some changes. I've been looking at some of the bills of lading, and it appears that Josh has been loading the wagons a bit light. From now on, we'll increase the loads."

"You'll bust wheels, break axles, and mire down in mud," said Dutch. "Josh knew what he was doing."

"And you're implying that I don't?"

"I'm implying nothing," Dutch said coldly. "I'm tellin' you straight. Josh had it all just right."

"Josh is gone," said Sneed, "and I'm calling the shots. Any of you who fail to find that satisfactory can move on."

Without another word, Dutch left the office, followed by his companions. They stood outside, near the freight warehouse, uncertain as to their next move.

"I reckon I'll stay on for a while," Dutch said. "I don't really have anywhere else to go, unless I join the army."

"Sneed don't know doodly squat about runnin' a freight line," said Rusty Karnes. "I'm of a mind to stick around just to watch him go under."

"Yeah," Jules Swenson said, "but when he goes under, the gal goes with him. I feel a mite sorry for her."

"Don't," said Dutch. "She's made her bed, and if it's her ambition to lie in it with a skunk-striped varmint like Sneed, then she deserves whatever she gets."

The five of them agreed to remain with Beckwith Freight Lines until the situation became intolerable, which it quickly did. Their very first run under Sneed's rules proved to be a disaster. They headed west in a pouring rain, and after two days, the five heavily loaded wagons were hopelessly bogged down in a sea of mud.

"I reckon we can't blame this on Sneed," said Brace Weaver. "With all this rain, we'd be mired down, even with lighter loads."

But the worst was yet to come. Sneed refused to hire the outriders as Josh Beckwith had done, and Dutch and his companions were attacked by Indians. The attack had come from the back trail, and the drivers had been forced to abandon the wagons to save their lives. The wagons had been looted and burned, and the hapless teamsters had been forced to ride mules for the two hundred miles back to Kansas City. Sneed was furious.

"You damned irresponsible bunglers. You'll pay for this. You'll work for nothing until you've paid for those wagons and their freight."

"I don't think so," Dutch said. "I'm through."

"Like hell you are," Sneed shouted. "You owe me money."

"I owe you just one thing," said Dutch, "and here it is."

He brought up a right that connected with Sneed's chin. The lawyer's feet left the floor and he crashed against the wall. He went limp, crumpling to the floor just as Christie entered the office.

"What have you done to him?" she cried.

"I reckon we reached an understanding," said Dutch. "In case he don't remember, when he wakes up, I'm finished. Quit. Done."

"I feel the same way, Miss Christie," Brace Weaver said. "Sorry."

Jules Swenson, Whit Sanderson, and Rusty Karnes said nothing. They followed Brace and Dutch out of the office, and Rusty closed the door behind them. It all had an air of finality that wasn't lost on Christie Beckwith. She regarded Jasper Sneed with disgust, and when he finally got groggily to his feet, she sat behind the desk, her face buried in her hands.

"So they've all quit, have they?" Sneed growled. "Damn them, they'll get no back pay from me."

"They didn't ask for any," said Christie bitterly. "They made it clear they didn't want anything from you or me."

"I'll hire more men," Sneed said. "I'll show them. I'll show everybody."

"Then you can start with the bank," said Christie wearily. "We owe them money, and there is none."

Dutch Siringo and his four friends sat in a saloon, each nursing a beer.

"Well, by God," Whit Sanderson said, "we done what we had to do, but where do we go from here?"

"Unless you got a better offer," said Dutch, "why don't you throw in with me? I aim to get together an outfit and call it Siringo Freight Lines."

They studied him in silence, wondering if he was joking. When he didn't smile, they concluded that he was serious. Silently, Brace Weaver extended his hand, and Dutch took it. Quickly, Jules Swenson, Whit Sanderson, and Rusty Karnes followed Weaver's example.

"By God," said Dutch Siringo, getting to his feet, "win, lose, or draw, we're goin' to give Jasper Sneed a run for his money."

CHAPTER 1

∽

*W*hile Dutch Siringo had saved his wages during his years with Beckwith, he found himself woefully short of what he needed to bankroll his own outfit.

"Amongst the four of us," said Brace Weaver, "we got fifteen hundred dollars. We're willin' to buy in for that much, taking nothin' until the outfit can afford to pay."

"I'm obliged," Dutch said, "and I'm accepting your offer. We're still shy of what we need, but it's that much less I'll have to raise. I'll go to the bank."

Dutch spoke to John McGruder, a longtime friend of Josh Beckwith. McGruder listened attentively, but had his reservations.

"While I appreciate your position, Mr. Siringo," said McGruder, "with times being as they are, we're forced to take a long, hard look at risky endeavors. I understand that you, along with some other teamsters, quit Beckwith Lines. May I ask why?"

"A change in policy," Dutch said, "and if you don't mind, I'd rather not be any more specific than that."

"I understand," said McGruder, "and I respect you for that. Asset-wise, what do you now have, and how much money do you need?"

"There's five of us," Dutch said, "all experienced Beckwith teamsters, and everything we own, we've put in the pot. We reckon we can afford four wagons, with necessary teams and harness. We're shy one wagon, teams, and harness. We're allowing a thousand dollars for that, and I figure we'll need another thousand for ammunition, grub, wagon parts, and spare harness.''

"You're putting up four thousand dollars of your own, then," said McGruder, "and you're willing to risk it all for the loan of another two thousand?''

"We are," Dutch said.

"Mr. Siringo," said McGruder, "I'm going to loan you that two thousand for a period of two years. At the end of a year, you will repay one half of it with interest, with the balance, plus interest, due at the end of two years. Will that be satisfactory?''

"Yes, sir," Siringo said.

Dutch signed the necessary papers, and McGruder wrote him a check. When Siringo departed, the banker watched him go. McGruder's head teller, Kendrick, had been waiting for McGruder to complete the transaction. Kendrick spoke.

"Mr. McGruder, late yesterday afternoon, after you had gone, Jasper Sneed was here on behalf of Beckwith Freight Lines. They're in arrears on their loan and are requesting an extension.''

"I'm not surprised," McGruder said. "Six months. No more.''

"Well," said Rusty Karnes, "we got wagons, mules, and harness, but no barn, no hay, and no office. Is anybody goin' to take us serious?''

"When we're in town, between freighting," Dutch said, "we can buy hay and sleep in the wagons. As for an office, we'll have to make do. Just startin' out, we can't depend on anybody coming to us, so we'll go to them. Since Beckwith has no drivers, we'll call on some of their contracts.''

But Sneed hadn't wasted any time making good his threat to hire new teamsters. In the Sunday edition of the

Kansas City Liberty-Tribune, he ran a large advertisement.

"My God," said Brace Weaver, "Sneed's offerin' seventy-five dollars a month. That's half again as much as we was bein' paid."

"There'll be a hell of a difference between what he's offering and what he'll be paying," Dutch said. "A man can't pay when he's broke, and if Sneed ain't already, he soon will be."

It was a prophecy soon fulfilled, for Sneed's first shipment with his new drivers was attacked by Indians. Two drivers were killed, the wagons were looted and burned, and the Beckwith insurance was immediately canceled.

"That's hurtin' him," Whit Sanderson observed, "but it'll hurt us too. Now everybody will likely be askin' about insurance, and we got none."

But while Sneed's fortunes seemed to have hit bottom, he had a hole card. Prior to his devastating loss to Indians, he had begun negotiating for government hauling contracts, and the contracts were approved. In desperation, three other freight lines began fighting for what remained of the Beckwith contracts, leaving Siringo and his comrades out in the cold. But while watching the newspaper for further Beckwith advertisements, Dutch came upon an unexpected opportunity. Haskel Collins, a miner's representative from Montana Territory was in town, seeking teamsters for a caravan to a new gold strike at the foot of the Bitterroot Mountains.

"I know where Montana Territory is," said Jules Swenson, "but where the hell is the Bitterroot Mountains?"

"This hombre's stayin' at the Frontier Hotel," Dutch said. "If he ain't already been swamped with offers, let's get over there and drop our names in the hat."

"We got word you're needin' teamsters," said Dutch, when Collins opened the door. "I'm Dutch Siringo, representin' the Siringo Freight Line. These gents—Brace Weaver, Jules Swenson, Whit Sanderson, and Rusty Karnes—

are my pardners and all of us are experienced teamsters.''

"Come on in," Collins said. "We can at least talk."

"You've already hired teamsters, then," said Dutch.

"No," Collins replied. "That's why we need to talk. Are you familiar with Montana Territory and the Bozeman Trail?"

"No," said Dutch. "I've only been as far north as Cheyenne, but others have told me something about the territory. It's Sioux country."

"It is," Collins said. "More than two hundred and fifty miles, from Cheyenne north."

"So you're looking for men with enough sand to face the Sioux," said Rusty Karnes.

"That's what it amounts to," Collins said, "but there's more."

"Just lay it all out for us," said Dutch. "Then we can ask questions, if need be."

"The Bitterroot Mountains are in western Montana Territory," Collins said, "and at the eastern foot of the mountains runs the Bitterroot River. Along the river, there's a new gold camp. I aim to build a mercantile there, but I need trade goods, provisions, clothing, everything. How many wagons do you have?"

"Five," said Dutch.

"That should be enough," Collins said. "Gentlemen, if you're willing to freight in these goods, I will pay one thousand dollars for each wagonload that arrives intact."

"No bids?" Dutch asked.

"No bids," said Collins. "In all fairness, I should tell you that nobody else is willing to consider my proposal."

"We'll consider it," Dutch said, "on one condition."

"That being?"

"That you hire outriders—mounted men with repeating rifles—to side every wagon. I know it's an added expense, but with a loaded wagon behind us, we can't watch the back trail. In case of Indian attack, we'll need time to rein in the teams, grab our rifles, and get off the wagon box.

The outriders serve two purposes. Their watchfulness can gain us the edge we need when there's an Indian attack and the added firepower necessary to survive it.''

"There would be ten men," said Collins. "Eleven, including myself.''

"You're going with us, then," Dutch said.

"I am," Collins replied. "I like the attitude of you and your men. Instead of backing off and saying it can't be done, you are suggesting ways that it can. Very well, I'm willing to pay extra for these outriders, granted that you can find such men.''

"We can find them," said Dutch. "When do you aim to go west?''

"A week from today," Collins said. "I'll need time to make the best deals I can. I'll be here in the evenings and at night.''

"Do you have a map?" Dutch asked.

"I have a copy of a map prepared by surveyors for the Union Pacific right-of-way," said Collins, "but that will be useful only as far as Cheyenne. Once there, the Bozeman is well defined. We travel north to Montana Territory, until we reach the Yellowstone River. We'll follow the Yellowstone due west, until we reach the Bitterroot.''

"One thing we haven't considered," Brace Weaver said, "and that's snow. I reckon we can make it to Cheyenne, but if I'm any judge, it'll be hell the rest of the way. We should have started this trek three months ago.''

"I agree," said Collins, "but I wasn't ready three months ago, and I can't wait until spring. If the snow drifts too deep for us to continue, we'll have to take refuge and wait it out. I'd suggest all of you outfit yourselves in heavy coats, gloves, woolen socks, and long handle underwear.''

"We have one hard and fast rule," Dutch said, "and that's don't overload the wagons. We can understand you wantin' to take as much a payload as you can, but you'll never get there on splintered wheels and busted axles. When you're loadin', don't forget we all have to eat. We'll have to save some room in the wagons for provisions and cooking utensils. If we're snowed in for days at a time, it'll take an almighty lot of grub for eleven men.''

''While we're talkin' grub,'' said Whit Sanderson, ''we'd best be considerin' our teams. If we're in snow country, and snow's so deep we can't move the wagons, how will our mules find graze? Starve our teams, and them wagons ain't goin' nowhere. Ever.''

''You gentlemen need work, and I need to move my goods to the Bitterroot,'' Collins said, ''but we seem to have overlooked some factors of extreme importance. Frankly, I'll need the five wagons you have, without considering provisions for ourselves or grain for the stock. You need a sixth wagon.''

''Or you need another freight line,'' said Dutch.

''That's impossible,'' Collins said. ''As I have already told you, nobody has the courage to haul my goods to western Montana Territory. What would be the cost of securing this additional wagon, with harness and teams?''

''A thousand dollars,'' said Dutch, ''and the hiring of a teamster.''

''The extra wagon wouldn't be fully loaded, then, with our provisions for the journey and grain for the stock?''

''No,'' Dutch said, ''but we can't afford an extra wagon just for that purpose.''

''I have agreed to pay one thousand dollars for every wagonload of goods delivered to western Montana Territory,'' said Collins. ''Suppose I advance you a thousand dollars for the purchase of another wagon, teams, and harness? Then, after loading provisions for our own use and grain for the stock, I would use the remaining available space for additional goods of my own. In return, upon reaching our destination, the extra wagon, teams, and harness would be yours. You will be responsible for an extra teamster, while I will pay an additional armed outrider.''

''I reckon we need time to consider,'' Dutch said.

''Tomorrow, then,'' said Collins.

"My God," Rusty Karnes said, when they had left Collins's hotel room, "we can pick up another wagon without it costin' us."

"Like hell," said Jules Swenson. "We got to pay a teamster."

"We don't pay him till we get paid," Whit Sanderson said, "and we purely got to have one more wagon."

"That's as square a deal as I ever heard," said Brace Weaver, "and I say we take it. Way I see it, if we come through for Collins, we got five thousand dollars and a wagon, teams, and harness that didn't cost us nothin'."

"Considerin' the other possibility," Rusty Karnes said, "we could all end up shot full of arrows and scalped, leavin' the Sioux with six wagonloads of fancy goods that didn't cost *them* nothin'."

"Hell," said Brace Weaver, "Karnes would go to a hangin' and take his own noose. It don't make a damn *what* the game is, the long odds always pay the most."

"Damn it," Dutch said, "we either accept his offer or we don't. Despite the risk we'll be taking, Collins is dealing the cards in our favor. Time we've loaded this extra wagon with grub for ourselves and grain for the teams, it'll be at least half full."

"How much grain are you countin' on haulin'?" Jules Swenson asked.

"Two thousand pounds," said Dutch. "I'm figurin' a pound of grain twice a day, for each animal."

"Damn," Jules said, "can't the varmints eat a little grass, like oxen?"

"If they can find it," said Dutch, "and if they can't, then we have to be prepared. In a warm climate they might survive on grass, but in extreme cold, they need grain twice a day. In the north country, the temperature can fall to forty below."

"We've thrashed this around long enough," Brace Weaver said. "Seein' as how there's not another damn thing in sight, and we're eatin' on borrowed money, I say we take what Collins is offering.''

"I agree," said Dutch.

"I'm in," Rusty Karnes said.

"Deal me a hand," said Jules Swenson. "It's the only game in town."

"What the hell," Whit Sanderson said, "I'll gamble my scalp against five thousand."

"Now that we've agreed on that," said Dutch, "we have a week to come up with those six outriders and another teamster with enough sand to throw in with us."

"Cass Carlyle might be interested," Rusty Karnes said. "He should have had a bellyful of Jasper Sneed by now."

"Tomorrow," said Dutch, "see if you can track him down. Now where are we goin' to find six hombres who are handy with long guns that ain't afraid of bein' scalped?"

"Maybe we can pick up some teamsters that ain't opposed to workin' as outriders," Brace Weaver said. "Some outfits cut back during the winter months."

"That's an idea worth considering," said Dutch. "All of you put your minds to it and let's find those six good men."

The following morning, Dutch Siringo knocked on the door of Haskel Collins's hotel room. When Collins opened the door, Dutch entered. He wasted no time in getting to the point.

"We're accepting your offer, Mr. Collins. If you'll advance me the funds, I'll arrange to buy the extra wagon, teams, and harness. The rest of my outfit's talking to some gents we're considering for outriders. We have a teamster in mind too."

"That is most gratifying," said Collins. "How much space within the extra wagon will be available to me?"

"At least half of it," Dutch replied. "Once we have the extra wagon, I'll begin searching for the necessary grain. Mules must be grained twice a day."

"I'll write you a check for the wagon, teams, and harness," said Collins.

"I don't know about that," Dutch said. "Will you be paying us by check, when we've reached the Bitterroot?"

"Yes," said Collins. "It will be written on a St. Louis bank. Is that a problem?"

"I don't know," Dutch said. "Write one for the wagon, teams, and harness, and I'll try it at my bank, here in town."

Collins wrote out the check and handed it to Dutch. Only then did he speak.

"At some point, Mr. Siringo, we must begin trusting one another."

"I'm willing," said Dutch, "but you have to look at it from my side of the fence. It's a hell of a long ways from western Montana Territory back here to Kansas City. After I get the bank to recognize this check, then I'll lean a little more in your direction."

Dutch Siringo went directly to the bank where he had borrowed two thousand dollars. After a few minutes, he was shown into John McGruder's office. Quickly, he explained the purpose of the check Collins had written.

"That's quite an accomplishment for a man in business less than a week," the banker said.

"When we reach Montana Territory," Dutch said, "I reckon we'll be paid with another check. Will you telegraph this bank in St. Louis and see just how good this check is? I'll pay for the telegram. If this check's good, then I'll feel better about taking the next one."

"I'll send the telegram," said McGruder. "This is a very sensible move. I may have an answer for you by this afternoon."

When Dutch returned to the bank, McGruder had news for him.

"I sent two telegrams," McGruder said, "one of them to a friend of mine in St. Louis. Haskel Collins is the son of the wealthiest man in St. Louis. His father owns a good part of the town, including a bank. I'll cash this check for you, and any future ones.''

Dutch waited for his partners at the boarding house where they had been living, and they all had supper at a nearby cafe. Over final cups of coffee, they compared notes.

"Cass Carlyle's throwin' in with us," Rusty Karnes said. "He'll hire on for his grub and ammunition, till we can pay. He's the last of the old Beckwith men. Sneed's got nothin' but new teamsters."

"I can't say I'm sorry to hear it," Dutch replied. "Maybe we can hire on some of the Beckwith men as outriders."

"We already have," said Brace Weaver. "Jules, Whit, an' me tracked down five of 'em. We got Dent Wells, Drago Peeler, Kirby Butler, and Gard Higgins. Gard's talkin' to an amigo of his, Tally Slaughter, about joinin' as a sixth outrider."

"They all know the money's at the other end of the trail, then," Dutch said.

"They know," Brace said. "All they're expectin' along the way is ammunition and their grub. Mostly, they're just glad to be shut of Jasper Sneed."

"Haskel Collins wrote a check for a thousand dollars," said Dutch, "which will buy our sixth wagon, teams, and harness. John McGruder telegraphed St. Louis and learned that Haskel's daddy owns a big chunk of the town, including a bank. There's nothing standing between us and five thousand dollars except maybe fifteen hundred miles of frontier, snow, outlaws, and the Sioux nation."

"Hell, if it was easy," said Jules, "everybody would be doin' it."

"In the morning," Dutch said, "we'll move out to the west of town, along the river, and set up camp. We'd as well leave the teams and the wagons where they are until we're ready to load. I reckon it's time for us to buy the warm clothes we'll need, and to begin loadin' up supplies and ammunition. How well are our outriders armed?''

"They've all been teamsters," Brace Weaver said. "Every man's got a Henry repeater, and they've all got at least one revolver."

"Be sure every man's sidearm is a Colt," said Dutch, "but most important is the long guns. In an Indian attack, if they're close enough for Colts, we're goners."

Two days later, Haskel Collins rode west to the camp Dutch Siringo had established. A dozen men watched Collins approach, and he looked more the frontiersman than Dutch had thought possible. He looked older than his probable thirty years, dressed in flannel shirt and Levi's. His boots had pointed toes and undershot heels, and his gray Stetson was uncreased. A revolver rode low on his right hip, while the butt of a rifle was visible in a saddle boot. When he dismounted, Dutch introduced him to the newly hired men.

"Tomorrow," said Collins, "we'll begin loading the wagons."

"I have reached an agreement with the government," Sneed said triumphantly. "We'll begin hauling army payrolls to the outlying forts immediately."

"We have no insurance," Christie Beckwith said, "and you know it."

"Ah, but you underestimate me, my dear. We have the necessary insurance. Without it, we could never do business with the government."

"Yes," Christie said, "but at what cost?"

"Don't let that concern you," said Sneed. "With the additional revenue, we can afford the insurance."

"The guards too?"

"No guards," Sneed said. "The payrolls will be hidden beneath false wagon beds."

"That will last as long as it takes the Indians to burn the wagon," said Christie. "Lose a couple of payrolls and see how long it takes your insurance and government contracts to follow."

"Damn it," Sneed said, "you're just like your stubborn old daddy, always backing away from every risk."

"My father took risks," said Christie, "but he had a head for business, and that's just a hell of a lot more than can be said for you."

"A shameful display of temper, my dear," Sneed said, "and swearing is so unladylike. I'm sure your father would be disappointed."

"Not nearly as disappointed as I am with him, for having left you in charge of Beckwith Freight Lines. Now get out. I want nothing more to do with you."

"Ah," said Sneed suavely, "I cannot allow you to dismiss me, for it would mean the betraying of your father's trust in me."

Words failing her, Christie Beckwith left the office and went into the livery barn. Leaning against the gate of an empty stall, she thought of the days when old Josh had been alive, when Dutch Siringo had sat beside her during Sunday dinner, when each new day dawned with promise. For all that was, and all that now seemed lost to her forever, she bowed her head and wept.

Kansas City, Missouri. September 12, 1863.

"Wagons, ho!" Dutch Siringo shouted, as the big mules drew his wagon into the lead. Each teamster had a saddled horse following his wagon on a lead rope, for if Indians were to attack in overwhelming numbers, they could ride for their lives. Haskel Collins trotted his horse ahead, until he was leading the column. Two of the outriders dropped back to the sixth wagon, while the others divided on either side of the caravan. Dutch watched them approvingly. They were young men, all under thirty, dressed and armed for the long trail ahead. They followed the Kansas River, covering what Dutch believed to be fifteen miles, before halting for the day.

"I've heard the trains always circled their wagons," Collins said. "Obviously, we don't have enough for that."

"No," said Dutch. "In more mountainous country, we can pitch our camp at the base of a butte or canyon wall, lining up the wagons as a barricade between us and any possible attackers. Out here on the Kansas plains, we'll have to keep watch, being damn sure nobody gets too close."

"We'll be in familiar territory until we take the Bozeman Trail," Brace Weaver said, "and from there on, we'll have to be almighty watchful. At least, water won't be scarce."

"As I understand it," said Collins, "we'll follow the Kansas River for perhaps eighty-five miles, to its confluence with the Big Blue. We'll then be following the Big Blue to within a few miles of the North Platte, which will serve all the way to Fort Laramie."*

"I'm concerned with the higher elevations, from Fort Laramie to the Bitterroot," Dutch said. "Have you traveled this country in winter?"

"No," said Collins. "My father sent me west with an expedition from St. Louis, so I could investigate the potential before reaching a final decision. I had been back in St. Louis only three weeks, when I started west again. With the possibility of heavy snowfall, Father believed I should wait until spring. I made the decision to go ahead. Am I being foolish?"

"Not as far as we're concerned," Dutch replied. "On the western frontier, folks need trade goods, grub, medicine, and ammunition the year round, fair weather or foul. If we limited ourselves to the summer months, we'd starve. You're paying us to get your goods to the Bitterroot. On the High Plains, there may be snow as late as May and as early as September. While this is our first train into western Montana Territory, it certainly won't be the last. We're

---

* From Independence to Fort Laramie, this is the same route as the Oregon Trail.

hauling plenty of grub for ourselves and grain for the teams. Heavy snow—like too much rain—will only slow us down. It won't stop us.''

"I like the attitude of you and your men," said Collins, "and I feel better about this venture. I'm thirty years old, and this is the first time I've stepped out of my father's shadow. He offered to set me up in business, back in St. Louis, but I want to make my own decisions, even if they're the wrong ones."

"That says a lot for a man," Brace Weaver said. "Any hombre worth his salt wants to ride his own broncs. Hell, we all walked out when we couldn't abide takin' orders from a slick-tongued varmint in town clothes that didn't know diddly about freightin' goods to the frontier."

"I'm thankful that you did," said Collins, "and I'll make you this promise. Deliver this caravan safely to the Bitterroot, and you'll be assured of my business. There's potential to justify a caravan every six months."

"If the diggings is that successful," Rusty Karnes said, "there should be miners with a stake that's needin' brought back to the States."

"Yes," said Collins. "I've been concerned only with getting my goods safely into the territory, and I haven't thought any further than that. Once you're there, what you will have done for me will be testimonial enough as to the value of your services. I'll be more than happy to recommend you to miners wishing to ship their gold out of the territory."

"We're obliged," said Dutch. "Startin' tonight, we'll stand watch from dusk to dawn. Two-hour watches won't be all that hard on any of us. We'll have to be especially watchful where our stock is concerned. Given a choice, Indians are likely to be more interested in stealing our livestock than in taking our scalps. It's a long trail, and they'll figure they can scalp us some other time."

The teamsters and outriders all laughed, and Haskel Collins regarded them in amazement. What kind of men were these, who could take so lightly the possibility of being scalped by hostile Indians? But the trail north to the Bitterroot would be treacherous, and before they reached the violent end, Haskel Collins would be thanking his lucky stars for the rough-around-the-edges frontiersmen who were his companions.

CHAPTER 2

✦

*T*hree days west of Kansas City, the caravan came upon the ashes of a recent fire and a profusion of tracks.

"Shod horses," said Dutch. "That rules out Indians."

"Soldiers, perhaps?" Collins suggested.

"No," said Dutch. "They're too far afield to have come from Fort Hays or Fort Dodge, and if they're from Fort Leavenworth, they'd be returning to the post. I reckon we ought to make camp here. There's still some daylight, and I aim to put it to good use. I'll back trail this bunch a ways. Where they're from can be as interesting as where they're going."

"They're potential trouble, then," said Collins.

"Until we know who they are and learn something to the contrary," Dutch said. "Rule out Indians and the military, and you're left facing the possibility of renegades."

"The varmints are more dangerous than Indians," said Cass Carlyle.

"Some of you go ahead and get supper started," Dutch said. "They rode in from the north, and when they left here, they rode south. I aim to follow their back trail a ways, and then swing back to the south."

Dutch mounted his horse and rode out. Haskel Collins watched him go. When he spoke, it was to nobody in particular.

"How can a man read so much from horse tracks?"

"It ain't so much the tracks," said Brace Weaver. "On the frontier, once you learn the whereabouts of suspicious hombres, it ain't all that hard to figure why they're around and what they're up to. We know this bunch ain't military and they ain't Indians. Takin' it from there, that don't leave nothin' but outlaws, and they ain't ridin' this far out, just to give their hosses a run."

"You think they're after the wagons, then?" asked Collins.

"That's what I think, and it's what Dutch thinks," Weaver said.

"Tonight," said Jules Swenson, "I think we better double the guard. I ain't even takin' off my hat, and I'm keepin' my Henry ready."

"Damn right," his companions agreed in a single voice.

"If these . . . ah . . . outlaws rode in from the north," Collins said, "how did they learn about us?"

"Mr. Collins," said Rusty Karnes pityingly, "the varmints keep a man on watch, and when a promisin' train goes west, he rides north and then northwest, so as not to leave a trail. He gets word to the rest of the gang, and they move in."

"But they left ashes from their fire and their trail is plain as day," Collins said. "How do they propose to take us by surprise, when we know they're coming?"

"They don't aim to take us by surprise," said Dent Wells, one of the outriders. "They know we've been over the mountain, that we'll be awake and ready. You foller their trail a ways, an' you'll see there's maybe twenty riders. They *want* us to know they're comin', an' they want us to know they outnumber us nearly two-to-one. They figure to intimidate us, so's we'll straddle our hosses an' ride for our lives."

"My God," said Collins, "we're out in the open, with no cover, but for the wagons."

"We'll have to shoot first, and shoot straight," Tally Slaughter said.

Dutch Siringo rode in from the south, dismounted, and unsaddled his horse. When he spoke, he told them what they had expected to hear.

"They're gathered to the south," said Dutch. "Nobody sleeps until we've settled with this bunch of coyotes. We'll hobble the horses and mules well away from the wagons. We don't have enough firepower to protect the stock, so we'll just have to gamble that these varmints are after the wagons."

"You've been through these attacks before?" Haskel Collins asked.

"Yes," said Dutch, "but you can't always anticipate the way it's likely to go. All we can do is hobble the horses and mules, so they don't scatter from hell to breakfast, when the shootin' starts."

"Just pray that none of the mules are hit," Kirby Butler said.

"Yeah," said Whit Sanderson. "These wagons ain't overloaded now, but they damn well can be, if we lose some mules."

"Gentlemen," said Collins, "I have never shot a man, or even considered it, but should these ruffians attack us, then I am prepared to respond in kind."

"Collins," Dutch said, "I'm pleased to hear you say that. If you aim to survive in the West, you got to have the savvy to know when to pull a gun and the sand to do it."

"You reckon they'll come at us from the south, then?" Brace Weaver asked.

"That's what I'm expecting," said Dutch. "We'll have the river behind us to the north, and we can line the wagons up in threes to offer some protection from east and west. All of you position yourselves between and under the wagons. Drop your saddles for cover and as a rest for your Henrys. There'll be a moon, but I expect them to wait it out. Make that first volley count, because your muzzle flash will make a damn good target."

Supper was eaten in silence, every man going to the river and washing his own tin plate, cup, and eating tools. Brace, Jules, and Whit then harnessed a team and lined up the wagons in threes, a few yards apart, their backs to the river. The mules were unharnessed, hobbled, and taken to graze with the rest of the stock. Each man chose a position for his saddle. Bellied down behind it, even on the flat Kansas plain, it afforded a man a little cover. The moon rose, and with the starlight, the prairie was light as day.

"Hell," said Levan Blade, one of the outriders, "they'll wait for moonset."

"I hope they do," Dutch replied. "They won't be able to see us any better than we can see them, and since we'll be firing first, we should be able to even the odds a mite, before they cut down on us."

Time dragged. The rising moon reached its zenith and began to recede toward the far horizon. A chill wind was out of the northwest, favoring the attackers if indeed they did approach from the south. The moon had set and by the stars, it was two o'clock in the morning when the renegades made their move. When it came, it was nothing like Dutch and his men were expecting. Reining up just out of rifle range, one of the renegades shouted a challenge.

"You hombres in camp, listen up. We're takin' the wagons. You kin back off an' go peaceful, or we kin drive enough lead in there to sink a steamboat."

The men with the wagons remained silent, waiting for Dutch Siringo to make the first move. As the renegade challenged them, Dutch was off and running. Instead of running directly toward the riders, he angled off to one side until he was near enough for a shot at the mounted men. He then bellied down and shot a man out of the saddle. It quickly drew the expected response, when the outlaws fired at his muzzle flash. But Dutch wasn't there. He had rolled away, and began firing from a new position. Returning his fire, the outlaws advanced, bringing them within range of Siringo's companions. As the renegades fired at Dutch, their own muzzle flashes became targets for the teamsters and outriders defending the wagons. Henrys roared, and the attackers were forced to retreat, leaving their comrades where they had fallen.

"Hold your fire," Dutch said softly. "I'm comin' in."

"Damn it," Brace Weaver said, "that was a fool thing to do. You had the whole bunch shootin' at you."

"That's what I expected," said Dutch. "Somebody had to draw their fire, so you would have targets. When no shots came from among the wagons, they had no way of knowing we weren't all scattered about."

"A remarkable maneuver," Haskel Collins said, "but dangerous."

"Not near as dangerous as waitin' for them to cut down on us," said Dutch. "When you must fight, choose your own time and place, and never do what the enemy is expecting you to."

"We emptied some saddles," Whit Sanderson said. "Reckon they'll be back tonight?"

"I doubt it," said Dutch. "We evened the odds some. You outriders sleep a couple of hours. Then you can stand watch while the rest of us catch a few winks. Come first light, we'll tally up some dead outlaws."

Soon as it was light enough to see, they found nine dead men.

"This ain't all of 'em," Dent Wells said. "Some of the varmints rode out trailin' blood. See them patches on the sand? At least two or three more was hard hit."

"My God," said Haskel Collins, "I can't believe we killed nine men."

Nobody said anything. While Collins had done his share of shooting, they all had their doubts as to whether or not he had felled one of the outlaws.

"Let's hitch up and move out," Siringo said.

Dutch estimated they had covered almost forty miles at the end of two days. Pitching camp well before dark, Dutch had taken to riding ahead and then circling back, seeking any sign of Indians or outlaws.

"There'll be rain before suppertime," Cass Carlyle predicted, as he and Tally Slaughter stood watch in the small hours just before dawn.

"I can't argue with that," said Slaughter, as lightning danced across the far western horizon. "That means hunkerin' down, waitin' for the sun to dry up the mud. I swear, I don't know which is more troublesome, hub-deep mud or hub-deep snow."

"Hell, I can answer that," Cass replied. "Snow takes twice as long. When it's deep, you're stuck, waitin' for it to melt. Then, when it finally does, you got mud."

"Damn it," Rusty Karnes growled from the darkness, "are you hombres standin' watch or havin' a tea social? A gent can't sleep through all that palaver."

"You'll likely sleep better with it rainin' in your face," said Slaughter. "There's a hell of a storm buildin' back yonder in the west."

"Since we're all awake," Siringo said, "we'll have an early breakfast and get the jump on that storm."

"Well, hell's bells," said Jules Swenson, "if I'd of wanted to eat breakfast in the dark, I'd of gone to Texas and took a job punchin' cows. Civilized hombres don't roll out of their blankets while it's still dark."

"Swenson," Drago Peeler said, "I've heard you called a heap of things, but nobody's ever accused you of bein' civilized."

As the day wore on, the building storm became a reality. A chill west wind drove in towering thunderheads, and by noon, the distant thunder had rumbled closer. Dutch waved his hat, seeking the attention of the outriders. Kirby Butler trotted his horse on back to the wagon.

"Take another of the riders with you," said Dutch, "and find some high ground, back away from the river. She's gettin' ready to blow, and we need time to rig us a shelter for the supper fire."

Having endured storms on the Kansas plains, Dutch Siringo had prepared for them as best he could. Stretched beneath each wagon bed was a canvas "underbelly" in which there was an ample supply of dry firewood. Within each wagon, there was a twelve-foot square of canvas, and secured to a heavy eyelet in each corner was a length of rope. Outside the wagon box—one on each side—was a sturdy hickory pole ten feet long. These extras had all been Dutch Siringo's doing, while he had been a Beckwith teamster. The rest of the teamsters had ridiculed him at first, but their laughter ceased when Dutch built his cook fire under shelter and escaped the pouring rain. Kirby Butler and Levan Blade waved their hats, and Dutch followed them with his wagon. They had found a plateau that would keep them out of high water, large enough for all the wagons. Dutch pointed his wagon into the rising wind and swung down from the box.

"On to the high ground," he shouted. "Front your wagons with mine. We'll hobble the horses and mules, so they don't drift with the storm."

Once the teams were unharnessed, the horses unsaddled, and all the animals hobbled, the men began erecting their shelters. Two corners of the protective canvas square were roped to the top of the last wagon bow which supported the wagon canvas. Finally, both the long hickory poles were driven into the ground a dozen feet behind the wagon, and to each of the poles was roped one corner of the canvas square. With the front pucker of each wagon canvas secured, the load would be kept dry, while the bulk of the wagon itself bore the force of the wind and rain. The extra square of canvas secured to the wagon bow and the sturdy poles was adequate shelter for cooking, while the wagon's lowered tailgate became a handy table for preparing the meal. Finally, there was room for two men to sit comfortably on the wagon's tailgate, out of the rain while eating.

"We've got just about enough time to get these shelters up," Dutch said.

Two men to a wagon, they spread the protective canvas. Quickly they secured two of the corners to the rear wagon bow, and the remaining corners to the upper ends of the two hickory poles. The overhead canvas was pulled taut and the sharpened ends of the poles were driven into the ground. The storm-bred wind whipped the canvas, threatening to rip it loose.

"After it's rained a while," Dutch shouted, "drive the poles in deeper."

The rain came with such force, that it seemed the sheer weight of it would collapse their shelters, but the canvas held. Using dry wood, their hats sheltering the first small flames, they soon had their supper fires going. Hot coffee lifted their spirits, and despite the storm, their morale was good.

"In such a storm," said Haskel Collins, "I would never have believed this degree of comfort possible."

"A man can stand being wet to the hide or froze three days at a time," Dutch said, "if he has hot coffee, grub, and it ain't rainin' or snowin' on him while he's eatin'."

"When it's stormin' like this, we ought to keep hot coffee on the fire all night," said Brace Weaver. "It'd sure make the night watch a mite easier."

"No reason we can't," Dutch said. "We got the coffee. Keep the fire down to coals. In weather like this, Indians ain't likely to smell the smoke."

Spreading their blankets in such weather was unthinkable, and except those on watch, the men sat on the wagon tailgates and got what sleep they could. The dawn broke gray and dismal. The rain had slacked to a drizzle, allowing Dutch and his men time to grain the horses and mules. They were eating breakfast when the storm again broke loose.

"God," said Brace Weaver, "it's a good thing we brought plenty of grain. Them poor brutes is goin' to be up to their bellies in water, if this don't let up."

"When it gets that deep," Rusty Karnes said, "you just take off your hat, turn it upside down, and hold it steady.

We'll build us a cook fire in it."

They all laughed, but they were uneasy, for the river had begun to rise. At the end of the second day, Dutch made the decision they had been expecting.

"Another day of this, and we'll have to move to higher ground."

"Hell," said Gard Higgins, "this is Kansas. There may not *be* any higher ground."

"Sure there is," Rusty Karnes said. "Nebraska."

"It occurs to me," said Haskel Collins, "that it won't matter, one way or the other. If the wagons bog down in deep mud, how will we move them?"

They looked at one another in embarrassed silence, and it was Siringo who laughed.

"Good point, Mr. Collins," Dutch said, "but I wasn't referrin' to the wagons. You're dead right. There may well *be* no ground higher than this. Leave here, and we risk getting bogged down in even lower ground. We can best protect our cargo by leaving the wagons where they are, and moving ourselves. I've never seen it rain this long without a letup. I reckon we can hold out until tomorrow."

Sometime before dawn the rain ceased, and by the time the outfit had finished breakfast, they were greeted by the welcome rays of the rising sun.

"We have lost three days," said Haskel Collins. "How much longer must we wait?"

"At least another day," Dutch said, "and maybe longer. Move out too soon, and the wagons will bog down to the wheel hubs. So we wait here, or after bogging down, somewhere else."

Fort Kearny, Nebraska. October 13, 1863.

"We're within a day of Fort Kearny," Haskel Collins said. "Will we stop there?"

"Yes," said Dutch. "It's always a good idea to lay over

a day or two. Since they have the telegraph, it's a good way of keepin' track of what the Indians are doing.''

"There is no telegraph once we reach the Bozeman,'' Collins said. "When we leave Fort Laramie, we're on our own. In fact, the government is discouraging civilian use of the Bozeman, entirely.''

"I reckon that don't bother you,'' said Dutch, "or you wouldn't be headed that way.''

"Oh, they don't forbid the use of it,'' Collins said. "They have issued warnings that the trail is unsafe, and that there is constant danger of attack by the Sioux.''

"Since we'll be traveling due north after leaving Fort Laramie,'' said Dutch, "why can't we stay off the Bozeman and make our own trail, farther west?''

"Because the Bozeman is the only sensible trail into Montana Territory,'' Collins said. "Move farther west, and even without snow, the mountains are impassable.''

While Kearny wasn't the largest of forts, it was adequate. Captain Bittner, the post commander, knew Dutch and most of his men.

"Sorry,'' said Bittner, "but I have no recent word on Indian activity. At least, none from Sioux country.''

Some of the outfit had to remain with the wagons, and Dutch allowed his men to visit the post three at a time. When Dutch rode in, Jules Swenson and Brace Weaver were with him. The sutler's store didn't have a full-fledged saloon, but there were three kegs of beer tapped and on-line. While Dutch Siringo's men weren't whiskey-minded, they often had an occasional beer. They ordered, and leaning on the bar, waited for the barkeep to draw their brew. There were three crude X-frame tables, each with a pair of hard wooden benches. Three men sat at one of the tables, their hard eyes on Dutch and his companions. Each wore a tied-down Colt. One of them leaned over and said something to the other two and then turned to face the three men at the bar. When he spoke, it was in a conversational tone.

"You hombres with them wagons that come in this mornin'?"

"We could be," Dutch said quietly. "Any particular reason you're wantin' to know?"

"Maybe. I got the feelin' we've met before."

"If we have," said Dutch, "it was of your choosing. You purely don't look like the kind I'd socialize with, unless we was both locked in the same cell."

"I reckon we ain't met. I've killed varmints with a more civil tongue than yours."

"I don't take kindly to threats," Dutch said.

"I don't like you, bucko. Ain't liked you since the minute I laid eyes on you."

"I reckon I'm not a very likable cuss," said Dutch. "Fact is, there's been some that disliked me so much, I had to shoot the varmints, to put 'em out of their misery."

"None of that, gents," the barkeep said. "There'll be no fightin' in here." He took a sawed-off shotgun from beneath the bar.

"We were about to leave," Dutch said. He placed his empty beer mug on the bar without taking his eyes from the three men at the table.

"Come on, Dutch," said Brace Weaver. "We'll cover you."

Swenson and Weaver had already reached the door, where they waited, thumbs hooked in their pistol belts. The tactic wasn't wasted on the three men at the table. Dutch joined his companions, and the three of them left the store.

"That's three of the bastards that come after our wagons," Jules Swenson said.

"We ain't done with 'em, either," said Brace Weaver. "I'd bet my saddle they'll be along right soon, and I couldn't sleep nights, if they was to get the idea we're scared of 'em."

"I don't hold with shooting an hombre unless he just won't settle for anything less," Dutch said, "and I'm inclined to believe these *busardos* would shoot us in the back at the first opportunity. If there's shootin' to be done, let's do it on our terms.''

They leaned on a hitch rail before the post orderly room, their eyes on the sutler's, a few yards away. They waited only a few minutes, and when the trio emerged, it was clear that they were prepared to fight. Dutch moved away from the hitch rail—Weaver to his left and Swenson to his right.

"I'll take the gent in the middle," said Dutch. "The one with the big mouth."

Jules and Brace said nothing, knowing what was expected of them. A soldier who had been standing in the open door of the orderly room suddenly became aware of what was about to happen, and quickly removed himself from the line of fire. Not a word was spoken as the three men began a slow walk from the sutler's store. When they drew, they seemed of a single mind, their weapons clearing leather simultaneously. But their three adversaries already had their weapons leveled and spitting lead. The trio who had just left the sutler's had died with their pistols in their hands, without firing a shot. Men appeared as though by magic, all of them talking at once. His office being in the same cabin with the orderly room, Captain Bittner was on the scene almost immediately.

"Quiet," the captain shouted. "First, I want to know what's behind this, and then I'll listen to those of you who witnessed it."

"They were spoiling for a fight, Captain," said Dutch. "We believe they were part of a bunch that attacked us on the trail, trying to take our wagons. They drew first."

"They did, sir," said the corporal who had been watching from the orderly room.

"Any more witnesses?" Captain Bittner asked.

"Me, sir," the barkeep shouted. "I watched it from a window, and I never seen anything more fair. These three didn't start their draw until them dead hombres was already pullin' iron."

"Regrettable," Captain Bittner said. "Corporal, have the

sergeant of the guard organize a burial detail. We will identify these men, if possible, Siringo, and I'll see that a report is filed regarding the incident. Be careful.''

"Thank you, Captain," said Dutch. "We'll be taking the trail tomorrow at first light."

Reaching camp, Dutch told the rest of the outfit about the shooting, minimizing it as much as possible.

"That accounts for twelve of them, then," Haskel Collins said. "Is it possible we'll be forced to kill them all?''

"I doubt it," said Dutch. "Those that were left must have split up. I reckon the three we shot today likely had friends or kin among the nine we killed during their attack. These three knew we'd be along, and they waited."

Kansas City, Missouri. October 13, 1863.

"Our first military payroll went through without a hitch, and without hiring guards," Jasper Sneed gloated, "and you said I didn't have a head for business."

"You don't," said Christie Beckwith wearily. "You gambled and won, but for every hand you win, you'll lose three."

"Some more of old daddy Beckwith's sage advice, I suppose," Sneed sneered.

"God knows, my father made his mistakes," she said. "I'm reminded of that, every time I look at you. Beckwith Freight Lines is only a shadow of what it once was, and I owe that to you."

"I might have done better if you had shown more confidence in me. When I asked you to marry me, you laughed in my face."

"I'd rather be dead and in hell than married to you," Christie shouted. "I *want* you to fail, damn you. I'm being dragged down with you, but I don't care. Whatever happens to me, it'll be worth it, seeing you hit bottom."

*   *   *

Honus Faulkner and Olney Sims had grown up in southern Missouri, friends of Jasper Sneed, joining the Confederate army the same day Sneed had left for Kansas City. Faulkner and Sims, during their months with the Confederacy, had accomplished just two things, neither of which would win them any medals. In the fall of 1863, their company had been virtually wiped out, and the pair of ne'er-do-wells had escaped by running for their lives. A twist of fate had left them with a payroll—twenty-five thousand in gold—that had been in possession of their headquarters company. The pair had promptly deserted, and stealing a munitions wagon, had taken the gold and lit out for Missouri. Aided by phenomenal luck, they reached northern Kentucky. There, they left the munitions wagon, stealing a rickety old farm wagon. In the dark of the night, they robbed a clothes-line, outfitting themselves in flannel shirts and overalls.

"You know," said Faulkner, as they sat eating raw turnips taken from somebody's fall planting, "we ain't gonna be safe in Missouri. Once them Rebs find out we wasn't kilt with the others, they won't be thinkin' kindly of us."

"I reckon they won't," Sims said, "but where else can we go?"

"California," said Faulkner. "They'll never find us there. We can live like kings."

"Hell," Sims said, "we don't know nobody in California, and we got no way of gettin' there. It gets God-awful cold in them mountains, with snow likely over our heads."

"All we got to do is get to Kansas City," said Faulkner. "We'll look up our old pard, Jasper Sneed, offerin' him a share of the gold, if he'll help us get to California. You think he won't jump on a deal like that?"

"Sure he will," Sims agreed, "but I don't trust him. He'll figger some way to grab all the gold, while gettin' us hung by the Rebs."

Faulkner laughed. "Why, we growed up together. Our old pard Sneed won't double-cross us, 'cause he ain't gonna get the chance. Once he's done all he can do for us, we'll shoot him.''

"Our old pard?"

"Through the head," said Faulkner. "Quick and merciful, for old times' sake.''

"Yeah," Sims said. "Let's not forget them old times.''

They set out, traveling by night, bound for Kansas City. Little did they know that they were about to arrive at a most opportune time, for Jasper Sneed was in desperate need of money.

CHAPTER 3

✑

Dutch and his outfit were three days west of Fort Kearny when they came upon the charred remains of a wagon. Clothing and personal goods had been scattered all around, and there were the bodies of a man and a woman. Both had been scalped, and the buzzards and coyotes had mutilated the bodies beyond recognition.

"My God," said Haskel Collins, staring in fascinated horror.

"We'll bury what's left of them," Dutch said. "It's all we can do."

The sun bore down from a sunny, cloudless sky, and for mid-October, it was almost uncomfortably warm. The burying had been done, and Dutch was wiping his sweaty face on the sleeve of his shirt, when he saw her walking toward them, along the river. Her long, red hair shone in the morning sun. She was sopping wet, from head to toe, the old shirt plastered to her in a way that left no doubt as to her gender. Speechless, all the men waited until she was within a few yards of them. Her green eyes shifted to first one and then the other, finally coming to rest on Haskel Collins. It was to him that she spoke.

"These are your wagons?"

"No," said Collins. "Only the freight. The wagons be-

long to Siringo Freight Lines. The gentleman to your right
is Dutch Siringo.''

"I'm bound for California," she said. "Can you take me
there?"

"No," said Dutch. "We're going to Montana Territory.
These people we just buried; are they your kin?"

"My aunt and uncle," she said. "We were going to California. Do you mind if I gather up some dry clothes? The
damn Indians didn't leave until they'd eaten all our food,
and I've been hidin' in the river since yesterday morning."

"Go ahead," said Dutch.

She began picking through the clothes strewn about, and
Haskel Collins edged close enough to speak to Dutch without being overheard.

"She's no more than a child, and we can't leave her here.
I believe you should make it plain to her that she can travel
with us only as far as Fort Laramie."

"I'll tell her," said Dutch, "but . . ."

He forgot what he had intended to say, joining the rest
of his outfit in openmouthed amazement. The girl had
found dry clothes, and having removed her sodden gar-
ments, was stark naked. First she donned a dry shirt, and
then the homespun trousers.

"Well, by God," Dutch said, turning to Collins, "what
was you sayin' about her being just a child?"

Collins actually blushed, and the rest of the outfit
laughed. Dutch approached the girl.

"Ma'am, what's your name?"

"Bonita."

"Bonita what?" Dutch persisted.

"Just Bonita."

"We'll need your family name, to return you to your
kin."

"I have no family, and I'm not returning anywhere,"
she said.

"We'll take you on to Fort Laramie," said Dutch.
"From there, the government will be responsible for you."

"I don't want the government being responsible for me. Take me with you, wherever you're going. I can pay my way."

"With what?" Dutch asked. "You have only the clothes you're wearing, and whatever you can salvage from the burned wagon."

She laughed, her green eyes twinkling. "I'm a woman, and all of you are men. If you can't figure *that* out . . ."

Dutch felt his face going red. "Ma'am," he said, "you don't owe us anything for takin' you on to Fort Laramie, but that's as far as you go. Now if there's anything you aim to take from the wagon, you'd best be gatherin' it up."

She took only a few articles of clothing, bundling it all up in a long-legged pair of ladies' bloomers. His companions all looked slanch-eyed at Dutch, grinning.

"Ma'am," said Dutch, "you're welcome to ride one of our horses, or you can ride the wagon box, with one of the teamsters."

"I can't ride a horse," she said. "I'll ride in the wagon with you."

Having little choice, Dutch boosted her up to the wagon box, acutely aware that all the outfit—even Haskel Collins—was giving him the horse laugh.

Dutch mounted the box, popped his whip, and took the lead. He kept his eyes straight ahead, grimly aware of the girl beside him. Finally she spoke.

"You don't talk much, do you?"

"A gent that keeps his mouth shut hardly ever ends up with his foot in it," Dutch replied. "If you feel like talking, tell me about yourself."

"There's nothing to tell."

"How old are you?" he asked.

"Eighteen."

"You don't look a day past sixteen," Dutch said.

"Seventeen, then."

"Sixteen," Dutch persisted.

"All right," she shouted, "sixteen, damn it."

She refused to look at him, and Dutch laughed. She ignored him as long as she could, and he caught her cutting her eyes at him while she faced straight ahead. She laughed and immediately put him back on the defensive.

"I may be just sixteen," she said, "but you'll have to admit I have everything in all the right places."

"I won't deny that," said Dutch. "Was that the purpose of the strip act, to advertise the goods?"

"Is there a better way?" she asked boldly. "I want to be somebody, go places, and I'll pay the fare any way that I can."

"I get your drift," said Dutch, "but a woman never betters herself by working cribs. Whores are old and used-up before they're thirty, and then they die. Does that appeal to you?"

"No," she said in a small voice, "but what am I going to do?"

"Find you a man, settle down, and have kids," said Dutch.

"To be old and used-up before I'm thirty, and then I die?"

"Damn it," Dutch said, irritated, "it happens to all of us, sooner or later, but don't you reckon, durin' them years in between, that a good man might make some difference?"

"I don't know." She sniffed. "Men only want to use a woman. I've been used, and I can't imagine it ever bein' any different."

"I've never used or abused a woman," said Dutch, realizing as he said it that he had hogtied himself.

"Do you want me?" she asked hopefully.

"Damn it, girl, don't be so quick to throw yourself around. Two hours ago, you had never heard of me."

"You don't want me, then. Maybe one of the others . . ."

"Bonita," said Dutch, sensing her misery, "you're inviting men to take advantage of you. You're a pretty girl, and I'm not rejecting you, but hell, we're practically strangers. I don't know you, and you don't know me. It takes time.''

"That's why I want to go on with you to . . . wherever you're going. By then . . .''

Dutch said no more. He was already in deep enough. She didn't speak again, ignoring him, and he preferred that to the delicate nature of their prior conversation. The sun was an hour high when Dutch reined his team and called it a day. By the time the horses had been unsaddled and the mules unharnessed, Bonita had a fire going and was busy preparing supper. It was a chore they all hated, and today the task had fallen to Dent Wells and Tally Slaughter. Dutch eyed them questioningly, and they shrugged their shoulders.

"She says she's payin' her way," said Tally, "and by God, if she can cook at all, don't you say nothin' to discourage her.''

Dutch said nothing and was left out on a limb by himself, when every man swore it was the best meal he'd had since leaving Kansas City. Without a word, when the meal was done, Bonita gathered up the tin plates, cups, and eating tools. These, along with the coffeepot, she washed thoroughly.

"Ma'am," said Brace Weaver, "if you wasn't a trail cook before, you should of been.''

Bonita cast a triumphant look at Dutch and flashed Weaver a smile that would have melted a High Plains snowdrift. Dutch sighed, dreading their arrival at Fort Laramie, for it had been his decision to leave Bonita there.

While Bonita had no proper bedroll, there were extra blankets, and she slept under Dutch's wagon. It was an arrangement that had worked well, until another storm struck and the ground was awash with muddy water. Enough of their provisions had been used to allow extra space in the supply wagon, and it was there that Dutch had told the girl to spend her nights until the storm had blown itself out. Drago

Peeler and Dutch had the just-before-dawn watch, and Haskel Collins dozed on the tailgate of the supply wagon. He was jostled as Bonita crept out.

"Where are you going?" Collins asked.

"Outside a ways," said Bonita. "Some things I can't do in the wagon."

Collins forgot about the girl for suddenly the mules began to bray, and one of the horses nickered. Every man who dozed was instantly awake, his Henry ready. But the commotion died down. The outfit came together, and Dutch spoke.

"This is Pawnee country. I'd not be surprised if that wasn't some of 'em usin' the rain for cover, taking our measure."

Only then did Haskel Collins remember Bonita.

"Damn it," said Dutch, "you shouldn't have let her go."

"She had personal business outside the wagon," Collins said stiffly, "and as a gentleman, I was in no position to forbid her."

"By God," said Dutch, "where Indians are concerned, personal business don't matter. She should have squatted on the wagon tailgate."

"Hell," said Whit Sanderson, "what's done is done, and us cussin' one another ain't gonna change a thing. The worst of the storm's over, and there'll be tracks."

"He's right," Brace Weaver added. "First light ain't more'n an hour off."

They waited, begrudging the time before the first gray light of dawn crept into the eastern sky.

"Brace," said Dutch, "I want you and Jules to ride with me. The rest of you stay here and keep your Henrys handy. This could be a trick to draw as many of us as possible away from the wagons."

"You could also ride headlong into a hundred Pawnees," said Tally Slaughter.

"That's a chance we'll have to take," Dutch replied.

"That many Pawnees could cut us down to the last man, while if there's not so many, three of us with Henrys can put up one hell of a fight."

The moccasin tracks and the tracks of the girl were plain enough, and they found where the Indian had mounted his horse. He had wasted no time in entering the river, and they had to make a choice.

"West," said Dutch. "He rode in from that direction, and it's away from our camp."

They followed the river for nearly three miles before finding where the horse had left the water.

"I hope this is the right horse," Jules said.

"It is," said Dutch. "It's carryin' two riders. And what other purpose would a single Pawnee have for ridin' around in the tag end of a storm? That commotion with the horses and mules could have been to get our attention, while this varmint grabbed Bonita."

Warily, they followed the tracks, and none of them were surprised when the single horseman was joined by three others.

"Them three varmints spooked the horses and mules," said Brace.

"This is goin' to be some trick, gettin' her away from them in broad daylight," Jules said. "Damn shame we can't wait till dark."

"Hell," said Dutch, "that's twelve hours. Wait that long, and we might as well let 'em keep her."

The wind—an occasional breeze—was out of the west, and it brought them the first warning of the nearness of the Pawnee camp. They were in south central Nebraska, and the flat Kansas plain had given way to ravines and rises. There was underbrush and thickets, offering some cover.

"We'd best leave the horses right here," Dutch said. "There may not be enough cover for us. Bring your Henry."

Leaving the horses behind was a calculated risk of which each of them was well aware, for discovery by the Pawnees could result in quick pursuit. But they had no choice, there being the need to first locate the camp and determine its strength. The sun was already up and beating down with a vengeance, and the three of them were wishing they had shucked their coats. Suddenly a horse nickered just a few yards away, and they froze.

"By God," Jules whispered, "their horses are between us and the camp. Suppose we was to circle around an' come in from the west? We could maybe grab the gal and spook their mounts on the way out."

"Depends on where they are," Dutch whispered back. "There may not be a scrap of cover to the west of their camp. We got to get as close as we can, and that means cover for us and our horses. The farther we got to ride after we're discovered, the better their chances of filling our hides full of arrows."

They crept closer, and reaching the crest of a short ridge, found themselves looking down on a shallow arroyo. There was a spring, with graze, and Dutch counted nineteen horses. On the rim, with virtually no cover, were seven tepees. Several cook fires were burned down to coals. Four Indians were stationed at intervals around one of the tepees.

"Damn," said Brace. "A sidewinder couldn't cross all that empty ground without bein' seen. Ain't no doubt the gal's in the tent with all the guards, but we can't get to her without scatterin' that bunch of Indians."

"That's what we're about to do," Dutch said. "First we get back to the horses. Jules, you and me will circle the camp, comin' in as close as we can from the west. Brace, you'll bring your horse up here where we are now. Jules, you'll come skalley-hootin' down that arroyo, scattering their horses. When you've done that, ride like hell. That should bring the whole bunch out like bees from a kicked-over hive. Brace, that's where it all depends on you. Cut loose with your Henry, first goin' after them four hombres that's outside the tepee where Bonita is. After that, take any target you can get. I'll be gallopin' across that open ground, goin' after Bonita.''

"You're taking the position where you're most likely to get yourself killed," Brace said. "Why not one of us?"

"My outfit, my choice," said Dutch. "When you get your own outfit, you can risk your own neck. Now let's jump that bunch, before they finish breakfast.''

Reaching their horses, Dutch had final words of caution.

"Jules, the first move is yours. Once those horses are running, get the hell out of there. Brace, some of them may manage to grab a horse. Don't set up here on this ridge and allow them to ride you down. I'll have just a few seconds to get Bonita out of there, before they discover what we're up to. If I fail, don't sell your lives trying to pay for my mistake. *Comprender?*''

"*Si*," they said in a single voice.

Dutch and Jules mounted their horses and rode south, while Brace led his horse up to the crest of the ridge. When Dutch and Jules were a mile to the west of the Pawnee camp, Dutch dismounted. Jules rode on, seeking to get as near the end of the arroyo as he was able. Dutch led his horse as near as he dared, and the open stretch over which he must ride seemed wider than ever. He mounted, waiting. Dangerous though it was, he believed it was a good plan. A man on the frontier—Indian or white—generally forgot everything else, when his horse was spooked. When Jules began shouting and shooting, the Indian mounts lit out toward the ridge where Brace Weaver was hiding. As soon as the horses started to run, Brace cut loose with his Henry. Some of the Pawnees chose to pursue the horses, and Brace ignored them, throwing lead at those who had decided to fight. But they faced a new danger. Thundering at them from the west, Dutch Siringo had a flaming Colt in one hand, and another under his belt. He cut down one of the Pawnees who tried to remain at his post, leaving the tepee unprotected. Reining up, standing in his stirrups, Dutch seized the upper end of one of the lodge poles. With a mighty heave, he toppled the tepee. With a glad cry, wearing only a blanket, Bonita sprang to her feet. Dutch caught her hand, lifting her to the saddle in front of him. But despite Brace's formidable accuracy with the Henry, some of the warriors had turned on Dutch. He shot one, and his Colt clicked on empty. He wheeled the horse, kicking it into a gallop, riding back the way he had come. His horse screamed as a lance raked its flank. He rode down two attackers, as the clawing fingers of a third seized Bonita's blanket. Dutch smashed the Pawnee in the face with his empty Colt, and the brave fell away, taking Bonita's blanket with him. Brace had ceased firing, and looking back, Dutch could have shouted. There was no pursuit! He slowed the heaving horse to a walk, very much aware that without the blanket, Bonita was completely naked.

"You're not returning to camp like that," Dutch said, reining up. "I just happen to have an extra blanket."

"Damn," said Bonita, "there goes my glorious return."

"This is no time to be funny," Dutch said. "You're lucky to come out of this alive. Do you have any idea what might have happened to you?"

"Ah reckon," she said, mimicking his speech. "I think they all would have taken their turns with me, but for my red hair. They were saving me for somebody important."

"Likely the chief," said Dutch. "Has this taught you anything?"

"Ah reckon," she replied. "Hold it till daylight, or squat on the wagon tailgate."

Despite himself, Dutch laughed, and accidentally or on purpose, she dropped the ends of the blanket.

"Now you stop that," said Dutch, gathering up the blanket. "We're quite a ways from camp, and that bunch of Pawnees will be rounding up their horses, mad as hell."

Dutch hoisted her to the saddle, mounted, and rode south.

"Dutch?"

"What?"

"Would it have bothered you, if they'd . . . had their way with me?"

"It would," said Dutch. "You're a damn good cook, and I reckon that might have distracted you from your work."

"Damn you, Dutch Siringo," she said, slapping his face, "you don't give a woman anything to hold on to, do you?"

"You have a blanket," said Dutch.

When they reached camp, they found the outfit anxiously awaiting them.

"You had us some worried," Brace said. "I fired as long as I could, but the varmints was comin' up the ridge after me."

"They'll be awhile roundin' up their horses," said Jules. "Most of 'em was ahead of me, and I run the hell out of 'em."

"They'll have rounded them up by tonight," Dutch said, "and unless they consider this bad medicine, they still could come after us. We need to cover as much distance as we can, and then post a strong watch for the next two or three nights."

"Hell," Cass Carlyle complained, "we ain't had breakfast."

"Is that a fact?" said Dutch. "What have you been doing for the past two hours?"

Rusty Karnes laughed. "Waitin' for you to bring the cook. What else could we of done?"

In quick succession, Beckwith Freight Lines lost two government payrolls, both to outlaws. Each time a teamster had been killed, and the others had quit. Frantic appeals in the newspapers were ignored, and Jasper Sneed became desperate. Occasionally, he met John McGruder, and the banker regarded him in cold-eyed contempt. His bank debt was more than three thousand dollars, and Sneed was only too well aware that time was growing short. Josh Beckwith had done a thriving business, and Sneed had believed he could do as well or better, with Christie Beckwith at his side. Now he was virtually face-to-face with two terrible truths. Christie Beckwith had been mildly rebellious toward her father, and she had used Sneed to that end. Now she had no further use for him. The second and most painful dose of reality had convinced Sneed he was riding for a fall. Not only had the Beckwith legacy denied him the riches he sought, but the few assets of his own had been swallowed up. His insurers had put him on notice. He had filed two enormous claims in two months. Another, and his coverage would be canceled. He had reason to believe there was a Judas in the upper echelons of the military, selling information on the payrolls to outlaws, but he had no proof. Slowly his devious mind began to conceive a plan. Suppose he, Jasper Sneed, *arranged* to have the payroll stolen? True, his insurers would be left holding the sack, but Jasper Sneed would have the money. He could then tell Beckwith Freight Lines and the uppity Christie Beckwith to go to hell. The more he thought of it, the more it appealed to him. While he had kept up a respectable front, he had maintained a relationship with the killers and thieves who frequented the saloons and dives along the river, and it was there that he went to put his plan in motion.

"Now let me git this straight," said the bearded man, with a patch over his left eye. "You'll be tellin' us when the payload's comin', and all we got to do is take it, bringin' it back here, where we divvy it up."

"That's it," Sneed said. "There's no risk, and you'll get a third. I expect it to be at least twenty-five thousand."

"Hell, Leech," said a companion, "we oughta git half."

"Shut up, Pig," Leech replied. "It's a deal, Sneed. You'll be tellin' us when?"

"I'll tell you when," said Sneed.

When Sneed had gone, the two ruffians looked at one another and grinned. Pig had an enormous Bowie knife, border-shifting it from one hand to the other.

"You come off like a damn fool, demandin' half," Leech said. "Hell, we ain't got to kill nobody but Sneed, an' we can take it all."

"That's why I allus liked bein' pards with you," said Pig. "You ain't satisfied with just a share of nothin'. You want it all. You got a real head fer business."

But Sneed's scheme never got off the ground. His government contracts were withdrawn, and he was hard-pressed to endure the knowing smirks from Christie Beckwith. Even after taking over Beckwith Freight Lines, he had maintained an office. He often went there, locking the door behind him. Following this latest double-barreled defeat, he needed seclusion, to think, to lick his wounds. When he lighted the lamp in the dingy office, his eyes fell on the sheet of paper that had been slipped under the door.

"Ole pard," the crudely printed message began, "we got big money. Help us git to Californy, an' we'll share with you. Be here at midnight."

It was signed, "Honus and Olney."

Sneed laughed, recalling the bumbling duo and his growing-up years. How could they have gotten their hands on the "big money" they spoke of? The last he had seen of them, they had joined the Confederate army. Had they possibly become successful thieves? He doubted it, for he still recalled them getting their behinds torn up with buckshot, just for stealing watermelons. Still, circumstances had reduced him to grasping at straws, and he settled down to await the arrival of Honus and Olney.

A week west of Fort Kearny, the fair weather ended, and a chill west wind suggested that something more ominous than rain lay ahead. Dutch and his outfit still followed the North Platte River, and the terrain was no longer flat.

"We'd best find us a place to hole up," said Dutch. "Overhead canvas ain't enough when the snow comes down from the mountains on a howling wind. We need a canyon with a high rim, water, and some not-too-distant windblown trees.''

"From the feel of the wind,'' Tally Slaughter said, "we ain't got much time.''

But to their surprise, they found just such a canyon. It obviously became a runoff from the Platte, during high water, but the river was at a low ebb. The canyon began in a shallow way a little more than a mile south, growing deeper and wider as the northern end of it neared the Platte. A seep from the river created a stream along the canyon floor that would be sufficient for the needs of Dutch and his outfit. Water had undercut the west bank, leaving a lip of rock thirty feet above the canyon floor.

"A remarkable piece of luck,'' said Haskel Collins. "The rim itself offers sufficient shelter to keep out the snow, as well as the wind.''

"It's still a couple of hours till dark,'' Dutch said, "and we may have to ride three or four miles to find enough firewood. We'll take axes with us and snake back as many windblown trees as we can. The way the temperature's dropping, it'll be almighty cold by morning.''

The snow began before dark, drifting in against the eastern rim of the canyon, where it was no inconvenience. Even the mules and horses came close to the fires to be fed their ration of grain. After supper, a coffeepot was kept on the coals, providing hot coffee. It became a pleasant time, with the cold and the roaring wind shut out.

"I've been thinking,'' said Whit Sanderson. "The real danger of freighting in winter is gettin' caught in a snowstorm on the open plains and freezin' to death. West of Kearny, as the country takes on hills and arroyos, there's got to be other canyons like this. All we got to do is find us a few more, and when we smell a blizzard blowin' in, shag out for the nearest shelter. We'll lose some time hunkered around a warm fire, eatin' good grub, but it makes more sense than settin' out on the prairie, your hands froze to the reins.''

"You're readin' my mind," Dutch said. "We can't change the weather, but we can adapt to it. Most freighters are so put out with the delays, they think only in terms of how much money they're losing while they wait out a storm. Yet, these same hombres set through a three-day rain, unable to move their wagons because of hub-deep mud. As long as freight moves in wagons drawn by mules or oxen, there'll be days when not a damn thing happens, and it won't matter if it's raining or snowing."

CHAPTER 4

✺

*T*he storm began its second day, and aside from tending the fires and seeing that the horses and mules were fed, there was little to do except talk.

"Before I left the diggings along the Bitterroot," said Collins, "I was told that nobody could freight in anything between September and April, because of the snow. I daresay my father is expecting word that my frozen body has been discovered somewhere on the High Plains. He all but commanded me to wait until spring, but I can't see that it would have made any difference. I've seen spring rains flood the Mississippi, with backwater extending for a mile on either side. Soak the earth with enough rain or snow, and it becomes mud."

"Amen to that," Dutch said.

"This is a bold thing to do, Mr. Collins," said Gard Higgins. "If I ain't pokin' my nose in where I got no business, do you aim to live in Montana Territory?"

"Yes," Collins replied. "There is potential on the western frontier like nowhere else on earth. I intend to become part of it, to build and grow with it."

"That's an admirable ambition," said Brace Weaver. "You'll likely have the only tradin' post between Fort Laramie and the Canadian border."

"There'll be an awful lot of work," Bonita said. "I have

no family, and nobody wants me. Could you make a place for me, Mr. Collins? I can keep house, I can cook, and I'd not expect any pay.''

For a while, nobody said anything. The girl's plea had touched them all, but it had gotten to Dutch Siringo in a way that he couldn't understand. He had to admit to himself that he would have a difficult time of it, leaving her at Fort Laramie, even if she agreed to stay, and even if the post commander agreed to take her. Finally, after a lengthy silence, Collins spoke. ''There will be a place for you, but I will want you to be more than a housekeeper and cook. I'll want you to become my wife.''

His words had a profound effect on them all. Dutch had trouble breathing, and his heart pounded with such force, it seemed the others might hear it. He leaned forward, his ears tuned to catch the girl's response, dreading the possibility that she might accept this strange proposal.

''I . . . I'm flattered, Mr. Collins,'' Bonita said, ''but I'd be afraid to . . . go so far . . . so . . . soon. Couldn't you . . . let me stay for a while . . . and see . . . ?''

''I will consider it,'' said Collins.

Bonita turned away, facing the darkness, and Dutch could have gut-shot Collins for his indifference. The tone of the conversation changed, losing something, and they all fell silent.

''We'll maintain our usual watch,'' Dutch said. ''Two men, two hours. I'll take the last watch before dawn.''

''I'll join you,'' said Brace Weaver.

''With the protection this canyon affords,'' Collins said, ''I see no need for watches.''

It was a foolish remark, and before anyone could counter it, there came the eerie cry of a prairie wolf. From a point not too distant, the cry was answered.

''Those of you on watch,'' said Dutch—and his eyes were on Collins—''pay attention to the shallow end of this canyon, and keep your Henrys ready.''

It was an indirect reprimand to Haskel Collins, for

Dutch's outfit well knew what the big gray predators could do to horse or mule. Collins stood looking into the fire, saying nothing, and Dutch wondered what the *real* Collins was like.

Kansas City, Missouri. November 2, 1863.

"Twenty-five thousand, in gold? By God, I got to see it to believe it," Jasper Sneed said.

"Ain't nobody seein' it," said Honus Faulkner, "till we got us the promise of a ticket to Californy."

"You don't trust me, your old pard, then," Sneed said, attempting to look as hurt as possible.

"We risked our damn necks to git this far," said Olney Sims, "an' we ain't takin' no chances now. Not even with old pards."

Sneed laughed. They had smartened up some. He would have to play on their egos.

"Times is hard," Sneed said, becoming serious. "I reckon it takes some brains, comin' up with twenty-five thousand."

"Damn right it does," said Olney, standing a little straighter. "Now how you aim to git us to Californy?"

"I have a freighting company," Sneed said. "We'll hide the gold in a false bottom, under the wagon box."

"Hell's fire," said Honus, "you sayin' we got to drive a wagon all the way acrost them plains an' mountains to Californy?"

"By God, you don't like my way, then just leave me out of it," Sneed said. "Get on a steamboat to St. Louis, take another to New Orleans, and from there, board a sailing ship. Of course, if you ain't got a legal claim to that gold, there may be a bounty on both your heads. The law may be watching the steamboats . . ."

"Aw, hell," Olney said, "Honus was just funnin'. Wasn't you, Honus?"

"Yeah," said Honus sullenly.

"That's better," Sneed said. "I'll be goin' with you. If it was dangerous, would I risk my own hide?"

"I reckon you wouldn't," said Honus grudgingly. "When are we goin'?"

"Be here with your wagon tomorrow at midnight," Sneed said. "We'll swap the gold from your wagon to mine."

"What makes your wagon any better than ours?" Honus asked suspiciously.

"Mine's a freight wagon," said Sneed smoothly. "I'll throw on a few pieces of freight bound for Fort Laramie, in case anybody gets nosey."

They parted company, neither Honus nor Olney speaking until they were well beyond Sneed's hearing.

"Hell," said Olney, "we didn't figger on him goin' with us."

Honus laughed. "That's all the better. It would of been risky, killin' him here in town. Now we can git him out on the plains, where nobody'll be the wiser."

Sneed was thinking similar thoughts, reared back in his chair, his feet on the desk. He felt a moment's regret for not having milked the anticipated fortune from Beckwith Freight Lines, but that couldn't be helped. Provided that Honus and Olney had the gold—and it made no sense for them to lie—he could arrive in California with a stake. Once they were far from town, it would be a simple matter to back shoot his ignorant companions. . . .

Two days after the storm had blown itself out, Siringo's outfit again took the trail west. They kept to the high ground as much as possible, for it was still bitter cold, and in shaded areas, the snow hadn't melted. For the lack of a coat, Bonita was wrapped in wool blankets.

"I miss the canyon," said Bonita. "It was nice."

"Better than being out in the storm," Dutch agreed.

"I didn't mean it . . . like that," she said. "It was . . .

almost like . . . we were a family, and for just . . . a little while I . . . felt like I . . . belonged.''

Dutch cut his eyes toward her, but she kept her eyes straight ahead, as though she hadn't the courage to face him. When she said no more, he spoke. ''You really don't aim to hitch up with Haskel Collins, do you?''

''No,'' she replied, still not looking at him. ''If I did, just for food and a roof over my head, wouldn't I still be a whore?''

''Not in the eyes of the world,'' he said. ''Many a woman has settled for that.''

''Maybe I could,'' she said, ''if he was . . . different. He talks so nice, but he talks one way and acts another. There's something about him . . . something false . . .''

''Don't say anything more about going to Montana Territory with him,'' said Dutch.

''But . . . what will I do? Where will I go, after . . . ?''

''Trust me,'' Dutch said. ''When we reach Fort Laramie, I'll have to report the deaths of your kin by Indians. Beyond that, I don't know . . .''

''Must you tell them about me?''

The pleading in her voice touched him, and when Dutch faced her, there were tears on her cheeks. He decided the anguish in her eyes was genuine, that it wasn't an act. When he spoke, it was with a question.

''Bonita, what are you afraid of? What haven't you told me?''

''I can't tell you,'' she cried. ''You'd . . . send me back. You'd have to. The law . . .''

''Because you're only sixteen?''

''That, and . . .''

''And what? You haven't killed somebody, have you?''

''My God, no. I . . . I ran away . . . from a foster home . . .''

''I noticed you wasn't too broke up over the man and woman killed by Indians,'' Dutch said. ''If they wasn't kin of yours, who were they?''

"Their name was McClellan. In Springfield, Illinois, one morning while it was still dark, I hid in their wagon. When they discovered me, I convinced them I was an orphan and begged them not to send me back. They let me stay when they found I could do all the hard work, the washing, and the cooking."

"Why are you so sure you'll be sent back to Illinois?" Dutch asked.

"This old bas . . . man and his woman make their living taking in orphans, wards of the state. The state pays them. They've already been paid to keep me until I'm eighteen, and if they don't find me, they'll have to give back the money."

"How much money?" Dutch asked.

"I'm not sure. A hundred . . . maybe two hundred . . . dollars."

"My God," said Dutch, "they'd hound you all across the western frontier for that? I can't believe there are people that greedy."

"They are," she said. "They fed us just twice a day, and there was never any meat."

"What is your name, besides Bonita?"

"I've told you everything else," she said. "It's Konda. Bonita Konda."

"Well, Bonita Konda, if you're telling me the truth, I aim to see that you're not sent back to any foster home."

Her eyes got big, her lip trembled, and she threw her arms around him, weeping. When she let him go, and Dutch again focused his attention on the trail, he saw Haskel Collins watching them. He had reined up a hundred yards ahead, and when he became aware that Dutch had seen him, he kicked his horse into a lope and rode on.

"Damn," said Kirby Butler, "it's been below zero for a week. Ain't it supposed to warm up after a blizzard?"

"Yeah," Whit Sanderson said, "but that wasn't a blizzard. She's got to blow at least four days to be an honest-to-God blizzard. I thought you was brung up in the West."

"I was," said Kirby defensively.

"Western Ohio," Drago Peeler said.

"You pecker woods better hope it don't warm up too much," said Brace Weaver. "Let 'er warm up enough, and there'll be more snow. Not that I don't enjoy hunkerin' in some desolate canyon and lookin' at your cheerful mugs for four straight days and nights."

Their humor—which occasionally became pretty crude—never ceased to amuse Bonita, but it seemed to have the opposite effect on Haskel Collins. Since the snowed-in days and nights in the canyon, he had said little, and Dutch Siringo suspicioned it had a lot to do with Bonita Konda.

Brace Weaver's prediction proved accurate. For the first time in days, the temperature rose enough for the men to remove their heavy coats, and by sundown, the big gray clouds had begun to gather in the west.

"Damn it," said Rusty Karnes, "here we go again."

"She'll be givin' us hell this time tomorrow," Tally Slaughter said. "If we aim to hole up somewhere, we'd best start lookin' for a place in the mornin'."

"There's a chance we'll find another dry runoff adjoining the Platte," said Dutch. "If nothing else, we'll dig in on the lee side of a hill and peg down our canvas."

But they weren't so fortunate, for the Platte had leveled out for as far as they could see. Drago Peeler rode ten miles—farther than the wagons could travel before the storm was expected to reach them—and found nothing more promising than a rise with a spring at the foot of it.

"Plenty of slope to break the wind," said Drago, "and there's downed trees for firewood, but we'll have to depend on our canvas for shelter."

"That's why every wagon has a shovel," Dutch said. "We'll peg the upper side of the canvas down, and shovel on enough dirt so the wind don't rip it loose."

"My mama would be proud of me," said Cass Carlyle. "She always wanted me to learn a trade, and I reckon I've exceeded her expectations. I can pop a whip over them mules' behinds, I can hire on to chop wood, or I can dig anything that's needin' to be dug.''

They reached the slope an hour past noon, and already the clouds had swallowed the sun. The wind from the west was cold. Quickly the men broke out the canvas shelters: six of them, each a dozen feet square, with eyelets along the edge, so they could all be joined together with heavy cord or rawhide.

"We'll lay down the first one near the spring," said Dutch, "joining the others in a line back along the slope. Some of you take shovels and begin piling dirt along those upper edges, while the rest of us secure the poles along the front."

Conscious of the impending storm, they quickly built the shelter. When the heavy hickory poles had been driven into the ground, the loose ends of the canvas were secured to the tops of the poles.

"Now," Dutch said, "a couple of you get under there with rawhide and begin lacing the edges of those canvas squares together. The rest of us will ride out and begin snaking in all the firewood we can find."

The wagon in which all their provisions were stored was backed up so that the tailgate let down under the overhead shelter. Most of the windblown trees were pine, a soft wood that could quickly be cut into suitable lengths. By the time sleet began rattling off the canvas, the outfit was ready. The wind rose to a shriek, driving before it a curtain of snow that seemed to shroud the world in white.

"This is almost as nice as the canyon," Bonita said, "but after awhile, won't the weight of the snow collapse the canvas?"

"No," said Dutch, "for two reasons. Our shelter is on a slope, and the canvas itself is sloped. But the most important reason is the wind. There's always wind on the High Plains, and the more violent the storm, the stronger the wind. Under this shelter, it's our friend. Without the shelter, it would just as quickly turn on us, becoming our deadly enemy.''

"Dutch gets all the credit for this,'' Brace Weaver said. "I never drove with anybody else that thinks ahead like he does. We're goin' to make some big tracks in the freightin' business, gettin' our cargo to the frontier in winter.''

Lacking a bedroll, Bonita still slept in the supply wagon. Recalling the near tragic episode with the Indians, she crept under the wagon at night, when there was personal need. Twice, on such occasions, she found Haskel Collins near the front of the wagon. While he was out of sight of the shelter, he could see Bonita. The second time it happened, she confronted him. It was far into the night, and Dutch and Brace were on watch. They were alerted by Bonita's angry voice.

"What's the commotion about?'' Dutch asked.

"Twice I have gone under the wagon to relieve myself,'' said Bonita, "and twice I have had him standing in front of it.''

"Merely a coincidence,'' Collins said. "I had business outside the shelter, myself.''

"Bonita is restricted to the wagon at night,'' said Dutch, "and you know it. The next time during the night, when you have business outside the shelter, limit yourself to the other end, well away from this wagon.''

Nothing more was said, and Collins returned to his blankets. Dutch helped Bonita back into the wagon. The storm was done, and the moon and starlight on the drifted snow made it light as day. Neither Dutch nor Brace spoke, but their eyes met, and each knew they shared the same doubt.

"Heavier snow, this time,'' said Whit Sanderson the following morning, "and with them big ugly clouds coverin' up the sun, she ain't likely to melt any time soon.''

"We'll wait it out,'' Dutch replied. "A couple more days won't make any difference, but the wolves might. The horses and mules have no protection here, except for us and our guns.''

"We could have us a wolf hunt," said Cass Carlyle. "Go after the varmints before they come after us."

"Snow's too deep for the horses," Dutch said, "and I won't risk it afoot. We'll shovel away enough snow to build another fire down the slope from us. Near that fire, we'll have all our stock where we can watch them. They'll get as near us as they can, if those wolves come on the prowl."

The howling began just after dark, spooking the horses and mules. Horses nickered and mules brayed, coming as near the lighted shelter as they could. Brace Weaver, Jules Swenson, and Rusty Karnes stood near the extra fire, between the frightened stock and the outer darkness, their Henry repeaters ready.

"Damn it," said Collins, "we'll never get any sleep with all that howling."

"You don't know how right you are," Dutch said grimly. "Don't you even think about closing your eyes. Those are our teams out there, and if anything happens to them, these wagons—loaded with your freight—will still be settin' here on Judgment Day."

The wolves came closer, the eerie howling seeming to come from every direction. In a single motion, Brace, Jules, and Rusty began firing.

"Come on," Dutch shouted, "they're comin' down the ridge above us."

The gray beasts made poor targets against the white of the snow, but Dutch and his companions accounted for five of the wolves. As suddenly as it had begun, the howling ceased.

"Thank God," said Collins. "They're gone."

"Collins," Jules Swenson said, "it's when you *don't* hear the brutes, you'd better keep your eyes open and your long gun ready."

As though to drive home the warning, one of the horses screamed. Bounding through the snow from above the spring came two snarling wolves. Dent Wells and Tally Slaughter, being the closest, fired.

"That's seven," said Gard Higgins. "God, there must be a hundred of them."

"The more we shoot tonight, the fewer of them we'll have to shoot tomorrow night," Dutch said.

"How many do you have to kill before it scares the others away?" Bonita asked.

"Honey," said Drago Peeler, "they're hungry, and when they're hungry, they purely don't scare easy."

"We'll sleep in shifts during daylight hours," Dutch said. "Tonight, and every night for as long as necessary, we'll defend our horses and mules."

The next day dawned clear and cold, and the sun rose in a brilliantly blue sky. The sun on the endless expanse of white had a blinding effect.

"Tomorrow, maybe," said Whit Sanderson, his eyes on the sun.

"Tomorrow, hell," Cass Carlyle scoffed. "It'll take two days for all this stuff to melt, and two more for the sun to dry up the mud. We could have our mail sent here, if they was any."

His prediction came close. There was a second night of shooting wolves, followed by a day of gradually melting snow. As the ground began to thaw, the stakes anchoring the upper side of their shelter began to pull loose, collapsing some of their protective canvas. Two days after the worst of the snow was gone, the sun had sucked enough moisture from the earth for the weary teamsters to resume their journey. There were occasional sloughs with mud, but they detoured, keeping the heavy wagons on high ground.

"We should have reached Fort Laramie by now," Collins grumbled.

"You've come down with an almighty short memory," said Dutch. "We've lost a good two weeks, waiting for mud to dry and snow to melt. What's happened to all your highfalutin cock-a-doodle-doo about becomin' a part of the frontier?"

Collins seemed about to respond, but thought better of it and said nothing.

"I wish Fort Laramie was behind us," Bonita said, when she and Dutch were alone on the wagon box.

"Stop worrying about Fort Laramie," said Dutch. "Remember what I told you."

"I am remembering, and I'm thanking you ever so much, but I can't help worrying. I was ten when Mama and Daddy died in a steamboat explosion, and after that, it just . . . seemed . . . nothing would ever be . . . right."

Dutch said nothing. He knew she was grateful to him for his promising to rescue her from the detested foster home, but beyond that, what were her feelings for him? Try as he might, he couldn't forget those first desperate words, when she had offered herself to him—or to any man in the outfit—just for the sake of escaping her past. He tried to get her off his mind, to think of those days with Christie Beckwith, which now seemed so long ago. He had reached the unhappy conclusion that much of his feeling for Christie Beckwith had resulted from his desire to live old Josh's dream, and Christie had been so much a part of Beckwith Lines, he had become lost somewhere between the dream and reality. Now that he had his feelings in order, where Bonita Konda was concerned, how could he ever be sure that she felt anything more for him than gratitude?

"What are you thinking about?" she asked.

"Why do I have to be thinking about anything?"

"Everybody thinks about something," she persisted.

"Maybe I was thinking about you."

"What would you be thinking . . . about me?"

"Someday . . . when the time is right, I'll tell you," he said.

"Tell me now," she begged.

"No. First, there's something I . . . have to hear from you."

"What? Tell me, and I'll say it."

"Damn it, that's exactly what I don't want you to do,"

he said. "Everything you say and do, you're trying to please somebody. Somewhere, down deep, there's the real Bonita, who talks true, sayin' what she means, and not what she thinks somebody wants to hear."

"What a . . . curious thing to say," she replied, studying his face. "How will I know the right words? How will you?"

"When the time comes," said Dutch, "if it ever does, you'll know what to say, and when you do, I'll have something to say to you."

She continued looking at him strangely, and he kept his eyes on the trail ahead. Deep down, he knew there was more to her than met the eye, but the false exterior must somehow be burned away. For the first time in his life, he felt frustrated, unequal to the task that lay before him. She interrupted his jumbled thoughts.

"How long will we be at Fort Laramie?"

"No longer than necessary. Overnight, maybe."

Haskel Collins still rode ahead of the wagons, preferring to distance himself from the outfit, and it was he who first saw the Indians. Wheeling his horse, he galloped back to meet the wagons. But the hard-riding Collins didn't have to shout a warning. Every one of Dutch's outfit had their rifles ready.

"Indians," cried the breathless Collins.

"How many?" Dutch asked.

"I don't know," said Collins.

"That's a help," Dutch said. "All of you take what cover you can find, and make your first shots count. If there's enough of them, they'll box us in. Bonita, squeeze yourself in behind that wagon canvas."

Dutch counted fifteen Indians, and they rode almost leisurely. The band was led by an old warrior Dutch suspected was a medicine man, for he wore buffalo horns. There was no evidence that they were armed with anything more than bow and arrow. The Henry cocked and in the crook of his arm, Dutch advanced to meet them. He raised his hand, a gesture of peace, and buffalo horns returned it. The band reined up, and the old one pointed at Dutch's team.

"*Mula*," he said. "*Cuatro*." To emphasize his demand, he raised four fingers.

"*Ninguno*," Dutch replied, shaking his head.

The bunch engaged in a heated discussion, some of them casting venomous looks at Dutch. Finally, without another word or backward glance, they rode away.

"They ain't done with us," said Whit Sanderson. "They was disagreein' as to whether they attack us now or later."

"I expect you're right," Dutch said. "They'll want to pick a place where they have the cover, and we have none."

"It don't make much sense, them ridin' up and demanding four mules. They knew that we'd never agree to a fool thing like that," said Brace Weaver.

"I've never come up against anything like it," Dutch replied, "but I suspect they want the mules for food. Since we don't know what their reasoning is, we'll have to assume that they're up to no good. The logical thing for them to do is attack after dark, stampeding the mules."

"Hobble 'em every one," said Cass Carlyle, "and we'll all stand watch. Put some lead in old buffalo horns, and the rest will run like coyotes."

"That's about all we can do," Dutch said. "In a way, that's better than having them come after us while we're strung out on the trail. At least we'll be able to group the mules and horses, and plan some kind of defense."

Again the wagons took the trail, but the hopes of the outfit for a better time and place were in vain. Shouting, the band of Indians swept out of a thicket. Hanging low over the offside of their horses, they began shooting arrows at the hapless teamsters. Haskel Collins rode frantically back toward the wagons, only to be struck by an arrow and driven from the saddle.

CHAPTER 5

❧

There was no time to organize a defense. Dutch, Brace, Jules, Whit, Rusty, and Cass leaped from their wagon boxes, rifles in hand. The mounted offriders bent low in their saddles and charged toward the Indian ponies. The men from the wagon boxes were at the greatest disadvantage, for there was little cover. The Indians preferred circling the wagons in a counterclockwise formation, for when they clung to the offsides of their horses, they offered virtually no target. Their arrows, fired under their horses' necks, could have a devastating effect. But they hadn't counted on the swift thinking of the offriders. While shooting from the back of a galloping horse was difficult at best, such was not the case with revolvers. Texas Ranger fashion, each of the outriders carried two fully loaded Colts, with an extra interchangeable cylinder, also loaded. With a Rebel yell that would have made a Comanche envious, the six riders rode beyond the circling Indians, cutting them down from the offsides of their horses. Dutch and his five companions were laying down a withering fire with their Henry repeaters. Nine of the attackers were down, including the buffalo-horned medicine man, before the rest galloped away. Bonita still sat on the wagon box, where she had remained during the fight.

"Damn it," Dutch said angrily, "you could have been shot full of arrows."

"But I wasn't," she said cheerfully.

The rest of the outfit came together, including the wounded Haskel Collins. The arrow had ripped a gash in his left shoulder.

"Rusty," said Dutch, "bring the medicine kit from the supply wagon."

"It's not that serious," Collins said.

"You were hit hard enough to pitch you out of the saddle," said Dutch, "and there's a possibility of infection. Shuck that shirt."

None of the rest of the men had been hurt, and after Collins's wound had been taken care of, the teamsters mounted their wagon boxes and the wagons rolled on. Dutch noted with some amusement that Haskel Collins no longer rode so far ahead of the wagons.

Kansas City, Missouri. November 25, 1863.

Jasper Sneed had taken one of Beckwith's newest wagons, recently equipped with a false bottom for concealing military payrolls, and it stood outside the shabby building in which his office was located. He could see the wagon from the first floor window of his office. A few minutes before midnight, he heard the clatter of a wagon, and it was drawn up behind the Beckwith freight wagon. He watched a shadowy form emerge from the newly arrived wagon and approach the building's entrance. A moment later, there was a cautious knock on his door.

"Who's there?"

"Olney."

Sneed opened the door, allowing Olney Sims into the darkened office.

"We got the gold," said Olney. "You want to see it?"

"No," Sneed said. "I want it loaded into that freight

wagon, and then we're getting the hell out of here. The floor of the wagon bed lifts up. You and Honus load it. I have a few things here I'll be taking with me, and then I'll join you."

Olney left without a word, and Sneed watched from the window. The pair hadn't told him where they had gotten the gold, and he hadn't asked, but he was more than a little certain it had been stolen. He feared the two might have been followed, and he would wait until the last possible minute to join them. After all, he hadn't stolen the gold, nor had he laid a hand on it. He could always swear that Honus and Olney had stolen the wagon, but not if he— Sneed—accompanied them. The moonlight allowed him to see them raise the floor of the Beckwith wagon. They were about to remove the chest of gold from their old wagon, when they were challenged.

"Don't move. You're covered. We're the Pinkertons, representing the government of the United States of America."

Sneed didn't wait to hear what Honus and Olney might have to say. He slipped out the door into the hall, only to hear footsteps on the porch. Fearfully he hid himself in the shadow of a stairwell. Two shadowy forms crept down the hall toward Sneed's office, and he slipped out the front door. In panic, Sneed ran toward the livery. He had to get away, and he dared not return to the Beckwith barn. He had not the slightest doubt that Honus and Olney would sing like mocking birds, implicating him in a crime that had been none of his doing. There was a buckboard and a pair of matched blacks that he often used on Sunday, and while the hostler obviously wondered where Sneed was going at so late an hour, he said nothing. Sneed had no money, and he knew there would be none at the Beckwith office, for Christie had begun keeping it at the Beckwith house. He drove there, finding it dark. Would she let him in? He decided she wouldn't, and began seeking a window through which he might enter. When he was finally able to force a window, it went up with a shriek that stood Sneed's hair on end. Entering the dark house, he kicked the leg of a chair. Despite his play for Christie, he had never been in the house, and he silently cursed various pieces of furniture that threatened to reveal his presence. He had no idea where the girl's bedroom was, and he paused when he reached a door that was closed. When he tried the knob, it turned easily, but when he stepped into the room, something came crashing down on his head. When he came to his senses, a lamp had been lighted, and Christie sat on the edge of the bed. He could have faced her, but she held a sawed-off shotgun, and that was another question. Its ugly snout was leveled at Sneed's throbbing head.

"What are you doing in my house?"

"Put the gun down, damn it. We don't have much time, and I have to talk to you."

"About what?"

"The Pinkertons . . . the government . . . is after us."

"Damn you," she shouted, "what have you done?"

"Nothing," Sneed lied. "I . . . I was workin' on a deal to get us some money. Friends of mine wanted to invest. I didn't know the money was stolen. Some kind of government payroll . . ."

"Get out," Christie said. "I own Beckwith Freight Lines, and I am in no way involved in any rotten, illegal scheme . . ."

"Ah, my dear," said Sneed, "I'm afraid you are. I allowed these friends to use one of the Beckwith wagons. By now, they have implicated me, and by this time tomorrow, I fear there will no longer *be* a Beckwith Freight Lines. The Federals will have seized it all."

Sneed thought she was going to kill him. The shotgun trembled in her hands. Finally she allowed the weapon to slide to the floor, buried her face in her hands, and wept. Sneed quickly regained his confidence.

"I have a buckboard hidden nearby," he said. "Take whatever you can gather up in a hurry, including clothes and all the cash you have. We're going west, and we'll make a new start."

"I'm not going anywhere with you," she sobbed. "I've done nothing wrong, and I—"

She was interrupted by a pounding on the front door. Sneed shook his head, but the pounding continued. Christie got up and started toward the front door.

"Damn it," Sneed hissed, "no."

But the girl ignored him. "Who is it," she asked, "and what do you want?"

"Sheriff Parker, Miss Christie. A bunch of Pinkertons arrested a couple of thieves with stolen goods in a Beckwith wagon. They claim they was workin' for you and Jasper Sneed. The Pinkertons is wantin' to talk to you. If you don't settle this somehow, they aim to attach Beckwith Lines in the name of the government of the United States. Will you talk to them in the mornin', in my office?"

"Yes," Christie said. "In the morning . . ."

Slowly she walked back into the bedroom and sat down on the bed. Sneed said not a word, for he was mentally assessing what had rapidly become a perilous situation. He had to suppress an overwhelming desire to gut-shoot his old pards, Honus and Olney, but it would mean sacrificing himself, and he wasn't ready for that. In an attempt to save their own hides, they had done only what he had expected them to do. Somehow, Sneed had to escape, and he must take Christie Beckwith with him. She *was* Beckwith Freight Lines, and fleeing with him would establish her guilt in the eyes of the law. While he hoped it wouldn't come to that, he could always use Christie as a hostage.

"How much cash do you have?" he asked.

"A little more than three hundred dollars," she replied. "There's a little more in the bank—"

"Damn the bank," said Sneed. "You heard what Parker said. Come morning, we've got to be far from here. Like I told you, none of this is my fault. These bastards I grew up with, claiming to be my friends, are dragging me down with them."

"Why can't you just explain that?" she asked.

"Because, like a damn fool, I allowed them the use of a Beckwith wagon, and when they get through lying, trying to save their own hides, we may be in the cells next to theirs. You heard Parker say the Federals are attaching the freight line, without talking to either of us. It's too late for talk. We have to run."

"I suppose so." She sighed. "Where are we going?"

"West," he said.

Sneed waited impatiently while she gathered up a few belongings. Reaching the buckboard, he hoisted her up, took the reins, and urged the horses into a lope. He dared not push them too hard, for he couldn't afford to attract attention. Come the dawn, he would stop at one of the villages west of Kansas City, buying food for themselves and grain for the horses. Christie nodded, leaving Sneed alone with his thoughts, and they drifted to the six heavily loaded wagons Dutch Siringo was taking to Montana Territory. It had seemed like a fool thing to do, with winter coming, but in light of his own failures, Sneed decided Dutch Siringo might just be resourceful enough to pull it off. Suppose he, Sneed, could somehow take over those wagons, using the freight to his own advantage? He conceded, however, that Siringo's outfit would be tough as whang leather, and there wasn't even the slightest possibility of his seizing the wagons without killing them all. For that, he would need men. Ruthless men who would kill to achieve his ends, for a share of the spoils. He knew something of the frontier, and there he would find the necessary killers to gun down Siringo's outfit and take the wagons.

"Dutch," said Brace Weaver, "when we reach Fort Laramie, our teams will have to be reshod. Horses too, maybe."

"We'll just replace those that need it most," Dutch said. "We'll take some extras with us when we leave here, for replacing thrown shoes along the trail."

"Who replaces the shoes?" Bonita asked.

"The teamsters," said Dutch. "That's one of the first things a whacker learns. A blacksmith will fit a horse or mule with shoes, and then make extra sets for front and rear, patterned after the first set. That allows a teamster to replace a worn or thrown shoe with one just like the original, fitted to the animal's hoof."

"Then we'll be at Fort Laramie longer than just a day or two."

"Yes," said Dutch. "Is that still bothering you?"

"Yes," she said. "I can't help believing they'll try to have me sent back."

"I'm not so sure," said Dutch. "With you gone, the folks who were paid to take care of you won't be out any money at all. Suppose they didn't bother notifying the state that you're no longer there?"

"That would be illegal."

"Sure it would," Dutch said, "but if the state knew you had disappeared, they would be sure to demand a return of the money that had been paid for your keep. If they don't lose the money they've been paid, do you reckon that foster family cares where you are?"

"No," she said. "I was just money to them. They won't miss me."

Fort Laramie, Wyoming Territory. December 5, 1863.

"We'll leave the wagons here by the river," Dutch said. "I'd best ride in and talk to the post commander, so he'll know who we are and where we're going. All of you will be able to visit the sutler's store while we're here. We'll be here longer than I intended, while the teams and horses are being shod. Maybe we can learn if there's been trouble with the Sioux to the north of here."

But before Dutch could visit the fort, their shelter had to be erected along the river in preparation for another snow-storm which was building along the western horizon. Because of the needs of the fort, wood had to be snaked in from a great distance, and it was the day after their arrival before Dutch was able to visit the fort. Snow had fallen most of the night, and it was less difficult to negotiate the distance on foot. While the snow had let up, the storm was far from over, and Dutch wished to meet with the post commander and return to the camp as quickly as possible. He was shown into the office of Captain Patterson, the post commander. Patterson remembered him, for they had met while Dutch had been a teamster with Beckwith.

"So you have your own outfit," Patterson said. "I must say you chose a glorious time for a journey to the High Plains."

"For some reason," said Dutch, "nobody wanted this run into western Montana Territory. This is our third snow-storm since leaving Kansas City. I'd have called on you yesterday, but we had to rig us up some shelter and snake in some firewood."

"You'd be welcome on post," Patterson said, "but believe it or not, we're finally up to strength, and our quarters are full. Believe it or not, Washington is expecting us to stand up to the Sioux."

"I had planned to ask you about the situation with the Sioux," said Dutch. "There has been talk of forts being built along the Bozeman."

"So far," Captain Patterson said, "there's nothing but talk. The war has taken its toll, and Congress has failed to appropriate the necessary money to build the forts. All I can tell you is what Washington has told me. Civilian use of the Bozeman Trail is dangerous in the extreme, and you travel at your own risk. While we're up to strength here, we're unable to police two hundred and fifty miles of

Sioux-infested territory. I don't know when or if the forts will ever be built.''

''We can't wait for the forts,'' said Dutch. ''I have never understood why the government negotiated a treaty with the Sioux without some provision for travel along the Bozeman. It's the only sensible way to reach Montana Territory without crossing the Continental Divide twice.''

''I can't allow you to quote me,'' Captain Patterson said, ''but I suspect that most of the land ceded to the Indians is considered useless to the white man. Who could know that Montana Territory would be shot full of gold and that there would be virtually no means of freighting in supplies except along the Bozeman Trail?''

''I reckon that pretty well accounts for the Indian belief that the white man's word just ain't worth a damn,'' said Dutch. ''While we're not harming them in any way, we are still in violation of their treaty with Washington.''

''Precisely,'' said Patterson. ''So many have violated the treaty, the damage has already been done, which is the reason the government is talking of building forts along the Bozeman. While we can't forbid you passage, it is our duty to warn you that we're unable to offer you protection.''

''I understand that, sir,'' Dutch said, ''and I'm not here to request it. I felt I should tell you that three days west of Kearny, we found the remains of the McClellans—man and wife—who had been murdered by Indians. We buried them, and brought with us the only survivor. She is Bonita Konda, an orphan from Illinois, who claims she ran away from a foster home. She claims she was abused and starved, and doesn't want to be sent back. Has there been any inquiry by telegraph?''

''None that I know of,'' Captain Patterson said. ''How old is the young lady?''

''Sixteen,'' said Dutch. ''She's sleeping in one of our wagons and cooking for us all.''

''I sense that you would prefer she continue doing that,'' Captain Patterson said, ''but you feel some obligation to those responsible for her care.''

"Only if they have inquired and tried to find her,'' said Dutch. "They were being paid by the state, and I doubt their concern went any further than collecting the money.''

"I share your doubt,'' Captain Patterson said, "and this being a civilian affair, I see no point in my becoming involved. I trust your judgment, so go with your conscience.''

"Thank you, sir,'' said Dutch. "I'll be talking to you again. Our teams and horses must be reshod, so we'll be here a while, after the storm subsides. We'll need the use of your livery barn and your forge, if that's all right.''

"You're welcome to it,'' said the officer.

The storm passed, leaving overcast skies and temperatures well below freezing.

"Damn it,'' said Whit Sanderson, "if the sun don't come out and the temperature rise, this snow will still be here come Christmas.''

"Three more weeks,'' Brace Weaver said, "but I ain't makin' any plans. I reckon we'll be busy shoein' mules and horses.''

"When my parents were alive, Christmas used to be so grand,'' said Bonita. "There was roast turkey, pumpkin pie, hot biscuits—''

"Keep talkin' about that kind of grub,'' Jules Swenson said, "and I'm goin' to cry.''

"With the fort here close by, we might be able to scare up something special,'' said Dutch. "That is, if we're here that long.''

"We'll be here,'' Tally Slaughter said. "This snow ain't about to melt without a week of sun. Then there's the mud.''

Most of the freighters traveling to Fort Laramie and beyond, were allowed the use of the post livery barn, for a forge was necessary to heat and properly fit shoes to horses and mules. Extra shoes for every animal could then be fitted and taken along for use on the trail. Once the storm had ended, Dutch and his men took turns—working in teams of two—replacing the worn shoes on their horses and mules. Bonita spent much time in the sutler's store, drawing the undivided attention of many a soldier. On one occasion, she met Captain Patterson, who introduced himself and invited her to his office. Only after she had talked to Patterson did she speak to Dutch. She didn't beat around the bush.

"Captain Patterson has invited us all to Christmas dinner. Can we go?"

"I don't know," Dutch said. "We ought to be on the trail before then. Whose idea was this, yours or his?"

"Mostly his," she said, "but I kind of . . . told him about the Christmas dinners that I remember . . ."

"I don't ever remember having a Christmas dinner," said Dutch. "Maybe it would be a good thing. By my figurin', we have maybe eight hundred miles ahead of us, and I reckon this will be our last chance to rest ourselves and our teams."

"Thank you," she said.

Being near enough, she stood on her tiptoes and kissed him. It embarrassed Dutch and drew knowing winks and laughter from his comrades. Unsmiling, Haskel Collins turned away.

By traveling all night, Jasper Sneed and Christie Beckwith were well beyond Kansas City when the eastern sky grayed with the first light of dawn. Sneed stopped at a village mercantile and bought bacon, beans, coffee, hardtack, and a ham. Having no utensils, he purchased a cooking pot, an iron skillet, a coffeepot, an iron spider, knives, and forks. When he returned to the store and emerged with an armful of blankets, Christie looked at them suspiciously.

"It's going to be cold, where we're headed," he said.

"And you rushed me off without a coat," she said.

"Wrap yourself in a blanket," said Sneed, without compassion.

Having forgotten something, he returned to the store a third time. While he had a .36 caliber Colt under his belt, he was very much aware of dangers on the western frontier. He bought a Henry repeating rifle and a tin of two hundred shells.

"We don't have any grain for the horses," Christie said.

"All right, damn it," said Sneed, returning to the store yet another time.

They drove on in silence, stopping only to rest the horses. It was Christie who finally spoke.

"You haven't told me where we're going."

"I haven't fully decided. Maybe to the gold fields, in Montana Territory."

"You haven't done an honest day's work in your life," Christie said contemptuously.

"Ah, my dear," said Sneed, unperturbed, "I am versatile. I'm sure you'll be surprised at what I can accomplish, given the opportunity."

"I haven't forgotten what you accomplished with Beckwith Freight Lines," Christie said bitterly. "I was a fool for allowing Dutch and the old Beckwith teamsters to walk out."

"They're on their way to Montana Territory with six wagons," said Sneed. "Maybe you can get together and talk about old times."

She said nothing, hunching deeper into her blanket. When they eventually stopped for the night, Christie remained on the buckboard's seat, allowing Sneed to prepare the supper.

"I'm damned if I'll bring it to you," Sneed said.

Without a word, she climbed down and took her share of the supper. By the time they had finished eating, it was sundown, and the west wind was cold.

"Where are we going to sleep?" she asked.

"I'm sleeping in the buckboard," he replied. "Suit yourself."

Taking all the blankets except the one Christie had about her shoulders, he spread them out in the back of the buckboard. Leaving her standing there, he climbed in.

"Move over, damn you," said Christie, swallowing hard.

Fort Kearny, Nebraska. December 5, 1863.

Jasper Sneed and Christie Beckwith reached Kearny barely ahead of the snowstorm that had stranded Dutch and his outfit at Fort Laramie. Using Christie to gain the post commander's sympathy, Sneed was allowed the use of a vacant officer's cabin.

"It has only one bed," said Christie.

"We only need one." Sneed smirked. "I told 'em you're my missus, and that you're in the family way."

"Is there no limit to your lies and deceit?"

"Not much." He chuckled. "You got the name, so you might as well play the game."

Her very bones ached from two weeks of lying on the hard floorboards of the buckboard. It all seemed like a nightmare from which she must soon awaken. With a sigh of resignation she began to get undressed, while Jasper Sneed waited.

While the saloon within the sutler's store at Kearny was nothing to get excited about, there was an adequate supply of beer and whiskey, with three crude tables for drinking or poker. While the storm raged, Sneed left Christie alone in the cabin and fought his way to the saloon through the drifted snow. There he drank the hours away, waiting for the storm to subside. He and Christie appeared to be the only civilians on the post, leaving him in a quandary as to where he would find the ruthless men he sought. After six days, Sneed was about to harness the horses to the buckboard and continue his journey, when nine rough looking men reined up before the sutler's store. Allowing them time to enter, Sneed followed, finding them lined up along the bar.

"I'm buying, gents," said Sneed.

As one, the nine turned and stared at him, observing his town clothes and narrow brimmed hat.

"What's the occasion, bucko?" one of them asked. "Are you celebratin' your first pair of long britches?" They all laughed uproariously.

"Better than that," Sneed said easily. "I got a pile of easy money waitin' for me in Montana Territory, and I'm drinking to that. Join me if you like."

"Well, now," said the one who had spoken, "that's a serious subject. I reckon we can all drink to that."

"Yeah," another said, "we was just fixin' to ride up yonder to the diggings and see if there wasn't room for us."

Taking their drinks, they crowded along the benches on either side of one of the long tables. Sneed ordered a drink for himself and joined them.

"Now," said one of them, wasting no time, "is this your own private claim, or would there be room for others?"

"I wouldn't consider taking on any pardners," Sneed said, "except that my missus and me are traveling alone, and I hear the Sioux are giving everybody hell on the Bozeman."

"They are, for a fact," said one of Sneed's newfound companions, "but we ain't used to hombres standin' in our way, Injuns or not. Now where is this here claim?"

"It's not the kind of claim you have in mind," Sneed said. "It's a sure thing for a man that's not afraid to use a gun."

"Do I look scairt to you?" one of the hard-faced men asked. In an instant he had a Colt cocked and its muzzle under Sneed's nose.

"No," Sneed said, swallowing hard.

"Then talk, damn it. I got no respect for a varmint that talks big an' can't deliver."

Sneed talked, not liking the looks on the faces of three

of the men, and when he had finished, it was one of the three who spoke.

"Me, an' Ham, an' Duro know that bunch. Our outfit went after 'em at night, and they just gunned the hell out of us. Nine men was killed, and the rest of us lit a shuck out of there."

"You sure it's the same bunch, Chug?" another man asked.

"Nobody else has come west since the cold started," said Chug. "Who else but them?"

"You're sayin' they're all nine feet tall and a yard wide, then," said another of the men.

"Hell, yes," Chug growled. "They all got repeatin' rifles, and they can shoot like hell wouldn't have it."

"Three of you are out of it, then," said Sneed, regaining his composure.

"I didn't say we was out," Chug snarled, leaning across the table. "I'm sayin' if we side you in this ambush, we aim to take a big enough share to make it worth the risk."

"I won't argue with that," said Sneed.

Chug bared broken teeth in a wolf grin. "I didn't reckon you would," he said.

CHAPTER 6

❧

Dutch and his outfit put their time to good use, taking advantage of the livery barn while the military had no need of it. It began to look as though the snow might still be around at Christmas, for the sky remained overcast and the sun became a stranger. There was a continuous wind from the west, and it was bitter cold.

"God," said Cass Carlyle, "I'm glad they're lettin' us use their livery barn to shoe our horses and mules. It's so cold out there, a man's fingers would just freeze and break off."

"That's why I'd like to see more forts on the frontier," Dutch said. "While they'll be handy for protection against Indians, they're more valuable in other ways. Besides allowin' us to come in out of the cold to shoe our teams, imagine the cost of hauling shoes all the way from Kansas City. They'd cost us three to four hundred pounds of freight."

The prolonged stay at Fort Laramie revealed yet another side of Haskel Collins that Dutch Siringo didn't like. Collins had taken to spending much of his time patronizing the saloon that was part of the sutler's store. But Collins didn't content himself with that. He went behind Dutch's back, with a foolish appeal to Captain Patterson, regarding Bonita. The captain found Dutch in the livery barn, where the horses and mules were being shod.

"One of your party—Haskel Collins—came to see me," Captain Patterson said, "and I thought you should know."

"I'm obliged," said Dutch. "What did he want?"

"He wanted me to keep the young lady, Bonita Konda, here at the fort, until such a time as she could be sent back east. His reasons, so he claims, are that she's underage, and he fears for her here on the frontier."

"Her being underage didn't bother him when he asked her to marry him," Dutch said, "and he'd be taking her to Montana Territory, likely the wildest part of the frontier."

"I take it she declined," said Captain Patterson.

"She did," Dutch replied, "and as for Haskel Collins's concern, put it out of your mind. I aim to look out for Bonita until she's of age, and I won't do that by forcing her to marry me."

"You won't have to force her," said Captain Patterson. "We've had some delightful conversations, and sixteen or not, she's as much a woman as she'll ever be. Take her with you, look out for her, and keep an eye on Haskel Collins."

"I aim to," Dutch said, "and thank you, Captain."

While Captain Patterson had not taken Collins seriously, Dutch had no intention of allowing Collins to get off scot-free. Not surprisingly, he found Collins in the saloon.

"Collins," said Dutch, "I've just had a talk with Captain Patterson, and I know what you tried to do to Bonita."

"I am concerned for the child," Collins said, looking at Dutch through bleary eyes.

"Don't be," said Dutch. "We contracted with you to freight your goods into western Montana Territory, and anything not directly concerned with that is no business of yours."

Jasper Sneed's newfound companions answered to Nemo, Pucket, Phelps, Shad, Griz, Chug, Ham, Duro, and Smoke. Sneed had no idea whether those were their last or first names, and didn't care. He anticipated a fight when he introduced the hardcase bunch to Christie Beckwith, and she didn't disappoint him.

"They look like thieves and murderers," she said. "I won't go anywhere with them."

"Oh, but you will," said Sneed. "We'll be traveling through Sioux Indian country, and we'll need all the extra guns we can get."

So the nine riders and the buckboard left Fort Kearny, heading west. There was still drifted snow in places where the sun didn't often shine, and the bitter cold became almost intolerable. Christie Beckwith said little, aware that nine pairs of eyes were constantly on her, dreading the time when Sneed's presence no longer made any difference.

Fort Laramie, Wyoming Territory. December 25, 1863.

Everybody—even the officers—gathered in the enlisted men's mess hall for Christmas dinner, and it was truly a grand occasion. Despite the delay, Dutch was glad they had stayed. The severe cold had remained, and although all the horses and mules had been reshod, Dutch was reluctant to move on until there was a break in the weather. There had been no sun to amount to anything since the last storm, and most of the snow remained, frozen hard as stone. After the Christmas festivities at the fort were done, Dutch and his companions were returning to their wagons when they saw the two riders coming in from the north. They were slumped over their staggering horses, and both had been wounded. One had the shaft of an arrow protruding from his shoulder, while the other had been hit in the thigh. Brace Weaver and Jules Swenson struggled through the snow, taking the reins from the frozen hands of the riders. The exhausted horses were led inside the stockade, and the wounded men fell from their saddles. Soldiers came on the run, helping the nearly frozen men to the dispensary.

"It looks like bad news along the Bozeman," said Dutch.

He didn't know just how bad until the next morning, when he returned to the fort and was able to talk to Captain Patterson.

"Eight men, heavily armed," Patterson said. "Miners trying to get out with their stake when they were jumped by a band of Sioux. Six men dead, and the two that made it could lose their hands and feet to frostbite."

"Where were they attacked?" Dutch asked.

"A day's ride north of here," said Patterson. "This spells out the danger better than I ever could."

Dutch and his outfit had some talking to do, for this latest development was serious enough to have sobered them all. Even Haskel Collins.

"We're in for it, I reckon," Brace Weaver said. "There was eight miners. There ain't that many more of us, and we got six wagons loaded with enough goodies to make this the biggest Christmas them Sioux has ever seen."

"We don't have to be in no hurry." said Whit Sanderson. "There's more snow comin'. It'll be here 'fore tomorrow night, if I'm any judge."

"We'd as well stay dug in where we are, then," Dutch said. "It'll mean more delay, but if we're snowbound, we're safer here. I don't want to spend any more time on the Bozeman than we have to."

"We're facing two hundred and fifty miles on the Bozeman," said Haskel Collins. "If we cover even fifteen miles a day, that's seventeen days. There's no way we're going to avoid snow and Indians for that length of time."

"I don't expect to avoid either, Collins," Dutch said. "The best we can hope for is to face them one at a time. Nothing but a damn fool would leave existing shelter with another storm blowing in, when we know there are marauding Sioux a day north of us."

Some of the teamsters eyed Collins with disgust, and he said no more.

* * *

The day after Christmas dawned cold and dismal, and dirty gray clouds marched in from the west on a rising wind.

"We'd best snake in some more firewood," Dutch said.

"Then we'd better start now," said Dent Wells. "We'll be ridin' out so far, it'll take us all day."

"Nobody rides alone," Dutch replied.

They rode east of the fort, snaking in as many windblown trees as they could find, for the temperature had already begun to fall. The men had axes, chopping the logs into usable lengths, when they first saw the approaching riders. Dutch drove his axe into a log and waited, for the newcomers would have to pass the teamsters' camp. Dutch's eyes were not on the riders, but on the buckboard trailing them.

"By God," said Brace Weaver, "that no-account Jasper Sneed's drivin' the rig, and he's got Miss Christie Beckwith with him."

Dutch said nothing, but he suspected the worst. Obviously, Sneed and Christie were traveling with the band of men who had ridden in ahead of them. He watched as one of the riders dropped back alongside the buckboard and spoke to Sneed. The nine men rode wide of the teamster camp, on their way to the fort. Sneed reined up a few yards shy of the shelters, and when the teamsters remained silent, Sneed spoke.

"Mr. Siringo and company. This is a surprise."

"What are you doing here, Sneed?" Dutch asked.

"Miss Christie and me got tired of the freighting business," said Sneed. "We're bound for Montana Territory and the diggings there. The Indian threat being what it is, perhaps we can travel together."

"I don't think so," Dutch said. "You seem to have an adequate escort. Besides, in case you're not bright enough to have figured it out, I don't trust you. I don't want you and that bunch that's ridin' with you within shoutin' distance of my outfit."

Sneed didn't seem surprised, but Dutch could see the disappointment in Christie Beckwith's face. Her eyes met Dutch's for only a second, and she seemed furious. Only when Sneed had driven on toward the fort did Dutch discover that Bonita had been standing to his right and a little behind him.

"From the looks of it," Rusty Karnes said, "Mr. Sneed put all his chips on the table, played out his hand, and was left with a busted flush."

"Yeah," said Brace Weaver, "and he lost Miss Christie's chips too."

"I'm going to the fort and see what I can learn," Dutch said. "I don't like the looks of this. The Indian threat's enough, without this bunch on our trail."

Civilians riding into a fort were required to report to the post commander, and Dutch waited an hour before going to Captain Patterson's office.

"I granted permission for the nine men to spread their blankets in the livery barn for the duration of the storm," said Patterson. "I have allowed Sneed and his wife the use of an officer's cabin. Do you know these people?"

"Sneed and the woman with him," Dutch said, "and I have my suspicions about all the others. I'd say they're about the same caliber of the bunch that tried to ambush us."

"I share your suspicions," said Captain Patterson. "But I was a bit partial to Sneed, since he said he knew you, and would be traveling with you to Montana Territory."

"He only told you half the truth," Dutch said. "He knows me all right, but it'll be a cold day in hell when he trails with my outfit."

"We can keep them in line here," said Captain Patterson, "but I suspect that when you take the Bozeman Trail, the Sioux may be only part of your trouble."

Dutch went on to the sutler's store and wasn't surprised to find Sneed in the nearby saloon. Christie wasn't with him, and Dutch wondered if Sneed had left her in the quarters that Captain Patterson had provided. But he found her at the sutler's wandering listlessly among tables stacked with bolts of cloth.

"Hello, Mrs. Sneed."

"I'm not his wife," Christie cried desperately. "Please take me with you."

"No," said Dutch. "You've made your bed, and now you'll have to lie in it."

"You have another woman," she hissed. "I saw her. You'd leave me here, taking that redheaded hussy—"

"You're damned right I will," said Dutch angrily. "That redheaded hussy ain't been cozied up to that skunk, Jasper Sneed. I'm just thankful I didn't shoot the bastard back in Kansas City. I owe him, because he showed you up for what you are."

He walked out, leaving her so furious that words failed her. She stalked recklessly into the saloon, and seizing the bottle before Sneed, smashed it on the bar.

"Get out of here," she shouted. "Get out!"

Without a word, shocked, Jasper Sneed followed her out of the saloon.

His anger had subsided by the time Dutch reached the wagon camp, and he felt only regret for those long-ago days when he had believed in Christie Beckwith. He had no idea what had become of Beckwith Freight Lines, and he didn't care. He had no doubt Sneed had run the outfit into the ground. Now he was about to play out his last hand, and when he went down, he would take Christie Beckwith with him. Just before dark, sleet began to rattle on the canvas of their shelters, and it soon changed to snow. Secure in the nearness of the fort, teams of two spent two-hour shifts keeping the fires going, for without them, the cold would have been intolerable. Far into the night, Dutch got up to take his turn, and before he could wake one of the men, Bonita stopped him.

"Let me help you. The only time I could talk to you was on the wagon box."

"Not much to talk about," Dutch said, "except snow and Indians."

"Let's talk about the nine men who rode in yesterday, followed by a wagon. You knew the man and woman in the wagon, and you didn't trust him."

"No," said Dutch, "I've never trusted him, and I'm wondering how deep he's involved with those nine hombres that rode in ahead of him."

"What about the woman? Is she his wife?"

"Far as I'm concerned, she is," Dutch said.

"I don't think she is," said Bonita. "When she saw me, if looks could kill, then I'd be dead. If she has a husband, then she has no reason to be jealous of me."

"Sit down over yonder where we won't wake the others," Dutch said. "It's a long story, and I might as well start at the beginning."

He told her all of it, from the day he had arrived, penniless and hungry, from Ohio, to the day he and the Beckwith teamsters had become pardners.

"This is the first run for Siringo Lines," he concluded, "and everything depends on the success of it."

"There is no way, then, that you could change your mind about Christie Beckwith?" Bonita asked.

"No," Dutch said. "Would you want me to?"

"No," she replied, "as long as you're sure. It's just that . . . I feel sorry for her. I have never had anyone want me since my mother and father died, and I know . . . the hurt. The same hurt I saw in her eyes, when she looked at you."

Dutch said nothing, touched by the earnestness in her voice. She had no claim on him and would have expected none, had he expressed any interest in Christie Beckwith. It was more than he could take without granting her the assurance that would mean so much to her. With a hand on each of her shoulders, he drew her close. Their eyes met in the rosy glow from the nearby fire, and her lips parted just a little. Not only did she not resist when he kissed her, she returned it with a ferocity that surprised Dutch. He had to break away for air, but he kept his hands on her shoulders. Her eyes were closed, and she was breathing hard.

"Does that tell you anything?" he asked softly.

"Yes," she replied, just as quietly, "but I'd like to hear you say it."

"I want you," he said. "I'm sorry for Christie Beckwith, but that's all I can ever feel. Remember when Haskel Collins asked you to marry him? I nearly choked to death on my tongue, and I knew that would never happen. Then, when the Pawnees grabbed you, I was scared to death of what they might do before we could rescue you. I knew then that if you would have me, I wanted you when you became of age."

"This is what you promised to tell me, when the time was right?"

"Yes," he said, "and I'd planned to do that when you came of age. But tonight, I had the feeling that you are as much a woman as you'll ever be. I believed it was something you needed to hear, because I don't know what the months ahead will bring. I only know that if I . . . if something happens to me . . . I'd want you to know."

Without a word, she threw her arms around him, and it was a long time before she let him go. Then, with her nose touching his, she spoke.

"I wanted to know," she said. "I'll be seventeen on January fifth. I only needed to hear you say that you want me. I've never . . . been with a man."

"I know," said Dutch. "All that bold talk after we found you was just talk. You were scared, and trying not to be."

"I want you to teach me to fire a gun," she said. "Now that we understand . . . how we feel, I couldn't bear it if something . . . happened."

"You aim to shoot Indians?" Dutch asked.

"If I have to," she replied. "I've heard all this talk about the frontier, and since I am to be part of it—beside you— then how can I hide in a wagon while the Indians or outlaws are trying to kill you?"

He kissed her again, long and hard, before he spoke.

"Tomorrow—provided the snow ain't neck-deep—I'll go to the fort and buy you a Colt pocket pistol and a Henry repeating rifle."

It was time to add more wood to the fires. That done, they sat down and continued their conversation until first light.

"My God," said Dutch, "we've been talking for more than four hours."

"I don't care," she said. "We needed to talk. If I died this very minute, I'd still be happy."

"So would I," said Dutch. "Somewhere in Montana Territory, there must be at least one preacher. I might not be able to resist you until we get back to Kansas City."

"I'll tell you a secret," she whispered. "I won't put up much of a fight."

Dutch kept his promise. Braving the storm, he went to the fort before the snow got any deeper. There he bought Bonita a .31 caliber Colt pocket pistol and a Henry repeater. While there, he called on Captain Patterson.

"There's nothing I can tell you," said Patterson. "Sneed and the men he's traveling with have caused no trouble. Of course, they can ill-afford to, this being a United States government outpost. So far, they've spent most of their time in the saloon, and as long as they remain orderly, we can't fault them for that. But I'm sticking to my earlier advice. On the trail, don't devote all your vigilance to the Sioux."

After Christie Beckwith's stormy encounter with Dutch, she spent most of her time in the tiny cabin alone. Sneed was more comfortable in the saloon, with the surly renegades with whom he had formed an alliance. Nemo appeared to be the spokesman for the bunch, and it was he who was engaged in an argument with Sneed.

"Damn it," Nemo growled, "you didn't tell us them teamsters was gonna be here at Fort Laramie, waitin' for us. They should of been in Montana by now.''

"I'm as surprised as you are," said Sneed. "I didn't expect them to be here, but this could be all the better. There ain't no way they can stop us from followin' 'em, and with all those loaded wagons, they'll be a prime target for the Sioux. Would it be more appealing to you if Siringo and his bunch was two hundred miles ahead, and we had to fight the Sioux on our own?''

"I reckon not," Nemo growled. "It'll be hard as hell, surprisin' 'em, when we're ready to grab the wagons."

"That's something we haven't talked about," said Sneed. "I can't see taking the wagons until we're well into Montana Territory, near the diggings."

"I won't argue with that," Nemo said. "We'll let them go ahead, catchin' hell from the Sioux and gettin' that freight over the worst of the trail. Then we'll gun them down and take the wagons."

Sneed swallowed hard. He could see nothing wrong with his plan, up to and including the murder of Siringo and his men. Beyond that, however, lay abundant opportunity for a double cross. The moment Nemo and his cutthroat band got their hands on the wagons, Jasper Sneed's life wouldn't be worth a plugged *peso*. Silently he cursed the fate that was forcing him to rely on treacherous, cold-blooded killers, it never once crossing his evil mind that he was no better than they.

Two days into the new year, Dutch and his outfit broke camp and prepared to move out. There had been very little sun, and temperatures hadn't risen enough to fully melt the last snow. There was a frozen crust that might remain for weeks, and after several days of warming, the temperature again plunged below zero.

"When it finally melts," said Dutch, "we'll be bogged down to the hubs, but there's no way we can delay any longer."

Jasper Sneed bought bedrolls for himself and Christie,

and a huge square of canvas to rig a shelter. As he and Nemo had agreed, they allowed Dutch and his wagons a full day's head start.

"There's no excuse for following them," Christie said angrily. "Why are they allowed to go on ahead of us?"

"This is Sioux country, my dear," said Sneed. "Why not let them go on ahead and blunt the edge of whatever hell the Indians intend to raise?"

In a brutal kind of way, it made sense, and Christie Beckwith said no more. Again and again she told herself she didn't *care* what happened to Dutch Siringo, but her heart knew better, and punished her unmercifully.

"We ain't gonna make much time as long as we're travelin' over this packed, frozen snow," Jules Swenson observed, while they had stopped to rest the teams.

"No," Dutch agreed, "but we had to move on. While I don't regret the layover at Fort Laramie, we're going to have to make the best of whatever lies ahead."

With the exception of Haskel Collins, the outfit approved of Dutch's teaching Bonita to shoot. He had bought her a holster and belt for the Colt, and she had spent an hour or more after supper, "dry firing" the weapons.

"As long as the Sioux are a threat," said Dutch, "we'll have to avoid actual firing. We don't want to do anything to draw attention to ourselves."

The second day after leaving Fort Laramie, they had firsthand experience with the frozen snow. The left rear wheel of Rusty Karnes's wagon slid off into a hidden depression and split the wheel rim. They even had trouble with the wagon jack, for it kept slipping on the frozen snow, refusing to support the weight of the wagon. Dutch finally took an axe and chopped through the frozen snow, so that the jack might rest on solid ground. Bitter cold numbed their hands and feet, and they continued only until they found a spring before stopping for the night.

"We'll continue with a two-man watch, two hours at a time," Dutch said, "but when you sleep, keep your guns handy and don't remove anything but your hats. We'll hobble the mules and horses so they can't be run off."

It was past midnight when there was a disturbance among the stock. Mules brayed and horses nickered, but by the time Dutch and Brace Weaver got to them, there was no sign of anyone.

"Could be the Sioux," Brace said, "but why would they come skulking around in the middle of the night? By now, they know we're here. What else is there to learn?"

"I don't know," said Dutch. "Maybe we're lookin' at it all wrong. Maybe it wasn't the Sioux. It might have been one of them varmints from Sneed's camp."

"For what reason?"

"I have no idea," Dutch said. "I think that bunch of hard cases may be planning to try and take over the wagons, once we're out of Sioux territory. What I'm not sure of is whether or not Sneed is involved."

"I can't imagine why they'd need him," said Brace, "and that gives them almost no reason to come sneaking around our teams. Without them, we'll never get out of Sioux territory."

"It's time to wake Rusty and Cass," Dutch said. "We'll have to keep a closer watch on our teams. We must learn who's stalking us, and why."

Two miles south, the Sneed camp hadn't kept any fires burning, depending on their bedrolls for warmth. While they had posted a sentry, he saw or heard nothing, and it was first light before the outlaw band knew anything had gone wrong.

"Damn it," Pucket shouted, "my horse is gone."

"So is mine," said Chug. "By God, somebody on watch ain't been watchin'."

"Hold it," Nemo said. "Who was on watch last night, startin' at dark?"

"I was," said Phelps, "and Shad follered me."

"Smoke come on after me," Shad said, "an' Ham was after him."

"Griz finished it, then," said Nemo.

"Yeah," Griz said, "an' there wasn't nothin' movin' out there."

"Well, if nobody saw or heard nothin'," Nemo roared, "why in hell are we botherin' to keep watch? Tonight nobody sleeps. You'll hunker next to your horses, keepin' your eyes an' ears open."

"That's a prime idea," said Pucket sarcastically, "but I'm left without a hoss."

"And me," Chug said. "What do you aim to do about us?"

"Not a damn thing," said Nemo. "I reckon after we reach Montana Territory and gun down them teamsters, you can take a couple of their horses. Until then, why don't the both of you talk real nice to Mr. Sneed? Maybe he'll make room in his buckboard for you and your saddles."

Sneed had heard the argument and Nemo's suggested solution, and as a result, he and Christie were subjected to the grumbling and cursing of Pucket and Chug, as they hunched uncomfortably in the crowded buckboard. Not until the trying day was over were Christie and Sneed rid of their ungrateful companions, and Christie turned on Sneed in a fury.

"I have never been subjected to so much filthy talk in my life," she shouted. "No lady should be forced into the company of a pair of dirty, ignorant animals such as these, and I won't tolerate them another day."

"You watch your mouth, miss high-and-mighty," Sneed snarled, seizing her arm. "On the frontier, ladies get drug down to a man's level damn quick. I got plans for these gents, and I'm more in need of them than I am of you. Trouble me, damn you, and I'll let them have you, taking their pleasure."

"You wouldn't dare," she said.

"Try me," said Sneed. When he released her arm, he slapped her, and she fell to the frozen ground. Ignoring her weeping, he began unharnessing the team from the buckboard.

Sneed's renegade companions watched the sorry episode, and some of them laughed. It was Nemo who finally spoke.

"When we're done with that slimy little varmint, I reckon we can sample the lady's talents. She can't sink no lower."

CHAPTER 7

*P*ucket and Chug—reduced to crowding into the back of Sneed's buckboard—became the butt of numerous jokes among their companions.

"Pucket," said Griz with a straight face, "if we meet anybody on the trail, you and Chug can always claim Sneed's your daddy."

"Pucket," Nemo shouted. "Don't!"

Pucket relaxed, his hand on the butt of his Colt. The moment passed, but Pucket and Chug were painfully aware of the ill-concealed grins of their companions. After supper, the two drifted away from the others, where they might talk without being overheard.

"I'm fed up with them giggin' me," said Pucket, "and tonight I aim to do something about it. Are you game?"

"Fer what?" Chug asked, interested.

"For sneakin' into that teamster camp and takin' us some horses," said Pucket.

"You reckon they won't come lookin' for 'em, and us? In this snow, froze or not, there'll be tracks."

"Yeah," Pucket replied, "but them tracks will go north. Hell, we'll circle back and hit our own trail, thirty miles south. They'll blame it on the Sioux."

"Injuns don't wear boots," said Chug. "How do you aim to get around that?"

"We'll rip up a blanket," Pucket said, "make pads, and tie 'em on the soles of our boots. We won't leave no tracks at all."

"I like that a mite better," said Chug. "S'pose we took two hosses an' stampeded all the others?"

"No, damn it," Pucket replied. "If they got any savvy at all—with so many mules—the varmints will be hobbled. We'll be almighty lucky if we can sneak away a couple of horses."

"When are we goin'? Just 'fore daylight, when they're sleepin' the hardest?"

"Use your head," said Pucket. "We got to grab them horses early as we can, 'cause we got a heap of ridin' to do before mornin'. If we don't get a good start, they'll ride us down. I don't look for 'em to trail us 'fore daylight, and by then we'll be back in camp."

"They'll come lookin' for us there," Chug said.

"Let 'em come," said Pucket. "They can't prove we took the horses. We'll say we saw 'em running loose, and demand a bill of sale. There ain't one rider in a hundred got one. Nemo and the others will have to side us, 'cause they want them teamsters kept alive. They'll be killin' mad, but who gives a damn? It's us that ain't got horses."

"Tonight," said Dutch, "all of us on watch will take a walk among the stock at least two or three times an hour. While the Sioux will be after our scalps, they'll figure they have plenty of time for that. I reckon they'd consider it a challenge, taking our horses and mules from right under our noses."

"For sure they can't stampede 'em," Dent Wells said. "There ain't an Indian alive who can cut all them hobbles without spookin' one of them mules. Hell, they see things that ain't even there."

"I hope you're right," said Dutch. "Just keep your weapons handy and don't sleep too hard."

*   *   *

Pucket and Chug lay in their blankets, waiting for moonset, begrudging the time they were losing. When at last they felt safe in the pale starlight, they got up, stumbling along in their heavily padded boots. It seemed they would never reach the teamster camp, for they were unaccustomed to walking long distances. Twice they stopped to rest. The fires had burned low, for temperatures had risen and the bitter cold had subsided. When at last they were near the grazing herd, they paused. The camp lay beyond, and try as they might, they were unable to locate any sentries. To their dismay, the horses were nearest the teamster camp. They must circle around, or risk working their way through all the mules, any one of which might spook and sound the alarm. Pucket crept along toward the south end of the grazing herd, Chug following. Each man had a knife in his hand, for they could tell by the movement of the animals, they were hobbled. They had made their way around the grazing mules and were nearing the horses, when one of the animals snorted. Even in the starlight, they could see the horse with its head up, ears perked, listening. It eventually settled down and began to graze.

"I reckon that horse just thought he heard something," Brace Weaver said.

"Keep your eye on that particular position," said Dutch. "I ain't so sure the horse was wrong."

The two were on watch, and within a few minutes, they would be relieved by Tally Slaughter and Drago Peeler. Dutch wasn't satisfied. Drawing his Colt, he crept beyond the wagons. Most of the horses grazed in the shadow of a stand of pines, for even the snow had not harmed the clumps of blue stem grass. There was a slight sound behind him, and Dutch froze.

"It's me," Brace whispered. "I thought I saw something, like a tiny flash of light."

Pucket had shoved his knife back under his belt, aware that even in the starlight, the well-honed blade might reflect. To his right, he could see Chug advancing toward one of the grazing horses. All they had to do was slit the leather hobbles and slowly lead the two animals into the nearby pines. Pucket was hunched over so that his head wouldn't be seen above the backs of the horses. He must get close enough to a horse to calm it before his shadowy presence spooked it. He was approaching a big black, and froze when the animal turned and looked at him. It was his undoing, for when the horse lifted its head and turned, it led Dutch Siringo's sharp eyes to the shadow that was Pucket.

"You're covered!" Dutch shouted.

Dutch had a poor target at best, but Pucket made a fatal mistake. He dropped to one knee and fired. While he missed his mark, Dutch Siringo did not. He fired once, at the muzzle flash. There was no return fire, and Dutch could hear the thump of boots. Brace was after a second man. The rest of the camp was up, with guns ready. By the time they reached Dutch, Brace had returned.

"There was two of the varmints," said Weaver. "He ducked in among the mules and made it into the brush. Who do you reckon they were?"

"They're not Sioux," Dutch replied. "Let's light a match and check out the one that I shot."

While the horses were hobbled and couldn't run, they had shied away from Pucket. He lay on his back, for the slug had hit him in the chest.

"Looks like one of them coyotes Sneed's nuzzled up to." Whit Sanderson observed.

"I reckon it is," said Dutch, "and that bein' the case, the one that got away is likely from the same pack."

"That was a fool thing to do," Drago Peeler said. "Hell, they're within hollerin' distance of our camp. Did they reckon we wouldn't recognize our own horses?"

"If they're needing horses," said Jules Swenson, "that means the Sioux has likely took some of theirs."

"I'd say you're right," Dutch replied, "and they'll be trouble enough. I don't aim to have this bunch of owlhoots stalking our horses and mules every night. Come first light,

I reckon we'll have to deliver that message in words they can understand. A couple of you drag this dead one far enough into the brush that his carcass don't keep spooking our mules and horses.''

The roar of a gun—distant though it may be—seldom goes unnoticed by men who ride outside the law, and by the time Chug reached the outlaw camp, the rest of them knew the probable cause of the distant shots. Chug fell into his blankets, exhausted, while the tattered remnants of a blanket thonged to his boots was eloquent testimony as to what he had attempted to do. Without a word, Nemo seized Chug by the front of his shirt and dragged the outlaw to his feet.

''Where's Pucket?'' Nemo snarled.

''I . . . I dunno,'' Chug wheezed.

''The hell you don't,'' Nemo all but shouted. ''Come daylight, we'll have that damn lot of teamsters after us, and if they want you, by God, they won't get any argument from me.''

There were growls of assent from the others, and Nemo shoved the terrified Chug to the ground. They were a somber lot. While one man might kill another and live, horse stealing called for the rope. While they didn't especially care what became of Chug, they could appreciate his unenviable position. As an unsuccessful horse thief, he didn't even have a horse on which he might ride for his life.

After breakfast, before harnessing the teams, Dutch called the outfit together.

''Rusty, Cass, Tally, and Drago, you'll ride with me,'' Dutch said.

Nobody had to ask what he had in mind, for they all knew of the attempt to steal their horses, and of the one thief who had paid with his life. The five of them saddled their horses and rode south.

''We have the right to take the varmint and hang him,'' said Dutch, ''but having shot one of them, that should be enough. I want to make it clear that next time—if there is a next time—that we'll hang the whole damn bunch. We won't start any trouble, but if they do, don't any of you be bashful about helping me finish it.''

They approached the camp, reining up a few yards shy of it. For a moment, Dutch said nothing. Allowing for the matched blacks that drew Jasper Sneed's buckboard, there were two horses missing. That accounted for the two horse thieves of the night before.

''I see that you're missing some horses,'' said Dutch, ''and that tells me why a pair of you coyotes came sneaking around our horses last night.''

''I don't know what you're talkin' about,'' Nemo said coldly.

''You don't lie any better than you steal horses,'' said Dutch. ''We'd likely be saving ourselves time and trouble if we stretched the necks of the whole damn lot of you, right now, but I'll forgive a man one mistake. Just don't make the second one.''

Eight of them stood there in silence, hating him, but the finality of Dutch's words had taken the edge off any response they might have made. Jasper Sneed stood beside the buckboard and a white-faced Christie Beckwith sat on the seat. Dutch Siringo and his five companions back stepped their horses out of gun range, and turning, rode away.

''Damn you,'' Nemo said, his eyes on Chug, ''I ought to hang you myself.''

Without a word, he turned away and began saddling his horse. The others followed his example, leaving the hapless Chug to another day in Sneed's buckboard.

Dutch increased the night watch to three men, but there were no more attempts to steal the horses. The most formidable threat of all arrived two nights later, while Rusty, Brace, and Jules were on watch. The weather had again turned bitterly cold, and the west wind brought the unmistakable feel of snow. It was near midnight, with no moon, when the horses and mules created a commotion that woke the entire camp. Rusty, Brace, and Jules were firing at a lumbering shadow that seemed ten feet tall. A mountain grizzly, it charged the attackers, slamming Rusty Karnes to the ground with a huge paw. Only when Dutch, Cass Carlyle, and Kirby Butler began firing did the enormous animal retreat into the surrounding brush.

"Some of you get a fire going," Dutch shouted. Even by starlight, as he knelt beside the wounded man, he could see the blood soaking the left shoulder of Rusty's coat.

By the light of the fire, they removed Rusty's coat and shirt, revealing dangerously lacerated skin. Bonita was there to help, and when the water was boiling, it was she who cleansed the terrible wound.

"This disinfectant is powerful stuff, Rusty," said Dutch. "and it's goin' to hurt like hell."

"I'm already hurtin' like hell," Rusty gritted. "Pour it on."

Following the disinfectant, they applied sulfur salve to the wounds, and Rusty was given a dose of laudanum. Belly-down, he slept.

"What'n hell is a grizzly doin' wandering around in January?" Dent Wells wondered. "I always believed the varmints slept through the winter."

"They do," said Whit Sanderson, "usually in a burrowed-out den beneath some windblown tree. We may have disturbed this critter's sleep while we was draggin' in dead trees for firewood. He got up, decided he was hungry, and discovered our livestock."

"Now that he's wide-awake and got some lead in him," Dutch said, "he's likely to be on the prod and on our trail. Rusty will need some time to heal, maybe to fight infection. I reckon we'll have to lay over a couple of days. That'll give us time to ride out tomorrow and finish off that grizzly."

"It seems like a waste of time to me," said Haskel Collins. "If the bear's going to be a problem, it will return on its own. Kill it then."

"Collins," Dutch said, "we already have a man hurt, and we're fortunate not to have had one or more of the mules injured or killed. In the morning, we're riding in search of that bear."

Collins said no more, and Dutch glared at him long and hard. The longer he knew Collins, the less he liked the man, and he longed to reach the Bitterroot, ending this less and less desirable alliance.

Sneed's camp was well aware of all the shooting that had resulted from the grizzly's visit, although they didn't know the reason behind it.

"We ain't goin' nowhere," said Nemo, "until they move on."

More and more, Christie Beckwith had come to question Sneed's purpose in traveling to the frontier. He and the ruffians who had been riding with him had become content to follow Dutch Siringo's wagons. She continually hounded Sneed.

"If we're going to Montana, why can't we go on? Why must we follow those freight wagons?"

Sneed laughed. "You really ain't figured it out, have you?"

"I've learned one thing, which I should have known from the start. You have no intention of pursuing anything honest. That's why you're in no hurry to reach Montana Territory."

"If you wasn't such a little fool," Sneed said contemptuously, "you'd understand. Damn it, every honest thing I've ever done has gotten me exactly nowhere, and from now on, I'm ridin' a different trail. We have no reason to reach Montana Territory ahead of those wagons, because when we get there, we're taking them."

"No," she cried. "You'd have to murder them all."

Again Sneed laughed. "That's the plan. Why do you

think I need Nemo and his gang?''

"You fool, even if you're successful, don't you know that band of killers will murder us and take everything for themselves?''

"Do you suppose I haven't thought of that?'' he snarled. "They can't do a thing to me that I won't do to them, and I'll do it first.''

It was Christie Beckwith's turn to laugh. "You? Jasper Sneed, who prides himself on slapping a woman around, is going to stand up to eight killers?''

"I have a plan,'' he shouted. "You'll see.''

"Dutch Siringo and his men will send you, your crooked plans, and all your outlaw friends straight to hell,'' Christie said.

"Then by God, you'll be along for the ride,'' Sneed gritted.

"I don't care anymore,'' said Christie. "You've destroyed me, and whatever happens to me, it'll be worth it, seeing you get yours.''

At first light, Dutch, Brace Weaver, and Cass Carlyle saddled up, preparing to track the grizzly, and if possible, shoot the troublesome animal.

"Whit,'' said Dutch, "you're in charge until we return. If Sneed's outfit moves out, see that they ride clear of our camp. Don't start any trouble, but stand your ground and keep your weapons handy.''

The trio rode north, having no trouble trailing the grizzly, for there were still patches of frozen snow. There was an occasional brown stain on the snow, evidence that the bear had taken some lead and was bleeding.

"God,'' said Cass, his eyes on the mass of gray clouds on the western horizon. "More snow's a-comin', maybe by tonight.''

"I should have had Jules and some of the others snaking in more firewood,'' Dutch replied. "And we'll have to rig our shelters in that stand of pines. We'll trail this grizzly a few miles, and if we don't have him in sight by then, we'll have to turn back. With a new storm blowing in, we'll need to get ready for it."

While the trail was plain enough, the occasional drops of blood had long since dried to brown stains. The trail was hours old, and the mass of snow clouds had come closer. Eventually the riders came upon a more ominous sign that took their minds off the grizzly entirely. Tracks of a dozen unshod horses crossed the bear's trail, leading west. The trio reined up, studying the tracks.

"The grizzly crossed their trail," said Dutch, "so that means they were through here probably late yesterday."

"They could swing south at any time," Brace said. "We'd better hightail it back and warn the others."

"If they've done that, we're already too late," said Dutch. "I reckon we'd best back trail this bunch. We need to know if there are more than the dozen who have crossed our trail. If there's a camp anywhere close, we may be in big trouble."

Dutch and his companions rode warily, their Henrys cocked and ready. The wind was from the west, growing colder by the minute, and clouds already shrouded the sun. The riders reined up, their eyes on the sky to the east. Half a dozen buzzards spiraled around, drifting downward.

"I'd bet my saddle them buzzards has got somethin' to do with this bunch of Injuns we're back trailing," said Brace Weaver.

"Come on," Dutch said. "They've killed something or somebody."

Dutch and his companions soon discovered what had attracted the scavengers. Along the bank of a creek lay the bodies of seven Indian braves.

"My God," said Cass, "They can't be Sioux, unless there's been a fallin' out within the tribe."

"I've never seen a Sioux," Dutch said, "but I've seen friendly Pawnees at Fort Kearny, and these hombres have the look of Pawnees. That would explain why the Sioux might have killed them."

"I reckon we ought to see if any of 'em are still alive," said Brace, "but I don't see how they could be."

Each of the men had been pierced with arrows, several with as many as four or five of the deadly barbs. One man—lying facedown—had been hit twice, with an arrow in his side and the other in his back, high up. Cass Carlyle knelt beside him and then rose with a shout.

"This one's still alive."

"He's a mite luckier than the rest," said Dutch. "They're all dead."

"We have to bury them," Brace said. "I won't leave any man for buzzard bait."

"Find an arroyo where we can cave in the banks," said Dutch. "We don't have any tools, and with a storm blowing in, we can't afford to come back."

While Brace and Cass sought a place for the burying, Dutch set about seeing to the badly wounded Indian who still lived. He broke off the arrow shafts, leaving just enough length to drive them through. The Indian's breath was ragged and his pulse weak, but he still lived. He was young, being not much out of his teens, if that.

"We found a place," Cass said, when he and Brace returned. "It ain't too deep, but it'll be better than bein' left to the buzzards."

"Bury them, then," said Dutch. "I'm going to wrap this one in blankets and take him with us. A man who's gone through a two-against-one fight with the Sioux deserves whatever chance we can give him."

"He must have put up some hell of a fight," Brace said. "He's the only one of the lot that wasn't scalped."

Dutch nodded. It seemed to be a universal show of respect among Indians, recognizing the bravery of an enemy by leaving him his scalp. By the time Brace and Cass returned, Dutch had the wounded Indian wrapped in several blankets.

"When I'm mounted," said Dutch, "hand him up to me. I'll have to take it slow, with a double load."

Brace Weaver leading out, Dutch and Cass following, they began the long ride back to camp. The temperature continued to drop, and by the time they reached the wagons, sleet was rattling off the brims of their hats and stinging their faces. Dutch was gratified to see that the rest of the outfit had taken it upon themselves to move the wagons into a nearby stand of pines and had erected their canvas shelters in anticipation of the gathering storm. Four of the outriders—Dent, Drago, Kirby, and Tally—had already begun snaking in fallen trees for the needed firewood. Jules and Whit were ready to take the Indian from Dutch.

"Belly-down," said Dutch. "He has arrows in his back."

Anticipating the need, Bonita brought the medicine kit. A fire was already going, and above it a coffeepot hung from an iron spider. The girl removed the coffeepot, replacing it with a pot of water to be heated for the cleansing of the Indian's wounds. Dried blood had stuck the buckskin shirt to the boy's wounds.

"Whit," said Dutch, "you and Jules lift him up enough for me to unlace his shirt. It'll have to be soaked loose from the wounds, when the water's hot."

"How are we going to remove the arrows?" Bonita asked.

"If they're barbed," said Dutch, "they can't be removed. They'll have to be driven on through, to the other side."

"I've heard of it," Jules said, "but I ain't never done it."

"Neither have I," said Dutch, "but if it must be done, one of us will have to do it."

None of them knew anything about the young Indian, except that he was near death from his wounds, and nobody questioned his need for attention except Haskel Collins.

"I don't understand you, Siringo," Collins said. "Obviously, he's been shot by his own kind and left to die. Must you nurse him back to health so he can join the others, when they come to murder us?''

''He's not a Sioux, Collins,'' said Dutch. ''Most of the Indians' hatred for the whites is justified, and I won't kill an Indian unless he's trying to kill me. This one was left for dead by the Sioux, and he's done nothing to harm us.''

''He doesn't look much older than me,'' Bonita said.

''I doubt that he is,'' said Dutch. ''We're going to do for him what we can. That water should be hot enough. Let's get this shirt off him.''

The arrows resisted all attempts to remove them, evidence that they were barbed, so it became necessary to drive them on through.

''This is going to be hard on him, and likely harder on me,'' Dutch said. ''Those of you who can stand it, gather around. Next time, one of you may be driving an arrow on through me.''

''You take the first one, and I'll try my hand at the second one,'' said Whit.

Dutch began with the arrow high in the shoulder, for it appeared the most difficult. It had to be driven out below the collarbone.

''God,'' Brace Weaver said, ''he's lucky, bein' unconscious.''

It was a slow, gut-wrenching procedure. Dutch had unloaded his Colt, and gripping the weapon by the barrel, was using the butt to drive the arrow through. Cold as it was, with snow already blowing in, the back of Dutch's shirt was soaked with sweat, and he had to pause, sleeving it from his eyes. The palms of his hands grew sweaty, and the big Colt slipped with every blow. When the arrow was finally driven through, he literally fell back in exhaustion.

''Here,'' said Whit, ''let me get rid of the next one. This needs doin', pronto. Strung out long enough, the shock could kill a man.''

While the wound in the side had bled more, it didn't take as long to drive the arrow on through.

"We'd better doctor the exit wounds first," Dutch said, "and stop the bleeding."

It was necessary to turn the Indian over on his back, and when they did so, it came as a shock to find the obsidian eyes open, and more of a shock when he spoke a single word.

"*Gracias.*"

The eyes closed, and those who surrounded him looked at one another, astonished. It was Whit Sanderson who finally said what they all were thinking.

"God Almighty. He was awake through all that, and he never grunted once. Indian or not, he's *uno bueno hombre.*"

"He knew what we were doing and what had to be done," said Dutch. "He has a will to live, and he had no other choice. A man with sand knows the odds and takes whatever chance he must."

Quickly they disinfected the wounds, applied sulfur salve, and bandaged them.

"Bonita," said Dutch, "you have a steady hand. I'm going to lift him up, and when I do, try to get some laudanum down him. He's got to be hurtin' like hell, and there'll be infection. He needs to sleep through that, if he can."

When the Indian had been bundled in blankets and placed near the fire, Dutch went to look in on the wounded Rusty Karnes. He was awake, his coat draped over his shoulders.

"My coat caught hell," he said. "Bonita patched it up for me."

"The bear got away," said Dutch. "We backtracked some Sioux and found what we think was a party of Pawnees. All but one was dead. He's down yonder near the fire."

"We can always get the bear next time," Rusty said. "Indian sign's what we got to look out for. You reckon there's a Sioux camp somewhere close?"

"We don't know," said Dutch. "We back trailed that bunch only to the place they had fought the Pawnees, so we don't know if they had left a camp somewhere to the east of us, or if they're on their way to one west of here."

"We can hold our own against a party of that size," Rusty said.

"I reckon we can," said Dutch, "as long as they don't surprise us."

"What do you aim to do with the Indian?"

"Turn him loose, I reckon," Dutch said, "when he's on his feet."

CHAPTER 8

∞

*T*he building storm broke in all its fury, the howling wind piling drifts head-high. The fires were kept burning, and the horses and mules gathered as near as they could, seeking the welcome warmth. The wounded Indian was moved into the provisions wagon, for it was the only one in which there was room. By dawn of the next day, he had a raging fever.

"He's ready for the whiskey," Dutch said. "He must sweat out the infection."

In the Sneed camp the whiskey was flowing, but it had nothing to do with care of the wounded. Besides provisions, the outlaws had bought a supply of whiskey, using the Sneed buckboard as a means of transporting it. For warmth, Sneed and Christie had been forced to gather with the outlaws around a common fire, as the temperature dropped below zero. Realizing their danger, should the fire die, Nemo had forbidden his men to partake too freely and too often of the whiskey. But he had said nothing to Sneed, and ignoring all Christie's pleas, he was soon dead drunk.

"Well," said Nemo, "it appears he ain't much in need of you, ma'am, but that ain't the case with the rest of us. Since you're cozy on this blanket here by the fire, why don't you just peel down and let some real men set your blood to boilin'?"

"Don't you touch me," Christie hissed, not believing her ears.

Grinning, Nemo took hold of the leather thong around his neck, drawing forth a huge Bowie knife with gleaming blade. When he again spoke, his voice was cold.

"One way or the other," he said, "you're goin' to do things our way. Be nice, and you won't be hurt. If you ain't, and need some persuadin', then I'll start by carving my name on your belly and maybe cuttin' off a couple of goodies you won't be needin' no more. Which way do you aim to go?"

Christie Beckwith stood up. Jasper Sneed had long since stripped her of her pride, so what—except for her life— could these men take? Slowly she unbuttoned her shirt and shrugged out of it. She then unbuttoned her Levi's and stepped out of them. His eyes alight with anticipation, Nemo came for her. The others waited their turn, while Jasper Sneed snored in drunken oblivion.

The wounded Indian fought the fever all day and most of the night, before it finally broke. After that, he slept, sweating under the blankets. Bonita had been looking in on him every two hours, while he had been feverish.

"Stay away from him, Bonita," Dutch said. "He'll be weak when he comes out of it, but we don't know how he'll react. He could still be dangerous."

"Maybe not," said Brace Weaver. "He'll know it wasn't us that done him in."

"Yes," Dutch said, "but we don't know how he feels about whites. To him, we may be as much an enemy as the Sioux."

"He spoke one word in Spanish," said Tally Slaughter. "Let me have a go at talkin' to him. I'm from south Texas, and I know some of the Mex lingo."

"I reckon it's worth a try," Dutch replied.

But their first experience with the Indian was far different than any of them expected. Despite Dutch's words of caution, Bonita continued looking in on the young Indian, and one morning—four days after he had been brought to their camp—the girl found him with his eyes open. Not knowing what to do, she alerted Dutch. He and Tally Slaughter went to the wagon.

"Ask him if he's hungry," Dutch said.

"*Alimento?*" Slaughter asked.*

"Paw-nee," the Indian said. "Paw-nee."

Dutch pointed toward the boy, and he nodded.

"He wants us to know he ain't Sioux," said Slaughter.

"Stay here with him," Dutch said. "I'll have Bonita fry some ham."

Bonita had already thought of that, and by the time Dutch reached her, she had the ham ready. She had filled a tin cup with strong black coffee.

"He ain't said nothin' else," said Slaughter.

"We'll leave him alone and let him eat," Dutch said. He placed the tin plate and cup on the wagon's floor without getting any response from the Indian.

When Dutch and Slaughter started back to the wagon, they were in time to see their patient climbing over the tailgate. Suddenly he fell into the snow.

"He's still weak," said Slaughter, "but he's trying to make a run for it."

"I don't think so," Dutch said. "After all that whiskey, followed by the ham, he's just almighty thirsty."

That seemed to be the case, for the Indian was scooping up snow by the handful. He didn't seem aware of Dutch and Slaughter, and they waited until he had apparently satisfied his thirst. He got to his knees, but was unable to stand. Only then did his eyes meet those of Dutch and Slaughter, and they understood, making no move to help him. With one hand he seized the upper edge of the wagon's tailgate, and with all the strength he possessed, he drew himself to his feet. He reached into the wagon and

* Food?

withdrew the tin cup, presenting it to Dutch.

"He wants more coffee," said Slaughter.

"He's still too weak to be on his feet," Dutch said. He pointed to the Indian, and then to the interior of the wagon. The Pawnee shook his head.

"He ain't goin' back into the wagon," said Slaughter.

"That's the impression I'm getting," Dutch said. "I reckon he can join us at the fire." He pointed toward the Indian and then toward the distant fire.

"Come on," said Slaughter. "He'll come in his own good time, if that's what he's wantin'."

They returned to the fire. The rest of the outfit had witnessed the drama, and they waited to see what the Indian would do. Slowly, one cautious step at a time, he started toward the shelters near where the cheerful fires burned. The Pawnee wore only buckskin trousers and moccasins. The windblown snow whipped about him, and he stumbled a time or two, evidence of his weakened condition. Reaching the first of the fires, he presented Bonita with his tin cup. He then sank to his knees before the fire, the protective canvas at his back a barrier against the howling wind. He sat cross-legged, staring into the fire, and when Bonita brought him the tin cup with more hot coffee, he took it and nodded.

"He acts downright civilized," said Whit Sanderson. "Any hombre comin' back for seconds of six-shooter coffee has got potential."

Bonita went to the wagon and returned with the empty tin plate. Whatever had befallen the young Pawnee, it hadn't harmed his appetite. He continued sitting before the fire as the storm howled about them, and while he didn't acknowledge their presence, neither did he seem afraid.

"What do you make of it?" Dutch asked Slaughter.

"He don't fear us," said Tally. "He knows that we saved his life, that if we had meant him harm, we wouldn't have doctored and fed him. The next move's his. Either he don't know any more Spanish words, or he's in no mood to talk. We likely won't know what he's of a mind to do until the storm's over. He ain't fool enough to light out in the middle of a blizzard.''

At suppertime, Bonita brought the Pawnee a tin plate of fried ham and beans, along with a tin cup of coffee. The Indian looked curiously at the fork and proceeded to eat the ham with his fingers. Then, with a look of disgust, he set aside the plate with the beans. He looked up in surprise when most of the men laughed. Bonita refilled his tin cup with coffee, and he continued staring into the fire.

Sneed awakened from his drunken stupor and sat up, rubbing bleary eyes. Christie sat by the fire regarding him with disgust. She wore nothing but a blanket, and it was draped carelessly about her. The storm still raged. Nemo and his men sat around drinking coffee and watching Sneed. He glared at her, and in a raspy voice, spoke. ''Damn it, why are you settin' around . . . like that?''

Christie laughed bitterly. ''What do you care? While you were piled up drunk, I've been entertaining your friends. All of them.''

''You . . . you whore!'' Sneed hissed.

Again Christie laughed. ''Why not? Any one of them's a better man than you, and it's better than having you take me for nothing. At least I'm serving a purpose, and I'll still be alive after you're dead.''

Nemo and his men laughed, and in their cruel eyes, Sneed could see the truth he had so long denied. His fury overcame his better judgment, and he snatched the Colt from beneath his waistband. It became his final act, as Nemo drew and shot him twice.

''Couple of you drag him off far enough so's he don't spook the horses,'' Nemo said. ''Chug, since you ain't got a horse, you'll drive the buckboard.''

''Hell,'' said Chug, ''why don't we leave the buckboard? They's two hosses. One fer me an' one fer the woman.''

"By God," Nemo snarled, "I said you'll drive the buckboard."

Christie Beckwith watched them drag Sneed's body away, and she felt nothing. She had no fear of these rough men. They had used her, and would use her again and again, until someone killed them, or until she ran away. But where would she go? She might have been safe with Dutch Siringo, but he wouldn't have her. Her moment of regret passed, and she recalled what had so recently happened to her. She realized she should be overcome with remorse, wishing herself dead, but she felt only relief at being rid of Sneed. He had stripped her of her pride, leaving her only the fear that when Nemo and his ruthless band killed Sneed, they would kill her as well. Now that fear was behind her, for she had something the outlaws wanted. It was that or her life, and she wanted to live.

"You ain't sheddin' no tears for the dearly departed," Nemo observed.

"He wasn't my husband," said Christie. "I'm glad to be rid of him."

Nemo laughed. "We wasn't all that bad, then."

"No," said Christie, "compared to him. I wanted someone to take care of me, and he couldn't take care of himself."

"By God, that's gospel," Nemo said. "Don't you worry none. We'll take care of you."

He eyed her with anticipation, and she knew what he meant, but she didn't care.

After three days, the storm subsided, leaving drifted snow as high as a man's head. The wind continued from the west, and the temperature dropped even lower.

"Damn," said Brace Weaver, "for every day we've been on the trail, we've spent two or three in camp, waitin' for mud to dry up or snow to melt."

"No help for it," Dutch replied. "We didn't accept this contract with any time limit on our arrival."

"An oversight on my part," said Haskel Collins shortly. "A man paying for delivery of freight should be able to expect it within a reasonable time."

"Collins," Dutch said, "you've been with us every mile of the way, and you know of every obstacle we've faced. We've just waited out a three-day blizzard, and God knows how long we'll be here before the wagons can so much as move. We're going to deliver your goods to the Bitterroot, but by God, we're going to decline any further business with you. You're welcome to buy your own wagons and freight your own goods through rain, snow, and Indians."

Collins laughed. "I am not a patient man, Mr. Siringo. As you know, I chose you and your outfit because nobody else wanted the job. I am not paying you to like it, but to do it, nor is it essential that you like me."

He said no more. Dutch and his men stared at him in amazement, and Dutch turned away just prior to losing his temper.

"He's been lookin' kind of slanch-eyed at the Indian," said Cass Carlyle.

"It's none of his affair," Dutch replied.

The Pawnee had regained his strength, yet he showed no inclination to leave. He was an enigma. He had shown his disdain for a wagon, and they had no extra horse for him. While each teamster led a saddled horse behind his wagon, he might need that horse at any time. Dutch was at a loss as to what to do with the Indian, for they had established no means of communication.

"Dutch," said Slaughter, "maybe if we gave him something, we could get through to him."

"I'm willing," Dutch said. "What do you suggest?"

"Certainly not a gun," said Slaughter. "What about a knife?"

Dutch believed it was worth a try, and haft-first, he offered the Indian his own Bowie knife. At first, the Indian didn't accept it.

"Pawnee," Dutch said. He pointed to himself, to the

Bowie, and then to the Indian.

"*Cuchillo*," said the Indian. Taking the huge knife, he ran his thumb along the blade. "*Gracias*," he said.

Dutch thought that was the end of it, but the young Indian found a place where the snow had melted and the ground was dry. Beckoning to Dutch, he knelt down, and Dutch joined him. With the point of the knife, the Pawnee drew seven crude stick horses. Then with the flat of his hand, he slapped the ground, destroying what he had drawn.

"Pawnee," he said, and with one finger, pointed to himself.

Dutch said nothing. He had just been told what had happened to the party of seven Pawnee, except for one survivor. The Indian quickly drew a dozen stick horses, using the point of the Bowie. Then, one at a time, he drove the knife into the images.

"Sioux," he said, spitting out the word with contempt.

Dutch nodded his understanding. The Pawnee wanted revenge on the Sioux, and since Dutch and his outfit must travel through Sioux territory, it seemed a perfect opportunity to communicate with the young Pawnee. Dutch pointed to himself, to one of the wagons, and finally, toward the north. He then pointed to the Pawnee, and then toward the north. The Indian nodded. The wagons were going north, through Sioux country, and he had been asked to go along. He had accepted. From his pocket Dutch took a small whetstone, and without a word, offered it to the Indian. He accepted it, sat down cross-legged next to the nearest fire, and began sharpening the already sharp Bowie.

"That was smooth, the way you got through to him," Tally Slaughter said.

"He's going after the Sioux alone," said Bonita. "That's terrible."

"It's also the Indian way," Dutch said. "We still have a good hundred and fifty miles on the Bozeman Trail. I reckon he'll get a bellyful of fighting the Sioux, along with the rest of us. Then when we finally reach the Bitterroot

and unload, we'll be coming back the same way, right
down the Bozeman.''

When the snow and the resulting mud permitted, Dutch
and his outfit broke camp and moved on, traveling north.
The Pawnee walked along beside Dutch's lead wagon,
wearing one of Dutch's flannel shirts. The wind was cold
and the ground was still frozen in places. At the end of the
day, Dutch had decided to allow the Indian to ride the horse
that followed Dutch's wagon on a lead rope. But some of
the outfit disagreed with Dutch's decision.

"You know he's got killing Sioux on his mind," Cass
Carlyle said. "He's likely to ride off, and you'll never see
him or your horse again."

"So far," said Tally Slaughter, "you've give him a
knife, a whetstone, and a shirt, so don't be surprised if he
thinks you're giving him a horse."

"I'll risk it," Dutch said. "When I'm on the wagon box,
I can't ride the horse, and it's foolish, him being afoot."

Despite the communication problem, most of the outfit
had developed a fondness for the young Indian, and
Dutch's trust was rewarded. The Pawnee rode the horse
bareback, and the first thing he did at the end of each day
was rub the animal down. Only Haskel Collins resented the
Pawnee.

"I'll be so glad," said Bonita, "when we're through
with that man. Did you mean it when you said you
wouldn't hire out to him again?"

"I did," Dutch said. It was late at night, a time when
he and the girl could be alone. "I'm thinking that when we
return to Kansas City, we ought to pool our money and buy
our own goods. We could freight them to the gold fields
and sell to the highest bidder."

"My God," said Bonita, "it would mean traveling the
Bozeman Trail through Sioux country twice."

"That's how it is," Dutch said. "If there wasn't some
risk, there wouldn't be any money in it. I aim to put a ring

on your finger, dress you up in finery, and leave you safe in Kansas City.''

''I want the ring, but I don't want to be dressed up in finery, and I don't want to be safe in Kansas City. I want to be with you. When am I going to actually shoot a gun?''

''When we're out of Sioux country,'' Dutch said, ''but I have more important things for a wife to do, besides fighting Indians.''

''You want to leave me behind, so I can worry myself silly, while *you* fight Indians.''

''Yeah,'' he said. ''That's kind of what I had in mind. I don't reckon there'll be time for much else on the trail. I just can't see us wrasslin' around under a wagon, me having my way with you, while the Sioux are shootin' arrows at us.''

She laughed. ''Can't you ever be serious? When I learn to shoot, there'll be one less man to pay, and you'll have someone to sleep with during these blizzards.''

''You purely know how to tempt a man,'' said Dutch.

Every morning, Nemo had sent a rider ahead, to report the status of the teamster camp. This time, Griz trotted his horse into camp with the news Nemo had been expecting.

''They're harnessin' the teams,'' said Griz.

''Saddle up,'' Nemo ordered.

Chug began harnessing the buckboard teams, and Christie Beckwith took her place on the wagon seat. She marveled at the person she had become, for she no longer cringed at the crude conduct of Nemo and his gang, and whatever liberties they took, she accepted. If she thought of Dutch Siringo at all, he seemed part of another world, and she no longer wept.

''Keep the wagons in sight,'' Nemo ordered, ''but don't get too close.''

It seemed the perfect defense against the Sioux, and Nemo grinned to himself. Should there be an attack, it was far more likely the Indians would go after Siringo's wagons.

Haskel Collins still rode ahead of the wagons, and now that the young Indian was riding Dutch's horse, Collins was more troublesome than ever. But the Pawnee appeared not to notice Collins, which Dutch's outfit found amusing.

"I've never seen a hombre with such a burr under his tail," said Whit Sanderson. "The Indian ain't even full growed, and he's still more a man than Haskel Collins."

But the time came when Collins was forced to recognize the Pawnee. Sundown was less than two hours away, and Dutch was concerned with finding a spring where they could spend the night, when the Sioux attacked. They came galloping in from the northeast, and grabbing their Henrys, the teamsters swung down from their wagon boxes. The outriders had split up, three to the north and three to the south, seeking to flank the Sioux. Dutch tried to count the Indians, and found there were more than thirty. They began riding in a circle around the wagons, spiraling in closer. Haskel Collins had wheeled his horse, trying to return to the wagons, when the horse spooked. It reared, throwing Collins directly in the path of the hard-riding Sioux. The Pawnee came galloping to Collins's rescue, riding into a hail of arrows, as the Sioux realized what he was attempting to do. On came the young Indian, but Collins didn't understand what was expected of him. Instead of extending his hand, he only stood there. The Pawnee, in a show of strength, seized the collar of Collins's coat, dragging him up onto the horse. Collins shrieked as an arrow ripped a painful furrow across his behind. The Pawnee shoved Collins off the horse, and he tumbled under Dutch's wagon. The outriders were beyond the circling Sioux, and their fire was beginning to have an effect. Some of the circling warriors broke toward the wagons, knives in their teeth and lances in their hands. Dutch saw one of them coming and shot the Sioux off his horse. The other was preparing to heave his lance into Dutch, when the Pawnee leaped from his horse to that of the Sioux, coming down behind him. With his left arm around the throat of his adversary, the Pawnee drove his Bowie into the belly of the Sioux. Withdrawing his Bowie, he shoved the dying brave off the horse and rode after yet another of the attackers. The attack ended as suddenly as it had begun. The outriders, all mounted, had not been hit. But the drivers hadn't fared so well. Brace Weaver had arrows driven into his left thigh and through his upper left arm. Whit Sanderson had one in his left side, just above his pistol belt, while Cass Carlyle had taken one through his upper right shoulder. The young Pawnee had not been hurt and was taking the scalps of the ten Sioux who hadn't been so fortunate. Haskel Collins stood with his back to the wagon, the seat of his trousers ripped from one side to the other, his backside bleeding. Bonita was watching him, striving to keep a straight face.

"We must reach water before we can treat your wounds," Dutch said. "Can all of you make it?"

"I can," said Brace Weaver.

"So can I," Whit and Cass said in a single voice.

Dutch looked at Collins, who was red with embarrassment. "I shall manage," he said.

The Pawnee, finished taking scalps, caught Collins's horse and returned it. Taking the reins, Collins said nothing. He began walking, leading the horse, not caring who witnessed his bare, bloody behind. Mounted on Dutch's horse, the Pawnee managed to catch one of the riderless Sioux horses. He then tied Dutch's horse behind the wagon and mounted the captured Indian pony. Dutch grinned at the Pawnee, and while he didn't return it, there was a crinkling around his eyes. They understood one another. The outriders had moved in close, and Tally Slaughter rode alongside Dutch's wagon.

"Want me to ride ahead and scout some water?" Slaughter asked.

"Good idea," said Dutch. "Take Pawnee with you."

Tally beckoned to the Indian, and they rode out. The

wagon rattled along for a distance, and finally Bonita spoke.

"You were right in the way you treated the Indian. He was magnificent."

"He was," Dutch agreed. "He did only one thing wrong. He should have left Collins where the damn fool fell off his horse."

"Oh, no," said Bonita. "Then we wouldn't have seen him get an arrow in his behind."

Dutch laughed. "I reckon that was worth something. Do you aim to patch him up?"

"If he asks me. He has too much pride, like he's better than anybody else, and I hate that."

"So do I," Dutch said. "We'll see what he does after we've made camp."

Tally and Pawnee were gone less than an hour.

"We're maybe three or four miles from water," said Slaughter. "We can make it easy before dark. Pawnee scouted around and found somethin' I missed. Them Sioux that come after us was near that spring yesterday. They come in from the north."

Reaching the spring, the rest of the outfit unharnessed the mules, allowing the men with wounds to rest. Everything else would wait until the wounded were attended to. Each of the arrows had to be driven on through, and since Brace had two of them, Dutch took the task for himself. Jules and Rusty began the grisly procedure on Whit and Cass, and darkness was upon them before they were finished. The wounds were disinfected, sulfur salve applied, and bandaged. Only then did Haskel Collins make his request.

"I have been wounded in a . . . ah . . . difficult place. I would attend to it myself, if I could, but I cannot. Would one of you administer the necessary treatment?"

"I will," said Bonita callously. "Drop your britches and bend over."

"Right here?"

"Hell, yes," Dutch said. "You want to go off in the

bushes a ways, where the Sioux can shoot some more arrows at you? The next one may be in your belly.''

Collins did as he was told, and Bonita took her time, prolonging his embarrassment. The Pawnee looked on with obvious amusement, and it was the closest he ever came to laughing. It was after dark before they were able to think about supper.

"Much as I hate to," said Dutch, "we'll have to lay over two or three days. Fevers have to burn themselves out and wounds must at least start to heal, and there's always a chance the Sioux may come looking for revenge. With some of you wounded, I want us all on the ground, with our guns ready.''

For the sake of water, Nemo and his band had traveled several miles to the east of Dutch's camp. The significance of the gunfire hadn't been lost on them, and Nemo had decided to post a double guard. Already they had lost two horses to the Sioux, and there was no way they could afford another loss. So far, the teamsters had blunted all the Sioux attacks, but how long could that continue before the Sioux came after Nemo and his band? The morning following the Sioux attack on Dutch's outfit, Nemo was in for an unpleasant surprise. Duro returned after checking out the teamster camp.

"They ain't goin' nowhere today," Duro said.

"Damn," said Nemo. While he didn't know what was causing the delay, he suspected some of Siringo's men had been killed or wounded. The longer the teamsters delayed, the more likely the Sioux were to expand their attacks to include Nemo and his men.

"Is the whiskey still off limits?" Shad asked.

"Damn right it is," said Nemo. "Them Sioux could come down on us at any time, and I don't aim to have a one of you soused on rotgut.''

Christie Beckwith had heard the distant gunfire, and she couldn't help wondering if one of the dead or wounded had been Dutch Siringo. She had heard Nemo's warning to his men, and she shuddered. Had she sought safety as the willing mistress to a band of outlaws, only to be murdered by the hostile Sioux?

A few miles to the north, the surviving Sioux had made their camp, were mourning their dead, and thirsting for revenge. A brave had been sent for more warriors, and when they arrived, the Sioux again would ride. This time, their medicine men assured them, their medicine would be good, their number great, and the scalps they would take would be many.

CHAPTER 9

❧

*T*he first two days after they had been wounded were the worst for Brace, Whit, and Cass. Brace, with his wounded upper left arm and Cass with his shoulder, were forced to exercise to overcome the stiffness and soreness. Whit, wounded in the left side, could do little except wait for the healing to begin. Pawnee, proud of the horse he had taken from the Sioux, was prouder still of the gruesome tangle of scalps.

"God," said Bonita, "I wish he would get rid of those things. They're giving me the creeps."

Dutch laughed. "He's just bein' an Indian."

Having sent Tally Slaughter and Pawnee in search of water had given Dutch an idea, and he shared it with the rest of the outfit.

"If I can get Pawnee to understand what I want him to do," said Dutch, "I'm thinking of having him ride well ahead of us, scouting for sign of the Sioux and for water for our next camp."

"There's not a man among us any better suited to the task," Tally Slaughter said, "but he should be armed with something more than a Bowie knife."

"I agree," said Dutch, "but we don't have any extra weapons."

"He can use my Henry rifle," Bonita said. "I can't practice shooting, as long as we're in Sioux country."

"That's the answer, then," said Dutch. "You still have the Colt, and I'll replace your Henry as soon as I can."

"Who's going to teach the Indian to shoot?" Haskel Collins asked.

"We don't know that he can't," said Rusty Karnes.

"Bonita," Dutch said, "bring the rifle."

Bonita brought the Henry, and when she handed it to Dutch, he threw it—without any warning—to Pawnee. The Indian caught the weapon deftly with one hand. Dutch then made a motion of raising a rifle to his shoulder, and pointed to Pawnee.

"*Comprender?*" Dutch asked.

Pawnee nodded. He raised the weapon to his shoulder, and while he had his finger on the trigger, he didn't fire. He didn't fear the Sioux. He didn't wish to waste ammunition.

"He'll get the hang of it," said Drago Peeler. "He has the touch."

"I think so too," Dutch replied. "Before we take the trail again, I'll try and tell him what we'd like for him to do."

After three days, the wounded men refused to be the cause of further delay. The outfit would take the trail again at dawn. Before moving out, Dutch beckoned to the Indian. He pointed first to Pawnee, to his horse, to the spring, and then toward the north. Pawnee nodded, and Dutch continued. He pointed to the ugly mass of scalps the Indian had tied about his middle, to the horse and mule tracks on the ground, and then to Pawnee's horse. Again Pawnee nodded. He understood. Without a word, he mounted the horse and rode north. The Henry rifle hung from a sling over his shoulder.

"Say good-bye to your Henry rifle, Siringo," Haskel Collins said.

Nobody responded. They had all begun dealing with Collins's sour disposition by simply ignoring him. Not once had he acknowledged his rescue by the young Pawnee, nor had he shown any friendliness toward the Indian. The teamsters mounted their wagon boxes and Dutch led out, heading north.

"When we stop tonight," said Bonita, "I want to take a bath."

"For God's sake, how?" Dutch asked. "The temperature's still below zero."

"I'll heat a pot of water and get in the supply wagon," said Bonita. "You'll stand outside and see that nobody comes around, won't you?"

"You're gettin' almighty shy," Dutch teased. "That day we found you on the plains, you stripped down to the hide before us all."

"That was when nobody wanted me," she said. "Before you said what . . . you did. Before that, I didn't care. I thought it . . . didn't matter. But it does . . . now."

"I doubt any of the outfit would bother you," said Dutch.

"I know one that might," she said. "Just stand outside the wagon till I'm finished."

"I'll be there," Dutch said, "but how do you know I won't look in on you?"

She leaned over and looked into his eyes. "I'd be disappointed if you didn't."

Pawnee was gone not quite two hours. He rode his horse alongside Dutch's wagon.

"*Agua?*" Dutch asked.

Pawnee held up both hands, fingers spread. Ten miles.

"Sioux?" Dutch asked.

Pawnee shook his head no.

"*Gracias*," Dutch said.

When they stopped to rest the teams, Dutch related to the rest of the outfit what the Indian had learned.

"Hell," said Whit Sanderson. "he's worth a Henry rifle to us. We need to know where the next water is, and who's better at readin' Indian sign than another Indian?"

Pawnee's estimate of ten miles proved amazingly accurate, and the wagons reached a swiftly flowing creek well before sundown. After supper, Bonita hung a pot of water over the fire to heat. When it was ready, she took it and headed for the supply wagon. A bit self-conscious, Dutch followed.

"Pards," said Rusty Karnes, loud enough for Dutch to hear, "I reckon they's about to be a happenin' in the supply wagon, and we ain't been invited."

"No," Dutch said, "you ain't. The lady's about to have herself a bath, and I aim to see that none of you shiftless varmints go lookin' in on her."

"Yeah," Cass Carlyle shouted, "but who's gonna stop *you* from lookin' in?"

"Nobody," said Dutch. "I've been invited to stand watch."

"Old Dutch is goin' to stand and watch," Kirby Butler shouted, and with the exception of Haskel Collins, they all laughed uproariously.

"Damn it," said Dutch, as he leaned against the wagon's tailgate, "you should have put this off until dark."

"Why?" she asked. "Don't they know what . . . you've told me?"

"Hell, no," said Dutch. "Not the way I told it to you. They'll just have to figure it all out. A man don't talk to other men about . . . such as . . . that."

She laughed, and despite himself, he looked at her. Standing on one foot, she raised her arms in a statuesque pose, with only a towel, and it was around her neck. He turned his back on her, and he could hear the laughter of the rest of the outfit. If they didn't know about him and Bonita before, he reckoned they would now. When she was finally finished, he helped her down and they returned to the camp. While none of his companions said anything, they flashed him knowing grins.

*   *   *

"There's more snow on the way," Phelps said.

"Thanks for the warning," said Nemo sarcastically. "Just what we need."

"Hell," Phelps said, "git off'n me. I didn't order it."

"We ain't never gittin' out of this damn Sioux country," said Duro. "I wish we'd of never laid eyes on Sneed."

Shad laughed. "You sure been takin' your turn with his woman."

Christie Beckwith seethed with silent anger. She didn't even want to be reminded of Jasper Sneed. Thunder rumbled far away, and the outlaws watched the western horizon with concern. It rankled them that they could travel no faster than the wagons, and that the wagons would invariably be brought to a standstill by snow.

In the teamster camp, the possibility of more snow was viewed with an equal lack of enthusiasm. Haskel Collins stood watching the western horizon, tight-lipped and silent.

"Look at him," said Rusty Karnes, under his breath. "If he could reach high enough, he'd try to slap God's face."

Dawn broke gray and dismal, with a cold wind from the northwest. There was no sun, nor was there the promise of any, for yesterday's cloud mass had moved in. Big gray clouds crowded one another from horizon to horizon.

"It's time for a decision," Dutch said. "Do we move out, getting as far as we can, or do we dig in where we are? There's water here. What do you think, Whit?"

"If you're wantin' a serious opinion," said Sanderson, "I'd say we move on. There's water here, but there ain't a lot of fallen timber anywhere close, and this ain't much of a place to set up a shelter. We got to have a ridge to break the force of the storm before it gets to us."

Dutch let his eyes roam the faces of the rest of the outfit, and nobody disagreed with Whit Sanderson's advice. They had weathered enough storms to relate to the wisdom of his words.

"Prepare to move out," said Dutch. "Pawnee?"

The Indian turned, and Dutch pointed to the massive clouds, to the nearby creek, and then to the north. Pawnee nodded. They must reach the next water before the impending storm struck. The Indian mounted and rode north at a fast gallop. Bonita was already on the wagon box. Dutch took his place, clucked to the teams, and led out. Bonita spoke.

"What if the next water's too far, and we can't reach it ahead of the storm?"

"We'll just have to find the best cover possible and hole up where we're forced to," said Dutch. "We can melt snow for water, if we have to. God knows, there's always plenty of it. I'm counting on Pawnee to keep his eyes open for some decent shelter, such as an arroyo or some shelving rock."

"How did you get him to understand that?"

"I'm not sure I have," Dutch said. "He knows this snow country better than we do, and he must know the importance of some natural break against a storm. This is the first time he's scouted ahead with a storm coming. I'm counting on him to think in terms of more than just water."

Within an hour, Pawnee returned. Wheeling his horse, he rode alongside Dutch's wagon, pointing to the northwest. Dutch nodded, pointed to the Indian and then northwest. Pawnee understood, and when he rode ahead, Dutch guided his teams in the same direction. Haskel Collins, again able to sit his saddle, still rode ahead of the wagons. When he discovered the wagons following the Indian, he cast a sour look at Dutch. While Dutch ignored him, Bonita laughed.

"He's jealous of Pawnee," she said.

"He should be," said Dutch. "The Indian was born to this land. My money's on him."

Dutch's confidence in the young Indian was more than justified. While they had gone a mile or two west of the trail, it had been necessary to take advantage of the water

and the shelter Pawnee had discovered. It was a box canyon, and as it deepened, there were natural stone parapets
rising up along the rims. At the head of it, water tumbled
down over stone, splashing to the canyon floor below.

"There's enough overhang for shelter, and to prevent us
from being ambushed from the canyon rims," said Dutch.
"That's more important than water or shelter."

"We should give some serious thought to hiring this Indian for a permanent guide, if he's willing," Tally Slaughter said.

"I've been thinking about that very thing," said Dutch,
"and I'm glad you agree. Since you speak some *Español*,
I'm assigning you the task of teaching Pawnee enough
words so that we can talk to him. I don't want him *too*
civilized, but we need to smooth off some of the rough
edges. Wandering around the soldier forts with a bundle of
scalps—even Sioux scalps—is enough to get him shot by
most white men."

"I'll have a go at it," said Tally, "but I ain't makin' no
promises."

"That'll give you something to do, while we wait out
this storm," Dutch said.

The outfit immediately rode out in search of fallen trees
for firewood. The wind had risen and seemed colder than
ever. With dry wood from one of the wagons, Bonita got
a fire started and began boiling water for coffee. While the
Indian had willingly taken to scouting, he did absolutely
nothing else. While the rest of the outfit snaked in logs for
firewood, Pawnee hunkered by the fire, helping himself to
a cup of newly brewed coffee. It was Bonita who complained to Dutch.

"How can he just sit here and do nothing, while everybody else is gathering wood?"

Dutch laughed. "He regards that as squaw work. He
thinks of himself as a scout, killing and scalping Sioux, and
anything less is beneath him."

"I was starting to like him," said Bonita, "but he's beginning to sound a lot like Haskel Collins.''

The snow began in the afternoon, worsening by nightfall. The box canyon was the best shelter they'd had since before Fort Laramie, on the Platte River. While they still had three fires as protection against the cold, they were free of the devastating wind, and only a little snow drifted in. Tally Slaughter began working with the Indian, speaking Spanish words, seeking some that were familiar. The rest of the outfit listened in silence, and the Indian seemed amused. He was delighted when he heard a word he understood, repeating it after Tally. Slaughter had a tablet and a stub of a pencil, and each time the Pawnee heard a word he understood, it was written down in the tablet. He took an interest in the written words, and by the time the lesson was done, he was referring to the tablet as the ''talking paper.''

''After this,'' said Drago Peeler, ''Slaughter won't be worth a damn for nothin'. He'll be wantin' to stay up here in Wyoming Territory, teachin' Injuns to talk *Mejicano*.''

''Give 'em a chance,'' Slaughter replied, ''and they might be more civilized than some other hombres that comes to mind.''

The Pawnee sat cross-legged before one of the fires, honing his Bowie on the whetstone. Finished, he began shifting the big knife from one hand to the other. Haskel Collins sat across the fire from the Indian and stared in disapproval. Without breaking his rhythm with the knife, Pawnee glared back, and Collins shuddered. Then he complained.

''He's no more than a savage, Siringo. I don't like the way he's looking at me.''

Dutch laughed, and it was Tally Slaughter who spoke.

''The Pawnee don't like you, Collins. God only knows why.''

''We have a hauling contract with you, Collins,'' said Dutch, ''but that don't entitle you to talk down to my men. The Indian's part of my outfit. Mistreat him, and you'll answer to me.''

Collins got up and walked down to the third fire, where he sat down. While the rest of their outfit retired to their blankets, Dutch and Bonita took their turn tending the fires. It was an opportunity to talk without being overheard. Bonita spoke.

"Did you mean that, about Pawnee being part of the outfit, or were you just saying that so Collins would leave him alone?"

"I want him as part of the outfit," said Dutch, "if he's willing to adapt. If his only ambition is to kill as many Sioux as he can, he won't be of much use to us, once we're off the Bozeman and into Montana Territory."

"How will you know what he intends to do?"

"By then, I'm hoping Tally Slaughter will be able to talk to him."

"Do you think he'll drive a wagon? He won't do anything else that's even close to work."

"I don't want him on a wagon box, even if he's willing. I want him on a fast horse, up ahead of the wagons, with a Henry repeating rifle," Dutch said.

"You believe in him, don't you?"

"Yes," said Dutch. "Nothing brings out the best in a man, like knowing somebody believes in him."

"That could be said for a woman, as well," Bonita said. "When I ran away, I decided to do anything I had to do— however terrible it was—just to get by. You remember the foolish things I said, that first day with you, on the wagon box?"

"I remember," said Dutch. "Would you have done that, taken up with any man in the outfit who would have had you?"

"Yes," she said. "From the time I went to the foster home, nobody ever cared about me beyond what they could get for themselves. When you found me, I had no money. All I had to give was . . . me, and I . . . thought . . . I never imagined . . ."

"That some can give without taking," Dutch finished.

"Yes," she said. "You were nice to me. You talked to me, told me I could be somebody, and you didn't try to use me. I'm ashamed of myself for some of the . . . things . . . I said to you."

"Sometimes we have to say those things before we realize just how God-awful they really are," said Dutch. "It's hell to be alone when you're young, with nobody to side you. I've been there, myself, and it's almighty easy to feel bitter, like the world owes you."

"You . . . were an orphan? You never told me that."

"I've never told anyone," Dutch said. "I'd feel better if I *had* been an orphan. The truth is, my mother abandoned me when I was five, leaving me with an old woman who wasn't even kin. I was big for my age, and I ran away, living on the streets of Cincinnati. I chopped wood, sold newspapers, swept floors, ran errands, and emptied slop jars. All for a few pennies to keep me alive. When I was ten, I got a job in a bakery, stoking the ovens at night. I lived on bread and water, taught myself to read, and managed to get a little schooling in the daytime."

"Now I'm *really* ashamed of myself," she said. "At least I had parents . . . for a while."

"I'm not telling you this to make you ashamed of yourself," said Dutch. "I want you to realize, once and for all, what I've come to understand. Life never stomps you down so low that you can't get up again, if you want to bad enough. I made up my mind I was comin' west, and I put aside nickels and dimes until I had enough for the steamboat fare to Kansas City, with a few dollars over. Of course, I lost the little I had to a crooked gambler on the boat, and when I got to Kansas City, I was broke and half-starved."

"That's why you sounded so sure when you talked to me," she said.

"Yes," he replied. "Maybe I overdid it some. I reckon it's more difficult for a girl, but I had to get you off the idea you had to sell yourself, just to live."

"Thank God you did, and that I believed you. Do you

suppose that where we're going, there'll be an honest-to-goodness bed, or will we end up sleeping under a wagon?''

"I ain't sure there'll be an honest-to-goodness preacher," said Dutch. "We may be shy of both until we're back in Kansas City."

"God," she said, in mock horror, "I'll be old and withered by then, and all my female parts will be grown up in weeds."

Dutch laughed. "The fields looked pretty well weeded when you was takin' that bath."

"Damn it," said Rusty Karnes, "if you two aim to talk all night, then make it loud enough so's the rest of us can hear."

"It's time for somebody else to tend the fires," Dutch said. "If everybody's awake, it shouldn't be too hard to find volunteers."

"I'll volunteer if the Indian will help me," said Karnes.

Nemo and his companions hadn't been so fortunate in finding shelter from the storm. They had traveled due north, unaware they were no longer behind Dutch Siringo's outfit. The wind whipped snow in under their staked-down canvas, and blew smoke and ashes into their faces. While they had adequate firewood, they were melting snow for water.

"My God," said Griz, as he melted yet another bucket of snow, "I never knowed hosses drunk so much water."

Christie Beckwith was bundled up in as many blankets as she could get, refusing to rid herself of a single one. The men who were not engaged in melting snow to water the horses were drinking coffee and trying to stay warm.

"I'm wonderin' where the hell Siringo's camp is," said Nemo. "We oughta be downwind from them, but there ain't been a hint of smoke."

"I don't know how you could tell," Phelps said sarcastically. "We've had our faces full of smoke and ashes from our own fires all day."

"Well, by God," said Nemo, "you don't like this camp, ride out and find another."

"Nemo," Duro said, "ain't it time to break out some whiskey?"

"No," said Nemo, "it ain't. I'd end up with the whole bunch of you owl-eyed, and I'd be feedin' all the fires by myself."

The outlaw called Smoke, who fancied himself a lady's man, approached the bundled-up Christie. He grinned, unbuckling his belt.

"No," Christie shouted, through chattering teeth.

"Aw," said Smoke, "it'll warm you up."

"Go to hell," Christie snarled. "That'll warm *you* up."

"Come on, damn it," Nemo shouted. "The fires are burning low, and I can't handle all the logs by myself."

It was a truly miserable day, and as it dragged on toward night, the storm seemed to grow in intensity. The wind squalled like a demented thing, swirling snow over, under, and around the taut canvas.

"God," said Shad, "if this keeps up more'n another day, we'll run out of firewood."

"No, we won't," Nemo said. "We'll get on our horses, storm or no, and snake in some more fallen trees."

The seven men looked at Nemo as though he had lost his mind, for the snow already was so deep, a horse couldn't move without somebody breaking trail. But the outlaw leader had other things on his mind. He had not anticipated the storms and resulting delays on the trail. As a result, the provisions they had loaded on Sneed's buckboard weren't going to see them through. As it stood, he was considering seizing Siringo's wagons as soon as the Sioux threat was behind them. Griz chose that particular moment to further fuel the flames of his anxiety.

"Nemo, we're low on bacon. Another week or two—"

"Damn it," Nemo roared, "you think I don't know that? I was just fixing to have you ride back to Fort Laramie and tote up another side or two."

"Why, that's a hunnert an' fifty mile," said Griz, taking him seriously.

They all laughed uproariously, but it died to an uneasy mutter at the stormy look on Nemo's face.

"Maybe we ought to grab Siringo's wagons a mite sooner than we planned," Phelps said. "When this Sioux country is behind us . . ."

"I'm considerin' that," said Nemo. "Let me do the thinking; the rest of you don't seem all that well suited to it."

He turned away, stalking to the fire, where Christie Beckwith lay bundled in blankets. Phelps and some of the others eyed him sourly, not liking his shouting and swearing, and the way he had taken to bossing them around. While the journey had its moments—there was the whiskey and Sneed's woman—Nemo's followers were beginning to doubt the wisdom of this pursuit which had stretched so far into the north country.

"If we was to start right after this storm's done," said Phelps quietly, "we got plenty of grub to get us back to Fort Laramie."

"With a hundred an' fifty miles of Sioux territory betwixt here an' there," said Shad.

"Hell," Phelps said, "it's near 'bout that far in the other direction, and before we see Montana Territory, we'll be ridin' on empty bellies."

It was a telling argument, and while none of them immediately sided with Phelps, the seed of discontent had been planted. But Nemo and his companions weren't the only ones waiting out the storm. Thirty miles to the north, more than a hundred Sioux had gathered. Their council fires burned brightly, and their medicine men assured the warriors of an impending victory against the intrusive whites.

While the storm roared across the High Plains, Tally Slaughter took advantage of the free time to further Pawnee's education. While most of the outfit knew little Spanish, they heard so much of it, they began picking it up as the Indian learned it.

"It won't be as handy as him knowin' English," Brace Weaver said, "but it's better than hand signs."

By noon of the third day, the storm had passed, leaving insurmountable snowdrifts and intense cold. The sky remained a leaden gray, and in the evening there was the distant, eerie howling of wolves.

"The canyon rim's high enough until they can't get at us without comin' in the same way we did," said Dutch. "It won't be hard to stand them off."

But it was a different situation at the outlaw camp. Nemo and his band were forced to spend the long night protecting their horses from the predators.

"God," Chug said, "come daylight, maybe they'll leave us be."

"Don't count on it," said Nemo grimly. "We can't risk it. Half of us will sleep, while the rest keeps watch. Then we'll all stand watch again tonight."

"If'n I ever git out of this damn snow country," Duro growled, "I ain't never comin' back."

"If them wolves get your horse," said Nemo grimly, "you won't have to worry about comin' back, 'cause you'll never get out. You'll be here till the Resurrection."

They spent the rest of the night in virtual silence, as the formidable howling seemed to come closer. For the sake of saving their dwindling supply of wood, they had cut back to only one fire, and with the outlaws standing off wolves, Christie Beckwith had prepared breakfast. She had donned every piece of clothing she could, including a pair of the departed Sneed's long handle underwear.

"Phelps, Shad, Griz, and me still sleep first," Nemo said, when dawn finally broke. "Wake us at midday."

"Might of knowed he'd be one of them that sleeps first," said Chug under his breath, his eyes on Nemo.

The howling of the wolves faded with the dawn. Christie Beckwith again retired to her blankets, leaving the four men with time on their hands, protecting horses that apparently were in no danger.

"By God," said Duro, "there's still three cases of whiskey. Who's goin' to know if we break out a bottle? We'll likely have to set fire to them hombres, just to wake 'em."

"I dunno," Chug said. "Nemo will raise hell."

"If he finds out," said Smoke, "let him. He ain't our daddy."

CHAPTER 10

❦

*D*utch and his outfit were watchful, but they were not
troubled by wolves. The day after the storm had
passed, the men had to brave drifted snow to snake in more
firewood. By nightfall, the ominous gray clouds had been
swept away, and twinkling stars bloomed in the purple
meadow that was the evening sky.

"She's got to warm up," said Jules Swenson. "With all
the wind, cold, and snow, we got some sun comin'."

"Good," Dutch said. "Order us up three straight days
of it. That's how much we'll need, just to make a dent in
those drifts."

"Well, hell," said Whit, "melt all this snow, and you
got hub-deep mud. Don't matter if you're mired up hub-
deep in snow or mud, you still ain't goin' nowhere."

Rusty Karnes laughed. "You cranky old varmint, just be
thankful if the snow melts. By then, she'll be gone cold
again, below zero. Mud, froze solid, ain't no problem."

There was much truth in that, and when the sun rose the
next morning, the cold had backed off. The wind, while
cold, was bearable, and the drifted snow showed definite
signs of melting. The stream cascading down the high stone
end of the box canyon took on the proportions of a waterfall, as the snow melted at higher elevations.

"Another day of this," said Dutch, "and the worst of the snow will be behind us."

"And if we don't have a hard freeze," Whit said, "the worst of the mud will be ahead of us."

"Whit," said Brace Weaver, "shut up. Any hombre that goes around forever expectin' the worst always runs headlong into it."

There were two more days of sun, without the bitter cold, and there were places where bare ground could be seen. Muddy bare ground.

"We'll move out in the morning," Dutch said. "There'll be mud, but we can overcome it by keeping to high ground. The low places are where we're likely to bog down."

"She'll be froze over again in a day or two," said Jules Swenson.

Contrary to Swenson's prediction, the warming trend continued, and there were times when it was impossible to avoid the hub-deep mud. In fact, as the frozen ground thawed, it wasn't easy to find a decent place to spread their bedrolls. Two days after leaving their shelter in the canyon, Dutch estimated they had traveled not more than twenty miles. The sun was an hour high when they stopped beside a creek at the end of the second day. The Indian had ridden out at dawn, and while he reported nothing unusual, he had spent most of the day riding far ahead of the wagons. Before supper, he did an unusual thing. He rode north and didn't return until after dark. Dismounting, he spoke to Dutch. "*Muchos Sioux. Ciento. Venir mañana.*"

Dutch had learned enough Spanish himself to understand what Pawnee had said, and so had most of the others. Tally Slaughter was the first to overcome his shock.

"*Como lejano?*" Slaughter asked.

Pawnee held up both hands, fingers spread. He then pointed north.

"My God," said Slaughter, "he says there's a hundred Sioux, camped ten miles north. They'll attack tomorrow."

"How can he know that?" Dutch asked.

The Indian either had begun to learn a little English or had anticipated the question. He pointed first to the eastern sky and then to a mass of horse and mule tracks in the mud. Finally, he pointed west and spoke a single word.

"*Campamento.*"

"He found their tracks when he rode out this morning," said Tally, "but he wasn't sure they were a threat to us. Tonight, he rode back and found their camp. I don't know why he reckons they'll attack tomorrow, but I trust his judgment."

"So do I," Dutch said, "and I don't aim for them to catch us strung out on the trail. We'll prepare for the attack right here and make them come to us."

"Group the wagons as best you can," said Dent Wells. "Levan, Drago, Kirby, Gard, Tally, and me will remain mounted, like before. When they begin circling you, we'll break out and circle them. They'll drop down on the offside of their horses where you can't get a shot at them, but the six of us can."

"That's throwing all the burden on you outriders," Dutch said.

"There's no better way," said Drago Peeler. "If all of us were mounted, they'd just ride us down until we were forced to hole up somewhere, and then they'd surround us. This way, they'll be drawn to the wagons, and when they attack, they'll be bunched. Our only hope is to gun down enough of them to intimidate the rest. Allow the attack to last too long, and they'll get some of us, sure as hell."

"That's good thinking," said Tally Slaughter.

"We'll go with that defense," Dutch said. "Why don't you include Pawnee? There'll be enough of us to defend the wagons, drawing their fire, while the rest of you move in on them from their offside."

"What do you wish me to do?" Haskel Collins asked.

"Stay off your horse and shoot Indians," said Dutch shortly.

The warming trend continuing, the fire had been allowed

to burn down to coals, just enough to keep the coffee hot. Conversation lagged, for they were in a somber mood. Not a man doubted the possibility that this might be his last night alive, for they would be outnumbered almost ten-to-one. Dutch and Bonita sat on the high box of Dutch's wagon, and she eased her hand into his.

"I won't have a rifle," she said. "I won't be much help."

"I want you behind the wagon canvas, where they can't see you," said Dutch. "You'll have your Colt. If any of them break through our lines, use it."

"This doesn't seem real," she said. "Before, there was never that many of them, and I thought . . . maybe . . . we could escape without . . . them all coming after us."

"That won't be all of them, by any means," said Dutch. "I reckon they could gather ten times that number, if they thought they needed 'em. They've held back as long as they have, only because they were waiting for reinforcements."

"God, I wish it was over." She shuddered. "If something should happen to you . . ."

"I can't promise that it won't," he said, "but my prayers have been heard before."

"I haven't said a prayer since Mother died. I'm afraid God's given up on me."

"He never gives up on you," said Dutch, "if you have the faith. Do you?"

"Yes," she said. "I believe."

"Then hold on to that," said Dutch. "See that star up yonder? That's yours and mine. There's a story—originated by the Indians, maybe—that says each of us are born under a star, and as long as that star's looking down on us, nothing can go wrong. Finally, when we ride that last trail—when we die—the star grows dim and flames out."

"That's beautiful," she said. "I'll remember it."

At first light, the Sioux rode south, more than a hundred strong. Half a dozen miles north of the teamster camp,

Chief Crazy Horse took half the force and rode to the southeast, a direction that would take him around and beyond the teamster camp. The rest of the Sioux rode on toward the wagons and the hated whites who had bested them in battle.

Nemo and his men had just finished breakfast, and Christie Beckwith had retreated to a distant thicket for personal reasons.

"Great God Almighty," Phelps bawled. He was the first to see the approaching Sioux, and the first to die. He got his hands on his rifle, but as he lifted it to his shoulder, two arrows thunked into his chest. Falling flat on his back, he watched in silent terror as his blood pumped out around the deadly shafts. His comrades were no more fortunate than he. Only Nemo got off a shot, and it slammed into the ground at his feet. It was over in no more than a minute. Some Indians had already caught up the horses, while others sacked saddlebags. There were shouts of glee when they discovered the remaining store of whiskey in the buckboard. In the distant thicket, Christie Beckwith bellied down, trembling. She was unable to take her eyes off the gruesome scene unfolding before her. Some of the Sioux were taking scalps. Distasteful as the outlaws had become, she was terrified at the thought that she no longer had them to rely on. Finally she closed her eyes and put her hands over her ears.

In the teamster camp, there was no fire, no coffee, no breakfast. Dent Wells, exactly as he had suggested, had taken Pawnee and the rest of the outriders to a position south of the camp. It was a good maneuver, but Wells didn't know that Crazy Horse and half the Sioux would soon be riding in from the south, following the slaughter at the outlaw camp.

"Here they come," Dutch shouted. "As soon as they're within range, fire."

Almost simultaneously, seven rifles opened up. Dutch

was a bit surprised that Haskel Collins was doing his share. Whatever his other faults, he didn't seem afraid. As expected, the Sioux began circling the wagons, each of them clinging to the offside of his horse, loosing arrows under the animal's neck. Wells and the outriders waited until the Sioux had established their circling pattern, and when they cut loose with their Henrys, it had a telling effect. Almost immediately a dozen horses galloped away riderless. Suddenly five of the Sioux broke ranks and rode toward the wagons. Their lances were poised and their intent obvious. Bonita shot one of them, and another flung his lance at the girl. Ripping through the wagon canvas, it narrowly missed her. Haskel Collins shot another of the lance bearers and the remaining two galloped away.

Suddenly the Sioux who had been circling the wagons drew away, pursuing Pawnee and the six outriders. Almost too late they saw their peril, for Crazy Horse and the rest of the Sioux were galloping at them from the south. It was a deadly crossfire in the making.

"Ride," Tally Slaughter shouted. "They're goin' to box us."

Kirby Butler's horse took three arrows. The animal screamed, faltered, and fell. Kirby kicked free, prepared to fight to the death, but Pawnee rode to the rescue. Kirby caught the Indian's extended hand, swinging up behind Pawnee. But the gallant deed was all in vain, as two arrows slammed into Kirby Butler's back. He was breathing his last as Pawnee reached the wagons. Dutch and the teamsters had mounted their horses and were taking the fight to the Sioux, but before they were within range, Gard Higgins was run through with a Sioux lance and driven from his saddle. It was enough to enrage the teamsters and the remaining outriders, and they charged the Sioux, firing their Henrys as rapidly as they could jack in the shells. Pawnee came galloping to catch up, a Sioux lance in each hand. He rode like a demon, driving each of the lances into the back of a fleeing enemy. The Sioux had lost more than a third of their warriors, and the others simply rode away. But it was a hollow victory for Dutch and his outfit, for it had cost them Kirby Butler and Gard Higgins, both longtime friends. Dutch rode back to where Gard Higgins lay. Cass Carlyle had caught Gard's horse, and they lifted Gard onto the saddle, belly-down. They all came together at the wagons. Bonita had an arrow driven into her upper left thigh, but she wept over the body of Kirby Butler. Rusty Karnes's face was a mass of blood from a scalp wound, while both sleeves of Brace Weaver's shirt were bloody. Haskel Collins had a gash in his right side, while Tally Slaughter had an arrow driven into his left shoulder.

"God," said Jules Swenson, "I just feel awful about Kirby and Gard."

"Imagine how I feel," Dent Wells said bitterly. "It was my fool idea that killed them."

"Neither of them would fault you," said Dutch, "and neither do we. By the time any of us knew the Sioux had split their forces, it was too late to back off. They must have circled around and wiped out that bunch of outlaws before comin' after us."

"Poor Miss Christie," Brace Weaver said. "She drove her ducks to a bad market."

"I reckon some of us will have to ride back and do some burying," said Dutch, "but not until we take care of our own. Them of you that's able, get some shovels and start digging graves for Kirby and Gard. I'll get a fire going, heat some water, and take care of our wounded."

"Cass," said Dent, "if you'll help, you, me, Levan, and Drago will dig the graves."

"That bein' the case," Jules Swenson said, "Whit an' me will help Dutch take care of the wounded. Dutch, you're elected to drive that arrow on through Bonita's leg."

With all that had happened, and with Bonita not complaining, Dutch had forgotten the arrow. The shock of it hadn't yet worn off, and the girl was distraught over the deaths of Kirby Butler and Gard Higgins.

"Dent," said Dutch, "while you all are digging the graves, keep an eye out for those Sioux. God knows, we're in no shape to fight them again today, but we must be ready."

Dutch took Bonita's arm and led her to the supply wagon, where there would be room and privacy to see to her wound. She went without a word, and he boosted her up into the wagon. He then climbed up on the box, delved into their supply of medicine, and came up with a quart of whiskey. Although the supply wagon was a third empty, it was crowded with Dutch and Bonita. He folded a blanket, placed it under her head, and stretched her out. He then broke off most of the arrow's shaft so that he could remove her Levi's.

"Now," he said, "here comes the hard part. I want you to drink half of this whiskey."

She tried to laugh. "You're going to get me drunk so you can have your way with me."

"I wish that's all it was," he said, cupping her face in his hands. "This is going to hurt like hell, babe. There's no other way."

"I know," she said. "Do what has to be done."

He drew the cork with his teeth and let her have only a little of the whiskey. Coughing and choking, she managed to get it down.

"I've never had . . . whiskey . . . before," she wheezed.

"All the better," he said. "It won't take as long or as much to knock you out."

It took awhile to get the whiskey down her, but only half as long for it to hit her. When her eyes closed and she began snoring, Dutch corked the whiskey bottle and went for a pot of hot water to cleanse the wound. Jules and Whit were doctoring the wounds of Brace Weaver, Rusty Karnes, Tally Slaughter, and Haskel Collins. Returning to the wagon, Dutch drew his Colt and punched out the loads. He climbed into the wagon, and kneeling in its close confines, began his grisly task. Even in a drunken stupor, Bonita grunted with pain, and Dutch gritted his teeth. The wound was in her extreme upper thigh, and he noted with satisfaction that it hadn't bled much. It seemed the arrow would never drive on through, and he sighed with relief when it finally did. He cleansed both the entry and the exit wounds with hot water. After a good dousing with disinfectant, he bound the wounds with white muslin. She groaned, and he leaned over and kissed her on the cheek. Washing his hands in what remained of the water, he covered Bonita with a blanket and went to see how Jules and Whit were doing.

"We done about all we can do," Whit said. "From here on, it's fevers up an' whiskey down."

When Dent, Levan, Drago, and Cass had finished digging the graves, Dutch decided to go ahead with the burying.

"Bonita's goin' to be almighty put out, us doin' the buryin' without her," said Jules.

"I reckon she will," Dutch replied, "but she'll be sleeping off the whiskey for the rest of the day, and by tonight, she'll be needin' more to kill the fever."

Kirby and Gard were laid to rest on a slope beneath the pines. From a worn Bible, Dutch read the Twenty-third Psalm. When the sad task was done, he returned to the wagon and found Bonita asleep. The rest of the wounded had partaken of the whiskey, as well, and there was little choice except to leave their camp where it was. Now it was time to do that which Dutch dreaded. They must ride to what had been the outlaw camp. He had no doubt that Christie Beckwith had been abducted or murdered by the Sioux. It would be a simple matter to bury her remains, but not so simple if the Sioux had taken her. Under the circumstances, where did his obligation to Christie end? Because of the weather, he was already behind schedule with the freight, and even without the loss of Kirby and Gard, he was ill-prepared to go looking for a Sioux-held captive. Even if that captive were Christie Beckwith. Dutch sighed and spoke.

"I reckon we'll have to check out that outlaw camp. Jules, you and Whit will ride with me. One of you bring a shovel. We may have to dig at least one grave. The rest of you stay with the wagons, keeping your guns handy. We'll be back as quickly as we can."

The three of them mounted, Jules carrying the shovel. He and Whit knew what Dutch was thinking, and despite Christie Beckwith having sold them out, they prayed that they weren't about to leave her in a lonely grave along the Bozeman. They were barely out of sight of the wagons, when they saw a distant figure stumbling toward them. Kicking their horses into a gallop, they rode on.

"My God," said Whit, "it's Miss Christie."

It was Christie Beckwith, and while her face was streaked with earlier tears, her eyes seemed emotionless and dead. Whit looked at Dutch, and Dutch nodded. Whit swung down from his saddle and went to the girl.

"Miss Christie," Whit asked, "what happened?"

Christie looked at Whit as though seeing him for the first time, and when he placed a kindly hand on her arm, she shied away. She wore men's clothes, muddy boots, and her hair was matted and dirty. Whit tried again.

"Miss Christie, we're goin' to help you, if you'll let us. What happened back yonder?"

"Dead," said Christie, without emotion. "All dead."

"Whit," Dutch said, "take her back to camp. Fix her some grub and hot coffee. Me and Jules will do whatever else needs doing."

Whit lifted Christie onto his horse and mounted behind her. He then rode back to camp, while Dutch and Jules rode south. The scene that awaited them was every bit as devastating as they had expected. The eight men had been scalped and their weapons taken.

"Great God," said Jules, "that means somewhere there's eight Sioux that's armed as well as we are. Do you aim to search this bunch?"

"No," Dutch said. "I want to be done with them and

back in our own camp. While I doubt the Sioux will return, we can't afford to gamble. Let's ride around and search out an arroyo that's deep enough. With the ground thawed, we can cave it in on these varmints and spare ourselves some digging.''

"What do you reckon happened to Sneed?" Jules wondered. "From what Miss Christie told us, I thought he was killed with the rest, but he wasn't among the dead."

"We'll likely never know the straight of it," said Dutch, "but I suspect Sneed was dead long before the Sioux showed up. Throwin' in with that bunch was Sneed's undoing. He was a weasel among lobo wolves."

They found the arroyo Dutch sought, and with the earth thawing, its high banks could easily be caved in. He and Jules roped the dead outlaws by their boots, and one at a time, dragged them to their final resting place.

"That'll keep the wolves and buzzards away from them," said Dutch, "and that's about all they deserve."

"The Sioux ain't done nothin' to the buckboard," Jules said, "an' the harness is still there. We got any use for it?"

"I think so," said Dutch. "We'll hitch our horses to it and take it with us. Some of the nonperishables from the supply wagon can be loaded on the buckboard. We'll be needing some room in the supply wagon, with two women along. I aim to keep Bonita off that wounded leg until it begins to heal, and then there's Christie. God only knows what's wrong with her."

"Pardner," Jules said, "you're one brave hombre, but not near as smart as I always thought you was. Did you ever drop two bobcats in a sack, to see how they'd get along?"

"No," said Dutch. "You reckon I'm about to find out?"

"In spades," said Jules. "I just hope you don't get clawed beyond recognition."

Dutch and Jules stepped down from the buckboard, and Jules unharnessed the horses. Christie Beckwith sat cross-legged on a blanket, staring off into the distance. While

Whit had told the rest of the outfit what Christie had said, regarding the fate of the outlaws, they gathered around to see what Dutch had to say.

"The Sioux got them all," said Dutch. "Jules and me buried the remains in an arroyo."

"What about Sneed?" Whit Sanderson asked.

"Sneed wasn't among the dead," said Dutch.

"So he wore out his welcome amongst that bunch before the Sioux got there," Brace Weaver said.

"That's what I figure," said Dutch. His eyes were on Christie Beckwith, and when she heard Sneed's name, her eyes had turned stormy. But only for a moment. She immediately slumped back into a state of indifference.

"We brought the buckboard," Jules said. "There's a big square of canvas with it, and Dutch aims to load it with some of the nonperishables from the supply wagon. He aims for Bonita an' Miss Christie to ride together."

Dutch could cheerfully have strangled Jules, for the rest of the outfit whistled and made absolutely no effort to hide knowing grins. Again Dutch noted a momentary storm in Christie Beckwith's dark eyes.

"Gard's hoss come in," said Cass Carlyle. "Him and one more, and we got us a team for the buckboard."

"By God," Drago Peeler said, "ain't he bright? We can't have all them smarts goin' unrewarded. Hitch up his hoss as the other half of the team and let him drive the buckboard."

It was an outrageous insult to a man who was a seasoned teamster, and Cass dug deep for some choice profanity, which he directed at Drago.

"Cass," Dutch said, "there's a lady present."

It silenced Cass, but if Christie Beckwith heard, there was no sign. Dutch returned to the wagon and found Bonita moaning. Feeling her forehead, he found there still was no fever. From the medicine chest he took a bottle of laudanum and got some of it down her. The medicine—almost pure opium—wouldn't take away the pain, but would result

in a deep sleep. By the time it wore off, she would have a
fever, requiring more whiskey. With so much on his mind,
Dutch had forgotten Pawnee, the Indian.

"Whit," said Dutch, "where's Pawnee?"

"Right after I brought Miss Christie in, he mounted his
horse an' rode off," Whit said. "She looked at him, an'
somethin' he saw in her just scared the hell out of him."

"The killing and scalping she witnessed has done something to her mind, I think," said Dutch. "There's a kind
of madness in her eyes, anyhow, and when she saw Pawnee, he may have seemed just another killer. Indians fear
what they don't understand, and what he saw in her eyes
must have been scary."

Pawnee rode north half a dozen miles and then circled
back to the southwest. It was his intention to ride in wid-
ening circles until he found where the scattered Sioux had
come together. He would then trail them far enough to be
certain they didn't intend to double back, revenge on their
minds. More than a third of the attacking Sioux had died,
and for the young Pawnee it had been a most satisfying
day. However, he regretted the loss of Kirby Butler and
Gard Higgins, for both men had been kind and respectful.
While he had his doubts the Sioux would return that day
or any day soon, he had needed to get away from the *diablo*
squaw with the haunted eyes. He had been aware of the
outlaw camp, and was in no way surprised that the Sioux
had ridden there first. Truly, the *diablo* squaw had been bad
medicine for the whites who had died at the hands of the
Sioux. Might she not be equally bad medicine for his
friends who drove the *carretas*?

Only Brace Weaver escaped the threat of infection from his
wounds. Rusty Karnes, Tally Slaughter, and Haskel Collins
all had to down a quantity of the whiskey. With a taste for
the stuff, Collins didn't mind. Dutch went to the wagon at
midnight and found Bonita with the expected fever. The

laudanum had begun to wear off, and he was able to wake her.

"No . . . more . . . whiskey," she begged. "I'm still sick . . . from the . . . other."

"I know," said Dutch, "but you have a raging fever, and there's nothing else we can do for it. You'll have to down the rest of this."

Somehow she got it down, and Dutch returned to the fire for some coffee. Christie Beckwith still sat cross-legged, staring into the fire. Since her arrival, she had spoken not a word nor had she accepted any food. It was an intolerable situation, and Dutch tried to think of a way to shock her out of the mental prison into which she had withdrawn. Whit Sanderson had taken over the cooking while Bonita was hurt, and he tried, again without success, to get Christie to eat.

Dutch poured a tin cup half full of coffee. Holding on to the upper rim of the cup, he offered it to Christie handle-first. To his surprise, she accepted it, and immediately threw it in his face. Dutch was kneeling, and grabbing the front of her shirt, he dragged her across his knee. With the flat of his right hand, while holding her down with his left, he administered a spanking that soon had her howling. Finally, grasping the collar of her shirt, he restored her to a sitting position. Tears streaked the dirt on her face, and if she'd had fangs, the venom in her eyes could have killed him ten times over. Dutch got a fistful of her shirtfront and drew her to him until they were face-to-face.

"By God," Dutch said, through clenched teeth, "if you're goin' to act like you're five years old, then I'll treat you that way. I know you've been through hell, but you can't go on livin' in it, and I won't let you drag the rest of us through it."

"Siringo," said Collins, who had slept off his fever, "must you be so brutal with her?"

"Collins," Dutch said, dangerously quiet, "stay the hell out of this." He then returned his attention to Christie

Beckwith. "Christie, are you ready for some breakfast and coffee?"

"Yes," she replied, almost in a whisper. "Please."

Without a word, Whit brought a tin cup of coffee, and a tin plate of fried ham. She accepted the coffee first, emptying the cup. While Whit went for more coffee, she started eating and didn't stop until the plate was empty. Dropping the plate, she took the coffee and drank it down. She then lay down on the blanket, and within seconds, was asleep.

"My God," said Tally Slaughter, "ain't he got a way with women?"

Dutch said nothing. He was thinking of the time when Bonita would be up and about, and what Jules Swenson had said about dropping two bobcats into a sack . . .

CHAPTER 11

❧

*P*awnee didn't return until near noon of the next day. Christie Beckwith was awake and the stormy look was gone from her eyes. She regarded the Indian without hostility, and he lost his fear of her. After two days in the wagon, Bonita refused to remain there any longer. While her leg was sore and she limped, she could walk, and she insisted on resuming her duties as cook. Whit Sanderson didn't argue. Christie Beckwith, while seeming normal, said little, speaking only when she had to. She turned away when Bonita was near, and Bonita spoke to Dutch.

"This is the last thing I ever expected to happen," Dutch said. "We had to take her in, because she had nowhere else to go."

"I'd never forgive you, if you hadn't," she said. "She may have made mistakes, but this is no fault of hers. Have you talked to her about . . . what she wants to do?"

"God, no," said Dutch. "I don't even know her. I thought I did, but she's changed, and I don't know what to say to her. All I can do is take her on to Montana Territory and hope something happens . . ."

"I'll talk to her," Bonita said.

"I doubt she'll talk to you," said Dutch. "We'll be taking the trail tomorrow, and I'm wondering what we're going to do with her. Do we hogtie her and chunk her into the back of a wagon?''

''Since we're taking the buckboard, maybe she'd like to drive it,'' Bonita said.

''I don't trust her with it,'' said Dutch. ''It'll be loaded with some of the durable goods from the supply wagon. I made some room in there, because I don't want you sleeping on the ground, with your wound unhealed. I aim to ask Haskel Collins to drive the buckboard. With his horse and Gard's, we'll have the necessary team.''

''Suppose he won't do it?''

''Then I'll have to do something else,'' said Dutch. ''We've had our differences, but I feel better about him, after he pitched in during the Sioux attack.''

''Collins,'' Dutch said, ''I've decided we'll take the buckboard with us. I'd consider it a favor if you'd drive it. We need one more horse to team with Gard's. Would you consider using yours for that purpose?''

''I'll consider driving the buckboard and including my horse as part of the team,'' said Collins, ''if you'll tell me why we *need* the buckboard.''

''I aim to shift some nonperishables from the supply wagon to it,'' Dutch said. ''I'd like to make room enough to keep Bonita off the ground until her wound heals.''

''What about the Beckwith woman?''

''I don't know,'' said Dutch. ''I aim to talk to her in the morning, before we move out. But she has nothing to do with whether you drive the buckboard or not. What about it?''

''Very well,'' Collins said.

The men made themselves scarce when Bonita approached Christie Beckwith. Christie stared straight ahead, saying nothing.

''There's room in one of the wagons, if you'd like to clean up,'' said Bonita. ''I'll heat some water and help you.''

''Are you saying I stink?''

"You're getting close," Bonita said carefully.

"You little wench," Christie snarled, "I want nothing from you."

"There's a change of clothes in the supply wagon," said Bonita. "You're welcome to them." She went to the creek, filled a pot with water, and suspended it above the fire.

"Well?" Dutch inquired.

"There's a change of clothes in the back of the supply wagon," said Bonita, "and I've put on some water to heat. I suppose we'll have to wait and see what she intends to do."

Christie Beckwith walked to the fire and stood looking into it. When the water began to boil, she took the pot and made her way to the supply wagon.

"Well, if that don't beat a goose a-gobblin'," said Whit Sanderson.

Bonita waited a few minutes before approaching the wagon. She found Christie out of her clothes, trying to do something with her tangled hair. She stared at Bonita a moment, and when she spoke, there still was no friendliness in her voice.

"Take a good look, damn you. It's all been used, but I'll match it against anything you've got."

"I brought you my comb," Bonita said. "You'll need it, fixing your hair."

Bonita dropped the comb on the wagon floor and turned away. She returned to the fire, and while the others looked at her questioningly, only Dutch spoke.

"It'll take more than a pot of hot water to straighten her out."

"I took her my comb," said Bonita. "Give her a chance. She might surprise you."

And Christie Beckwith did exactly that. While she still wore ill-fitting men's clothing supplied by Bonita, there was a world of difference in her. Despite what she had suffered, she looked much like the old Christie. Her hair looked clean, curled down to her shoulders, and she had scrubbed her hands, arms, and face. Without a word, she returned the comb to Bonita and set the empty pot down on the ground. Pawnee looked at her, not believing she was the *diablo* squaw of the day before. To everybody's surprise, Haskel Collins spoke.

"Miss Beckwith, you are looking especially attractive tonight. Since you will be going on to Montana Territory with us, will you accompany me in the buckboard?"

"Yes," said Christie, and she almost smiled. "Thank you."

Taking her blankets, she spread them under the supply wagon, where she had been sleeping. Collins retired to his own bedroll.

"By God," Dutch said, under his breath. "I never seen such a turnaround."

The weather turned cold again, as the wagons again took the trail north. Collins had helped Christie Beckwith to the seat of the buckboard, and they trailed Dutch's wagon.

"I'm surprised he didn't cut in ahead of me and take the lead," Dutch said.

Bonita laughed. "Then we could see every move they made."

"What kind of moves are you expecting?"

"I don't know," said Bonita. "Is it bothering you?"

"Hell, no," Dutch said. "Until yesterday, she'd never seen Collins before in her life, while the rest of us drove for her daddy. I can't imagine why she'd ride with Collins instead of one of us."

"Well," said Bonita, "he *did* ask her, and in an especially kind way. How long do you suppose it's been since anyone told her she looked nice?"

"How long do you reckon it's been *since* she looked nice?" Dutch asked. "Hell, she shows up after weeks of doin' God knows what with Jasper Sneed and that gang of thieves and killers, looking like she's been dragged through a chaparral thicket by the heels. How in hell can Collins overlook what she's . . . become?''

''He's not judging her,'' said Bonita, ''but accepting her as she is. You—and all the others—who once worked for her father, feel you were betrayed by her. You'll never forget that, and she knows it. She's not comfortable with any of you.''

''But she's comfortable with Collins.''

''I'm glad for her,'' Bonita replied. ''He's said and done things I didn't like, but there's no reason for Christie to dislike him, as long as he's nice to her. I think we should leave them alone. By the time we reach Montana Territory, you might be surprised at what can happen.''

Pawnee again rode out far ahead of the wagons, seeking more than the next suitable water. While the Sioux who had most recently attacked them hadn't returned, there was always the possibility of encountering another war party farther north. Pawnee had never traveled to the land of the far north, beyond Sioux country, but he was aware that these men whom he accompanied were bound for that region. When they were beyond the reach of the Sioux, would there not be other enemies of a similar mind? His father and brother had died at the hand of the Sioux, and Pawnee had no ties. These whites had saved his life, given him a fine knife, one of the white man's weapons, and had allowed him the use of a horse until he had captured one of his own. He would remain with these people, if they would allow him to do so. While he knew not what trail they followed, he had none of his own. . . .

Virginia City, Montana Territory. January 20, 1864.

Sheriff Henry Plummer reached the Nebraska House Hotel, where George Ives waited. Ives, one of Plummer's most trusted men, was a lieutenant in Plummer's outlaw gang, the most ruthless band of thieves and killers in Montana Territory. Miners were murdered for their gold, usually as they were about to quit the territory.

"George," said Plummer, "we got to back off for a while. There's talk of a vigilance committee."

"Hell," Ives said, "you're the sheriff. Ain't vigilantes breakin' the law?"

"Not when half the damn territory's ready to join up," said Plummer.

"There's at least five men gettin' ready to sell out, take their gold, and vamoose," Ives said. "You aim to let them get away?"

"Not necessarily," said Plummer, "but I can't afford for them to be robbed and killed as the others have been. It's hurting my reputation as a lawman."

Ives laughed. Plummer being sheriff while leading a band of outlaws had become a standing joke among members of his gang, "The Innocents."

"From now on," Plummer said, "I want miners to leave the gulch unharmed, with their gold. You will assign the necessary men to follow them until they're well out of the territory. There you will perform your necessary duties. You will take the gold, leaving no witnesses."

"You're expectin' us to ride two hunnert miles to do what we've been doin' here in the gulch?"

"It's that or get your necks stretched," said Plummer. "We may already have gone too far. Get enough men headed in the same direction, and they become the law."

"All right, damn it," Ives growled. "Is that all?"

"No," said Plummer. "Grande Oso's in town."*

"I saw the varmint," Ives replied. "He's so totally soused, he don't know where or who he is."

Plummer laughed. "He brought news, and I paid him in whiskey."

"I wouldn't trust that renegade Sioux as far as I could walk on water," said Ives.

"I do," Plummer said. "If he lies to me, there'll be no

* Big Bear

more whiskey, and he damn well knows it. He tells me there's six wagons headin' this way, along the Bozeman.''

"Hell, I don't believe that," said Ives. "It's the dead of winter, and if that ain't bad enough, there's the Sioux.''

"Oso tells me Crazy Horse and more than a hundred braves attacked them, and while they lost two men, Crazy Horse lost near forty. They're a hell-for-leather bunch, and it won't be easy, takin' them wagons.''

"My God," Ives said, "they fought off a hunnert Sioux, and you're expectin' *us* to go after them? I reckon not.''

"I reckon you will," Plummer said. "You're here in the territory under my protection, and it's subject to being withdrawn. That freight—if it's supplies and trade goods—can be worth thirty thousand dollars and more, in the mining camps.''

"You aim for us to follow the miners out of the territory, take their gold, and then meet the wagons, I reckon," said Ives.

"Perhaps there's hope for you yet, George," Plummer replied. "That's exactly what I have in mind. Take nine men with you, armed with repeating rifles. Is that clear enough, or must I draw you a picture?''

Saying nothing, Ives got up and stalked out. Henry Plummer sighed, his thoughts returning to the ominous possibility of vigilantes. George Ives set about visiting the various saloons, seeking men who didn't dig their riches from the ground. Before the day was ended, he had spoken to the men he needed, arranging a time and place to meet them.

Pawnee continued to ride out ahead of the wagons as they took the trail, and there was no sign of the Sioux. After the third day, the outfit began to breathe easier.

"Another week should see us out of Sioux territory," Dutch said.

"Don't bet money on it," said Whit Sanderson. "It's been nigh bearable for too long. Two days—mebbe sooner—an' there'll be snow.''

It was a safe enough prophecy. As the sun sank toward the western horizon, it was soon lost behind dirty gray clouds. The wind grew colder, and it became yet another night of hunkering behind shelters and tending fires for warmth. Since Christie Beckwith had begun spending her days in the buckboard with Haskel Collins, there had been a marked difference in the two of them. At night, they rarely spoke to one another or to anyone else, retiring to their blankets early, except when Collins took his turn tending the fires. Dutch was satisfied the two had formed some kind of an alliance. He never spoke of them, except to Bonita, and then only when she brought them up.

"They must do all their talking during the day," said Bonita. "They never talk around the rest of us."

The truth of it was—which none of the others would ever know—Christie and Haskel Collins hadn't spoken half a dozen words to one another their first two days together. It was the third day, when suddenly she startled him with a question.

"Why did you say . . . what you did to me?"

"Because I meant it," Collins replied.

"Don't you know what I am?"

"All I know is what my eyes tell me," said Collins.

"I'm used goods. Western men look down on women who have been used."

"I'm not a Western man," Collins said. "I'm from St. Louis. I can't see that it makes you less of a person because you've been with a man."

"Not just one," she cried. "Don't you understand?"

"Why don't you tell me?" said Collins. "I'd never seen you before, until three days ago, and I have no prejudices."

Slowly, reluctantly, she began telling him of the days when old Josh Beckwith had been alive, when Beckwith Freight Lines was a thriving business. It became more painful as she told of her alliance with Jasper Sneed, of his failed schemes, and their forced departure from Kansas City.

"For a while," she said, "it was just . . . him . . . Sneed. It was always . . . so cold, and I slept with him. Then . . . three weeks ago . . . they . . . they killed him. They'd have killed me if I hadn't given in to them."

"You're a brave woman, a strong woman," said Collins.

"I'm a coward and a weakling," she cried. "I allowed them to use me, to share me like they'd share a bottle of whiskey, until I no longer cared."

"You did what you had to, then," said Collins. "Now you're reviling yourself, not for what you feel, but for what you expect others to feel, to think of you."

"Yes," she said. "How can anyone who knows me think of me as anything less than a whore?"

"I don't see you in that light," said Collins. "In exchange for your life, you bartered the only thing you had. Why condemn yourself for doing what any other woman might have done under similar circumstances?"

He kept his eyes straight ahead, saying nothing more. Finally she spoke.

"I believe you," she said. "Maybe it's because I want to. Maybe it's because you're so unlike any man I've ever known. Then maybe down deep, you're like all the others. You're building me up, because there's something you want."

"Maybe there is," he replied.

She laughed, and it had a bitter sound. "Haven't you heard anything I've told you? It's true, damn it. There's nothing left for you. Not for any man."

"I don't know what it is about me," he said. "Maybe it's because I'm not a Westerner. Nobody takes me seriously. I've had every man in this freight outfit down on me because of things I've said and done. I gained a little ground, I think, when I joined in the fight against the Sioux, when I met these Westerners on their own level. Now, when I fail to condemn you as you feel you deserve, you doubt me. I intend to live on the frontier, to become a Westerner, but I refuse to adopt any prejudices such as you suggest.''

"I'm sorry," she said quietly. "You're right. I am condemning you without a trial. So what *do* you want from me . . . of the little that's left to give?''

"I'm opening a trading post in Western Montana Territory,'' Collins said. "I want you to join me there.''

"You want me to sleep with you. I am to resume my status as a whore, on a higher level.''

"No," he replied. "I'll expect nothing of you that leaves you uncomfortable. In time, if the feeling is there, you'll become a partner in the fullest sense of the word. Only then will I expect you to sleep with me.''

Again he kept his eyes straight ahead, but she thought there was just the ghost of a smile at the corner of his mouth. Seizing his arm, she leaned over until she could look into his eyes. Finally she caught her breath and was able to speak.

"You mean it? Would you . . . knowing what I . . . I've done . . .''

"I will," he said. "I'll put a ring on your finger, but on one condition. You're to say nothing to any of these men in Siringo's outfit. Especially Siringo.''

"That's a promise I can keep," said Christie, "but why, if you're not ashamed of me?''

"Because none of them think highly of me," Collins said. "Despite what you think, all these men are concerned about you, and they're sure to doubt my intentions.''

Christie laughed, this time with humor. "What could they possibly expect you to do that hasn't already been done to me?''

"They can't change what's happened," said Collins, "but they'll be careful to see that nobody else takes advantage of you again. They'll be especially wary of me.''

"Why?" she asked. "If I'm to take you seriously, don't I have a right to know?''

"Yes," said Collins, "I suppose you do. The truth is, I took a fancy to Bonita, before Siringo stepped in. She turned me down, after I made the same proposal I offered you."

For a moment, Collins feared he had said too much. She looked ahead, at the trotting horses, but when she finally spoke, there was no anger in her voice.

"She's not sleeping with Dutch?"

"No," said Collins. "He's an honorable man, as far as I know."

"Then she's everything that I'm not," Christie said, "and you're offering me all that you offered her."

"I am," said Collins. "Ask her."

"I won't need to," Christie said. "I believe you."

"Then you're willing to consider my offer."

"I'm willing to accept it," she said, "if you still feel the same way when we reach the end of this journey."

"I will," said Collins, "and I'm all the more anxious to reach the Bitterroot diggings."

Virginia City, Montana Territory. January 20, 1864.

On a street that ran along Virginia Gulch, George Ives paid fourteen dollars a week for board and lodging at the Missouri House, one of Virginia City's hastily erected log structures. It was into Ives's room that Ives and nine men gathered. There was Prinz, Vick, Stem, Hadsell, Aten, Dyer, Font, Mull, and Borg, all of whom were part of the infamous Plummer gang.

"Gents," said Ives, "this won't be close to home. We got to do some ridin'. We may be away two weeks or more."

There was immediate grousing and cursing.

"Damn it," Ives said, "it ain't my doin'. There's been vigilante talk, and Plummer's got the jitters. You'll all get a bigger share."

"Hell," said Prinz, "them miners ain't goin' nowhere anytime soon. There's more snow comin'."

"We don't ride until the miners have a day's start," Ives said. "Plummer wants 'em a hunnert miles away from here, before we relieve 'em of their gold. If they're snowed in here, them wagons will be snowed in somewhere to the south of here. Just hole up with a bottle until the weather breaks. When them miners ride out with their gold, we follow."

With yet another storm about to move in, Pawnee again rode north, aware of the need for adequate shelter. It was he who had found the secluded arroyo with water, and he prided himself on his ability to successfully seek water and shelter, while scouting for the tracks of the hated Sioux. While the terrain had become more rugged and mountainous, there had been fewer arroyos suited to the needs of the teamsters. As Pawnee well knew, the *carretas* could travel only so far in a day, and that limited him as to how far ahead he might seek shelter. Prior successes had taught him he must range to east and west of the trail, for it led over mostly level terrain which posed few obstacles. There was a mountain range to the west, and building toward it was a series of ridges which grew progressively higher. Again Pawnee was limited, for the *carretas* were unable to climb beyond a certain elevation. By deviating not more than a mile west of the trail, the Indian found what he was looking for. While it wasn't an arroyo, it was a steep ridge with a shelving rock ledge that leaned out over a swift stream. Upstream, as the ridge became less steep, its slope was littered with fallen trees, victims of storm-bred winds or heavy snow. This Pawnee observed with satisfaction, for the cold that accompanied the storm would require massive amounts of firewood. The Indian wheeled his horse and rode back to meet the wagons. They would reach this shelter well ahead of the impending storm.

"The wind's getting colder," Bonita said, hunching into her blanket.

"We're in for another blue norther, I reckon," said Dutch. "I just hope Pawnee's been able to find us some decent shelter. That last storm caught us almost unprepared."

Pawnee rode into sight half a mile ahead of them, and when Dutch's wagon reached him, the Indian rode alongside. He held up his right hand, fingers spread, and then pointed northwest.

"*Bueno?*" Dutch asked.

"*Bueno,*" the Indian replied.

"Another five miles," said Dutch, "and he says it's good shelter. That's what I wanted to hear."

Pawnee rode ahead, and Dutch followed him in the lead wagon. With sundown a good two hours distant, the gray clouds were herded in from the west ahead of a rising wind, and already the sky was overcast.

"I hope there's time to gather firewood," said Bonita. "I'm already freezing."

Topping a lesser ridge, they could see the stream below, sheltered by the steeper ridge and its towering rock overhang.

"I couldn't ask for better," Dutch said. "Look at those fallen trees along the lesser end of that ridge. There'll be firewood in abundance."

The teamsters drew their wagons along the creek, beneath the protective overhang, and unhitched their teams. Removed from the icy clutches of the wind, it already seemed warm, even without a fire.

"Saddle up your horses and bring your lariats," said Dutch. "There's plenty of fallen trees upstream, where the ridge gentles down. Let's snake in some firewood ahead of the storm."

They quickly secured the camp, and with no shortage of firewood, soon had three fires going in defense of the approaching storm. The wind howled across the crest of the ridge, driving flurries of snow ahead of it. Bonita had coffee ready, and Whit Sanderson had begun helping her with supper. Haskel Collins had spread a blanket near one of the fires, where he and Christie Beckwith sat drinking coffee. Little was said during supper, and immediately afterward, Dutch spoke. "We'll tend the fires in pairs, two hours at a time. It may be a little soon for the wolves to be a problem but keep your weapons close at hand. Bonita and me will take the first two hours."

"Christie and me will take the second two," Haskel Collins said.

That came as a surprise, but nobody said anything. Dutch knew Bonita would likely have something to say, once the others had turned in for the night. But for tending the fires, there was little else to do during a storm except sleep, and most of the outfit spread their blankets near one of the fires. Coals were kept live under one coffeepot, so that the fire tenders would have hot coffee during the night. Having added more wood to the fires, Dutch and Bonita sat down near the coffeepot, and Dutch refilled their cups.

"What did you think of what Collins said?" Bonita asked.

"I think Christie and him will be tending the fires after we finish," said Dutch.

"You *know* what I mean," Bonita said.

"I think they've reached some kind of understanding with one another that's none of our business," said Dutch.

"It doesn't have to be our business to be our concern," Bonita said. "The poor woman has been through so much, I want her to find a home. It's just that I'm not so sure about Haskel Collins."

"Hell," said Dutch, "he could have horns, a spike tail, and cloven feet, and still be head and shoulders above anything she's throwed in with, so far."

"I know," Bonita said, "but I can't imagine him being kind to her, after all she's been through. Do you suppose he . . . knows . . . what must have happened . . . while she was with all those men?''

"How could he *not* know?'' Dutch asked. "He's been with us ever since Christie and Sneed caught up to us, and he knew they were with that bunch of outlaws. There's things I don't like about Haskel Collins, but as far as we know, he's been nice to her, and we all know he's not sleeping with her. Don't sell the man short. He's got a hell of a lot to overlook, where Christie's concerned, and if he can do it, he's a better man than I am, because I'm not sure I could.''

CHAPTER 12

❧

Dutch and his outfit weathered the storm for the first night and all the next day, and by the second night, there had been no sign of the expected wolves.

"Unless the wolves show up," said Dutch, "the team tending the fires can keep watch. All of you have your weapons close at hand."

The ridge with its overhang—while protecting them from the elements—offered little protection from predators, for it was vulnerable on three sides. The creek ran deep, and there was snow drifted high along the east bank, but the only protection from up- or downstream was the vigilance of the sentries. The horses and mules were bunched toward the upper end of the ridge, for it was here that the overhang offered the most protection from the storm. Brace Weaver and Cass Carlyle were adding more logs to the fires, when there was a commotion among the stock. Horses neighed, mules brayed, as every one of the frightened animals attempted to crowd in between the protective ridge and the fires. As a result, neither Cass nor Brace could get a clear shot at the lumbering grizzly that had come downstream under cover of the howling wind. Desperately the men fought their way through the ranks of rearing horses and mules. Dutch, Jules, Whit, and Rusty were ready with their Henrys, but unable to get a clear shot. Cass Carlyle broke through, but before he could fire, a mule sidestepped into him. Off balance, he dropped to one knee. Before he could get to his feet, the bear seized him in a pair of mighty paws. Dutch fought to get through the tangle of horses and mules, to get behind the grizzly. Every man held his fire, for from their positions, they couldn't shoot the bear without risking killing Cass. For a few agonizing seconds—to the ticking of an invisible clock—Cass Carlyle's life hung in the balance. Then with a leap, Pawnee was bounding over the backs of the milling horses and mules, his Bowie in his right hand. He pounced like a cougar onto the back of the big grizzly, his left arm around the animal's massive throat. The bear dropped Cass Carlyle and began swiping at this new enemy that clung to his back like a burr. Pawnee drove the knife again and again into the grizzly, just below its throat. But one mighty paw ripped into the Indian's shoulder, and he was thrown free, over the bear's head. But Cass Carlyle, the sleeves of his coat shredded and bloody, had seized his Henry. Once, twice, three times, he fired. The grizzly paused, as though confused, and finally sank down, dying. Dutch and the rest of the outfit had managed to drive the mules and horses on down the creek, away from the fires, calming the animals.

"My . . . God," Cass Carlyle groaned, staggering.

At least he was on his feet. Pawnee lay facedown, having struck his head on a rock. The bear's claws had gone deep, ripping him from his shoulder blade almost to the elbow of his left arm. While Cass had been wearing a coat, the Indian's only protection had been the flannel shirt given him by Dutch. Cass sank down by the nearest fire, while Jules and Whit carried Pawnee in, lowering him belly-down on a blanket. Bonita had removed the coffeepot, stirred up the coals, and had water on to boil.

"Get what's left of that shirt off him," said Dutch. "We have to stop the bleeding."

Brace Weaver and Dent Wells began stripping off the shirt, while Dutch went to the creek, seeking a particular kind of mud. It was all they had to stop the bleeding.

"Lord God," Wells said, "I never seen a man clawed so deep. We may not be able to save him."

"We got to try," said Weaver. "What he done took more guts than I've ever seen, and he don't deserve to die like this."

By the time the water was boiling, Dutch had a pot two-thirds full of mud. As soon as Bonita washed off the accumulated blood, more welled up from the terrible wound.

"Hold off with the water," Dutch said. "We can't do anything else for him until we've stopped the bleeding."

He applied handfuls of the mud, laying it on thick. Finished, he returned to the creek, rinsed the pot, and washed his hands. Levan Blade and Drago Peeler had saddled their unwilling horses, roped the bear's carcass, and had dragged it as far from the camp as the drifted snow would permit. The horses and mules, still fearful of the bear scent, were far down the creek.

"They ain't wantin' to come back up here where the bear was killed," Tally Slaughter said.

"Then we'll have to drive them back and hobble them," said Dutch. "If there's wolves within ten miles, they'll be drawn to that bear carcass. We must keep our stock as near as we can, for their protection."

"There likely won't be another bear," Drago said. "That's the same one that come after us before. He had some lead in him before Cass shot him."

Cass Carlyle sat hunched over, bare to the waist. While his coat had protected him, and he hadn't been clawed as badly as the Indian, he was hurt and bleeding. Bonita washed the wound with warm water and applied disinfectant. Soaking white muslin in more of the disinfectant, she spread the pads over the wound until the bleeding ceased. Removing the muslin pads, she then applied a thick coat of sulfur salve.

"Best leave him uncovered for a while," said Dutch. "Dose him with laudanum, so's he can sleep."

"A wounded man needs whiskey," Cass grumbled.

"A wounded man with fever needs whiskey," said Dutch.

Dutch found that the mud he had applied to the Indian's wounds had begun to dry. He hunkered down beside Pawnee and found the Indian's eyes open.

"*Oso muerto*," Dutch said. "*Valiente Indio. Medico herida.*"*

"*Gracias*," said Pawnee.

"Rusty," Dutch said, "you and Tally build up this fire some more. Soon as that mud dries, we'll peel it off and tend to his wound."

Through it all, Haskel Collins and Christie Beckwith had remained silent. When Collins spoke, he surprised them all.

"There are some sheepskin-lined coats in one of the wagons. When the Indian heals, I will see that he is given one."

While Christie Beckwith said nothing, her eyes were on Haskel Collins, approving this unselfish act. It proved contagious.

"I got an extra shirt the Indian can have," said Dent Wells.

"So have I," Drago Peeler added.

Dutch sighed with satisfaction. In the face of near tragedy, the heroic act of a homeless Indian had drawn them together as nothing else ever could have. For courage went beyond the color of a man's skin, touching him to his soul, reviving in him some long forgotten brotherhood that perhaps he didn't fully understand.

"The mud's dry now," Bonita said.

"Bring some warm water and the disinfectant," said Dutch.

Peeling the mud away from the wound, Dutch found the bleeding had stopped. There was the possibility that cleansing with water and applying disinfectant would cause

_____
* Bear dead. Brave Indian. Doctor wound.

bleeding to start anew, but it was a chance they had to take.

"Use plenty of warm water," Dutch said.

Bonita gently cleansed the torn flesh with muslin soaked in hot water, and immediately Dutch followed with muslin pads soaked in disinfectant. The pads were left in place for a few minutes, and then sulfur salve was applied to the clean, dry wound.

"Bring me the laudanum," said Dutch. "He has to be hurting, and he needs to sleep some of it off."

Bonita brought the laudanum and a large bone spoon.

"Pour him a dose of it," Dutch said. "I'm going to lift him enough for him to swallow the stuff." He then spoke to the Indian. "Pawnee."

Pawnee opened his eyes, and Dutch pointed to the laudanum bottle Bonita held. More than once the Indian had seen the wounded teamsters given the medicine, and while he had no idea what purpose it served, he knew it had to do with healing. Carefully, Dutch lifted him up enough to swallow the laudanum Bonita offered. He lay on a blanket between the fire and the protective wall of the ridge, and Bonita covered him with another blanket. He became less conscious of the pain and more aware of the warmth of the fire, and then he slept.

"Dawn can't be far off," said Whit Sanderson. "We might as well just stay up."

"I reckon," Dutch agreed. "The horses and mules are still skittish."

"Them jug-headed mules will be spooked this time tomorrow night," Rusty Karnes said. "Long as that bear smell is around."

"Somebody tell me when it gits daylight," said Jules Swenson. "With a storm roarin', I can't never tell."

"This storm ain't costin' us any time," Tally Slaughter said. "With Cass and Pawnee hurt, we'd have to lay over a couple days anyhow."

The storm continued unabated, and by suppertime of the next day, the two wounded men were burning with fever.

"It's good that you brought plenty of whiskey," said Bonita. "I just hope I never have to drink any more of it."

Cass Carlyle was the first to sweat out his fever and begin healing. He sat up and began to eat the day the storm finally blew itself out. Pawnee took a day longer. Immediately the Indian began exercising his arms and shoulders, working out the stiffness. Just when it seemed the wolves weren't going to return, they did. Although the storm was gone, the bitter cold remained. There was a full moon, and the stars twinkled like particles of ice on a heavenly field of purple. The mournful cries of the wolves seemed to come from everywhere. The horses and mules overcame their fear of the bear scent, hovering as near the fires as they could, terrified by the cries of the hunting wolves.

"Just our damn luck," Tally Slaughter grumbled. "Enough bear carcass out there to feed every wolf in Wyoming Territory, and we draw a bunch that don't like bear meat."

"We'll double the guard," said Dutch. "All of you keep your rifles handy. If they try to move in on us, make every shot count."

The wolves found the bear carcass, but Dutch and his men were unable to relax their vigilance, for they feared their mules and horses would continue to be a temptation. There was a continual commotion, as the big gray predators fought among themselves.

"There's likely more of the varmints than can find a place around the bear carcass," said Jules Swenson. "Some of 'em will git pushed out, and they'll come lookin' for our livestock."

It was a safe prediction, and the third day after the killing of the bear, wolves began stalking the camp. Brace Weaver shot one, driving the rest back to a safe distance.

"My God," Whit Sanderson said, "there must be more'n a hundred of them, it they've finished off that bear. With 'em comin' in this close in daylight, what'll they do when it's dark?"

It was a question that was on the minds of them all, and nobody had an answer. While an anemic sun had made occasional appearances during the several days since the storm had blown over, gray clouds still marched from horizon to horizon. Little if any of the snow had melted, for the temperature remained below zero, and a bitter wind swept in from the northwest. Pawnee had recovered to the extent that he sat before the fire drinking coffee from a tin cup. He had donned one of the several flannel shirts that had been given him, as well as the sheepskin-lined coat which Haskel Collins had promised. While the Indian had said nothing, he had accepted the gifts and seemed as pleased with the concern of his benefactors as with what they had given him.

"While it's still daylight," said Dutch, "some of us had better snake in some more firewood. I don't see this cold lettin' up anytime soon."

By the time the cold finally let up and the worst of the drifted snow was gone, Cass Carlyle and Pawnee were able to ride. As usual, mud became a problem, and the second day after they had again taken the trail, there was a rash of trouble with the wagons. The left rear wheel of Dutch's wagon slid off a stone and slammed into another, splintering the oak rim. Replacing the wheel, they had traveled not more than a mile when the right rear wheel of Brace Weaver's wagon met with an identical fate.

"My God," said Whit Sanderson, "another day like this, and we'll be packin' all this freight the rest of the way on mules."

Pawnee had ridden on ahead, seeking water for the night's camp. A warming trend had lifted the temperature to the extent that shelter wouldn't be necessary for a while. The Indian rode slowly, looking for tracks. While the teamsters cursed the abundance of mud, Pawnee saw it as beneficial, for it readily revealed the tracks of potential enemies. With the passing of many days since the attack of the Sioux, it began to appear that Crazy Horse and his fierce warriors had given up, but Pawnee wasn't ready to accept that. He believed that before Dutch Siringo's wagons were free of the Bozeman, that the Sioux would make one more attempt to avenge some of the braves they had lost. While there were plenty of wet-weather springs, as a result of melting snow, Pawnee sought a permanent water source which might afford some cover. At these higher elevations, springs often gushed out from beneath stone plateaus, with surrounding pinnacles securing men with rifles. Pawnee had just found such a place, when he became aware that he wasn't alone. The wind was from the northwest, and though the sound was faint when a horse's hoof loosed a stone, Pawnee heard it. The Sioux, aware they had been discovered, kicked their horses into a run, and fifteen of them came galloping toward Pawnee. While the spring he had just discovered was within an area easily defended by several men, a single man would quickly be surrounded. If he must, Pawnee would sell his life as dearly as possible, but to die so great a distance from the approaching wagons would betray the trust of his newfound comrades. When he was dead, the Sioux could then swoop down on the unsuspecting teamsters. Pawnee rode for his life and for the lives of his comrades, knowing that if he was close enough when he made his stand, the sharp ears of Dutch Siringo would hear the thunder of his Henry. And Siringo would understand . . .

Far to the south, Dutch reined up his teams, listening.

"What is it?" Bonita asked.

"Gunfire," said Dutch. "Pawnee's in trouble."

Dutch leaped down from the wagon box, as the rest of the teamsters reined up. Dutch loosed the reins of his horse from the wagon bow and swung into the saddle. The four outriders were there, and he spoke to them first.

"Dent, Levan, Drago, and Tally, you'll ride with me. The rest of you stay close by the wagons, keepin' your guns ready."

Dutch rode out, kicking his horse into a fast gallop, his four companions following.

Pawnee's horse was tiring. He could feel the valiant animal heaving, and he knew there wasn't much time. Ahead was a windblown pine, the root mass torn out of the ground. A substantial hole remained, and leaping from the back of the horse, Pawnee took cover. The Henry was fully loaded, and in a leather bag around his middle, the Indian had more than a hundred rounds. Arrows ripped into the root mass of the fallen tree, showering Pawnee with dirt. He fired, and had the satisfaction of seeing one of the Sioux tumble from his horse. They were riding in an ever-lessening circle, bringing them nearer their quarry, with every Sioux clinging to the offside of his horse. Pawnee had nothing at which to fire, and while he presented no target to the attackers, they had the advantage. Circling, some of them were always behind him. Once they were near enough, one of them would drop from his horse and come after Pawnee with a knife. But time ran out for the Sioux. There was the thunder of galloping horses, as five riders approached from the south. One of the riders—Siringo—came straight on, while the remaining four split, flanking the attacking Sioux. Each of the five men accounted for one of the enemy, while Pawnee—free from immediate danger—shot another Sioux off his horse. With seven warriors dead and several wounded, the Sioux retreated. Dent Wells caught up Pawnee's horse.

"*Gracias*," said Pawnee, crawling out of the hole where he had taken refuge.

The five men grinned at him, appreciating what he had done. No further words were spoken and none were necessary. The six of them rode back toward the wagons.

Virginia City, Montana Territory. January 28, 1864.

Five miners had gathered, the night before their planned departure from the diggings. There was Hugh McCulloch,

Gus Pryor, Julius Blackburn, Irv Robb, and Alvin Taylor.

"There's been no robberies or killings for two weeks," Taylor said. "Maybe talk of the vigilantes has scared the varmints off."

"Hell," said McCulloch, "you know better'n that. Nobody's made a move because of head-high snowdrifts and below-zero weather. Now that it's warmed up enough fer us to make a break, them lobos will be after us."

"I'm for ridin' out in the mornin' 'fore daylight," Pryor said, "an' not sleepin' till we got this territory behind us."

"They can still ride us down and shoot us in the back," said Blackburn.

"Well, if you got a better idea," Robb said, "let's hear it."

They looked at one another, uncertain, yet knowing it was their only chance.

A similar meeting was taking place in George Ives's room at the Missouri House Hotel. The nine men Ives had chosen were there, and Ives was delegating duties.

"Prinz, I want you to keep an eye on Hugh McCulloch. Vick, you'll watch Gus Pryor. Stem, don't you let Julius Blackburn out of your sight. Hadsell, you'll trail Irv Robb, and Aten, keep your eye on Alvin Taylor. They may not come together until they're well away from the gulch, hopin' to throw us off. If they don't try to run tomorrow, for sure they'll do it the day after."

"If they don't ride out in the mornin'," said Prinz, "we'll be stuck with tailin' 'em day and night, until they do."

"You're damn right we will," Ives said. "There's ten of us. If they're still here after tomorrow, the rest of us will take a turn watchin' them. They're not to get away without us knowin'. Lay off the booze and keep your eyes and ears open."

*   *   *

Without incident, Dutch and his outfit made it to the spring Pawnee had found, and as a precaution, the Indian rode a five-mile circle around the camp. He wanted to be sure the Sioux had not doubled back, and it was a precaution Dutch didn't overlook. Half the outfit stood watch until midnight, and the rest took over until dawn. But the night passed without incident, and when the wagons again took the trail, Pawnee rode far ahead, again searching for good water. Despite the unquestionable presence of the Sioux, the Indian had no fear. Hadn't he held off the cursed Sioux until his companions arrived, and hadn't they triumphed over the enemy and driven them away? While he no longer had kin among his tribe, he had won the friendship of white men, and had made a place for himself. He had been given a treasured weapon that fired many times from a single loading, killing quickly from a great distance. On impulse, he reined up, turning his horse to face the rising sun. Knowing no words, he lifted his arms toward the heavens, giving silent thanks to the Great Spirit in the only way he knew how.

The fair weather held, and after supper, a single fire was maintained only to keep the coffee hot. Dutch still kept a double watch, which he intended to do as long as they were anywhere close to Sioux territory.

"God," said Whit Sanderson, "it seems like we been in Sioux country forever. How are we goin' to know when we cross the line into Montana?"

"You've been here before, Collins," Dutch said. "How will we know?"

"As I recall," said Collins, "we'll cross the Little Missouri River. It flows from Dakota Territory across the southeastern corner of Montana Territory."

"That should free us of the Sioux," Dutch said. "Montana is Crow country. I've heard they're friendly."

"That's what I've heard," said Collins, "but they are notorious thieves. They're partial to horses, but they'll take mules too. They'll ride into camp and eat with you, then return after dark and steal every animal you own."

"That means we'll all be pulling a lot of sentry duty," Dutch said. "They'll plunder the wagons too."

"That they will," said Collins.

Southeastern Montana Territory. February 6, 1864.

The weather held until the wagons crossed the Little Missouri. There was little doubt another storm was building, forcing them to spend their first day in Montana Territory in search of shelter.

"Perhaps we should search the river for an overhang," Collins said.

"You're right," said Dutch. "It would provide the best and quickest shelter. It's much too shallow along here. Tally, take Pawnee with you and ride upstream a ways."

While Slaughter and the Indian failed to find a suitable shelter within the river's banks, they eventually found something better. There was an arroyo that angled off from the river's west bank, and the farther it led from the river, the higher its banks became. A runoff from the river itself provided a stream down the arroyo. Slaughter looked at Pawnee, and the Indian nodded. It would offer adequate protection against the coming storm. They rode southwest, along the floor of the arroyo, until the walls diminished to level ground. The wagons could easily enter from the lower end, advancing until the walls became high enough to hold the storm at bay. Reaching the waiting wagons, Slaughter and Pawnee led the rest of the outfit into the low end of the arroyo. From there, they went on to the point where the rim became protective, some twenty-five feet overhead.

"This could be the best of them all," said Dutch approvingly. "Now we have to ride out and begin snaking in firewood."

The riders snaked in fallen trees until it became too dark to see. Already the sky was overcast with billowing gray clouds, and the familiar wind had begun to moan. Fires had been built, the coffee was ready, and supper was underway. The snow soon began, dusting the floor of the arroyo, but not reaching beneath the overhang. Just when their camp seemed the most secure, there came the *clop-clop-clop* of horses' hooves from the shallow end of the arroyo. Every man had his Henry cocked and ready, and when the first of the Indians came within the light of the fires, he had his right hand raised as a sign of peace. Nine more rode behind him, single file.

"Hold your fire," Dutch said cautiously.

The mounted men reined up, and the lead rider spoke.

"Crow. Much hungry. Want eat."

Dutch raised his right hand in a sign of peace. He then turned his thumb toward the ground in what he hoped was an invitation to dismount. The Indians dismounted, turning their lank, spotted ponies loose.

"Whit," said Dutch, "slice off some ham and put it on to fry. Bonita, put on three pots of coffee."

The Indians squatted near the fire where Whit was slicing ham into an iron frying pan. The ham began to sizzle, and with grunts of satisfaction, the Crows began eating the ham from the pan. Whit looked on in disgust, and began slicing more ham. Bonita brought enough tin cups, and when the coffee was ready, began filling them with coffee. The only one of the Indians who had spoken took one of the cups, drained it in a single gulp, and repeated the procedure with a second one. Bonita looked on in disbelief. Finally she went for another pot and began filling the cups again. The Crows drank all three pots of coffee, scalding hot, and sat there smacking their lips in anticipation of more. Bonita looked helplessly at Dutch, and he shook his head. Whit had ceased frying ham and was scouring the pan with sand. Several of the Indians looked questioningly at Dutch, and he shook his head. He had a forbidding suspicion they would be snowed in with this gluttonous bunch for the duration of the storm, requiring a rationing of food. Convinced there would be no more food or coffee, the Crows grumbled among themselves. They were dressed in buckskin, each with a blanket about his shoulders. Spreading their blankets, they stretched out near one of the fires and were soon snoring.

"My God," said Whit Sanderson, in awe, "we was better off with the Sioux. All we had to do was shoot them."

"If they stay until this storm blows itself out," Brace Weaver predicted, "we'll all be eatin' mule, and glad to get it."

"I won't," said Bonita, shuddering.

"We'll need double sentries as long as they're here," Haskel Collins said. "If we don't, we may not *have* any horses or mules."

"But it's snowing," said Bonita. "They wouldn't sneak off with our horses and mules in a storm, would they?"

"We don't know," Dutch said, "because we've had no experience with Crows, but I'd say we can't risk it. Four of us will have to be awake at all times, not more than two tending the fires."

Pawnee kept his distance from the Crows, not trusting them. When he spread his own blankets, he positioned himself at the fire next to the visitors, and Dutch grinned to himself. While the Crows might get past the rest of the outfit, they wouldn't escape Pawnee.

"We'll do sentry duty and fire-tending four hours at a time," said Dutch. "Brace, you and Cass join Bonita and me for the first watch. Jules, you and Whit take the second four hours with Collins and Christie. Dent, Levan, Drago, and Tally, you'll have the last watch. All of you, while you're sleeping, keep your weapons close by, and don't remove anything except your hats. When you're on watch, see that our horses and mules stay as near the fires as possible. Don't allow any of them to drift down the arroyo, where you can't see them."

Except for the four on watch, the camp soon slept. Bonita and Dutch hunkered down near one of the fires. Bonita spoke quietly. "This is such a good camp. Why did they have to show up and ruin it?"

"I don't expect any trouble out of them," said Dutch, "beyond the possibility they may eat us all into starvation."

"How will the rest of us manage to eat?" Bonita asked. "They eat it right out of the pan, before it's even done."

"I don't know," said Dutch. "I just hope this storm won't be a three-day affair, with another three or four days until the drifts subside."

CHAPTER 13

⌘

The ravenous Crows remained only until the storm had gone. To the everlasting relief of Dutch and his outfit, they rode out on the third day following their arrival, without so much as a word of thanks or farewell.

"Thank God," said Whit Sanderson. "I hope we've seen the last of them."

"Don't count on it," Dutch said. "While they were in no position to make off with our horses and mules, they know how many we have. They can always visit us again when we are on the open plains."

"They're an ungrateful lot," said Haskel Collins. "What kind of men would devour our food for three days, and then come back and rob us?"

"Crows," Brace Weaver said.

They all laughed, but it was short-lived, for the possibility of such disgraceful conduct by the Crows was very real. Once Dutch and his outfit left the protective arroyo, they dared not relax their vigilance for a minute.

"We'll continue to hobble the horses and mules at night," said Dutch, "and we'll leave our horses saddled. Don't remove anything but your hats, and be ready to ride at any time. When you're on watch, don't overlook anything. That shadow—when you think your eyes are deceiving you—may be a Crow with a knife. And we can't devote all our time to the livestock. We must watch the wagons. The varmints can slit the canvas on the offside and steal us blind, before we know they're about.''

Dutch took the trail a day early, knowing they would have trouble with remaining snowdrifts and mud, but refusing to lose another day. The cold remained, keeping the ground frozen, sparing them hub-deep mud. Drifted snow, however, concealed gullies and drop-offs, increasing the possibility of smashed wheels and snapped axles. What appeared to be level ground was often treacherous ruts filled with snow, and it was into one of these that the left rear wheel of Whit Sanderson's wagon slid. They could tell it wasn't a broken wheel, for the wheel leaned outward at a drunken angle.

''Busted axle,'' said Whit.

''Better that than another wheel,'' Rusty Karnes said.

It was a truth to which they could all relate, for among all the wagons, they had but two more spare rear wheels. Without complaining, they jacked up the wagon and began the tiresome job of removing the axle. As was always the case, it had broken at a slender end where it went through the wheel's hub.

''These damn things ought to be made of solid iron,'' said Jules Swenson.

''Some are,'' Dutch said, ''but they're not popular. They add too much weight to the wagon, reducing the payload.''

The cold continued, requiring shelter at night, for the wind rose to gale strength. The Crow being a threat, sentry duty required moving among the horses, mules, and wagons at regular intervals. Two days north of the crossing of the Little Missouri, Dutch headed the caravan due west.

''From what I recall,'' said Haskel Collins, ''we're a hundred and seventy miles west of the Yellowstone. We'll follow it about eighty-five miles, until it turns south.''

The bitter cold began to retreat and the sun turned the frozen ground into a veritable sea of mud. Wagons bogged down, requiring the use of additional teams to free them.

The mules brayed their frustration, nipping at one another, and the wagons advanced less than five miles. Finally, when they reached some stony high ground with a spring, Dutch gave it up and called a halt.

"Damn it, we've worn out ourselves and the teams, and have gotten virtually nowhere. We'll give the sun a day to dry up some of this mud."

While the teamsters cursed the mud, Pawnee took advantage of it to scout ahead. The bothersome Crows were strong on his mind, and tracks—if he found them—could tell him much. Half a dozen miles beyond the wagon camp, he found the tracks of many horses and some of them were shod. The trail led in from the north, turning west where Pawnee had first come upon it. The Indian followed the tracks for three miles. He wished to know if they changed course, and how many Indian riders there were. The tracks of the shod horses told him the animals were riderless and being driven, and with the tracks of the unshod horses dominant, he determined there were a dozen or more Indian riders. While the trail continued on, it was only a few hours old, and Pawnee reined up. He might ride many miles without finding a camp, allowing some of the riders ahead of him to circle back to the wagons and the unsuspecting teamsters. He might yet follow the trail, but the men with the wagons needed to know of the party ahead of them. The Indian wheeled his horse and rode back the way he had come.

"Crow," said Dutch, as Pawnee pointed to the tracks of his own unshod pony. Raising both hands, he spread his fingers. He then lowered his hands and raised his right, showing two fingers.

"*Todo?*" Dutch asked.

Pawnee shrugged. He didn't know if it was all. There might be more. To justify his uncertainty, he pointed to a shod track of Dutch's own horse. He then raised both hands several times, spreading his fingers each time. The sign was clear enough for them all to understand.

"Injuns drivin' shod horses," said Tally Slaughter. "By God, that bunch has been busy since they left us. There's a bunch of mad-as-hell white men somewhere, and they're likely all afoot."

"If it's the Crows," Dutch said, "they've increased their number. Pawnee figures at least a dozen, and there could be more. They'll have a camp somewhere."

"The Indian should have followed them to the camp," said Haskel Collins. "My God, there may be several hundred, and we need to know."

"You're only half-right," Dutch replied. "We do need to know where the camp is, but Pawnee did exactly the right thing by first riding back to tell us what he had learned. He didn't know that some of the bunch ahead of him wouldn't double back and lay an ambush for anybody on their back trail, which could have included us. I think Pawnee, Tally, and me will follow that bunch to their camp. While we've heard the Crows are friendly to whites, I can't believe they won't fight for a herd of horses they've gone to the trouble of stealing."

"Them's my feelings, exactly," said Slaughter, "and we need to know just how friendly that bunch is, since they're headin' the same way we are. If we was to come up on their camp unexpected, and they're hunkered there with a bunch of shod horses, they might just forget all about bein' friendly to whites."

"We're not going to pick a fight with them over somebody else's horses," Dutch said, "and to avoid that, we might have to alter our course some. But we can't do that until we know where they're going."

"It kind of rubs me the wrong way," said Brace Weaver, "knowin' they've took them horses from ranchers or miners that's needin' 'em. Just think what a hell of a mess we'd be in, if they managed to steal some of our stock."

"If they had taken our stock," Dutch said, "we'd take them back, if we had to shoot every Crow in eastern Montana Territory, but only a damn fool gets himself killed in somebody else's fight. We're going to learn where these peckerwoods are, not so we can fight them, but avoid them. Saddle up, Tally, and let's ride.''

Dutch and Slaughter saddled their horses. Dutch pointed west and then to Pawnee, and when the Indian rode out, Dutch and Tally followed. Pawnee rode at a slow gallop, for he knew where he was going. The need for caution would come when they reached the point where the Indian had turned back. Pawnee reined up when he reached the place where the trail had come in from the north, allowing Dutch and Slaughter to study the mingled tracks of shod and unshod horses. They needed only a moment to confirm what Pawnee had told them. When Dutch nodded, Pawnee again led out, following the trail west.

Virginia City, Montana Territory. February 7, 1864.

The five miners seeking to escape Virginia City with their gold met ten miles east of town, each unaware that he had been trailed by a member of Henry Plummer's gang, ''The Innocents.'' They must reach the Bozeman Trail— more than three hundred and twenty miles eastward—before they would feel safe from the Plummer gang. But when the five came together, their most immediate concern was what had happened the night before in a Virginia City saloon, and how it might affect them. Hugh McCulloch was the only one of the five who had actually been present, and he fleshed out the rumor with facts.

''Last night,'' said McCulloch, ''I was in the Gulch Saloon, when this renegade Sioux come in. Big Bear, he's called, and he's been layin' around here since before the storm, payin' for his whiskey with gold. Well, last night, the varmint got more'n a little soused, and he tells where he got the gold. Henry Plummer give it to him, and do you know why?''

There wasn't a sound except the creak of saddle leather,

as one of the five shifted his position. McCulloch continued.

"There's freight wagons—six of 'em—comin' up the Bozeman, loaded to the bows. The Sioux said he's seen 'em, that they're bein' drove by a mean-as-hell bunch that beat Crazy Horse and more'n a hundred Sioux."

"That's damn hard to believe, on two counts," said Gus Pryor. "First, that this bunch is fool enough to bring wagons to the High Plains in the dead of winter, and second, that they run off Crazy Horse and a hundred Sioux."

"Charlie Edenbaugh didn't believe it, either," McCulloch said. "He laughed, and this Sioux—Big Bear—pulled a Bowie and near killed Charlie, 'fore the barkeep floored the Sioux with a bung starter. Plummer showed up, took the Indian to jail, but turned him loose this mornin'. Plummer put him on a fast horse and told him to get the hell out of town. Does that suggest anything to any of you, Plummer payin' for information about a bunch of loaded freight wagons headin' this way?"

"He aims to bushwhack them teamsters and take the wagons," Julius Blackburn said.

"Has any of you seen George Ives and that scruffy bunch of his?" Alvin Taylor asked. "I ain't seen 'em in more'n two weeks."

"I reckon that goes along with what Julius just said," Irv Robb growled. "When they come, there'll be enough of the varmints to take them wagons and their freight. But they'll ride us down, first. Ives has got a dozen of them coyotes that rides with him."

"We still got a chance, gents," said McCulloch. "If we ride like hell, maybe we can get to them oncoming wagons before Ives and his killers get to us. If that bunch of teamsters stood off Crazy Horse and a band of Sioux, they're just the gents we need to side us agin the Plummer gang. Let's ride."

*   *   *

Once the Plummer outlaws stalking the fleeing miners knew where their quarry was bound, Prinz rode back to join George Ives and the remaining men. They all then rode eastward to join their comrades. While they had followed Ives's orders and stayed out of the saloons, they all had heard of the incident of the night before, and how Big Bear had revealed the information he had sold to Henry Plummer.

"Damn it," Hadsell said, "when we gun down them teamsters, that ties Plummer in, and us along with him."

"You worry too much," said Ives. "Who's goin' to know the teamsters wasn't done in by the Sioux?"

Borg laughed. "Just about ever'body, when we go drivin' them wagons into Virginia City. Did you ever hear of Injuns attacking teamsters and not lootin' the wagons?"

"What's done is done," Ives said irritably. "First thing we got to do is run down them miners and take their gold. Then we'll go lookin' for the wagons."

"It's gonna be after dark before we reach that Crow camp," said Tally Slaughter, "if we make it by then."

"I'm counting on that," Dutch replied. "Then if they happen to discover us, we'll have a better chance of escaping them."

"There's no moon tonight," said Tally, "which is good for sneakin' up, but not worth a damn for followin' tracks."

"I doubt we'll be trailing them after dark," Dutch said, "but if we are, we won't need tracks. They're headed due west. Maybe their camp is along the Yellowstone."

Something kept bothering Pawnee. He slowed his horse, his eyes to the south, riding on only when he became aware Dutch was watching him. The camp, when they found it, was in a grassy canyon, protected from the elements by lofty rims. It had a permanent look about it, with two dozen tepees. Some fifty horses grazed along a stream, a third of them wearing brands.

"That ain't a box canyon," said Tally. "They can ride

in or out either end. I reckon we'd ought to circle around and see if that trail picks up at the other end.''

"You're dead right," Dutch said. "By God, that's what Pawnee's had on his mind for the past hour.''

The Indian was ahead of them, riding northwest, preparing to circle to the south. The trail leading out of the canyon might be vastly more important than the one they had been following to it. Dutch and Tally galloped their horses after Pawnee, riding wide of the rim, lest they be seen from the canyon below. The terrain began to level out, as the sun dipped below the western horizon.

"If there's anything to see, we'd better be findin' it pronto," said Tally. "It'll soon be dark.''

There was plenty to see, and Pawnee reined up when he found it. There were tracks of more than thirty unshod horses leading from the canyon in a direct line to the east.

"Damn," said Dutch, "they knew we'd strike their trail and likely follow them. Unless I'm dead wrong, they're somewhere near our camp, just waitin' for dark. Let's ride.''

They had ridden a great distance and were forced to rest their horses. Then, they could hear the distant rattle of gunfire.

"Whatever they're up to, they won't get off scot-free," Dutch said. "Let's ride.''

The scene was about what Dutch had expected. Haskel Collins, Brace Weaver, and Drago Peeler sat without their shirts, bloody from knife wounds. Bonita had pots of water heating on two fires, while Christie Beckwith was using shears to cut muslin from a bolt into short lengths. Jules Swenson and Whit Sanderson stood with their rifles under their arms, staring angrily into the darkness.

"Who's hurt, and how bad?" Dutch asked.

"Them that you can see," said Whit shortly. "They was prowlin' around the wagons, usin' them as a diversion, I reckon. The bastards split up, an' when we went after them in the wagons, the rest of 'em was amongst the horses an' mules.''

"And they took how many?"

"Three mules," Whit said, "along with mine and Jules's horses."

"You and Jules will stay here with those who are wounded," said Dutch. "The rest of us are going after those horses and mules."

"Wouldn't it be better to wait until dawn?" Collins asked.

"No," said Dutch. "Large as that camp is, they'll have killed and eaten the mules by then. We know where their camp is. Cass, Rusty, Dent, and Levan, saddle up. You'll be riding with Pawnee, Tally, and me. Collins, do you have any black powder?"

"Yes," Collins said. "There's a ten-pound keg in the number two wagon."

"Good," said Dutch. "We need an edge. Rusty, go roust out that keg of powder."

Bonita and Christie were attending the wounded men. Dutch took the shears and began cutting yard-long lengths from the bolt of muslin. He spread a blanket as far from the fire as possible, while still having light enough to see. There he doubled each length of muslin, and when Rusty Karnes brought the keg of black powder, Dutch poured an estimated half pound onto each of seven muslin squares. He then brought the corners of each of the squares together, forming a poke. Snapping lengths from a ball of twine, he tied the neck of each poke securely.

"All of you who are riding with me," said Dutch, "take one of these pokes of black powder. We're going to be considerably outnumbered. I'll tell you what I aim to do as we ride. Let's go."

They rode out, Bonita looking anxiously into the darkness, as the sounds of their going faded to silence. Pawnee rode ahead, setting the pace, every man riding close enough to hear Dutch as he spoke.

"It's a big village," said Dutch, "and they're in a canyon, so they'll feel safe. I doubt they'll expect pursuit before morning. It's still early enough in the evening for them to have supper fires going. Dent, I want you and Levan on one of those canyon rims. Rusty, you and Cass will be on the other. Pawnee, Tally, and me are goin' to charge right down that canyon, stampedin' every animal there. A second before we do, I'll fire one shot, and that's when I want you to drop those black powder bombs into the supper fires. Each of us charging through the canyon will have one, and we'll try to use them to our advantage."

"What about shootin' the varmints?" Rusty asked.

"I'm not as concerned with killing as I am recovering our stock," said Dutch. "After you've thrown the black powder, cut loose with your Henrys, forcing them to run for cover. If we can scatter their horses from hell to breakfast, that should be lesson enough."

"You'll be scattering our stock with them," Cass pointed out.

"No help for that," said Dutch, "but we'll be charging in the western end of that canyon, and that means the stampede will run to the east. Once they're off and running, and you're no longer needed on the canyon rims, all of you mount up and help us keep the stampede going. Run them far enough, and we'll be able to gather our horses and mules long before the Crows find theirs."

"Friendly or not," said Tally Slaughter, "they won't let this pass. Sooner or later, they'll round up their horses, and you think they won't give us hell?"

"I reckon," Dutch said, "but what can we do, short of lettin' them get away with two of our horses, three mules, and the cutting of some of our outfit?"

Tally laughed. "I wasn't meanin' we had any choice. They started this, and we can give as good as we get."

"Ride alongside Pawnee a ways," said Dutch, "and see can you get him to understand he's to ride with you and me. We won't get a second chance at this."

Slaughter rode ahead, catching up to the Indian. The others dropped back, allowing Slaughter to converse with Pawnee. Eventually, Slaughter slowed his mount until he was again riding alongside Dutch.

"He knows he'll be riding with you and me, down the canyon," Tally said. "He's one sharp Indian, and from the first whoop, he'll know what we have to do."

They rode on, stopping only to rest the horses, and when they neared the east end of the canyon, Pawnee reined up. Nobody spoke, for each man knew what was expected of him. Dent and Levan rode west. When they were well beyond the canyon, they would then ride back along the south rim. Cass and Rusty would remain on the north rim, working up close enough to view the activity below. Dutch touched Pawnee's arm with his right hand and Tally with his left, and the three rode along the north rim until the canyon leveled out. Dutch then led the way back toward the western end, from which they would start the stampede. In the distance there was a glow from many fires, and Dutch sighed with satisfaction. The black powder bombs—accompanied by fire from four repeating rifles—should create the stampede they needed while allowing them to get out alive. While there was no moon, the starlight allowed them to be aware of one another's movement, and Dutch took the black powder bomb from his shirt. He could see Tally Slaughter doing the same, while Pawnee followed their example. Dutch had no idea that the Indian understood what the bombs were for, or their destructive potential, but as Slaughter had pointed out, Pawnee learned fast. Dutch had failed to work out a time schedule, and could only wait until he was sure his companions were in position on the canyon rims. He began trotting his horse slowly forward, drawing his Colt. Raising the Colt, he fired once, kicking his horse into a fast gallop. Almost immediately, one of the black powder bombs from the canyon rim was dropped into a fire, and there was an explosion that exceeded Dutch's wildest expectations. Fire was flung in every direction, horses screamed, and a second bomb was dropped from the other canyon rim. Dutch flung his own bomb against a canyon wall, and it rebounded into one of the fires. The resulting explosion caused his horse to rear, and the animal almost threw him. Almost simultaneously, the last two bombs descended from the canyon rims, and total chaos reigned. Toward the eastern end of the canyon, some of the Crow made a futile attempt to catch some of the fleeing horses. Tally and Pawnee flung their bombs toward the same fire, and the explosion literally shook the earth. Then the three of them were free of the canyon, pursuing the many horses. Their four companions, riding in from each of the canyon rims, joined them in a moving line. Strung out half a mile wide, they pushed the horse herd ahead of them. The herd split around their camp, and by the time they had unsaddled, their two missing horses and three mules, recognizing the camp, had drifted in on their own. Many of the other horses, no longer being driven, grazed close by.

"By God," said Jules Swenson, "I wouldn't of believed it. You brung 'em back in the dark, along with a bunch more."

"Hell," Tally Slaughter said, "you wouldn't believe what we pulled off, and we didn't shoot nobody. When we dropped that black powder in their supper fires, them Crows just went plumb crazy, along with all their horses. We drove off ever' damn horse they had."

Pawnee was actually grinning, although he understood little of what Tally Slaughter had said. While they had taken no scalps and counted no coup, they had recovered their own stock, while taking every horse the Crow claimed. Pawnee regarded the black powder as more of the white man's magic, and was still in awe of what he had witnessed.

"If you've driven away all their horses," said Collins, "is there a chance we'll have to fight them?"

"I don't really know," Dutch replied. "If they're anything like the Plains Indians, they may regard this as bad medicine, and leave us alone. Most Indians are superstitious, and they fear what they don't understand. We had four men on the canyon rims with repeating rifles, and we could have killed all or most of them, but we didn't. That's going to puzzle them no end, but not nearly as much as having their supper fires explode.''

''Superstitious or not,'' said Whit, ''if you left them all afoot, that's gonna be mighty hard for them to swallow.''

''Some of their horses will probably wander back,'' Dutch said. ''If they've been in that canyon long enough, their horses will consider it home.''

''After what happened tonight,'' said Cass, ''that bunch of Crows won't be able to get far enough from that canyon.''

''Wherever they go, they'll need horses,'' Dutch said, ''and we can't afford to take any chances. Indians are unpredictable. They may show up here before morning, trying to take our horses. I think we'll continue posting a double guard. Be sure all those horses and mules are hobbled, and the next time there's a commotion at the wagons, some of you get out there among the horses and mules.''

''Damn it,'' said Jules Swenson, ''don't rub it in.''

Tally Slaughter laughed.

''Don't be too hasty with your criticism, Siringo,'' Collins said. ''We were protecting this freight, which you contracted to deliver intact.''

''That I did,'' said Dutch, ''and I can't very well do that, if there are no mules to pull the wagons. I'm segundo, and when I believe criticism's needed, I'll pass it around.''

It was a rebuff that every man understood, and Collins's mouth tightened in anger. It wasn't lost on Dutch, nor was the stormy look in Christie Beckwith's eyes. He said nothing more, pouring himself a tin cup of coffee from one of the suspended pots.

''No hard feelings, Dutch,'' said Jules Swenson. ''You was justified.''

"Damn right," Whit Sanderson said. "We was snook-ered, and a man hates to admit it. Hell, I've out-fought and out-thought Comanches and Apaches, only to git took by a bunch of horse-thievin' Crows."

Dutch laughed. "Tally and Pawnee's wide-awake, and if Bonita will join me, I think I'll stay up a while. The rest of you get some sleep."

Tally and Pawnee walked out among the horses and mules, leaving Dutch and Bonita alone. The girl spoke. "Just when I begin to feel better about Haskel Collins, he does something to spoil it."

"Don't mind him," said Dutch. "He's still a long way from being a frontiersman. In a way, it was my fault, for not being here. None of us are perfect."

"But you had no way of knowing," Bonita said.

"Actually, I did," said Dutch. "I should have suspected something, when those Crows left such an obvious trail. They wanted to attract our attention, at least long enough to get some of us out of camp."

"They would have eaten our mules?"

"They would," Dutch said. "I think that's what they were after, since they took only two horses."

"I hope they'll leave us alone. I'm tired of Indians, ex-cept for Pawnee."

At first light, Dutch was amazed to find many of the Indian spotted ponies grazing a few hundred yards from camp. Even closer were the shod horses the Crow had obviously stolen. Dutch counted fifteen, all wearing the same brand: an F-V on the left flank. The outfit was finishing breakfast when they saw three men riding in from the north. Each had a Henry rifle across his saddle. All were dressed in cowboy garb, and they reined up forty yards away, awaiting an invitation to ride in or an order to leave.

"Ride in and step down," Dutch invited. "Breakfast is done, but there's coffee."

"I'm Frank Valenti," said the oldest of the trio, "and

these are my sons. We're a mite particular about who we set with, until we know which way the stick floats. I reckon there is some good reason why you have fifteen of my horses?"

"There is," Dutch replied. "We don't have them. They're just here, waiting for you to claim them. The Crow stole some of our stock, and we stampeded every animal they had, just to recover our horses and mules."

Valenti looked at his sons and they looked at him. Then they all laughed.

"I reckon we'll have some of that coffee, now," said Valenti. "We got a place north of here, on the Yellowstone, and it's been some ride. I'd admire to hear how that bunch of Crows that robbed us got the tables turned, and ended up afoot."

CHAPTER 14

✦

*W*hen the rancher and his sons had departed with their horses, Dutch's outfit again took the trail, heading west. As had become his custom, Pawnee rode ahead in search of water. But Dutch suspected the Indian was anxious to scout the canyon where the Crows had been camped the night before.

"I'm surprised we haven't seen any of the Crow horses," Bonita said.

"We drove most of them ahead of us," said Dutch, "but there were just a few of them around this morning. Most of them likely returned to the canyon, or were on their way there, when the Crow found them. I reckon those black powder bombs put the fear of God into them. They'll go after the rest of their horses when they're sure we're gone."

Pawnee approached the canyon cautiously, peering down from the north rim. There was only the blackened remains of the fires. He pondered the situation. The Crows having no horses, there was no way he could trail them from the canyon. They would be forced to pursue their horses on foot, and finding them, would have no reason to return to the canyon. Pawnee rode along the rim until it leveled down. He then rode up canyon, studying the ground, finding the drag lines he had expected. Lacking horses, squaws were pulling travois loaded with tepees and personal belongings. When they eventually recovered their horses, they would move on, and Pawnee doubted they would follow the wagons. Again he thought of how they had taken every Crow horse, and the strange customs of the white man. While they had taken many horses, Dutch Siringo had claimed only the two they had lost, and the three stolen mules. A man's medicine was indeed strong, when it allowed him to spare his enemy's life, as well as his horses. Pawnee wished to know more about the white man's medicine that had caused Indian fires to erupt with mighty thunder, scattering coals and flaming embers like vengeful lightning bolts.

The wind had again turned cold, sweeping down from the mighty mountains to the west, bringing a promise of more snow. The gathering clouds were evidence enough that it wasn't too distant. George Ives and his men had stopped to rest their horses, and there was much grousing and complaining, as the outlaws watched the darkening sky.

"Damn it," said Borg, "we shouldn't of let them miners git a day ahead of us. There's another storm comin', sure as hell. We'll have to hole up till it blows over."

"So will they," Ives said, "and I told you it was Plummer's idea, lettin' them get ahead of us. There's been too much killin' near the gulch. Would you rather set out a blizzard, or risk gettin' strung up by vigilantes?"

Miles ahead, the five wary men with a fortune in gold watched the darkening skies, knowing what was coming.

"We'd best be lookin' for shelter where we can have a fire," Alvin Taylor said. "This time tomorrow, she'll be blowin' like hell wouldn't have it."

"If that renegade Sioux was telling the truth about those freight wagons on the Bozeman," said Hugh McCulloch, "there's a chance we might reach them ahead of the storm."

"And an even better chance that we won't," Gus Pryor said. "Stake everything on that, and we could be caught in a blizzard, with no shelter, and none in sight.''

"Gus is right," said Irv Robb. "When that storm hits, it can drop the temperature forty degrees in an hour, blowin' in enough snow to make it tough goin' for a horse.''

"All of you are missing the point," McCulloch said. "There's a good chance that these Plummer outlaws trailing us have intentions of taking those wagons and their freight. I'd say the teamsters will be grateful if they're warned. Grateful enough to throw in with us in gunning down those outlaws.''

"You got a powerful lot of confidence in these men with the wagons," said Julius Blackburn.

"I do," McCulloch said, "because I was once one of them. Until two years ago, I was ridin' the box for Josh Beckwith, out of Kansas City. Then I took a notion to come out here and get rich.''

"I'm for holin' up somewhere and waitin' out the storm," said Alvin Taylor. "After it blows over, we can still reach the wagons and warn the teamsters.''

"I'm with you," Gus Pryor said.

"Me too," said Julius Blackburn.

"I'm buyin' in," Irv Robb said. "Sorry, Hugh.''

McCulloch said nothing, but he believed they were making a mistake in not trying to reach the wagons ahead of the storm. While the pursuing outlaws would be forced to wait out the storm, might they not push on until the very start of it, and then continue almost immediately after its end? They had purposely been allowed to get ahead, and he had little doubt their pursuers would waste any time in cutting down their lead.

"Mount up," said Gus Pryor. "Let's ride.''

"The storm won't reach us until sometime tomorrow," McCulloch said. "If we got to hole up, then let's cover as many miles as we can. Let's ride all night, tonight, and start lookin' for shelter tomorrow.''

"That ain't unreasonable," said Pryor. "What do the rest of you think?"

"Let's do it," Blackburn said, "stoppin' just long enough to rest the horses."

"Good move," said Robb.

"*Bueno*," Alvin Taylor said. "We can't be sure how much snow will be dumped on us, or how hard the goin' will be after the storm. Let's get as far ahead as we can."

"Thanks for that much," said McCulloch. "I can't help feeling this storm is going to help the Plummer gang and hurt us, because we don't know how far behind they are."

Before the coming ordeal was over, they would remember McCulloch's words. On they rode, thonging down their hats against a rising wind: a northwesterly wind that was growing colder by the hour.

George Ives and his outlaw companions hurriedly cooked and ate their supper, grained their horses, and rode on. Their coat collars were turned up against the cold wind at their backs, and they spoke only while stopped to rest their mounts. Ives had suggested they ride all night, and his decision had proven highly unpopular.

"You could of at least let us bring some whiskey," Mull growled.

"Yeah," said Borg. "A man needs somethin' to keep his gut warm."

"The whole damn lot of you are soft," Ives said. "It'll do you good, sufferin' through a blizzard on snow water and jerked beef. Now, mount up and let's ride."

Dutch and his outfit had settled for the night on the lee side of a ridge, out of the cold wind. Aware that yet another storm was building, Dutch had considered going ahead and taking shelter, but was reluctant to lose any more time than he had to. He believed the storm wouldn't break for another day, allowing them to cover a few more miles. Haskel Collins had seemed certain enough that, once they entered

Montana Territory, they were within two hundred miles of the Yellowstone, where it dipped south before turning west. It was Dutch's hope that they might reach that particular point before the storm blew in.*

"We ain't likely to git a full day, tomorrow," Whit Sanderson observed, as he poured himself coffee from the suspended pot.

"I don't expect to," said Dutch. "Pawnee will be lookin' for shelter when he rides out in the morning. I was hopeful we might reach the Yellowstone, where it drops in from the southwest and heads due west."

"Somethin' to shoot for," Whit agreed. "Decent rivers is likely to have them deep side canyons branchin' off, like the one we shared with the Crows, on the Little Missouri."

"We'll never reach the bend in the Yellowstone tomorrow," said Collins. "I doubt we have come more than a hundred and fifty miles, since entering Montana Territory."

"I expect you're right," Dutch agreed, "but we'll travel as far tomorrow as we can, before the storm forces us to take cover."

Pawnee rode out at dawn, very much aware of the gathering storm far to the west. A cold wind still blew in from the northwest. While the sun rose in a clear blue sky, nobody doubted it would vanish early in the day, behind the gray clouds on the distant horizon.

"She's gonna be another big one," Jules Swenson predicted. "I just hope the Injun can find us a good, deep canyon, and that we don't have to share it with a passel of them half-starved Crows."

Pawnee rode cautiously. While they had seen no more Crows, he didn't know them, or their habits. While he had found the presence of the Crows in their camp distasteful, and he had understood Siringo's purpose in feeding them, he had no respect for them. He saw it as treacherous, par-

---

* Near present-day Billings, Montana.

taking of the white man's food, and then stealing his horses and mules. More and more, he believed that Siringo had been too generous, that while they had the chance, they should have killed every Crow within the canyon. He rode on, and around him the land was changing. There were hills, many of them so steep the *carretas* could not climb them, and with that in mind, he sought a way around them. While an occasional canyon offered shelter, there was no water, and no fallen trees in sight for use as firewood. The first suitable water was the tag end of a runoff, and Pawnee followed it for almost a mile before reaching the spring. Water tumbled off a rock ledge forty feet high, pooling at the base. While the shelter would be open to the east, there was a virtual mountain of stone to the west. There was a natural cutback in the stone that stretched along the face of the mountain for a great distance, with a cavern behind the waterfall. Pawnee considered the possibility that beyond the cavern there might also be a cave in which a grizzly might be hibernating, but it was a chance they would have to take, for it was a perfect shelter. There were ashes from old fires, and even some firewood. Pawnee mounted his horse and rode wide of the bluff, climbing a ridge until he was above it. On the downside of the ridge there was a forest of pine and cedar, many of them windblown, others standing gray and dead among their living counterparts. There was the wood that would feed their fires while the storm raged. Satisfied with his find, Pawnee wheeled his horse and rode back to meet the wagons. It seemed the wind had become even colder, and far to the west there was a rumble of thunder.

"Thunder," said Jules Swenson. "I always heard that means cold weather's a-comin'."

"Comin', hell," Cass Carlyle snorted, "it's here. Ain't you feelin' that wind that's been smackin' us in the face all day?"

They had stopped to rest the teams, and the storm moving in from the west was on their minds. Their eyes were on the trail ahead, for it seemed Pawnee had been gone much longer than usual. While Dutch hadn't become alarmed, he was anxious, for after Pawnee's return, there must be time to reach the shelter he had found. He marveled at how much they had come to depend on the Indian, and his willingness to scout for them.

"He don't usually take this long," said Tally Slaughter. "That could mean we got a far piece to go, before reaching shelter, and we got to snake in firewood after we get there."

"Back to your wagons," Dutch said, "and let's be on our way."

They moved on, and there were many sighs of relief when Pawnee came galloping to meet them. Dutch reined up. They would rest the teams while the Indian told them how far they must go before reaching shelter. Pawnee reined up, raised his right hand, and spread his fingers. He then elevated one hand in an angle.

"Five more miles," said Tally Slaughter, "over steeper trails."

"Let's roll, then," Dutch said. "We don't have that much time."

They were less than halfway when the storm assaulted them, rattling sleet off the wagon canvas like buckshot. But the sleet was temporary, and it soon made way for the snow. It rode in on a screaming wind, the force of it stinging their faces. Mules brayed and balked, forcing the teamsters to shout and slap them with the lines.

"Move, you jug-heads," Dutch shouted.

Slowly the wagons rolled on, the mules seeking to turn their backsides to the storm. Pawnee rode ahead, guiding them around steep ridges and dropoffs, until at last they were at the runoff that led to the bluff with its hollowed-out shelter. As they progressed and the bluff grew higher, it shielded them from the driven snow, lessening the cussedness of the balking mules. Dutch and his men quickly unharnessed the mules, and the animals went to water to drink.

"Come on," Dutch said, "and let's snake in some firewood before it gets any worse."

Haskel Collins was unharnessing the buckboard team, while Christie Beckwith waited. Bonita made use of some of the wood within the cavern, starting a fire so there would be hot coffee when the men returned with their snaked-in logs. Collins and Christie entered the shelter, and Bonita eyed Collins in disgust. Pawnee leaned against a stone wall, his dark eyes expressionless. Christie turned on Bonita with a snarl.

"I saw the way you looked at him," she hissed.

"And what way was that?" Bonita asked calmly.

"Like you hate him," said Christie venomously.

"I don't especially like him, but I don't hate him," Bonita replied. "I just wonder why he considers himself too good to help the rest of the men snake in firewood."

"Having financed this expedition," said Collins coldly, "I feel that I am fulfilling my responsibilities rather well. I am truly sorry that I don't measure up to your expectations."

"You're a fine one," Christie shouted. "All you've done is make coffee and become Dutch Siringo's whore."

It was exactly the wrong thing to have said. Bonita had a two-gallon coffeepot full of cold water, and she drenched Christie Beckwith from head to toe. Christie screeched like a wounded cougar. Bonita dropped the coffeepot, and the two of them engaged in a kicking, shrieking, hair-pulling affair. Haskel Collins tried to calm them, only to have a foot driven into his groin. Christie and Bonita were down on the stone floor, fighting like a pair of bobcats. Pawnee continued to watch with interest. If these squaws wished to thrash about, scratching and clawing one another, who was he to interfere? Haskel Collins had adopted the same attitude. The combatants got to their knees. Christie Beckwith's shirt had been ripped off, and she bled from many cuts and scratches. She seized the front of Bonita's shirt, only to have Bonita slam a fist into her jaw. Bonita broke loose, and Christie fell facedown. Bonita got to her feet and stood there swaying. When she caught her breath, she turned to Haskel Collins.

"You'd best get her a blanket to cover herself. That is, if it makes any difference to you."

Bonita took the coffeepot to the pool and refilled it. She then put more wood on the fire and suspended the coffeepot from the iron spider. Collins had Christie on her feet, a blanket around her shoulders. She glared at Bonita, her nose dripping blood, and then she spoke through clenched teeth.

"I'm not finished with you."

"I must disagree with you," said Collins. "No woman of mine is going to engage in such disgraceful conduct."

"Then maybe I won't *be* your woman!" Christie shouted.

"Maybe you won't," Collins shouted back.

"Stop it," said Bonita, in a tone that got their immediate attention. "The two of you deserve one another."

The two of them looked at her as though they couldn't believe their ears, and all the hostility went out of them. Dutch and the rest of the men had returned with their first load of snaked-in firewood. Taking axes from the wagon, they began chopping the logs into manageable lengths. Christie Beckwith washed the blood off her face, and Collins gave her one of his shirts. Bonita stuffed the tail of her shirt back into her Levi's and brought more wood to add to the fire. Without coming into the shelter, the men rode back for more logs, for the storm was worsening. Bonita brought in supplies and cooking utensils from the wagon and began preparing supper. By the time Dutch and the men had snaked in what they hoped would be enough firewood, there were three fires going, and supper was almost ready. There was no evidence of the fight, except that Bonita's left eye slowly was turning purple, and Christie's nose was twice its normal size. Dutch looked at Haskel Collins, who kept his head down. In the dark eyes of Pawnee, there was only what might have been considered amusement.

*   *   *

The five fleeing miners paused at dawn just long enough for a cold meal from their saddlebags. When they rode out, the sun was rising in the east, while the storm continued to build in the west. An hour later, when they stopped to rest their horses, the wind was much colder, while the dirty band of clouds had widened across the horizon.

"It ain't too soon to start lookin' for a place to dig in," Gus Pryor said. "We'll need time to gather up firewood."

"What bothers me," said Hugh McCulloch, "is that while we're gathering firewood, that bunch of outlaws will still be in their saddles, comin' closer."

"Damn it, Hugh," Julius Blackburn said, "they're human, like us. They got to stop and dig in, just like we have. You don't survive a blizzard on the High Plains without some shelter and a fire."

"Sorry," said McCulloch. "After all these months of digging a stake, I can't swallow the idea of givin' it up. Not to a bunch of thieves and killers, or to a High Plains blizzard."

"I can't help feelin' we ought to be farther north, following the Yellowstone," Julius Blackburn said. "That's likely the way those wagons will be comin', and there'll be a better chance of findin' shelter in arroyos or under overhangs."

"We ain't more than thirty miles south of the Yellowstone," said Alvin Taylor. "Hugh, what do you think?"

"I think it might be worth our while to ride north and follow the Yellowstone," said McCulloch. "There's a good chance that any freight wagons on their way into the territory will follow the river, for they'll be needing shelter too."

"It might confuse Plummer's outlaws for a while," Gus Pryor said. "Next creek we come to, let's cut north, to the Yellowstone. It might gain us some time, while costing them."

Reaching a suitable creek, they rode north, keeping

within the water and leaving no tracks. The creek flowed out of the Yellowstone, and reaching the river, they rode eastward along it.

"This bein' mountainous country," said Blackburn, "these riverbanks ought to soon be high enough for an overhang, especially if we can find some stone outcroppings and ledges."

But when they found their sanctuary, it was an arroyo that angled southwest from the Yellowstone, serving as a runoff during high water.

"We won't find any better than this," said McCulloch. "Now we'd best begin searching for logs and fallen timber we can use for firewood. It won't be easy, once the snowdrifts are deep."

They rode out, roping and dragging in anything that would burn, and long before they had enough, the storm struck. They toiled on, and each time they returned to their shelter, their tracks had already been snowed out.

"About one more load," Alvin Taylor said, "and we'll have to give it up. I can't feel my hands or feet."

Their horses' hooves slipped on unseen stones, and the animals were fighting drifts the storm-bred wind had already flung in their path. Irv Robb's horse plunged a leg into a hole, and Robb had to dismount and lead the horse.

"Come on," said McCulloch, "and let's get back while we still can. That's all we need, is one of the horses to break a leg."

George Ives and his band of outlaws had been forced to back off in their pursuit and seek shelter from the impending storm.

"Damn it," Ives growled, "this is goin' to cost us. Snow will spoil the trail."

"Hell," said Prinz, "we don't need a trail. They're ridin' east, toward the Bozeman. How many ways can they go?"

"It's near fifty miles from the foothills of the Absarokas north to the Yellowstone," Ives said. "They could be anywhere in that stretch, and we could ride in circles for a week without findin' 'em.''

"The same snow that'll hide their trail will make a new one, soon as they ride out," said Hadsell. "We got to ride out this storm, and I aim to do it as comfortable as I can."

Even Ives couldn't deny the wisdom in that, and they set about finding shelter.

"Up yonder, ahead," said Stem. "Might be room for us among that bunch of rocks."

"Ain't high enough, there's no overhang, and no water," Dyer said.

Stopping to rest the horses, they found the ominous cloud mass from the west had moved closer. Uneasy, they mounted and rode on.

"We're too far north," said Mull. "If we was more to the south, among the Absaroka foothills, there'd likely be some caves."

"We don't need a cave," Ives said. "Hell, we ain't lookin' for a homestead. All we need is an overhang to keep the snow and wind off, with plenty of wood for a fire."

But they found nothing suitable, and Ives was forced to give in. They angled back to the southeast, where the northern end of the Absaroka Range extended from northwestern Wyoming Territory into southern Montana. What they eventually found was an overhanging bluff with a nearby stream. It would shelter them from the wind and the snow. They had just begun to gather wood for their fire when the snow started. They complained about the snow, the cold, and the unaccustomed hard work. George Ives grunted in disgust, dreading the enforced companionship of the disgruntled bunch in the days to come.

Not until well after supper, when the outfit had settled down, did Dutch get a chance to speak to Bonita in private. Her purpled eye was now almost swollen shut.

"What was the fight about?"

"She said some things I didn't like," Bonita replied, "and I sloshed a coffeepot full of cold water on her. It just kind of went downhill from there."

Dutch laughed. "I'm glad you stopped short of killin' one another."

"We wouldn't have, but for Haskel Collins," said Bonita. "She was kind of . . . missing some of her clothes, and he made her back off."

At another of the fires, a more heated conversation was taking place between Haskel Collins and Christie Beckwith.

"All that was uncalled for," Collins said.

"I was defending you," said Christie heatedly.

"I don't need defending," Collins replied. "She wouldn't have said a word, if you had not pushed it. She's never been unkind to you."

"I don't care," said Christie. "I don't like her."

"Why? Because she took your place with Dutch Siringo?"

"I never *had* a place with Dutch Siringo," she said bitterly. "When my father died, he walked out on me, taking the rest of the drivers with him."

"I haven't made it my business to inquire," Collins said, "but I've heard talk among these men that, following your father's death, you turned everything over to this Jasper Sneed. By your own admission, he bankrupted Beckwith Freight Lines and then ruined you. Mind you, I am not being critical of you, but these former Beckwith men didn't have any confidence in Jasper Sneed, and they could rid themselves of his influence only by quitting Beckwith Freight Lines. Knowing what Sneed is—or was—I can't fault them for that, and neither can you. Can you?"

"No," she said in a small voice. "I . . . let him do what . . . he did, and then I . . . I hated him for it."

"That, my dear," said Collins, "is precisely why I don't want you standing up for me, or attempting to manipulate me. I am not another Sneed, and I am by no means weak. If you are to stand beside me, then you must be strong enough not to throw yourself into verbal and physical battles that accomplish exactly nothing. Do you understand?''

"Yes," she said, "I understand, and I . . . I'll try."

"Good," said Collins, "and just to be sure that you're sincere, I want you to go make amends with Bonita. Tell her you're sorry, and mean it."

"Oh, God," she said, "do I have to?"

"Yes," said Collins, "you have to. I want you to become friends with her, and I'm not prepared to tell you why. Just do it."

Christie got up and approached the other end of the camp, where Dutch and Bonita were talking. They became silent as she approached. Her eyes were on Bonita, and there was a painful silence before she was able to speak.

"I . . . need to talk to you . . .''

"I'd best go check on the horses and mules," said Dutch.

Neither of them spoke until Dutch was gone, and it was Christie who finally broke the silence.

"I'm sorry for what I said . . . for what I did."

"Are you," Bonita asked, "or is this Haskel Collins talking through you?"

Christie fought to control her temper, resenting this younger woman who seemed to understand her better than she understood herself.

"Mostly him," she admitted, her eyes not meeting Bonita's. "He thinks I'm jealous of you . . . that I resent you . . . because of Dutch."

"Do you?" Bonita persisted.

"Perhaps . . . a little," said Christie, "and I have . . . no right. He didn't leave me. I turned away from him . . . to Jasper Sneed."

"And Collins reminded you of that," Bonita said.

"Yes," said Christie. "He's everything . . . that Sneed wasn't, and he wants me . . ."

The words were difficult, and her voice trailed off. She swallowed hard, her eyes not meeting Bonita's and in the firelight, tears silvered her cheeks.

"Sit down," Bonita said, touched.

Christie sat down, looking much older than her twenty-four years. She wiped her eyes on the sleeve of her shirt before she finally spoke. "Could you . . . would you . . . cut my hair and help me do . . . something with it?"

It was the first time Christie had ever seen the younger woman smile. In a friendly gesture, she placed her hand on Christie's arm, and then she spoke. "I'll cut yours and help you fix it, if you'll help me with mine."

Dutch Siringo watched from a distance, shaking his head in wonder.

CHAPTER 15

❧

"The next damn one of you that gets testy with me is goin' to get the muzzle of my pistol upside his head," said George Ives. "By God, I didn't ask for this storm, and I'm almighty tired of the lot of you diggin' the gut hooks in me."

His nine companions glared at Ives in silent anger. They had been snowed in for one night and most of a day, and cabin fever was consuming them. They had slept until they could sleep no more, for even with a roaring fire, the ground was cold. Traveling light, they hadn't brought coffee or coffeepot. All they had in abundance was jerked beef and water.

"God," said Aten, "I'd give fifty dollars for a pot of hot coffee."

"I'd give a hundred for a quart of whiskey," Hadsell said. "Even rotgut."

"I'd give five hundred," said Font, "if I was back in Virginia City."

George Ives said nothing. Weary as he was of their complaining, he understood their frustration, for he shared it. The more he thought of phony Sheriff Henry Plummer living a life of comfort back in Virginia City, the angrier he became. Once this grueling task was finished, he promised himself that he would quit the territory, going to California.

There had to be a limit as to how long a man could wear a lawman's badge, while heading up the most notorious band of outlaws in the territory. Henry Plummer's time was running out, and George Ives didn't intend to be around when the sand reached the bottom of the glass.

On the Yellowstone, McCulloch and his four comrades weren't faring much better. The cold was so intense, they sat around in their heavy coats, hands and feet to the fire. Wind whipped snow into the arroyo, and the five horses huddled together for warmth. Starting its second night, the storm continued unabated.

"God," said Gus Pryor, "it's pilin' up an almighty lot of snow out there. We're goin' to be stuck here a while, after the storm's done."

"Maybe not," McCulloch said. "If the cold continues, the snow will freeze. We'll have to ride slow, so's the horses don't slip and fall, but we can go on. We must, because that bunch trailing us won't wait."

"They'll have a hell of a time trailin' us over frozen snow," said Irv Robb, "and with us followin' the Yellowstone, they'll have to ride some, before crossin' our trail."

"That's all the edge we have," McCulloch said. "While they know we're bound for the Bozeman, they won't know whether we're following the Yellowstone, or trailing east along the foothills of the Absarokas. We could just as easily have gone there, seeking shelter."

"If they are in the foothills," said Blackburn, "when the storm plays out, we could be more than a day's ride ahead of them. More, when we consider the snow."

"But we don't know where they are," Alvin Taylor said. "They may be holed up here on the Yellowstone, not twenty miles behind us."

"Somehow I doubt it," said McCulloch. "Seeking shelter, most men tend to search for caves, and they're more common in mountainous country."

"Hell," Irv Robb said, "I ain't seen much of Montana

Territory that wasn't mountainous. There's some bluffs overlookin' the Yellowstone, east of here.''

"All the more reason for us to follow the river," said Blackburn. "If them teamsters ain't familiar with the territory, they're likely followin' the Yellowstone. It's important that we reach them ahead of Plummer's outlaws.''

Thirty miles east of the anxious miners, beneath a bluff overlooking the Yellowstone, Dutch Siringo and his outfit waited out the storm. The men took turns feeding the fires, privately speculating as to how long the truce would last between Christie and Bonita. All their bruises had healed, and Bonita had spent the morning cutting Christie's hair, using shears. Finished, they traded places, Christie working with Bonita's hair. Neither of the women had spoken a word, and none of the men had seen fit to interrupt them. Pawnee had spread his blankets near one of the fires, and spent most of his time sleeping. Haskel Collins, for some reason none of them understood, seemed especially pleased. Finally, when Christie had finished cutting Bonita's hair, the two of them sat on a blanket near one of the fires, talking quietly. Not until after supper did Dutch have a chance to speak privately with Bonita.

"I've never seen such a turnaround in my life," said Dutch.

"It was her idea," Bonita said. "I understand her better. She's been through a lot.''

"Most of it by her own choice," said Dutch.

"She admits that," Bonita replied. "She now believes that this Jasper Sneed falsified her father's will, that he had nothing to do with leaving Sneed in charge.''

"I've thought that from the very first," said Dutch, "because I knew Josh Beckwith a hell of a lot better than she did.''

"Then why didn't you say something, instead of just walking out?"

"She wouldn't have believed me," Dutch said, "and it's

too late to undo all that's been done. It's generous of you, being her friend. I reckon she needs one.''

Later that night, while the night watch was feeding the fires, Haskel Collins spoke to Christie Beckwith.

"I'm proud of you, my dear. That was quite a performance.''

"It was no performance,'' Christie said. "I told her the truth and said I was sorry. She was nicer to me than I deserved, and she treats me like a friend. Why are you trying to make something else out of it?''

"I see nothing but good coming of it,'' said Collins. "There's nothing I'd like better than for you and the young lady to become friends. Despite the hardship of freighting in goods along the Bozeman, I can see this kind of venture becoming very, very profitable. I intend to double the size of the next load, and I want Siringo and his men hauling it. You being friends with Bonita could have a profound influence on Siringo.''

It took a moment for the significance of what he had said to register. When it did, she got to her feet and stomped away into the darkness, into the snow that the wind swept in from above. Collins got up and went after her, taking her by the shoulders. Angrily freeing herself, she slapped him. Hard.

"What the hell?'' he exclaimed. "Don't you understand anything?''

"I understand everything,'' she hissed, her eyes boring into his. "I'm tired of being used, damn it. Today, for the first time in my entire, sorry life, I was honest. It was like a breath of fresh air, speaking as a friend and being spoken to by a friend. Now you tell me it's an act, a means to an end. Well, I'm through betraying those who have trusted me. I'm going to tell Dutch Siringo what you've told me to do, and why.''

"No,'' he said. "Christie, forget what I told you. I'm going to make Siringo a genuine, legitimate offer. I just thought . . . if you and Bonita were friends . . . Damn it, what I'm trying to say is, I fear Siringo may not feel too kindly toward me, and once this contract has been fulfilled, he may just tell me to go to hell.''

"He should," said Christie, "and so will I, if you don't mend your ways. Don't you ever again try to use me to better yourself.''

Again she turned away from him. He returned to the nearest fire and stood there warming his hands. It was awhile before Christie again took her place at the fire and sat there staring into it. Somewhere in the distant darkness, a wolf howled, low and mournful.

The storm ceased near dawn of the third day, but the wind and the bitter cold continued. George Ives and his companions were faced with the terrible fact that they had failed to gather enough firewood. The cold had become so intense, they had built a third fire, and it had consumed even more of their dwindling supply of wood.

"We need more wood," said Ives. "Who's gonna saddle up and go with me?"

"I'll go," Hadsell said. "If I don't get out of here, I'll go crazy.''

"We'll go two at a time, then," said Ives.

Ives and Hadsell saddled their horses and led them out into the howling wind. There was an expanse of blinding white, stretching as far as they could see in any direction. They slipped and slid up a rise, seeking windblown timber. Everything else—every log, branch, and pine knot—would be under the snow. Sighting the root mass of a windblown pine, they fought their way to it through drifted snow. They sank over their boot tops in the drifts, and the snow soon numbed their feet. The tree had broken in half, and with their hands numb inside their gloves, they each knotted a lariat around half of the tree. They had to tug on the ropes, helping the horses, for the snow had begun to freeze. Tearing the broken halves of the pine loose, they led their horses. Time after time, the animals slipped, often going to their knees. When Ives and Hadsell finally reached the shelter with their prize, they were scarcely able to move arms or legs. It was awhile before either man was able to speak.

"The rest of you get a turn," Ives said, "and you'd best not wait too long. It's gettin' colder all the time, and the wood ain't that close."

"I'll take my turn now," said Prinz. "Vick, are you game?"

"Hell," Vick said, "let's be done with it."

They got up and saddled their horses. Somewhere a wolf howled, and one of the horses nickered in fear.

The hapless miners huddled around their fire, listening to the howling wind. While the snow had ceased, the cold seemed more intense than ever.

"We got to get out of here," said Gus Pryor. "The snow's stopped."

"But the wind ain't," Irv Robb said, "and it's cold enough to freeze a man to death in his saddle."

"It's a temptation to move on," McCulloch said, "but there's three things against us. First, we'd have to walk our horses, maybe even lead 'em. Second, we got no idea how far we are from those wagons, and third, we have no way of knowing that we could find another shelter, once we leave this one."

"That's the gospel truth," Blackburn agreed. "We can't travel far, and there's no way we could stand a night of this cold, without shelter or fire."

"So we got to sit here and wait some more," said Alvin Taylor.

"Suits me," Irv Robb said. "Hugh's right. We got no sure destination ahead of us, and if it's cold in here, with a fire, I know what it'll be like in the open, without one."

Then there was a sound—blending with the moan of the wind—that chilled the very marrow of their bones. It was the howl of a wolf. Rising, falling, rising, and then fading away to silence.

"God," said Gus Pryor, "another reason for stayin' put."

"We can stay put," said Alvin Taylor, "but suppose the wolves don't?"

None of them attempted to answer that question, nor did they need to. Every one of them had heard tales—grim accounts they knew to be true—of the big wolves stalking a man for the horse that he rode. Again the wolf howled, closer this time, and like a distant echo, there was an answer.

"We'd best bring our horses in as close as we can," said Hugh McCulloch, "and ready our rifles. We're goin' to have to fight, maybe for our lives."

The wind being from the west, sound carried for many miles, and the mournful, haunting cries of the wolves were heard in Dutch Siringo's camp.

"The varmints ain't come no closer," said Whit Sanderson, "meanin' they've found somethin' or somebody nearer than us."

"I expect they have," Dutch said, "but we can't count on them leaving us alone. This is the worst storm, so far. It's colder today than it was yesterday, and if I'm any judge, it'll be colder tomorrow than it is today. Those wolves are hungry, and God knows how many there are. We'll continue with a double watch. This is good shelter from the cold, but let's not forget it's vulnerable on three sides, where our horses and mules are concerned."

As further evidence of the bone-chilling cold, long shards of ice clung to the stone where water tumbled down from the ledge above, while there was thin ice along the edges of the runoff. While the snow had ceased, there was the rattle of sleet, and they couldn't be sure there wasn't a second storm brewing. The sky remained a leaden gray, without hope of sun to melt the snow, and as darkness closed in to end a third day, there was yet another sound to accompany that of the howling wolves. Sounding faint and far away, there was the unmistakable rattle of gunfire.

"Them wolves is movin' in," said Brace Weaver, "and some poor devils has got a hell of a fight on their hands."

"They're on their own," Dutch said. "Even if we weren't snowed in, we could never reach them in time."

"I can't imagine anyone being out in weather such as this," said Collins, "unless it's a matter of life and death."

"Perhaps it is," Dutch replied. "We'll listen for more shooting during the night, and in the morning, have another look at the situation. Whatever's happened, it's to the west, and that's the way we're going."

"If the snow freezes rock-hard," said Drago Peeler, "a couple of us might ride a ways ahead, and see can we help."

"Kind of what I was thinking," Dutch said, "as long as that storm don't pick up where it left off. But it'll be slow going, and we can't ride so far that we can't make it back before dark."

"Is that practical?" Haskel Collins asked. "You may be risking your lives for a cause that's already lost."

"No cause is ever lost, Collins," said Dutch, "as long as there's one man alive, fighting for his life. Always go with the gut feeling that tells you it's right, and to hell with what's practical."

The howling of the wolves seemed to come from everywhere. The five men sat with Henry rifles cocked and fully loaded.

"God," said Alvin Taylor, "they're all around us. That howling is enough to give a man heart failure."

"You don't worry, as long as they're howling," Julius Blackburn said. "It's when the howling stops, that you know they're movin' in."

"One thing we have going for us," said Hugh Mc-Culloch, "is the high rims of this arroyo. If they come after us or the horses, they'll have to come in through the lower end of the arroyo, like we did. I don't look for them to leap off the rim on us or the horses.''

But Hugh McCulloch was wrong. Suddenly the howling of the wolves ceased, and the five men stepped out from beneath their overhang, into the arroyo. Straining their eyes into the gathering darkness, they faced the lower end of the arroyo, whence they expected the wolves to come. But they came from above. A horse screamed as a clawing, snarling fury landed on its back. Simultaneously, a second wolf slammed Gus Pryor to the ground, while a third came down on Irv Robb. McCulloch shot two wolves crouching to spring, while Blackburn shot the one off the back of the terrified horse. Pryor and Robb fought for their lives, their companions fearing to risk a shot, lest they kill their friends. Other wolves snarled on the rim, as Blackburn and Taylor fired as rapidly as they could jack in the shells. Hugh McCulloch dropped his Henry, and seizing his Bowie knife, went after the wolves that had attacked his companions. He killed the wolf that had jumped Robb and went after the second one with whom Pryor struggled desperately. Killing the wolf and freeing Pryor, he dropped the Bowie and seized his Henry. But the attack was over. Alvin Taylor and Jules Blackburn seemed almost in shock. Four of the horses huddled against the highest portion of the wall at the upper end of the arroyo, while the horse attacked by the wolf lay mortally wounded. Pryor and Robb struggled to free themselves from the bodies of the dead wolves, and McCulloch hurried to help them.

''God,'' Pryor groaned, ''I'm done for. I'm bleedin' like a stuck hog.''

''Maybe not,'' McCulloch said. ''Your coat protected you some.''

''I reckon I'm pretty well ripped open,'' said Irv Robb. ''I can't feel nothin'.''

''We'll get both of you in by the fire,'' McCulloch said, ''and see what can be done. At least, we can stop the bleeding.''

Alvin Taylor already had added wood to the fire, for the

wounded men would have to be stripped to the waist. While their heavy coats had provided some protection, Pryor and Robb had been clawed deep. With both men belly-down on blankets, their companions took water and half-frozen soil and created thick mud. It would help stop the bleeding, but there was nothing more that could be done, without medicine. The same unspoken concern was on the minds of them all, especially Pryor and Robb. There would be infection, a high fever, and not a drop of whiskey to counter it.

"Taylor," said McCulloch, "go ahead and shoot the horse."

"My God," Taylor said, "they'll be comin' back after the horse."

"Hell," said Pryor, "you might as well shoot me too. That's my horse. I'll never make it afoot, even if this clawin' don't kill me."

Taylor shot the horse, and the echo of the shot was the sound of finality, of doom.

"I'll saddle up and drag the horse down yonder as far as I can," Blackburn said. "If they can get at it, maybe they'll leave us alone."

"For a while," said McCulloch. "When you've done that, drag these dead wolves down there with it. That'll give them somethin' more to gorge on."

"God," Taylor said, "do they eat their own kind?"

"I reckon," said McCulloch. "Better them than us."

Pryor and Robb slept, mumbling in their sleep, as the fever began to get a grip on them. McCulloch, Blackburn, and Taylor sat awake, their Henrys ready. From down the arroyo came the growling and snarling of wolves, as they feasted on Pryor's horse.

"My God," Blackburn said, "we're goners. Gus and Irv ain't goin' to make it without medicine, and even if they do, we're one horse shy. We'll be easy pickings for that bunch of outlaws Plummer's sent after us."

"Maybe not," said McCulloch. "I figure we're safe for another day. Tomorrow, I aim to ride east until I find those teamsters and their wagons. It's our only hope.''

Blackburn and Taylor said nothing. They knew the risk. McCulloch was playing a long shot, not knowing when or where he might meet the oncoming wagons, whether they were traveling along the Yellowstone or somewhere between it and the Absarokas. But they all knew he was right. Somewhere those teamsters had holed up to wait out the storm. Hugh McCulloch must find that camp, for time was running out.

After a hard day of fighting the bitter cold for needed firewood, George Ives and his outlaw companions were in a surly mood. If nothing else, they had learned the futility of a hasty departure from their shelter. However much they hated it, they must remain where they were until there was a break in the weather.

"Long as we're stuck here," said Hadsell, "we know them miners won't be ridin' away, either."

"Yeah," Stem said, "that's a real comfort, ain't it, gents?"

"Damn right," said Borg.

The rest of them only grunted, their hard eyes on George Ives. But Ives ignored their sarcasm, thinking of his return to Virginia City and his planned breakup with the outlaw sheriff, Henry Plummer.

"You'd better get a little sleep, Hugh," said Blackburn. "Alvin and me will stay awake and keep watch."

McCulloch stretched out before one of the fires. First light wasn't more than two hours away, and that's when he must ride out. It seemed that he had dozed only a short time, when he was awakened by the groans of one of the wounded men. He sat up, rubbing his eyes.

"Their fever's on the rise," said Blackburn, "but it ain't peaked yet."

"It's light enough for me to be on my way," McCulloch said.

"I wish there was a better way, Hugh," said Blackburn.
"I'll go, if you want me to."

"So will I," Alvin Taylor said. "At least, let's draw
lots."

"No need for that," said McCulloch, swinging into his
saddle. "I'll bring help, if I can."

Wordlessly, Blackburn and Taylor offered their hands for
luck, and McCulloch took them. McCulloch rode out into
the cold, dreary first light of dawn. The sky was gray and
the High Plains wind seemed colder than ever. McCulloch
allowed his horse to set its own gait, slipping and sliding
along the south bank of the Yellowstone. While it was hard
going among the brakes, the underbrush hadn't allowed the
snow to drift quite as deep. While Hugh McCulloch wasn't
sure he could even find the teamsters, they offered hope,
and since he had once been one of them, he believed they
would come to the aid of his wounded companions. He rode
on into an unending expanse of white, broken only by the
course of the Yellowstone.

Dutch Siringo hurriedly ate his breakfast and downed a
second cup of coffee. There was less than an hour until first
light. Bonita offered Dutch more coffee, but he shook his
head.

"You're riding west to see about the shooting we heard
last night, aren't you?" she asked.

"Yes," said Dutch. "I believe it had something to do
with the howling of the wolves. There may be somebody
in trouble. On the frontier, you help when you can. Tally,
I want you and Pawnee to go with me. I want the rest of
you to keep your weapons ready. Those wolves haven't
bothered us yet, but they're still out there somewhere."

Tally Slaughter had saddled Dutch's horse and was saddling his own. Pawnee wore his white man's coat, its collar
turned up against the wind. While Dutch and Tally had
heavy gloves, Pawnee had none.

"One of you hombres loan Pawnee your gloves," said Slaughter.

"There are plenty of them in one of the wagons," Collins said. "I'll get him a pair that fits."

Nobody said anything, and Collins brought several pairs of heavy gloves, allowing the Indian to choose a pair in his size.

"*Gracias*," said Pawnee.

The three men mounted their horses and rode out into the wind and the unrelenting white of the unbroken snow. Their horses slipped, forcing the riders to dismount and lead them down the slope.

"I just hope we can keep our sense of direction until we reach the river," Slaughter said. "After awhile, one stretch of snow looks like another."

"It's the only use I've found for this High Plains wind," said Dutch. "Just be sure it's always roaring into your face, and you know you're headed west."

Without the sun, the snow had frozen rock-hard, and they had only to avoid the deep drifts. They were forced to ride around an occasional ridge which was too steep to afford any grip for their horses' hooves. Even in the terrible cold, it was necessary to stop and rest the horses, and they tried to find the lee side of a ridge, to shield them from the ever raging wind.

"Slow going," said Slaughter. "How far you reckon we can ride, before we have to turn back?"

"Not more than fifteen miles," Dutch replied. "I'm hoping we can get at least as far as the Yellowstone, where it comes in from the northeast and heads west."

"That gunfire we heard last night could have come from twenty miles or more," said Slaughter, "with the wind to carry it."

"I know," Dutch said. "This may have been a fool thing to do, now that I think about it. If there's people hurt, we didn't bring any medicine or whiskey."

The three of them rode on, covering what Dutch believed

was ten miles, in about two hours.

"We'll give it another hour," said Dutch. "When we stop to rest the horses again, if we haven't seen anybody, I reckon we'll turn back."

Even with the terrible wind at his back, Hugh McCulloch realized he was losing his battle with the cold. His legs were numb to the thighs. He must rest the horse, and stamp some feeling back into his limbs. He reined up, and when he slid out of the saddle, he was forced to cling to the horn, for his numbed legs wouldn't support him. He tried to stamp his feet, only to have his legs fail him, for they felt like lead. After he had rested the horse, he tried to mount and found that he could not. He had no strength in his legs, and after many failed attempts to regain his saddle, he leaned against the horse, gasping for breath. His brow was bathed in sweat, his teeth chattered, and it seemed colder than ever. He urged the horse ahead, and clinging to the saddle horn, he forced himself to walk beside it. But the time came when he could go no farther. With his failing strength, he drew his Henry rifle from the saddle boot and sank to the snow. His arms and hands refused to obey his will, feeling wooden. Somehow, he jacked a shell into the chamber and pulled the trigger. The wind swept the sound away. He fired a second time, and then lay back on the snow. He must rest. But he could not, for his mind told his half-frozen body there was something left undone. With all his remaining strength, he fired the Henry a third time. It was a frontiersman's last desperate appeal for help. He began losing consciousness, then, as the howling wind seemed to invite sleep. His horse stamped its feet, heeding the dropped reins, its eyes on the still form that lay on the frozen snow.

Dutch and his companions reined up at the sound of the first shot, waiting for the second. It came, and just when they had decided there wasn't going to be a third shot, there was.

"Come on," said Dutch. "He can't be more than four or five miles ahead of us, and I reckon he's in a bad way. He almost didn't get off that third shot."

They rode on, traveling as fast as they dared, unaware that the desperate man who had fired the shots was being stalked by a pair of gray wolves . . .

CHAPTER 16

ᐱᐧᐸ

P awnee in the lead, the three riders rode as fast as they dared. While the terrain had leveled out, the frozen snow was still treacherous. Ahead of them, to the right, was the Yellowstone, where it began its journey west. They moved nearer the river, and somewhere ahead, a horse screamed. Pawnee was nearest, and in an instant he was off his horse with his Henry rifle ready. Kneeling on one knee, he fired once, twice, three times.

"*El Lobos*," said the Indian, as Dutch and Tally reined up beside him.

Riding on, they soon saw the horse, its eyes wild with fear. A few yards beyond was the body of a wolf, but their concern was the body of a man, his hands still clutching his rifle. He lay on his back, and his thonged-down hat had slipped over his face. Slaughter and Dutch knelt beside him, and Tally removed the hat.

"My God," Dutch said, "it's Hugh McCulloch."

"You know him, then," Tally said.

"You bet I do," said Dutch. "He was one of Beckwith's best teamsters, until he left in 'sixty-one for the diggings in Virginia City."

Slaughter was seeking a pulse, but found none. He tried the big artery in the neck and found life.

"He's near froze to death," Tally said. "He may not last until we get him to camp."

"All we can do is try," said Dutch. "There may be others needing help, but we don't know that, nor do we know where they are. We'll have to coax him back and see what he can tell us."

Pawnee had brought McCulloch's horse, and for the lack of a better means, they tied him belly-down across his saddle. They then set out for their camp, pushing their horses into as fast a gait as they dared. Despite the slipping and sliding, with the vicious wind at their backs, they made better time than Dutch had expected. Their arrival created considerable excitement, for Brace Weaver, Jules Swenson, Whit Sanderson, and Rusty Karnes knew McCulloch from his days with Beckwith Freight Lines. They stretched him out on a blanket near the fire and began rubbing his hands and feet. Bonita brought hot coffee, and Dutch managed to get some whiskey down him. Bad off as he had been, McCulloch quickly responded. When he eventually opened his eyes, he studied the faces surrounding him.

"I must have died and gone to hell," he said, "seein' as how I know most of you."

"Drag the ungrateful varmint back out there in the snow," said Brace Weaver.

"I'd favor that," Whit Sanderson said, "but the carcass might attract wolves."

Bonita knelt with a tin cup of hot coffee, and McCulloch took the cup in both hands.

"Ah," he said, his eyes on Bonita, "I reckon everybody here ain't been beat with an ugly stick."

"To all of you who don't know him," Dutch said to the rest of the outfit, "this is Hugh McCulloch, once a driver for Beckwith Freight Lines. We found him half-frozen, on the banks of the Yellowstone, maybe ten miles west of here. Hugh, do you feel like talking?"

"Yes," said McCulloch. "We don't have much time."

Quickly he told them of the situation in Virginia City

that had forced him and his four companions to flee for their lives, pursued by Henry Plummer's outlaws. Dutch and his outfit listened incredulously as McCulloch related Plummer's intention, not only to murder five men for their gold, but to seize the wagons and their freight.

"What's bothering me most," McCulloch concluded, "is that I left four men behind, two of them burning up with fever. The wolves jumped us, clawing Gus Pryor and Irv Robb almighty bad. They got one of our horses too. I must get back to them with some whiskey, and maybe some medicine, if you can spare any."

"I reckon you'd better stay right where you are," said Dutch. "We'll have to bring your pards here, and all of us prepare to welcome that bunch of outlaws. How far do you figure you'd come, when we found you?"

"I'm not sure," McCulloch said, "but guessing, I'd say fifteen miles. I made it that far by staying near the river, where there were fewer ridges. But it won't be easy, moving Pryor and Robb, and you'll be working against time."

"I know," Dutch said. "I figure it'll be close to twenty-five miles, and since we'll have two wounded men, I aim to take the buckboard. I'm countin' on it being light enough not to break through the frozen snow. Now you'd better tell me how to find those men. Tally, harness the buckboard team."

McCulloch gave directions. When he had finished, Christie Beckwith approached and spoke to him.

"Miss Christie," said McCulloch, "what in the world are you doing out here?"

"Going west," Christie said.

Most of the outfit had gathered around Dutch, volunteering to help with the proposed rescue. Haskel Collins said nothing.

"I'm taking Tally, Brace, and Pawnee," said Dutch. "Brace, I want you to handle the buckboard. You'll have to avoid ridges, taking the long way around. That means you'll keep the team at not much more than a walk. One slip can break a horse's leg.''

"The buckboard's ready," Tally Slaughter said.

"Brace will be driving," said Dutch, "and you'll be riding with Pawnee and me. Brace, put a gallon of whiskey in the buckboard, and some extra blankets."

"You and Tally will need fresh horses," Jules Swenson said. "Whit an' me are offerin' ours. What about Pawnee?"

"Tally and me are obliged," said Dutch. "Tally, see if you can find out if Pawnee will want another horse."

Slaughter conversed with Pawnee in Spanish and by sign, and the Indian shook his head. He would ride his own horse.

"We're ready, then," Dutch said, "and we'd better get started."

Pawnee led out. Brace followed with the buckboard, Dutch and Tally trailing him.

"God, I hope that renegade Sioux wasn't lying to Plummer about them wagons on the Bozeman," Alvin Taylor said. "Hugh findin' them is our only chance."

"It's his only chance," Julius Blackburn replied, "and without some means of whipping this fever, Pryor and Robb are done for. Hugh McCulloch is a strong man, but these High Plains blizzards are hell. The wind blowin' across solid ice, a man can't endure that kind of cold for long. Hugh's too good a man to cash in this way, and if he does, it's goin' to lay one God-awful decision on our backs."

He didn't have to spell it out. If Hugh McCulloch failed to find and bring help, Alvin Taylor and Julius Blackburn would be forced to choose between saving their own lives and those of their two wounded companions. Without a miracle, Pryor and Robb would die, leaving Taylor and Blackburn at the mercy of Plummer's outlaws.

"I reckon we'll know before this day ends," said Taylor.

"After that, it won't make any difference to Pryor, Robb, or us."

"This damn cold, with the ground froze, might last another month," Hadsell said. "I'm for pullin' out, come first light, and findin' where them miners is holed up. They can't be that far ahead of us. We can gun them down and take their camp."

"I've been considering that," said Ives. "I've enjoyed about all I can stand of you and the rest of these coyotes. As long as this snow's froze hard, we'll be moving slow. One more day here, and we'll be gathering more firewood."

"We'll be gatherin' firewood somewhere else," Prinz said, "and we may not have near as good a shelter as this."

"Luck of the draw," said Ives. "Lay around here till it warms up, and there may be another storm by then. If we can ride, even takin' it slow, so can them miners, and I ain't about to spend all this time for nothing. Tomorrow, we ride."

Despite their impatience and concern for the time it was costing them, Dutch, Tally, and Pawnee were limited to the progress of the buckboard. Brace Weaver, being one of the most experienced teamsters Dutch had ever known, was forced to make allowances for the conditions. Even the slightest rise caused the iron rims of the buckboard's wheels to slide sideways on the frozen snow. The horses' hooves slipped repeatedly, dropping the valiant animals to their knees. The wind still roared out of the west, and for yet another day, there had been no sun. It took them almost two hours to reach the place along the river where Pawnee had shot the wolf. There, the terrain leveled out, with fewer obstructions to slow the buckboard.

"It's goin' to push us to reach our camp before dark," Tally Slaughter observed.

"We'll have the wind at our backs, goin' back," said Dutch.

Riding ahead, Pawnee was the first to discover the arroyo they sought. Knowing they were seeking white men, and being an Indian, he wisely waited for his companions.

"*Cañon*," Pawnee said.

Dutch and Slaughter caught up to the Indian, and the three of them rode on. Nearing the head of the arroyo, they reined up.

"Hello, the camp," Dutch shouted. "We're friends of Hugh McCulloch."

Two men slipped and slid up the lower slope of the arroyo, apparently not believing their eyes, for Brace Weaver had come in sight with the buckboard. Dutch and Tally dismounted, and Dutch performed the introductions.

"Thank God," said Blackburn. "This is Alvin Taylor, and I'm Julius Blackburn. Gus Pryor and Irv Robb are inside, burnin' up with fever."

"There's a gallon of whiskey in the buckboard," Dutch said. "We'll dose them with it and be on our way. It's a good twenty-five miles to our camp."

"You've made a considerable sacrifice," Blackburn said, "and we're obliged. I'd never have believed you could bring a wagon over solid ice."

"This is Brace Weaver," said Dutch. "He's one of the best teamsters on the frontier."

"Here's the whiskey," Brace said. "We'd best get the wounded men loaded up and be on our way. I ain't promisin' I can get this contraption back to camp in the dark."

Pryor and Robb were dosed with whiskey, wrapped in blankets, and taken to the buckboard. Blackburn and Taylor saddled their horses, and the extra horse was tied behind the buckboard. Slowly, carefully, they began the return journey beneath a sky of big gray clouds that created an atmosphere of perpetual twilight. Occasional sleet, driven by the ever aggressive wind, stung their cheeks. Despite the lateness of the hour and the press of time, they stopped to rest the horses.

"I don't like the feel of this sleet," said Blackburn. "It has the feel of another storm in the making."

"Neither do I," Dutch said. "All I want is to reach our camp before it gets any worse."

"I reckon Hugh told you about Henry Plummer's bunch of outlaws, and what they got in mind," said Alvin Taylor.

"Yes," Dutch replied. "I've heard that killings are common in a boomtown, but this is an almighty long way for outlaws to ride."

"Not when there's vigilante talk," said Taylor. "Plummer's about played out his hand, and as sheriff, he can't afford to have any more killing and robbing anywhere even close to Virginia City."

"We're obliged for the warning," Dutch said. "They sound like the kind who would gun us down from cover. Now we'll be ready for them."

They moved on, the buckboard continuing to slip and slide, their horses stumbling. To their horror, the occasional sleet was replaced with snow, and there was every evidence of a new storm in the making. Still they pressed on. But darkness came early, and there was no moon and no stars to light their way through the deepening snow.

Dutch's outfit anxiously awaited some sign or some sound of his return, as the wind drove flurries of snow down the face of the bluff that sheltered them. It was so dismal a day, they could scarcely tell when twilight came.

"It's snowing out their tracks," Bonita said. "How will they ever find their way back?"

"It'll be so blasted dark they couldn't see their tracks, anyhow," said Rusty Karnes. "All they got to do is keep their backs to the wind."

"I'm sorry to have been the cause of this," Hugh McCulloch said. "We'd have had a chance, if it hadn't been for the wolves."

"There's some things a man can't avoid," said Whit Sanderson. "On the frontier, we got to help one another, because we never know when we'll be needin' help ourselves. I've lost count of the times Dutch Siringo saved my bacon. I'd give my life for him, if it ever comes to that."

It was a moving testimonial, and while the rest of the men who knew Dutch were silent, there was a fierce resolve in their eyes that said they shared Whit's sentiment. The wind howled over the stone pinnacles that sheltered them, and darkness descended on a land that seemed a never-ending panorama of white.

"Damn," George Ives swore, when the wind began swirling new snow in among them.

Borg laughed. "You still aim to ride out in the morning?"

"I don't see nothin' funny," said Ives. "Tomorrow, we got to scrounge more wood, if we can find it. Another foot of snow on top of what's already there, and it'll be hell."

"At least we know them miners ain't goin' nowhere," Stem said.

"Yeah," Prinz replied, "that'll make us all feel a heap better, knowin' them jaspers is freezin' to death along with us."

"What bothers me," said Vick, "is the thought that them miners have somehow got to the teamsters. They may all be settin' around a fire, drinkin' coffee, and laughin' at us."

Ives struck without warning, his fist slamming against Vick's chin. Vick stumbled over a pile of wood and fell. His hand froze on the butt of his Colt, for Ives had him covered.

"Don't let me hear no more of that talk," Ives gritted. "Not from any of you. We got a job to do, and by God, we're gonna do it."

Vick got to his feet, sleeving blood from the corner of his mouth. His eyes were cold, and they said this wasn't over. The rest of the outlaws were careful not to look at Ives, lest he see the rebellion in their eyes.

Dutch again ordered a halt to rest the horses. Straining his eyes, he tried to look into the gray-white curtain of swirling snow that had limited visibility to only a few feet. While they were still traveling eastward—with the storm at their backs—they had left the river where it curved to the northeast. Somewhere in the murky dark, there had to be a mighty stone butte that sheltered their camp. But the very security of the camp prevented them from seeing the glow of a fire, and the force of the wind swept away the smoke. There was nothing they could do except move on, their bodies half-frozen and becoming more and more unresponsive. Finally, Dutch reined up. Even with the wind at their backs, he had no real sense of direction, and feared they were straying from their course. Lost in the swirling snow and intense darkness, they might pass within a hundred yards of their camp and still be unaware of it. Cocking his Henry with nearly frozen hands, Dutch fired once, twice, three times. Somehow—and soon—they must regain their sense of direction. He waited, listening, but there was no answer to his desperate appeal. While his shots might be heard by his companions, their response would be swept away by the wind.

"Listen," Jules Swenson shouted.

There were two more shots in quick succession.

"They're close," said Whit Sanderson, "but they've lost their sense of direction."

Jules Swenson cocked his Henry rifle and fired three answering shots, but there was no response, no indication they'd been heard.

"The wind's carryin' the sound of the shots away to the east," said Drago Peeler, "and they ain't hearin' 'em. We got to send 'em a signal they can see. Couple of you come with me."

Drago selected a long pine branch, dry and resinous.

Thrusting it into the coals, he waited until the fire took hold. Rusty Karnes and Cass Carlyle had gotten the idea and were lighting torches of their own.

"The wind may swallow 'em pronto," said Drago, "but old Dutch won't need more than a second or two, and he'll know where we are. Let's go."

They crossed the spring runoff and climbed the ridge, walking along the crest of it until they looked off a shoulder of the bluff, toward the west. Shielding their torches with their bodies, they kept them burning until they had advanced enough to be seen from a distance.

"Now let's hold 'em high," Drago shouted. The wind whipped his voice away, but his companions followed his example.

The weary, half-frozen men on the plains saw the three distant points of light, and lifted their voices in shouts to the fury of the wind. Dutch drew his revolver and fired once, hoping his companions with the torches would hear and know they had been seen. The trio with the torches heard the shot and shouted in response. Drago's torch flamed out, but the other two held strong for a little longer, and that was enough. Borne on the wind, they heard the rattle of the buckboard, and Jules Swenson appeared with yet another torch. Brace Weaver gave the horses their heads the rest of the way. While they stumbled from weariness and the deepening snow, they sensed their trial was almost done. There was a shout from the sheltered camp, as the buckboard, its accompanying riders, and the men on foot made their way down the ridge. Pawnee was first off his horse, followed by Dutch and Tally. Hugh McCulloch was on his feet, greeting Julius Blackburn and Alvin Taylor. Jules Swenson, Whit Sanderson, Dent Wells, and Levan Blade carried the wounded Pryor and Robb from the buckboard and into the shelter, placing them near one of the fires. Bonita and Christie had three pots of coffee ready, and with the exception of the two wounded men, they all accepted tin cups of hot coffee.

"Thank God," said Hugh McCulloch. "I was starting to fear that I had sent you all to your deaths."

"You didn't know about the new storm coming," Dutch replied. "That's what almost got us. Once we left the Yellowstone, we weren't sure we hadn't wandered too far north. I knew some of you would answer my three shots, but the wind carried the sound away from us. Thank God for the torches. They made the difference."

"That was Drago's idea," said Whit Sanderson. "A damn shame none of us thought of 'em sooner."

"They wouldn't have been helpful to us any sooner," Brace Weaver said. "Close as we were, we could barely see them. The timing was perfect."

Bonita had heated water and had begun cleansing the wounds of Pryor and Robb.

"You'd better bring that jug of whiskey, Brace," said Dutch. "These hombres are well past the time they're needin' another slug of it."

"Their fever's down some," Julius Blackburn said, having checked it.

Bonita had doused the wounds of both men with disinfectant and was smoothing on a layer of sulfur salve.

"I think you'd better leave off the bandages for a while, Bonita," said Dutch. "We'll have another look at them in the morning. I reckon the rest of us have thawed out enough to be needin' some grub. Hugh, why don't you introduce these pards of yours that just rode in?"

Everybody pitched in, preparing supper for the rescuers and the rescued. They sat around the fire eating bacon and beans, and drinking hot coffee, and only when they had their fill did McCulloch, Blackburn, and Taylor relate all the details regarding their flight from Virginia City, the intent of the outlaws pursuing them, and the attack by the wolves.

"You're among friends," said Dutch, "and your pards that tangled with the wolves will heal, once their fever breaks. Now I want to know—if we're to believe it—how serious is this outlaw threat?''

"Believe it," Hugh McCulloch said, "because it's damn serious. You know me, Dutch. I'd face up to the devil, given an even break, but these Plummer outlaws are bushwhackers who kill from cover. When you're out-gunned and don't stand a prayer, only a damn fool hangs around to play out the hand.''

"I won't argue with that," said Dutch. "You say the sheriff of Virginia City is head of the gang?''

"There's no proof," Blackburn cut in, "but there's enough certainty in everybody's minds that vigilantes will ride before this year's done.''

"Talk of vigilantes is all that saved us bein' murdered before leavin' Virginia City," said Alvin Taylor. "Plummer wanted us well away from there, before we was killed and our gold taken.''

"That makes sense," Dutch said, "but what of this plan to take our wagons? Is it all riding on the word of a drunken Sioux?''

"Yes," said McCulloch, "and Big Bear was telling it plain that Plummer wanted to know all about your wagons. That was when Plummer run the Sioux out of town. We got word on our own that Plummer was sendin' at least ten men south, and being the killers they are, they wouldn't need that many men to bushwhack five of us. That makes sense to me.''

"It makes sense to me too," Haskel Collins said. "In the gold camps, in winter, the goods and supplies in these wagons will be worth more than all your gold combined. While I hadn't anticipated this problem, I can readily see the possibility of it.''

"It's a threat we can't overlook," said Dutch. "Once your compadres are able to ride, you can be on your way. You'll be able to escape these outlaws, and if they're serious about comin' after us, we'll be ready for them.''

"You know me better than that," McCulloch said. "Once the odds are evened up some, I don't run from a fight. Besides, we're one horse shy. The wolves got Pryor's mount, and we'll have to find him a horse. I figure, with you and your outfit and the five of us, when these bush-whackers ride in, some of them won't be ridin' out. We'll just replace Pryor's horse with one of theirs.''

Dutch laughed. ''Hugh, why in tarnation did you ever give up the trail? An old catamount like you ain't happy unless he's clawin' and bein' clawed, shootin' and bein' shot at.''

''There's some truth in that,'' McCulloch said. ''If I get out of here with my hide in one piece, I'll have me a stake, but what am I going to do? Lay around in town until the money runs out, and hire on as a bullwhacker?''

''You can always buy into Siringo Freight Lines,'' said Dutch. ''You can be out here on the High Plains, enjoying wind, rain, and snow, freezing your behind off, and fighting Sioux. There's no way you can equal that, living in town.''

''You shouldn't tempt a man like that, my friend,'' McCulloch said. ''Some damn fool like me might take you up on it.''

''Hugh,'' said Dutch, ''you're a man to ride the river with. Money or not, you'll never belong on the front porch in a rocking chair. You belong on the high box, with the reins in your hand and a Henry rifle under the seat.''

McCulloch laughed. ''You know me better than I know myself. When all the dust has settled, and we've shown Plummer's outlaws the error of their ways, we'll talk again. I'll be ready for some new direction, and it won't be toward a rocking chair.''

One of the wounded men groaned. On his belly, Gus Pryor raised up on his elbows, looking around in confusion. His eyes were dull, and there were beads of sweat on his brow. McCulloch knelt down beside him.

''Hugh? Where . . . am I?'' Pryor asked, slurring the words.

''We're all with Dutch Siringo's freighting outfit,'' said McCulloch. ''Yours and Robb's wounds have been taken care of. You need to sleep off the whiskey."

"God, yes," Pryor mumbled. "Feel like I . . . been on a three-day drunk. Water . . ."

Bonita brought a tin cup of water, and Pryor drank thirstily. He then relaxed and said no more.

"If these outlaws kill from ambush," Collins said, "they could kill some of us before we get to them. Have you a plan to prevent that, Mr. Siringo?"

"Yes," said Dutch. "If they're serious, they'll come after us just as soon as the storm lets up and the weather permits. You have the right idea, Collins. We'll have to get them before they get us, and that means picking up their trail and taking the fight to them. I'm not the kind to let somebody else choose the time and place. Do that, and you're forever on the defensive."

"Damn right," Julius Blackburn agreed. "Bushwhackers would pick us off one at a time, with no danger to themselves."

"That's why we must move before they do," said Dutch, "and the snow will be a help to us. How far behind do you think they are?"

"We figured they were a day behind us," McCulloch replied. "Once we were far from Virginia City, they would have caught up. Now, I reckon we've gained on them. I doubt they'd be out in the storm, like we were. With Pryor and Robb facing death, I really had no choice."

"They have to be holed up somewhere west of here," said Dutch, "and they can't be sure where we are. We must keep it that way, discover where they are, and call their hand before they begin bushwhacking us."

"If they intend to ambush us," Collins said, "I see nothing wrong with fighting fire with fire. Let us set up an ambush of our own."

"I don't think so," said Dutch. "While they may be skunk-striped, murdering coyotes, I don't aim to sink to their level. We'll corner them, challenge them, and if they won't have it any other way, we'll gun them down."

"You are an ethical, courageous man, Siringo," Collins said, "but I don't favor allowing a reptile to bite me so that I may be certain of its intentions."

"Things are a mite different on the frontier, Collins," said Dutch. "You don't stomp a snake just because he *is* a snake, but when you know damn well he aims to bite you."

George Ives and his outlaw band were forced out into the driving snow and howling wind in search of more firewood. Tempers were on short rein. Ives and Prinz had ventured out in search of wood, and the others were criticizing Ives.

"I'm ready to gut-shoot Ives," said Hadsell, "bushwhack the miners, take their gold, and quit the territory."

"What about the wagons?" Borg asked.

Hadsell laughed. "They'll be Henry Plummer's problem."

CHAPTER 17

❦

*T*he storm continued through the night and was still going strong at dawn. The two wounded men—Gus Pryor and Irv Robb—were awake, their fever broken. McCulloch introduced them to Dutch and his outfit, and breakfast was an interesting affair. Talking to Pryor and Robb, the teamsters became more sure than ever that the threat from Plummer's outlaws was very real. The wounded men told the same graphic tale of miners who had been murdered for their gold. Now that Pryor and Robb were able to participate in the discussion, Dutch felt it was time to decide how they would move against the outlaws.

"I reckon we'd better lay some plans," said Dutch. "All the evidence we have that the outlaws aim to ambush us and take our wagons is the word of a renegade Sioux, but we can't afford to laugh it off. Hugh McCulloch and his pards are in danger of being murdered for their gold, and it's starting to make sense to me that if a bunch of killers will ride them down, they'll come after us. I've already suggested to Hugh that he and his pards are welcome to take their gold and ride, that we'll take our chances with Plummer's outlaws, but Hugh wants to stay and fight. The rest of you gents—Pryor, Blackburn, Taylor, and Robb—how do you feel?"

"We're with Hugh," they said in a single voice.

"Good," said Dutch. "Now here's what I have in mind. We don't know when or where we'll have to face up to these outlaws. Hugh, why don't you and your boys ride on to the Bitterroot with us? Then it won't matter whether these outlaws are after your gold or our wagons, or both. We can handle them. Then we'll be returning to Kansas City, and there'll be more of us to face up to the Bozeman Trail and the Sioux."

"We've been so determined to escape Plummer's gang and get out of the territory, we forgot about the Bozeman Trail and the Sioux," Blackburn said. "I like the idea of being part of a bigger outfit."

"So do I," McCulloch said.

"Count me in," said Alvin Taylor. "Escaping Plummer's outlaws won't do us no good, if the Sioux shoot us full of arrows."

"I like the bigger outfit," Irv Robb said. "I'll go."

"So will I," said Gus Pryor, "but I reckon I'll have to beg me a ride in a wagon. The damn wolves got my horse."

"Since you'll be going on with us," Dutch said, "you can ride my horse. I just wanted to know where everybody stands."

"A good move," said Hugh McCulloch. "I feel better than I have since before we left Virginia City. Even if we had escaped Plummer's outlaws, our chances of slipping through the hands of the Sioux were pretty slim. I don't mind a good fight, but I don't like the idea of being outnumbered twenty-to-one."

"You have the right idea, Siringo," Jules Blackburn said, "freighting in goods to the diggings in Montana Territory. You can become a wealthy man, without ever digging an ounce of gold."

"I think you're right, Blackburn," said Dutch, "but this freight doesn't belong to me or my teamsters. We contracted to haul it for Haskel Collins. I've about decided that when we return to Kansas City, we'll buy some more wagons and teams and freight in some of our own goods, selling to the highest bidder.''

"I'll want you to do some more hauling for me, Siringo," Collins said. "We'll go with the same per-wagon deal, adding more wagons, if you're agreeable."

"We'll have to wait and see, Collins," said Dutch. "I can get the wagons, but I may not be able to find the drivers."

"You'll have at least one more," Hugh McCulloch said, "but not for wages. I want to put some money in the pot and own a piece of the line. I know some other gents that will come in with me, if you're willing."

"Then we'll talk," said Dutch. "I reckon by the time we reach Kansas City, we'll have the teamsters, as well as money for more wagons and teams."

Sometime during the third night after the storm began, the snow ended. The dawn broke clear, and while the wind was still cold, there was a change coming. The first rays of the rising sun painted the eastern horizon a dusty rose.

"My God," Drago Peeler shouted, "look yonder!"

"I see it," said Rusty Karnes, "but I ain't believin' it."

"You varmints shut up," Whit Sanderson said, "or you'll scare it away. The sky will cloud up, an' it'll start snowin' again."

"There's nothin' to get excited about," said Brace Weaver. "Once all this snow and ice melts, we'll be in mud up to our ears, and us settin' our saddles."

"We'll be waitin' a spell," Dutch said, "but it won't be time wasted. I reckon that bunch of outlaws will be able to ride long before we can move our wagons, and if they're half as tired of waiting as we are, they'll come looking for us. Under a clear sky, I'd say we can see a far piece from the top of this butte that's shelterin' us. Startin' today, I want a lookout up there, watching the plains to the west. Right now, it's a Mexican standoff, with neither party knowing where the other is. Somebody's got to make a first move, and they're in a better position to do it than we are.

There's enough of us so that we can keep a daylight watch in two-hour shifts. Who wants to go first?''

"I will," Brace Weaver said.

"Take some hot coffee with you," said Dutch, "and after awhile, one of us will climb up and bring you some more."

Breakfast was over, and Bonita put on some more coffee to boil. She then brought the medicine chest. Gus Pryor and Irv Robb had gotten through the night without pain, and it was time to see to their wounds and change the dressing.

"You got a good touch, ma'am," Pryor said. "I'm still sore as all tarnation, but I can feel it gettin' better."

"Me too," said Robb, "and I'm obliged."

"When I was a teamster," McCulloch said, "I don't recall this kind of attention, eatin' this well, or sleeping warm and dry."

"You wasn't drivin' for my outfit," said Dutch, "and I make my own rules. I was all but told I was a damn fool for accepting a contract from Collins and headin' for the High Plains in winter."

"There was a time when I'd have agreed with whoever said that," McCulloch replied, "but I wouldn't now. A thing is only impossible until somebody does it, and you're well on your way."

Haskel Collins had been listening with interest, and finally, he spoke. "The journey takes longer in winter, because of the storms, but that's when the goods are most needed in the mining camps. A second trip, starting in the spring, wouldn't take nearly as long."

Dutch said nothing, knowing what Collins was leading up to. The man's moods seemed to change with the weather, and Siringo wasn't sure he wanted another hauling contract. It was later in the day, when Dutch was able to talk to Bonita, that the subject again came up as a result of something Christie Beckwith had said.

"I know you said you wanted nothing more to do with Collins, once this contract has been fulfilled," said Bonita, "but Christie's hoping you'll change your mind."

"Why?" Dutch asked. "Is she throwin' in with him?"

"I think so," said Bonita. "I have the feeling she wants to stay on the frontier, and she knows she can't do it alone. She wants Collins to be successful, so she can make herself a place with him."

"I can see how it might improve her position with Collins," Dutch said, "but I'm not so sure it'll do much for us. Today he talks sense, and tomorrow I'll have one hell of a time talking myself out of bending a pistol barrel over his head."

"Christie says he wants to bring in ten wagonloads, next time," said Bonita, "and he plans to double his offer to you."

"The more wagons, comin' through Sioux country, the safer we'll be," Dutch said. "I believe we can enlist Hugh McCulloch and his four amigos. We haven't talked money, but I suspect they'll buy in for enough to purchase as many wagons and mules as we'll need. I want to reach some agreement with them, if I can, before we get to the Bitterroot. Then I reckon all of us will have to take a look at what Collins is offering. Hugh and his pards ain't had to tolerate the varmint all the way from Kansas City, and I purely don't want to agree to that again, unless everybody's willing, money or not."

Following the storm, there was sun every day, and the frozen land began to thaw. As Dutch had planned, they kept a lookout near the top of the butte, with a view toward the west during daylight hours. The wind had died to a breeze, and there was no need for the three fires for warmth. There was a single fire at night to light their shelter and for coals to keep the coffee hot.

"If those outlaws haven't given up," said Dutch, "they should be showin' up. While we still can't move the wagons, there's nothing to stop mounted men."

"They won't give up," Hugh McCulloch said. "We

don't know how far behind us they were when we all had to take shelter from the storm.''

"All the more reason they should be coming, if they're coming at all,'' said Dutch. "As soon as we're able to take the trail again—maybe tomorrow—we'll be going, outlaws or not.''

McCulloch said nothing, but he sensed some doubt among the teamsters. They were beginning to wonder if the presence of Plummer's outlaws was real or imagined.

"Tomorrow,'' said George Ives, "we move out.''

"Hell,'' Hadsell said, "we should of done that two days ago. Them miners will be in Sioux country before we catch up to 'em. If we ever do.''

"Hadsell,'' said Ives, "I'm doing the thinking, which is a good thing, because none of the rest of you seem capable of it. We don't know where those hombres are holed up, and until they make some tracks, there's no way in hell of ever findin' them. Do I have to tell you what damn fools we'd be, gettin' *ahead* of them?''

"No bigger damn fools than we'll be, if they meet them wagons before we catch up to 'em,'' said Borg.

"Them wagons are likely stranded somewhere along the Bozeman,'' Ives said. "I expect we'll have to wait for them, after we ambush McCulloch and his pards.''

None of the men said anything, but they furtively eyed one another, reaffirming what they had agreed upon while Ives had been absent. They had no intention of attacking the teamsters and seizing the wagons, as Henry Plummer had ordered. Instead, they would kill the miners, take their gold, and quit the territory. Plummer would blame the failure on George Ives, but it wouldn't matter to Ives, for he would be dead. Nobody had argued with that, for the stolen gold would be split nine ways, instead of ten.

"This has been a nice shelter,'' said Bonita. "I almost hate to leave it.''

"God, I don't," Cass Carlyle said. "It seems like we been here for a year."

"I reckon we'll all be missin' it before we reach the Bitterroot," said Whit Sanderson. "These few days of sun will be gone 'fore you know it, the wind blowin' like hell wouldn't have it, and we'll all be hunched around a fire, wonderin' if the snow's ever gonna quit."

"You're a cheerful cuss," Brace Weaver said. "Why didn't you dig a little deeper and remind us that we're all goin' to die, and anything we do between now and then won't make a damn anyhow?"

"When you varmints are done cheerin' one another up," said Dutch, "harness your teams and let's move out."

With Pawnee riding ahead, Dutch led out with his wagon. Haskel Collins followed him with the buckboard, the rest of the wagons trailing him. Hugh McCulloch and his four companions rode alongside the wagons, with the outriders.

"Do you really believe there are outlaws planning to attack us and take the wagons?" Bonita asked.

"Yes," Dutch said. "I'm sure Hugh McCulloch and his friends are in danger, or they wouldn't have left Virginia City on the run. If these outlaws are willing to ride this far to kill for gold, I don't have any trouble believing they'd ambush us and take our wagons. I don't think Collins is stretching it when he estimates the worth of these goods and supplies at thirty thousand dollars. Not a bad haul for a bunch of outlaws, this near the diggings."

"Now that we're out in the open, and we don't know where they are, there's nothing to stop them from ambushing us, is there?"

"One thing, I reckon," said Dutch. "They won't know McCulloch and his pards are with us, and I figure they'll go after the gold first. That means they'll light out toward the east, believing McCulloch and his pards are still ahead of them. They can pass us without ever knowing we're here. I aim to have Pawnee ride south every day, as far as the foothills of the Absarokas. Somewhere, he'll pick up their trail, and before they learn that the men they're chasing are with us, we'll make our move.''

''Suppose they give up on getting the gold, and come after us?''

''We're not taking any chances,'' Dutch said. ''We'll post a double guard every night, until we know where they are, and then we'll challenge them.''

''How will we do that?''

''Get the drop on them and demand a reason for their being here,'' said Dutch. ''What we do after that will depend entirely on them.''

''What will we do with them, if they just surrender?''

''They won't,'' Dutch said. ''We'll likely have to shoot some of them, to make believers of the rest. Given a chance, those who survive will run.''

''But what's to stop them from coming after us again?''

''Nothing,'' said Dutch. ''I'll expect them to, and when they do, we'll gun them down to the last man.''

''God.'' She shuddered. ''Life on the frontier is so . . . brutal. Is it always like this, kill or be killed?''

''Pretty much,'' said Dutch. ''I don't believe in killing a man, unless he won't have it any other way. Greed—men killing and stealing from other men—is the same the world over, I reckon. It just seems worse here in the West, because there's no law, forcing us all to stomp our own snakes.''

''Some think it's wrong to kill, for any reason.''

''Maybe they need some varmint to shoot them a couple of times, or drive a Bowie in their bellies,'' Dutch replied. ''It's easy to preach against hurtin' somebody, until that somebody comes after you with killing on his mind. I'll protect myself and what belongs to me, and I'll do it by whatever means I have to. We had to kill the Sioux, or they would have killed us, like they did Kirby and Gard. Doesn't that make sense?''

''Yes,'' she said. ''I heard Tally Slaughter talking to the other men about the way you ran off the Crows' horses, taking back the ones they stole from us. Tally said you could have killed them all from the canyon rims. He said that other men might have done that, but you didn't. I don't much like the Crows, but they didn't hurt us, and I'm glad that you spared them. I'm proud of you for that."

"They're mostly a nuisance," said Dutch, "and if I killed for that, I'd have gut-shot Haskel Collins before we ever reached Fort Laramie."

She laughed. "For Christie's sake, I'm glad you didn't."

"You think he has plans for her, then."

"Yes," Bonita said. "They've had a misunderstanding or two, but he's always managed to patch things up. She told him everything, from the time Sneed took over her father's freight line until she watched the Sioux murder the men she was with. I think she wanted to see if she could scare him away, but she couldn't. Now she's sure of him."

"I'm glad for her," Dutch said. "I don't fully understand what he aims to do, once we reach these Bitterroot diggings. I believe he can sell everything right from the wagons, to the highest bidder. If he can do that, why does he need a trading post?"

"I don't know," said Bonita. "Christie thinks they're going to live there, somewhere."

"We'll have to split up," said Ives, "until we pick up the trail of them miners. Prinz, you take Vick, Stem, Hadsell, and Aten, and ride north until you reach the Yellowstone. As you ride, watch for a trail and for riders. The rest of us will ride east for another ten miles, and from there, ride north. We'll meet at the bend in the river, where it turns to the west. Anybody got a problem with that?"

"Hell," Hadsell said, "this ain't goin' to get us nowhere. Them miners is farther ahead of us than that. All we're doin' is searchin' the plains behind 'em, after the storm's wiped out their tracks."

"Maybe you're right," said Ives grimly, "but since we're not sure where they are, we got to cover some useless ground until we find a trail. Get to that bend in the Yellowstone as quick as you can, but don't overlook nothin'. Wait there until we double back and meet you. Then if none of us has found a trail, we'll split up and ride east, coverin' another fifteen miles.''

Ives and his companions rode eastward, while Prinz and the rest of the gang rode out toward the north.

"Prinz," said Hadsell, "them miners was a day ahead of us when we took their trail. We don't know that they didn't ride out yesterday, bound for the Bozeman. Damn it, that puts 'em a good two days ahead of us. We ain't never gonna catch up to 'em, thisaway.''

"We sure as hell ain't," Vick agreed. "Plummer's had some fool plans before, but this one—with Ives the segundo—purely rips the rag off'n the bush.''

"We had an agreement," said Prinz. "Once we find them miners, we rid ourselves of Ives, take the gold and quit the territory. Well, we ain't found the miners, and there's a chance we won't. If they got away clean, then we can take them wagons or ride back to Virginia City empty-handed. Now, by God, if we got to bushwhack them teamsters, we'll need every man we got, includin' Ives.''

"Damn the wagons," said Hadsell. "I want the gold, so's I can get the hell out of here for good.''

"So do we all," Prinz replied, "but if them miners has outrode us and escaped, then it's neck meat or nothin'. You aim to quit the territory with your pockets empty? We ain't got enough grub to see us to Fort Laramie.''

Prinz and his four companions rode to the bend in the Yellowstone without finding any sign or seeing any riders.

"Now we got to set here, waitin' for Ives and the others," Hadsell complained, "and I'd bet my saddle, when they show up, they'll be as empty-handed as we are.''

Hadsell's prediction was accurate. They saw the answer in the faces of Ives and his companions, before any of them spoke.

"Nothin', I reckon," said Ives.

"Another great idea shot to hell," Hadsell said.

"We'll spread out in a line to the south," said Ives, "and ride eastward. Sometime between now and dark, we'll catch up to them. If we don't catch up, then we should be close enough to see their fire."

They spread out, riding toward the east. The sodden earth had dried to the extent that tendrils of dust rose, to be caught up by the wind. Half a mile ahead of them, a lone Indian sat his horse, concealed by boulders. Shading his eyes with his hands, he watched the oncoming riders for a moment. He then wheeled his horse and rode back the way he had come.

Dutch and his outfit had reined up to rest the teams, when they saw Pawnee coming at a fast gallop. He dismounted on the run.

"Trouble," said Dutch.

"*Hombres*," Pawnee said. He raised both hands, spreading his fingers.

"It's Ives and his bunch," said Hugh McCulloch. "They're after us; why don't you let me challenge them?"

"Go ahead," Dutch replied. "Just bear in mind that if they're who you think they are, we'll have to fight them now or later. They'll try to bluff their way out and come after us later."

"Fight them now," said McCulloch, "and they'll get some of us. We'll hold out for a better time and place and take them on our terms."

"We'll wait for them here," Dutch said. "There's seventeen of us, not counting Bonita and Christie. Fan out, all of you, and nobody fires unless they start it."

They were in a favorable position, not visible to Ives and his bunch until the outlaws topped a ridge three hundred yards beyond. It was the very last thing Ives and his riders expected to see, and they reined up in confusion.

"By God, it's the wagons," Hadsell said. "Where'n hell is them miners?"

The answer came almost immediately.

"Ives? George Ives. This is Hugh McCulloch. Pryor, Blackburn, Robb, Taylor, and me have thrown in with some friends of ours. Dutch Siringo and his teamsters have invited us to ride on to the Bitterroot and then return with them to Kansas City. We aim to do just that. We have seventeen men with repeating rifles. Listen, and listen good. We're invitin' you to turn your horses around and ride back the way you came. Tell Henry Plummer he's lost this one."

"We got no idea what you're talkin' about," George Ives shouted. "We're mindin' our own business."

"Have it your way," McCulloch shouted back. "That's the only warning you're going to get from us."

Ives led his nine men to the northeast, and they circled the wagons and riders at the foot of the ridge. McCulloch watched them out of sight, before he spoke.

"We took them by surprise, but they'll be back."

"And we'll be ready for them," said Dutch. "Let's go. We can still reach that bend in the river before dark."

Well beyond the wagons, Ives and his men reined up. Hadsell and some of the other men eyed one another, silently conceding that their plan to rid themselves of Ives and take the gold had fallen through. To a man, they were in a surly mood, and it was Ives who spoke.

"We just had a change in plans," he said. "We'll take the gold and the wagons, all in one swoop."

"They'll be waitin' for us," said Dyer, "and we're outgunned nearly two-to-one."

"That don't make a damn bit of difference in an ambush," Ives said. "They're headed for the Yellowstone, and that's where they'll set up camp. We'll come in from the north, and take them from the river brakes."

"I don't like the way this is shapin' up," said Prinz. "We had the element of surprise, and we had 'em outgunned. Now we got neither. This whole damn thing has gone sour."

"Why don't you ride back and tell that to Plummer?" Ives asked.

"I ain't tellin' Plummer nothin'," said Prinz. "It was you and him that kept us behind them miners, allowin' 'em to throw in with the teamsters."

"We come here to gun them all down," Ives said, "and that ain't changed. We'll just be doin' it all at once."

None of his companions said anything, but they no longer had any confidence in Ives, and no enthusiasm for attacking seventeen armed men, even from ambush.

"Too bad we can't make it to the arroyo along the Yellowstone, where we fought off the wolves," said McCulloch. "It would be a perfect place to stand them off."

"That's exactly what we don't want," Dutch said. "If we holed up there tonight, they'd just wait until we move on, to a more vulnerable camp. The sooner they come after us, the sooner we'll be done with them."

McCulloch laughed. "You set up the defense, and we'll follow your lead."

The wagons reached the bend in the river, where the Yellowstone turned to the west.

"I want the wagons and the camp well away from the river," Dutch said, "without any cover anywhere within rifle range. If they come after us, we'll make it damned expensive."

Dutch had the wagons lined up in a row at the foot of a low rise a quarter of a mile south of the river. To the south, beyond the wagons, was another rise, with no cover.

"There'll be no moon tonight," said Dutch, "and it's warm enough that we won't need a fire. For coffee, we'll dig a fire pit and keep the coals burned down. Bonita, I want you and Christie in the supply wagon. The rest of us will position ourselves within the shadows of the wagons, with our rifles. North, east, south, or west, there's not enough cover for them to surprise us. Tally, I want you to talk to Pawnee. I want him out there in the dark, using his

own judgment and his Bowie. Get it across to him that
these men are our enemies, just as much as the Sioux.
They've been warned, and if they come wolfing around,
we'll show them no mercy."

Slaughter spent some time with Pawnee, and the Indian
nodded, shifting his big Bowie from one hand to the other.

"My God," said Bonita, "when he has that knife in his
hand, he becomes another man, a killer."

"Tonight," Dutch said, "we may all become killers."

Fifteen miles north, on the Yellowstone, George Ives and
his gang sat around their supper fire. They had eaten in
silence, and it was Ives who finally spoke.

"I'm as tired of this search as any of you," said Ives.
"That's all the more reason to shoot hell out of the teamster
camp and wrap this up."

Still none of the men responded. They owed George Ives
nothing, and strong on their minds was their recollection
of this salty bunch having stood off Crazy Horse and more
than a hundred Sioux.

"We'll ride after midnight," said Ives.

CHAPTER 18

✦

"*P*erhaps they aren't coming tonight," Haskel Collins suggested. "It's past midnight."

"I believe they will," said Hugh McCulloch. "We know they're here, and that's cost them whatever advantage they had. Further delay will gain them nothing."

By the stars, it was two o'clock in the morning when Pawnee brought the word. Like a shadow, the Indian appeared.

"*Bandido lobos*," Pawnee said. The starlight being sufficient, he pointed toward the distant river.

Quickly Dutch visited the position of every man, preparing them. Pawnee had vanished into the night, and Dutch had no idea what the Indian intended to do. He soon found out. Somewhere between the wagons and the river, there was a scream of agony that trailed off into silence.

"My God," said Collins, "what was *that*?"

"Pawnee, working his magic," Dutch replied quietly.

George Ives and his men were belly-down, each of them familiar enough with Indian tactics to know what was happening.

"My God," Hadsell gritted, "they got Injuns stalkin' us with knives. I'm gettin' the hell away from here, while I can."

The attackers were still more than three hundred yards

from the wagons, and not a shot had been fired. Suddenly George Ives found himself alone, for his companions were on their feet, hunched over, and running for their lives. Ives followed, relieved, for their flight justified his own. To hell with what Henry Plummer thought; the deal had gone sour. The outlaws reached their horses, pausing just long enough for a head count.

"Borg ain't here," said Hadsell. "The damn Injuns got him."

Not another word was spoken. The outlaws mounted their horses and rode southwest, toward Virginia City and whatever retribution awaited them. But every one—George Ives included—was more willing to face the potential wrath of outlaw Sheriff Henry Plummer than death-dealing Indians in the darkness, with Bowie knives in their hands.

"Are they gone?" Bonita whispered.

"Maybe," said Dutch quietly. "We'll soon be hearing from Pawnee."

The Indian wasn't long in coming, and he summed it up with a few well-chosen words.

"*Bandito lobos vamoose. Uno muerto.*"

"By God," Hugh McCulloch said, "I'd never have believed it. I want to shake that Indian's hand."

But Pawnee wasn't there. While he was aware of their appreciation, he had done no more than he believed was expected of him. Just as the white man played upon the Indian's superstitions, so did the Indian play upon the white man's fear of the unknown. Nothing intimidated an enemy more thoroughly than hearing his comrade's death cry, and knowing that the next might be his own.

"We owe Pawnee a big one," Dutch said. "Tally, what did you tell him?"

"Not much," said Slaughter. "He knew they were the enemy, and I told him to handle them his way."

"I've never seen anything like it," Collins said. "If it had come to shooting, some of us would have surely been wounded or killed. Are those outlaws gone for good, or should we expect them back?"

"We'll post a double guard for the next few nights," said Dutch, "but my guess is that we're rid of them. I believe their plans began falling apart when Hugh and his pards got to us before Ives and his outlaws got to them. It's one thing to go gunning for five men, when you have them out-gunned two-to-one, and another to jump seventeen armed men who are fully expecting it. Their cause was lost, and Pawnee convinced them."

"I never seen anything as slick," said Drago Peeler. "Them varmints didn't know there was just one Indian after them."

"That's all we needed," said Whit Sanderson. "With Pawnee stalkin' 'em, they couldn't of kept their minds on attacking us. When a gent thinks there's a chance of havin' his throat slit, he ain't likely to think of nothin' else."

"We'll need sentries till daylight," Dutch said, "which is maybe four hours away. We'll need four men for the next two hours and four for the last two. Who'll join me for the first two?"

"I will," said Bonita.

"So will I," Jules Swenson said.

"And I," said Whit Sanderson.

"Us five from Virginia City will take the last two," Hugh McCulloch said.

"*Bueno*," said Dutch. "The rest of you turn in and get what sleep you can."

Bonita had stirred up the coals in the fire pit, and there was fresh coffee brewing. The rest of the outfit not on watch took Dutch's advice, seeking their blankets. Lightning ran its jagged fingers across the horizon, far to the west.

"It's been decent for too long," Whit said. "Yonder is the start of another blizzard."

"I don't think I've ever seen lightning except when there was rain," said Bonita. "It's a little strange to see it when there's snow on the way."

"I reckon it's raining out there where the lightning is," Whit said. "I just hope we can get another good day behind us, before we get bogged down again."

Jules and Whit wandered out among the horses and mules, leaving Bonita and Dutch alone.

"Where do you suppose Pawnee is?" Bonita asked.

"Trailing that bunch of outlaws," said Dutch. "There's always a chance they might ride a few miles and double back. Pawnee doesn't trust them."

"He's very smart, for an . . ."

"Indian," Dutch finished.

"I didn't mean it that way," she said. "He's as good as any man here, and I'd trust him with my life."

"I know," said Dutch, "and so would I. What he did tonight was pure genius, yet he saw it as no more than his duty. He can become a legend on the frontier, if whites will accept him as a man, instead of looking down on him as an Indian."

"We must help him."

"I intend to," Dutch said, "if he'll let me. A lot will depend on Tally Slaughter, and the Spanish he's teaching Pawnee. The real test is going to come when we return to Kansas City. Then there'll be the soldier forts, where Pawnee may be seen as just another Indian, good only when he is dead. His only hope, I reckon, is to remain with us as a scout, and there are some who won't accept him, even then."

Pawnee rode out at dawn, aware of the growing mass of clouds in the west. Dutch led out, the rest of the wagons following.

"I hate to see another storm coming," said Bonita. "How far do you suppose we are from the Bitterroot?"

"Going by what Collins has told me, about two hundred miles," Dutch said.

"Without bad weather, traveling fifteen miles a day, we could be there in two weeks."

Dutch laughed. "We could, but there's going to be bad weather, and there'll be days when we won't cover ten miles. There's nothing certain out here but the uncertainty."

The wind was from the west, and in the buckboard behind Dutch's wagon, Christie and Haskel Collins could hear Dutch's laughter. Regarding Christie with some amusement, Collins spoke. "Jealous, my dear?"

"Yes," she said. "When he walked out on me, I had everything, while he had nothing. Now it's all turned around."

"You haven't forgotten my promise, when we reach the Bitterroot?"

"No," she said. "It's just . . . that I can't believe I have nothing to show for my father's lifetime of hard work. If Dutch Siringo had taken over . . ."

"You wouldn't be here," Collins finished. "I think you are quite right, when it comes to Mr. Siringo's abilities. All the more reason we must win his confidence to the extent that he will continue freighting goods for us."

"When you speak of a trading post," said Christie, "is it ready, or to be built?"

"To be built," Collins said.

"Dutch is going to want to unload these wagons and be on his way back to Kansas City. What do you intend to do with all these goods?"

"Frankly," said Collins, "I haven't thought beyond just getting them to the Bitterroot. Now that you mention it, I foresee a problem. Men who are stricken with gold fever do not have time for anything else. Consequently, they live in mud huts, under bits of canvas, and in caves."

"So nobody will stop digging for gold long enough to build you a trading post."

"I'm afraid that's how it's going to be," said Collins. "As I recall, during the gold rush in California, sailing ships sat in the harbor, lacking men to unload them. Soldiers and sailors deserted to hunt for gold, and men sent after them followed their example. It's a kind of sickness that washes everything else from a man's mind."

"You've been to these Bitterroot diggings," Christie said. "Why didn't you stay there and dig, instead of taking on this dangerous freighting venture?"

"I considered it," said Collins, "but I doubt more than one man in a hundred will ever strike it rich. On the other hand, I have a pretty good idea what these five wagonloads of trade goods are worth."

Christie laughed, and Collins looked at her with appreciation before he spoke. "Do I take that as a sign of approval?"

"I suppose," said Christie. "This is a far more dangerous undertaking than mining, and the mark of a strong man. I like strong men."

"Such as Siringo."

"Yes," Christie replied, "and I'm starting to see some of the same strength in you that I've seen in him."

"I will take that as a compliment," said Collins. "While I don't always agree with him, I respect his judgment."

"Once we reach the Bitterroot, what are we going to do for a building to house these wagonloads of goods?"

"I'm considering some alternatives," Collins replied. "Would it bother you a great deal if we didn't remain on the frontier?"

"I suppose not. But where would we go?"

"Back to Kansas City, for more trade goods," said Collins. "I'm considering selling the current loads directly from the wagons."

"Then there won't be a trading post."

"No," Collins said. "That was mostly my father's idea, and thinking about it, I'm just not sure it's practical. Suppose I put up a building, unloaded all these goods, and sold out to the bare walls in two weeks? I'd be out of business until another load could be brought in from Kansas City. Suppose I just sell out and return for another load?"

"I see nothing wrong with that, if Dutch and his teamsters are willing to wait for you to empty the wagons.''

"It's one of the things we'll have to resolve," said Collins.

Riding west, Pawnee was gratified to see many bluffs and rock formations to the south. If nothing better presented itself, they could leave the river and seek possibly a cave or bluff overhang. There were runoffs from the Yellowstone, one of them substantial enough that Pawnee followed it through a forest of stone pillars, and beneath a wide stone arch, twenty feet over his head. While the shelter might have to be supplemented with canvas, it would do. Turning his horse, he rode back to meet the wagons.

"It'll do," said Dutch, when they came within sight of the great stone arch. Starting at the western end of the bluff, it spanned a distance of twenty yards, connecting to an even larger stone fortress. On the open sides of the arch, stone spires stood as barriers to the wind, which already was growing cold.

"*Bueno*, Pawnee," Tally Slaughter said.

"Line the wagons up, three to a side, on the open sides of the arch," said Dutch. "We can set our spare canvas up, wagon-bow-to-wagon-bow, for extra protection from blown-in snow."

When the wagons were in position and the teams unharnessed, most of the men rode out, seeking firewood. There was a natural stone floor, with a channel through which ran the stream from the Yellowstone.

"There's been plenty here before us," Whit Sanderson said. "Ashes from old fires."

"Crows, likely," said Hugh McCulloch.

"God, I hope the varmints don't ride in while we're here," Jules Swenson said. "Three days of them is enough to last a lifetime."

"There'll be snow before dark," said Whit. "I reckon the rest of us had better mount up and join the search for firewood. It's been warm too long. This storm's gonna lay some snow on us.''

The snow began before dark, becoming heavier as the evening wore on. After supper, they built up the fires. Christie helped Bonita wash out the coffeepots and get more coffee started.

"We'll start with two of us on watch at a time, for two hours," said Dutch. "We'll be doubling or tripling the guard if the wolves come around.''

Sometime during the second night after it began, the storm subsided. While the wind blew cold, it didn't seem as severe as it had following previous storms.

"If ever'thing don't freeze solid," Whit predicted, "we'll be out of here and on our way in two days."

The sun rose in a clear, blue sky, and before the end of the day, the snow had begun to melt. There were no massive drifts, and the fierce prairie wolves hadn't shown up. Even with much of the snow still present, they were at a higher elevation, and the resulting mud didn't seem that much of a problem. Dutch made a decision.

"Harness the teams. We're movin' out."

They took the trail, keeping to high ground, avoiding the sloughs. The weather held, and two days later, they reached the bend in the river where the Yellowstone turned south into northwestern Wyoming Territory.*

"It's due west from here to the Bitterroots," said Collins.

"Leaving the Yellowstone, it's the end of ready water," Dutch said. "We'll be depending on Pawnee."

"As I recall," said Collins, "there's an abundance of water. As the terrain becomes more mountainous, there are many springs."

"If there are no more storms," Dutch said, "I'm predicting we'll reach the end of this trail on March first. Five-

---

* The river flows into Yellowstone Lake, now a part of Yellowstone National Park.

and-a-half months, with all but two months of it snow. I reckon that ain't bad.''

"Indeed it isn't," Collins agreed. "Sometime before we reach the Bitterroot, I want to talk to all of you about some future business. I'm talking about doubling your money, over what you will earn with this contract.''

Christie Beckwith had her eyes on Dutch, while Bonita watched Haskel Collins. None of the outfit spoke, leaving it to Dutch.

"We'll talk," said Dutch. "There are some questions I'm wantin' answered, starting with how do we unload our wagons, when this trading post of yours is yet to be built?''

"We'll talk," Collins said. "I may have to ask you to bend some on this first contract, but I'll see that it's worth your while.''

"We don't aim to bend, when it comes to the money," Dutch said. "Anything else, and we'll talk.''

The conversation took place around the supper fire, and nothing more was said. Dutch and Bonita talked during the night.

"I'm thinking there's at least one thing we didn't nail down, that we should have," said Dutch. "We should have set a limit on how long this freight can occupy our wagons, after we reach our destination. How in thunder is Collins goin' to build a trading post in a boomtown where everybody's there to dig for gold?''

"He didn't tell you the trading post hadn't been built?''

"No," Dutch said, "and none of us thought to ask. We were so damn excited, getting a decent contract, we didn't think to ask what we were going to do with the freight when we reached the gold camp. I'm not even sure Collins had given it any thought. I reckon all of us were so concerned with getting it here, we forgot everything else.''

"Then what are you going to do with it?''

"I don't know," said Dutch. "It's not as though he tricked us. If he had, I'd unload it all on the ground.''

"He has something in mind," Bonita said, "and maybe

it won't be all that bad, since he's wanting you to continue hauling.''

"Maybe," said Dutch. "For the lack of a better choice, I'll wait and see."

While there was no more snow, the nights were bitter cold, and each night it seemed the howling wolves came closer. Mules brayed, horses nickered in fear, and Dutch doubled the guard. Tally Slaughter, Drago Peeler, Brace Weaver, and Cass Carlyle were on duty the night the wolves attacked the camp. Since there was no snow, there was no shelter except the canvas wind-breakers stretched between the wagons. There was no moon, and the night was deathly still. Their only warning was the terrified scream of a horse, as one of the big gray predators sprang. Brace Weaver shot the wolf off the horse's back. Around him, rifles roared, his companions firing as rapidly as they could jack in the shells. Christie Beckwith wasn't even free of her blankets, when a wolf leaped on her. She screamed as mighty claws raked her from neck to crotch. Pawnee leaped astraddle of the wolf, his left arm around the beast's neck. In his right hand was the deadly Bowie, and he drove it repeatedly into the wolf's chest. Bonita shot a wolf with her Colt, and wounded, the animal sprang. Claws raked her shoulder, as Tally Slaughter shot the wolf. The terrible ordeal ended as suddenly as it had begun. Dutch threw more wood on the fires, to better see what damage had been done. Christie Beckwith lay on her back, bloodied, the clothing stripped from her. Bonita's shirt was minus a sleeve, her arm and shoulder bleeding. Haskel Collins had a thigh-to-knee gash on his left leg. Both sleeves of Dutch's shirt were shredded from the shoulder, his arms bleeding. Collins was kneeling over Christie, covering her with a blanket. There were two shots, and Dutch saw Rusty Karnes step out of the darkness into the firelight.

"Had to shoot two horses," said Rusty. "Mine and yours."

"We may have lost more than that," Dutch said. "Get

everybody together that's able, in case the varmints come after us again. We got some God-awful wounds to tend.''

Whit Sanderson and Jules Swenson had emptied both coffeepots, filling them with cold water and hanging them over the fire. Despite her own wound, Bonita was trying to tend the severely wounded Christie. Dutch had blood dripping off the ends of his fingers and was forced to allow others to do what had to be done. Brace Weaver had taken a pot to the stream and collected mud to stop the bleeding. Because Christie was more severely clawed than any of them, Collins seized the pot of mud and began spreading it over the girl's upper body. Only when that was done did he allow his own wound to be tended. Dutch removed his shirt, allowing Jules Swenson to cover his bleeding arms with mud, while Whit Sanderson was caring for Bonita's wounded arm and shoulder.

"My God," said Hugh McCulloch, "there must have been more than a hundred of the varmints. We got fifteen of them."

"Some of you saddle up and drag those dead horses as far away as you can. We don't want any more wolves tonight," Dutch said.

By the time the bleeding had stopped, the water was boiling. Collins took a pot of it and was about to remove the blanket from the wounded Christie, when Bonita spoke.

"I'll see to her, if you want me to. You have a wound of your own."

"So do you," Collins replied, "but I'd appreciate you tending her."

Ignoring her own pain, Bonita washed the mud and the dried blood from the terrible wounds. She then doused them with disinfectant. Christie groaned, biting her lower lip. The wounds cleansed, Bonita then applied sulfur salve. From the medicine chest she took a bottle of laudanum and a spoon.

"This will help you to sleep," said Bonita. "When you wake, you'll probably be needing whiskey."

Christie swallowed the medicine and Bonita covered her with several blankets. Dutch had his wounded arms bandaged, while Collins lay on a blanket, wearing only his shirt. His wounded leg had begun bleeding again, and Brace Weaver was again applying mud. Bonita removed her shirt, allowing Whit Sanderson to cleanse the wound, apply sulfur salve, and finally, a bandage.

"A man ain't worth a damn with two clawed arms," said Dutch. "I reckon we'll have to stay here until some of us heal."

"I've never seen wolves so God-awful bold," Brace Weaver said.

"I have," said Gus Pryor. "The varmints got my horse, and near got me and Robb."

"I think," Blackburn said, "whether we need the shelter or not, we'd better arrange our camps with an eye to security. Canvas keeps the wind off, but not the wolves."

"After tonight, I can only agree," said Dutch. "Where's Pawnee?"

"He saved Christie's life," Collins said. "He may be hurt."

But the Indian soon returned, the Henry rifle slung over his shoulder, saying nothing. He apparently was unhurt.

"He's been scouting for wolves," said Dutch.

Those wounded by wolves were feverish by morning, and before the end of the day, were ready for whiskey. While they would have preferred a more secure camp, it was no time to consider moving. Christie Beckwith's fever hadn't broken, despite repeated doses of whiskey. Dutch could scarcely move either arm, while Collins was unable to stand on his wounded leg. Only Bonita's wound seemed to be responding, and she often knelt beside the wounded Christie. Bonita approached Dutch with a strange request.

"Christie wants to talk to you."

"Why?" Dutch asked. "Is she out of her head?"

"No," said Bonita. "The fever's burning her up, but she knows what she's saying."

The others had discreetly moved away, leaving Christie alone. Dutch knelt beside her.

"How do you feel?" he asked.

She tried to laugh. "Like I've been chewed and clawed by a wolf."

"What do you want to say to me?" he asked awkwardly.

"I just wanted . . . to say . . . I'm sorry."

"You have nothing to be sorry for," said Dutch. "We all make mistakes."

"You didn't," she said so softly he almost didn't hear. "I don't think . . . I'm going to make it . . . and I . . . wanted you to know . . . I . . . never stopped . . . caring."

Dutch lifted the blanket and looked at the wound. Despite the continued fever, there was no discoloration that suggested infection. On her lower belly, where the clawing hadn't been quite so severe, the wound had scabbed over. Dutch replaced the blanket and placed his hand on her brow. It was slightly moist.

"Christie," he said, "the fever's broken. It'll take awhile, but you'll heal."

"Damn," she said, "I can't do anything right."

Dutch got up and went to Bonita. "Give her some more whiskey. She's sweating just a little. The fever will break before suppertime."

Four days following the attack by the wolves, Dutch made the decision to move on. Christie was wrapped in blankets and placed in the supply wagon, out of the wind. Haskel Collins's leg was stiff, but he was able to drive the buckboard. Bonita's shoulder was almost healed, and while much of the soreness was still there, Dutch could move his arms. Tally Slaughter had taken some time to talk with Pawnee, and the Indian would begin looking for shelter that offered some security. Pawnee rode west at first light.

"Christie's feeling pretty low," said Bonita, as the big wagon jounced along.

"Why?" Dutch asked. "She's alive."

"I think that's what's bothering her," said Bonita. "Why don't you talk to her?"

"I've already talked to her," Dutch said, "and she told me she was dying and that she's sorry. I think she exaggerated the former and lied about the latter."

"I suppose she has a lot of regrets," said Bonita, "and it might make her feel better if she confesses some of them. After supper, why don't you talk to her?"

"I'll talk to her before supper," Dutch said. "I don't want to be alone with her after dark, in that wagon."

Pawnee, aware that they needed a secured shelter, began looking for one. He followed every stream until he found one that flowed out from under a rock ledge. While there was no overhang, the ledge was high enough to offer protection from above, and was part of a formation that was closed in on three sides. Satisfied, he rode back to meet the wagons.

"*Bueno*, Pawnee," said Dutch. "That's wolf-proof from above and on three sides. If we can't protect ourselves here, we might as well surrender."

True to his word, while supper was being prepared, Dutch went to the supply wagon where Christie Beckwith had been confined. He peered in through the canvas pucker and found her looking at him.

"Now that you're feeling better," he said, "I reckoned I'd stop by and talk a spell."

"There's room for you in here, unless you're afraid of me."

"I'm not afraid of you," he said.

"Then come in here with me," she said angrily. "Show the rest of them you still consider me human. That is, if you do."

With a sigh, he climbed in over the wagon's tailgate.

"I don't know that we have anything more to talk about," she said. "I've already told you I'm sorry, that my life's been a mistake. I suppose I can show you my wound.''

She flung back the blanket, and she was still naked beneath it. She laughed bitterly.

"It all looked better before it was clawed," she said, "but there was so little left, I suppose it doesn't matter. You and me never got this far before."

Dutch said nothing. Stepping over the wagon's tailgate, he dropped to the ground and returned to the supper fire.

CHAPTER 19

*D*utch continued sending Pawnee ahead each day, and just when it seemed there was nothing else that could go wrong, the Indian reported riders from the south.

"*Indios?*" Dutch asked.

Pawnee shook his head, holding up both hands, fingers spread. He then raised his left hand, extending three fingers.

"I don't like the sound of this," said Hugh McCulloch. "It could be Plummer men."

"We'll remain where we are until we know what their business is," Dutch said. "While we're givin' 'em the benefit of the doubt, we'll keep our weapons ready."

The thirteen men reined up well out of rifle range, and the lead rider hailed the camp.

"We're from the Bonanza diggings, to the south. Are we welcome?"

"That depends on your purpose for being here," Dutch shouted. "A couple of you are welcome to ride in and talk. The rest of you stay where you are, until we know why you're here."

Two of the men rode forward, reining up a few yards away. The rider who had hailed the camp spoke. "We hear by way of Virginia City that your wagons are loaded with trade goods. We want to be sure you don't pass us by."

"Sorry," said Dutch, "we're bound for the Bitterroot."

"We'll pay a fair price for anything we take," the rider persisted.

"I don't own this freight," said Dutch. "This is Haskel Collins, and we're hauling for him. Collins?"

"That's correct," Collins said. "We're bound for the Bitterroot."

"Well, that don't strike us as fair," the stranger persisted. "We're as entitled to them goods as that bunch on the Bitterroot. Our boys ain't goin' to like this."

"That's how it is," Dutch said. "We contracted to deliver this freight to the Bitterroot diggings, and unless Collins changes his mind, that's where it's going."

"I'm not changing my mind," said Collins. "We're going to the Bitterroot."

"My name is Emil Hankins," the stranger said, "and I'm talkin' for near three hundred miners. It's a far piece to the Bitterroot, an' this ain't over."

He and his companion joined the eleven men who waited, and they all rode back the way they had come.

"Well, by God," said Hugh McCulloch, "I've never seen hombres with so much gall. Is the frontier so uncivilized that a mob can tell a man what he can and can't do with his own goods?"

"I hope all the miners in this Montana Territory ain't of the same mind as these was," Whit Sanderson said. "We'll spend more time fightin' the civilized whites than fightin' the uncivilized Indians."

"A regrettable situation," said Collins. "It's enough to set me to reconsidering my plan to contract for more goods."

"It's not going to change our plans for hauling to the diggings," Dutch said. "We've contracted with you to take these wagons to the Bitterroot, and that's where they're going. If we have to shoot some varmints to live up to our end of the deal, then so be it."

They took the trail again, watchful lest the miners return. Pawnee ranged far ahead, his eyes to the south, more aware than ever of their need for a secure camp. While much of the territory was mountainous, it wasn't always possible to find a walled location with a single entrance. Dutch continued to post four sentries in three-hour watches, but there was no further trouble.

"Siringo," said Collins, one night after supper, "I've been thinking about this situation involving the Bonanza diggings. It seems to me that, with enough wagons, we could freight in goods to more than one camp at a time."

"Maybe," Dutch said. "How many camps are we talking about?"

"Perhaps a dozen," said Collins.

"Sixty wagons, then, figurin' five to a camp."

"Why not?" Collins said. "That's roughly a thousand dollars for each wagon, teams, and harness. That's sixty thousand. Another sixty thousand would cover the freight. I'd say a hundred and twenty thousand."

"A hundred and fifty thousand," said Dutch.

"How so?"

"For starters," Dutch said, "you'll need at least two wagons—maybe three—to carry grain for the horses and mules and grub for the outfit. While you won't need outriders for every wagon, I'd say you'll need an armed force of maybe forty fighting men. The Bozeman Trail is nothing like the Sante Fe or Oregon trails, which are mostly broad enough to travel three or four wagons abreast. On the Bozeman, and over most of Montana Territory the best you can do is one wagon behind the other. With sixty wagons, they'll be strung out for more than a mile, and the Sioux could strike any one of those wagons. I believe a mule remuda and a pair of wranglers will be necessary too. We've been almighty lucky, not losing any mules. In winter, with so many mules, you'd almost have to devote an entire wagon just to hauling grain."

"I haven't considered all that," said Collins. "I suppose there's such a thing as biting off more than one can chew."

"I think so," Dutch said. "Another thing to consider is

that, with many wagons, you'll not be able to take shelter in arroyos and beneath overhangs, as we have done. The best you'll be able to do is circle the wagons and erect canvas against rain, wind, and snow."

"God," said Jules Swenson, "I don't want no part of that train."

"Me, neither," Brace Weaver said. "I even had my doubts about this High Plains with snow and ice, but I got to admit it ain't been all that bad. We've had decent shelter durin' the storms, good grub, hot coffee, and warm fires."

"We could of done without that three-day visit from the Crows, and all that attention from the wolves," Rusty Karnes said, "but I got no complaints."

"We wasn't with you on the Bozeman," said Julius Blackburn, "but it appears you've overcome many of the hardships on the trail."

"Mostly we rely on common sense," Dutch said. "It's foolish to take the trail when you know mud or snow will bog the wagons down to the wheel hubs. You're better off to wait it out, allowing your teams to rest."

"Since there is no place to unload this freight," said McCulloch, "may I suggest what might be a solution?"

"Please do," Collins replied.

"Sell it right off the wagons, to the highest bidder," said McCulloch. "I'll venture you can empty the wagons in a day. Two, at most."

"Hugh," Dutch said, "that might be the answer. Not just this time, but for other times as well."

"I heartily agree," said Haskel Collins. "Perhaps word will get around to the other camps and there'll be some competition."

"That might be what it'll take to defuse Emil Hankins and his bunch from Bonanza," Dutch said. "Let them compete against one another for gold, instead of coming after us with guns."

"That Sioux that carried word of us back to Virginia City done us a big favor," said Cass Carlyle. "Next time, we ought to send a rider to all the gold camps, tellin' 'em we're on the way, that ever'thing's for sale to the highest bidder.''

"That'd give 'em all time to get together and bushwhack us," Jules Swenson said.

"I reckon we'd better play out this hand," said Dutch, "before we bet our roll on the next one."

It had been the most civil and productive discussion they'd had since leaving Kansas City, and Dutch found himself feeling better about the disposition of the freight, once they reached the Bitterroot. Christie Beckwith eyed Haskel Collins with more confidence, and it seemed that Collins was a little more sure of himself. Tally Slaughter, Cass Carlyle, Jules Swenson, and Brace Weaver had the first watch. The rest of the outfit took to their bedrolls and blankets.

"Dutch," Bonita whispered, "are you asleep?"

"Yes," said Dutch.

"Then I won't wake you," she whispered back.

"Damn it, what do you want?"

"I'm glad all of you talked tonight. It's what Christie's been wanting."

"I reckon it cleared the air some," said Dutch.

Breakfast was done and the men were harnessing their teams, when Rusty Karnes made a startling discovery.

"Some varmint's tampered with my wagon," he shouted.

Someone had, indeed. There was a sifting of sugar on the ground, and when Rusty bumped the underside of the wagon, more followed.

"Damn Crows," Tally Slaughter said, "but how did they know where to cut the hole?"

"I don't know," said Dutch. "Never underestimate an Indian, when it comes to stealing something. We'd better have a look at the rest of the wagons."

But none of the other wagons had been bothered. While

Haskel Collins wasn't pleased, he wasn't nearly as disturbed as Pawnee. He acted as though he was personally responsible for another Indian having successfully pilfered one of the wagons while he slept. Leading his horse, he set out to track the culprit.

"That's the first time I've ever had that happen," said Dutch. "Of course, this is the first time I've been in Crow country. Sorry, Collins. We'll just have to keep a closer watch on the wagons. When we return to Kansas City, I reckon we'll have to line our wagon beds with tin."

They were two hours into the day, when Pawnee returned, looking more mortified than ever. Obviously he had lost the trail. Without a word or a look, he rode out ahead of the wagons, bent on his usual scouting mission.

"He's acting like it was all his fault," said Bonita.

"If it had been anybody but another Indian, it wouldn't bother him so bad," Dutch replied. "It's likely there was only one Indian, since none of the other wagons were disturbed."

To his credit, Pawnee located a secluded, protected site near a spring, and directed the wagons to it. As a precaution, Pawnee rode out several miles, and circling the camp, it was he who spotted the lone rider on the back trail. He watched long enough to learn that the stranger was an Indian. Resisting an urge to kill and scalp the newcomer, Pawnee rode back and reported to Dutch Siringo.

"*Uno Indio*," said Pawnee, pointing along their back trail. "*Matar?*"

Dutch shook his head. There was no point in killing a lone Indian, even if he had taken a little sugar from one of the wagons. Besides, they had no proof. They all waited until the stranger rode in, Pawnee with a grim set to his jaw, and the Bowie in his hand. The newcomer rode hunched over, a blanket draped over his bony frame to partially protect him from the chill wind. There was no sign of a weapon except a bow that had been shoved down into a quiver of feathered arrows. He didn't look like any of the

Crows, and the teamsters quickly learned the reason. He spoke. "Sioux. Grande Oso."

Dutch had his hand on Pawnee's shoulder and had to physically restrain the young Indian. Dutch nodded, and the Sioux slid off his horse, his eyes never leaving Pawnee. He again spoke, and the single word came as a question.

"Whiskey?"

"No whiskey," said Dutch, shaking his head.

"Eat?" he asked, trying a different approach.

"*Si*," Dutch said. "Eat."

"By God," said Gus Pryor, "it's that same drunken, no-account Sioux that's always in Virginia City, swappin' trail gossip for whiskey. I've never seen the varmint, but this has got to be him."

Silently, Bonita offered Big Bear a tin cup of coffee, which the Sioux accepted. Supper was in the making, and Big Bear hunkered down, sipping his coffee. While he appeared at ease, he never once took his eyes off Pawnee. While Pawnee did nothing to aggravate the situation, he clearly was ready to finish anything the Sioux might start. They warily eyed one another like a pair of hostile hounds, neither quite sure of the other's intention. Dutch hadn't needed to speak a word, for his outfit had enough Indian savvy to be prepared for whatever might ensue. Tally Slaughter and Rusty Karnes stood with thumbs hooked over their pistol belts. While their readiness might have been overlooked by Pawnee, Big Bear was very much aware of it. A leather thong about his neck suggested that he had a Bowie down the back of his shirt, but he made no hostile move. Slowly Pawnee relaxed, knowing that if he remained with these white men, he must adopt some of their less-than-desirable customs. He could ill-afford to kill and scalp an enemy who chose not to fight, but who squatted before the fire like an old squaw of many winters.

"They'll fight, if that Sioux don't move on," said Brace Weaver.

"Won't do him much good," Tally Slaughter said.

"Pawnee will likely follow, and the fight will take place somewhere on the plains."

"That mustn't happen," said Bonita. "Pawnee could be killed."

"He's aware of that," Dutch said, "but I don't think he'll force the Sioux into a fight, if Big Bear's unwilling."

"Big Bear may not be unwilling for long," said Drago Peeler. "Even a renegade Sioux has some pride, and to be thought a coward by a Pawnee half his age ain't goin' to set well with him. If Big Bear stays the night, they're goin' to have at it, and it'll be with Bowies. It ain't for anybody with a weak stomach."

"My God," Christie whispered in Haskel Collins's ear, "the young Indian saved me from the wolves. This is so foolish. Must they fight?"

"It's a barbaric custom," Collins replied, "but I think we'll allow Siringo to decide how deeply he wishes to become involved."

Finally, supper was ready, and hostilities were set aside. Whit Sanderson had taken it upon himself to help Bonita, not because she required it, but to purposely separate Pawnee from Big Bear. Whit served the Sioux his supper, while Bonita fed Pawnee from another fire. The Sioux was more courteous than the Crow, accepting what was offered without demanding seconds. Whit brought him a second helping and refilled his tin cup with coffee.

"We have a secure camp," said Dutch, as he spoke with the men in the outfit, "but I want double sentries for tonight and for as long as that Sioux remains with us."

"You're expectin' trouble, then," Brace Weaver said.

"I don't know what I'm expecting," said Dutch. "I just don't believe this Sioux has any fondness for whites, and with that in mind, I'm suspicious. I can't imagine Big Bear staying beyond breakfast in the morning. He's already a long way from Sioux country, and if he takes the trail with us, he'll be going even farther."

"He's likely worn out his welcome in Virginia City,"

Hugh McCulloch said. "When he got likkered-up and started talkin' about wagons on the Bozeman, it didn't take us long to decide that Plummer's gang was after more than just our gold. By the time they caught up to us, we'd joined your outfit, and everything went sour for them. They lost out on the gold they expected to take from us and found you with seventeen fighting men standing between them and the wagons. Big Bear will get the blame for having spilled the beans, and that could account for his sudden decision to travel west."

"It could," Dutch agreed, "but that won't mean doodly to Pawnee. Big Bear is still a Sioux, and the Sioux is still the enemy."

The following morning, following breakfast, Big Bear made it obvious he hadn't the slightest intention of leaving Siringo's outfit. Ignoring the hated Sioux, Pawnee rode out in his customary quest for water and a secure camp, and when the wagons again took the trail, Big Bear joined the outriders.

"He's going with us," said Bonita, standing on the wagon box so that she might see the back trail.

"Damn it," Dutch said, "I was afraid of that. I reckon McCulloch put his finger on it, when he suggested that Big Bear is avoiding Plummer and his outlaws."

"In a way, I feel sorry for Big Bear," said Bonita, "but why couldn't he be something other than a Sioux? If he was a Crow, Pawnee might not see him as an enemy."

"Hell, if he was a Crow," Dutch said, "we couldn't afford to feed him."

"Drago says Pawnee and Big Bear are going to fight. Suppose they do?"

"Let them, I reckon," said Dutch. "If they're hell-bent on a fight, let them have it and be done with it. I can't see that it would help if I ran them off and they went out on the plains and whittled on one another with their Bowies, can you?"

"No," she said. "I just wish it . . . didn't have to be this way."

"But it does," said Dutch. "Pawnee is walking a thin line between savagery and civilization, and he must go one way or the other. If he kills without specific cause, riding the old trails, pursuing tribal hatreds, then we've lost him. If he is to ride the other trail, then he must learn that a man with strong enough medicine doesn't have to kill in the name of the old ones whose deaths he seeks to avenge."

"I've often wondered what he thought," said Bonita, "when you spared the lives of the Crows who stole our horses and mules. Surely he realizes you could have killed them all."

"He knows," Dutch said. "That's one of the reasons I had him riding with us, when we raised hell in that Crow camp. I wanted him to understand two things. The first, that a raid on an Indian camp should have some purpose, other than a bloody attempt to right old wrongs. We went after the Crows because they had taken our horses and mules, and for no other reason. The second lesson I hoped he would learn is that there's more honor and strength in sparing a man's life than in killing him. I have no way of knowing, but I believe it's a lesson the Crows learned. Nothing humbles a man—if he *is* a man—like knowing he's alive because another man was strong enough to spare his life."

"You talk like a preacher I once heard," Bonita said, "but he was a lot older than you. Where . . . how . . . did you come to understand so much?"

"When I came west," said Dutch, "I was just a kid, big for my age, who had almost never had enough to eat. But I had one hell of an advantage. While I was dumb as a corral post in a lot of ways, I knew it. I listened to old-timers who had been over the mountain, I asked questions, and I learned. I learned to use my fists on the streets of Cincinnati, and I mastered the Bowie, the Colt, and the Henry rifle on the frontier. I'll fight when there's no other way, but I've never hurt or killed a man who didn't force me to.''

"I hope Pawnee has learned from you," said Bonita, "if only just a little."

"I reckon we're goin' to find out," Dutch said. "As long as he has a killing hatred for the Sioux, and there's one right under his nose, the lid could blow off anytime."

And it did. That very day, after supper . . .

Pawnee and Big Bear eyed one another across the supper fire, and as Drago Peeler had predicted, it seemed that if the Sioux remained, the two must clash. While Dutch could have intervened, he had not, nor did he intend to. While he might have driven the homeless Sioux away, he could have done nothing to prevent Pawnee from following. Instead, it had become a trial in which Pawnee would accept or reject a measure of civilization. It was a decision the young Indian must make for himself. In a deft movement, the Sioux drew his Bowie by its thong from down the back of his buckskin shirt. He began border-shifting the formidable weapon from hand-to-hand, his eyes never leaving Pawnee. Not to be outdone, Pawnee drew his own Bowie, matching Bear's hand-to-hand movement. There wasn't a sound except the crackle of the fire and the sigh of the wind, and it seemed that death hovered over that isolated camp on the High Plains. As though obeying a simultaneous order that only they could hear, the antagonists sprang to their feet and circled the fire. Big Bear made the first move, slashing empty air with his Bowie, as Pawnee back stepped.

"*Cobarde*," Big Bear hissed. "*Perro*."*

Pawnee ignored the insult, responding with a thrust of his own weapon. It slashed the right sleeve of Big Bear's buckskin shirt from elbow-to-wrist, drawing blood. In his fury, the Sioux lunged. It was the perfect opportunity for a death thrust, but Pawnee ignored it. Instead, he did a

---

* Coward. Dog.

strange thing. Stepping aside, he tripped the Sioux, and Big Bear plunged belly-down into the fire. He rolled free and bounded to his feet, but not without damage to his dignity and some obvious burns. He paused, seeking to control his fury, while his adversary waited. Pawnee's attitude itself had become a weapon, an insult, and he used it to the fullest advantage. It said that he was more than a match for the Sioux, that Big Bear needed an edge.

"By God," said Tally Slaughter quietly, "he's playin' with the Sioux."

Nobody was more aware of that than Big Bear, and his slash with the Bowie would have beheaded Pawnee, had it connected. But Pawnee had countered with a move of his own, and the flat of his Bowie struck Big Bear's wrist a numbing blow, causing him to drop his weapon. It could have—should have—been the end, but Pawnee didn't pursue his obvious advantage. Clearly, Big Bear would have preferred to die, as opposed to having had his life spared by a hated enemy, but he had little choice. Seizing the big Bowie, he again came after Pawnee. But Pawnee had grown tired of the conflict, and with his left hand he caught Big Bear's right wrist. Driving a knee into the Sioux's groin, they went down, Pawnee on top. In his agony, Big Bear had dropped his Bowie and was unarmed. He expected death, welcomed it, for Pawnee's blade was at his throat.

"Please, God," Bonita whispered, "don't let him do it."

It was a plea that echoed the unspoken feelings of Dutch Siringo and all of those who had become fond of the young Indian. For a few heartbeats, Big Bear's life hung in the balance. Then slowly—almost as though he regretted it—Pawnee got to his feet, shoving the big Bowie beneath his waistband. It was the most difficult thing he had ever done, sparing the life of a hated Sioux, enemy of his people. He vanished into the darkness, only wishing to be alone with his conflicting emotions. Big Bear took his Bowie, got to his feet, and mounted his spotted pony. He then rode away, back the way he had come, toward the traditional land of the Sioux.

"That was truly a noble act," said Haskel Collins.

"I've never seen the equal of it," Drago Peeler said, "an' I can't talk about it, 'cause nobody but us that seen it would ever believe it."

"That young Indian has judgment and compassion," said Hugh McCulloch, "something lacking in some white men I have known. It would be a mistake not to have him with us, if only as a scout."

"I expect him to become much more than that," Dutch said. "He's already mastered the Henry rifle, and I aim to teach him to draw that Colt in a hurry and to hit what he's shootin' at. As for the Bowie, when he learns a few more words, I'm hopin' he'll teach me just half of what he knows."

It was the kind of humor they could appreciate. Dutch was elated, and volunteered for the first watch. To nobody's surprise, Bonita joined him. The others took to their bedrolls to get what sleep they could.

"Where could Pawnee have gone?" Bonita wondered.

"I expect he's doing some thinking," said Dutch. "What he did tonight seemed sensible to us, but probably not to him. I reckon he feels like he's forsaken his heritage and all the teachings of the old ones."

"Somehow, we must tell him he did the right thing," Bonita said, "that we're proud of him."

"I reckon he'd find that embarrassing," said Dutch. "What he's done is contrary to his nature, and it'll take some time for him to get used to it. We won't act any different toward him, allowing him to adapt as he becomes more confident."

"I can't tell him," Bonita said, "but I can tell you. I'm proud of him for what he did, and I'm proud of you for believing in him."

On the plains, Pawnee sat with his back to a stone. He faced the east, the direction in which Big Bear had ridden.

The Sioux had been at his mercy, and he knew not what had stayed his hand. Something had touched him, and despite a superstitious nature, he didn't fear it. He only wanted to understand. While there was some guilt for having spared the life of a hated Sioux, there was something stronger. He had held his enemy's life in his own hands, a thing the Sioux would never forget, for he would live within the shadow of a man who had bested him in battle. While it was much like counting coup, it was immensely more satisfying, and he again recalled that night Dutch Siringo had spared the Crows. With a measure of satisfaction, he got to his feet and made his way back to the sleeping camp.

At dawn, Pawnee rode out in search of water as well as shelter, for yet another storm was building. The wind already had a chill to it, detracting from the warmth of the rising sun, as a band of dirty gray clouds marched in from the west.

"I had hoped we might reach the Bitterroot before another storm immobilized us," said Haskel Collins. In the buckboard, he and Christie trailed Dutch's wagon.

"Maybe this will be the last one," Christie said. "We've done well, having good shelter as often as we have, and we owe it all to the Indian."

"I quite agree," said Collins. "All the more reason to enlist Siringo and his outfit for future delivery from Kansas City. Believe me, I have come to appreciate Siringo's ability to influence others to do his bidding. I'm sorry to say that I was highly critical of him when he brought in the wounded Indian. I have concluded that, rather than criticizing the man, I should keep my mouth shut and learn from him."

Christie laughed. "That's what I like most about you. You're honest with yourself. And I'd have to agree with you, when it comes to Dutch Siringo. I've gone from hating him to admiring him, and I understand now why he wasn't satisfied to run a freighting outfit from Kansas City. He belongs on the frontier."

CHAPTER 20

⁓

The west wind grew colder, sweeping before it a mass of clouds that swiftly changed the blue sky to dirty gray. Stopping only to rest the teams, Dutch kept the wagons rolling, his eyes ever on the trail ahead for some sign of Pawnee. The Indian never wasted any time, particularly when a storm was brewing, but this morning he had been gone much longer than usual.

Pawnee had ridden well beyond the distance the *carretas* could travel before the storm and had failed to find water with adequate shelter. He had begun working his way back, a mile south of the trail the wagons would take. He had found no stream and had ventured into higher elevations in search of a spring. Eventually he came upon a canyon that was deep enough for shelter, and at the box end, there was a spring. Besides high rims, there were large pines growing around the spring, which gushed from beneath a wall of stone. Evidence of old fires was plentiful, but nobody had been there recently enough to have left tracks. Still Pawnee wasn't satisfied. He rode out the lower end of the canyon and back up along the rims, seeking tracks. He found none, but on the west rim, he found something even more ominous. There were two human skulls and a scattering of bones. Wolves and other predators had long since stripped away all flesh. Pawnee remained only long enough to de-

termine if there was any Indian sign—perhaps lance or arrow—but found none. He wheeled his horse and galloped
back to inform Dutch Siringo of his discovery. While there
was a language barrier, the Indian had learned that Hugh
McCulloch and his companions had been pursued by
thieves—George Ives and his men—intent on killing them
and taking their gold. From what remained of their clothing,
it seemed that the duo who had died on the canyon rim had
also been miners, leading Pawnee to the conclusion that he
had found the bones of men who had been murdered for
their gold. Carefully he sought a way back to the trail by
which the *carretas* could reach the box canyon. From there,
he kicked his horse into a fast gallop, aware of the nearness
of the approaching storm.

"He must have discovered something of importance,"
said Dutch, for Pawnee was riding hard. He wheeled his
horse, trotting it alongside Dutch's wagon.

"*Malo?*" Dutch inquired.

"*Bueno cañon. Hueso. Malo.*"

With that, he rode on ahead, expecting them to follow
and draw their own conclusion.

"Good canyon I understood," said Bonita, "but what
was the rest?"

"Bones," Dutch replied, "and he considers that *malo*.
Bad."

"Perhaps it has to do with Indians."

"No," said Dutch. "He didn't mention Indians. This has
to do with whites."

Pawnee led them off their course almost a mile to the
south. The terrain was rough, but the Indian had found a
way around enormous boulders and across the shallow ends
of gullies. While this protective canyon was much like the
others, it was deep enough at the box end to prevent any
wolf attacks from above, a fact the teamsters were quick to
appreciate. Pawnee remained mounted, evidence that Dutch
needed a horse to accompany him.

"Jules," Dutch said, "I need to borrow your horse. Pawnee's found something he wants me to see. Tally, maybe you should come with us. The rest of you begin snaking in firewood.''

Tally and Dutch followed Pawnee back to the shallow end of the canyon and up along the west rim. The Indian reined up, allowing the scattering of human bones to speak for themselves. Dutch and Tally dismounted, and Dutch gathered up what remained of a sheepskin coat. Dutch poked his fingers through three holes in the back of the garment.

"That one was shot in the back," said Tally, "and I'd gamble the other got the same treatment."

"From their clothes and boots, I'd say they were miners," Dutch said. "This has all the earmarks of killings such as those McCulloch and his pards spoke of. These hombres may have struck it rich along the Bitterroot, only to lose it to thieves and killers when they tried to leave the diggings."

"It makes sense to me," Slaughter said. "You aim to bury them?"

"I reckon not," said Dutch. "The wolves can't do anything more to them, and we're in for a blue norther just any time. Let's get back to camp."

The wind whistled through the pines, bringing with it fine particles of snow that soon became a blinding torrent of white. Dutch waited until enough firewood had been snaked in before he told the others about the human bones on the canyon rim.

"I reckon all the boomtowns have a common problem," said Julius Blackburn. "Those unfortunate hombres were likely trying to escape the diggings with their gold. Instead, thieves and killers from the diggings followed them, murdered them, and took their gold."

"That brings us back to what I've already suggested," Hugh McCulloch said. "Why not offer protection and grub to miners wantin' to escape the diggings with their gold and their lives? It should be worth two hundred dollars a man."

"That's a mite expensive," said Brace Weaver. "We're returning to Kansas City, anyhow. Besides, they'd be a help, standin' off the Sioux on the Bozeman."

"The more I think about it," Dutch said, "the more I think Hugh's got something. I'd say there's not a miner in Montana Territory who wouldn't pay to escape the killers and thieves who would kill him for his gold. Those who aren't ready to leave this time would be prime candidates when we return."

"Sounds like good business," said Whit Sanderson, "but we ain't prepared to do more than feed ourselves from here back to Kansas City. That three-day visit from them Crows has ruint us, grub-wise."

"I might remind you that I have provisions for sale," Haskel Collins said. "I could be persuaded—for a modest profit—to part with enough provisions to make this proposal of Mr. McCulloch's possible."

The first reaction to Collins's bold proposal was anger, but almost imperceptibly, Dutch shook his head. Nobody spoke, allowing Dutch to respond.

"I reckon we'll accept your offer, Collins, but I'm expecting you to bear in mind that some things have changed. We'll be stuck in the diggings until you dispose of the freight in the wagons, and during this time, all of us and our stock have to eat."

"I assure you I will consider your every sacrifice," said Collins, "and let us not overlook my plans to return with you to Kansas City. Christie will be going with me, and I do not intend for either of us to go hungry. Before we reach the Bitterroot diggings, we will determine the needed provisions for our return to Kansas City. These provisions will then be removed to the supply wagon. Agreed?"

"Agreed," Dutch replied, "and at that time, we'll discuss the possibility of a new hauling venture."

It was a move none of them had expected, the result of

a surprising turnaround by Haskel Collins, and some of Dutch's longtime companions were openly resentful. Christie Beckwith was obviously pleased, but having known the men who had once driven for Beckwith, she sensed their discontent. In their eyes, Collins still hadn't proven himself. Christie caught Bonita's eye and believed the younger girl sympathized with her. After the storm, the Bitterroot diggings would be only a few days away. Somehow, before a decision had to be made, Dutch Siringo's men must be persuaded to follow Dutch's lead. Otherwise, Dutch would allow his loyalty to his pardners to crush any potential alliance with Collins, whatever the cost. The storm roared over the canyon, the vicious wind whipping in flurries of snow and causing the flames from the fires to leap in excitement.

"I reckon Bonita and me will take the first watch," Dutch said.

Bonita refilled a coffeepot and hung it over the fire, so the sentries would have their hot coffee during the night. When enough time had elapsed for the camp to be asleep, Bonita spoke. "I thought it was a good thing, your accepting Collins's offer. What's going to happen if the others don't agree with you?"

"Then there'll be no deal," said Dutch. "We're pardners. Collins got on the bad side of some of them, and he has yet to redeem himself. His offer tonight was fair, but still not enough to square him with the outfit."

"Then perhaps they should talk to Whit Sanderson," Bonita said. "He was right when he said we're in trouble, and it wasn't just the Crows eating everything in sight. Since you left Kansas City, you've had three more of us to feed. There's Christie, Pawnee, and me, and since two weeks ago, Mr. McCulloch and his friends. All eight of us will be returning to Kansas City, and there simply won't be enough food, if you refuse Collins's offer. There is no more whiskey or laudanum among our supplies, even for the rest of the way to the Bitterroot. That means traveling through Sioux country, along the Bozeman, without food or medicine."

"By God," Dutch said, "you got it all figured out, ain't you?"

"It didn't take much figuring," she replied. "It's got Whit worried."

"And you," said Dutch.

"Yes," she admitted. "I know Haskel Collins has often been less than he should be, and there have been times when I hated him, myself. But people can change. I did, and I know Christie has. Why not Collins?"

Dutch laughed. "If I'm ever on trial for my life, I want you handling my defense. I'll talk to the rest of the outfit, and I'll ask Whit to do his share. You're right. We're dead center between a rock and a hard place, and Collins is offerin' us a way out."

The storm roared for another day and night. Dutch quietly enlisted Whit Sanderson in his effort to convince the others of their need to accept Haskel Collins's offer. Jules Swenson was an easy convert who quickly won over Brace Weaver. Rusty Karnes and Cass Carlyle, faced with Whit Sanderson's logic, made it unanimous. Nothing negative had been said to Collins, and Bonita passed the good news to Christie.

"Thank you," said Christie. "He . . . Haskel . . . realizes he's made some bad moves, that some of the men don't like him, and he's really trying to make amends. He knows that the sacrifices Dutch has made have been for the good of us all. What he tried to do tonight is to help without seeming to, without creating hard feelings."

Western Montana Territory. March 1, 1864.

Waiting out the storm, Dutch and Whit spent some time in the supply wagon, weighing their remaining provisions against the many days it would take them to return to Kansas City.

"Twelve more days, and we'll have been on the trail six months," said Whit. "Now we know that sixth wagon should have been loaded with nothin' but grub for us, and grain for the horses and mules."

"I reckon that explains why nobody fought us for the privilege of freighting into the High Plains in winter," Dutch said. "The layovers cost us, and having to buy provisions from Collins for the return trip will eat into our profit."

"Maybe not," said Whit. "McCulloch has been talkin' to them pards of his, and they're plannin' to put up two hundred dollars a man, in return for travelin' with us. That's a full thousand dollars, and there may be more miners wantin' to leave the diggings, without having to fight for their lives and their gold. When you think about it, two hundred ain't a lot to pay for grub and a company of fighting men to see you along the Bozeman, through Sioux country."

"You're right," Dutch conceded. "We owe McCulloch for that. If freighting's goin' to pay, there almost has to be a return load. In our case, instead of freight, it'll be miners paying for passage out of the territory."

"That's workin' in Collins's favor, where Brace, Jules, Rusty, and Cass are concerned," said Whit. "If it wasn't for Collins offerin' us grub from his freight, we wouldn't be able to feed even ourselves, when we leave the territory. If he don't do nothin' stupid from here on, he'll be in solid. For Miss Christie's sake, I hope he turns out as solid as he's appearin' to be."

"I think he's got the makings of a man," Dutch replied, "but his daddy's got money, and that's a handicap. From what he told us, he's thirty years old, and this is the first time he's stepped out of his old man's shadow. For his sake, I hope he stays away from St. Louis and repays any money his daddy's loaned him."

The elder Collins and his holdings in St. Louis had become the subject of more than one conversation between Haskel Collins and Christie Beckwith. Following Collins's offer to sell provisions to Dutch Siringo, Christie was more and more sure there would be a working alliance between Siringo and Collins. Thus she felt more confident when she again spoke to Collins about St. Louis.

"Since you're going to be freighting more and more goods west," said Christie, "you'll be working out of Kansas City instead of St. Louis, won't you?"

"Yes," Collins said, "but I'll be seeing my father occasionally. Does that bother you?"

"Some," she admitted. "I have the feeling he'll be expecting better of you than . . . me."

"I'm past thirty," said Collins irritably. "Don't you think I'm man enough to make my own decisions, to override my father's wishes?"

"Yes," she replied, in a small voice. "I'm just uncertain . . ."

"You have a low opinion of yourself," said Collins, "and you're allowing that to cloud what you expect others to think of you. While I know all about you, must you confess your past to everyone else? My father won't know anything more about you than what one of us tells him, and I plan to tell him virtually nothing. Now for God's sake, stop creating problems where there are none."

He said no more, for he had raised his voice, and Bonita was watching. It was for Bonita's benefit that Christie tried to smile, but doubts still plagued her.

Sometime during the third night after it had begun, the snow ceased, but the wind continued to howl, and the cold seemed more intense than ever. Fighting boredom, men cleaned and oiled weapons that had already been cleaned and oiled. A blanket about his shoulders, Pawnee sat hunched over, sleeping or appearing to. Christie and Bonita spent considerable time in the two-thirds-empty supply wagon during daylight hours. Darkness brought them all near the roaring fires, as the howling wind united with the howling of distant wolves.

"What's that I hear?" Cass Carlyle asked, as they sat around the breakfast fire.

"Nothin'," said Rusty Karnes. "The wind ain't even blowin'."

"Hell," Cass said, "that's what I mean. When the wind howls for three straight days and nights, ain't that a beautiful sound, when all of a sudden it's gone?"

"I think the little varmint's losin' it," said Jules Swenson, loud enough for everybody to hear.

They laughed, but they all understood Cass Carlyle's feelings. On the High Plains, the wind was like a thing alive, rarely ever calm. When they stepped out of the canyon where they could see the sky, it was so blue it almost hurt their eyes. There was not a cloud in sight. On the eastern horizon was the golden glow of the rising sun.

"I got me a feelin'," said Whit Sanderson. "This here was the last storm between us and the Bitterroot. The next ring-tailed blue norther that blows in, we'll have the varmint at our backs, on our way to the Bozeman."

"I think tomorrow we'll move out," Dutch said. "There'll be mud as the snow melts, but we'll keep as much to the ridges as we can."

It was solid thinking, for much of the prairie was hard, with stone outcroppings. The earth hadn't frozen, and while there would be mud with the melting of the snow, it would not bog the wagons down if they avoided low places.

The dawn again broke clear and mild, and as had become his custom, Pawnee rode west. There would be little need for shelter from the elements, but the Indian rode warily, looking for sign. They were bound for a white man's village, and had not the whites killed two of their own kind back on the canyon rim? When Pawnee found water, it was a spring at the base of a towering butte. It was a magnificent thing, a monument, and Pawnee rode around it. While the face of it was virtually straight up, it sloped back to the west, shot full of ravines and tumbled-down stone. For no reason other than the prodding of his Indian nature, Pawnee dismounted and began the climb to the top. He knew not what he expected to see. He yielded to a caution that was centuries old, as had his brothers, for he—as they—knew not whence the enemy might come. He continued until he reached the uppermost tip of the butte, a finger of solid stone, and stood there in awe.

"*Grande Espiritu*," he whispered.*

Far to the west rose a thin tendril of smoke. Pawnee closed his eyes for a moment, opened them, and looked again. The smoke was still there, within the path the *carretas* traveled. Could it not be the very camp they were seeking? Facing the east, shading his eyes with his hand, he tried to find the slow-moving wagons. While the terrain was such that he could not see them, he could see occasional ridges that rose above the prairie, and it was on the westward slope of a ridge that he saw the riders. At first he thought his eyes were deceiving him, but when he looked again, the tiny figures were still there. Even as he watched, they descended a ridge and were lost to his view. He had lost them just as suddenly as he had discovered them, and while he hadn't been able to count them, he was sure of two things: There was an alarming number of them, and they were trailing Dutch Siringo's outfit. Scrambling down the rugged butte to his horse, Pawnee kicked the animal into a fast gallop, riding to meet the oncoming wagons. When Dutch saw Pawnee coming, riding hard, he reined up. The other teamsters drove in as close as they could, the outriders following. Haskel Collins helped Christie down from the buckboard. Pawnee summed it up quickly.

* Great Spirit.

"*Humo*," he said, pointing west. He then pointed east. "*Mucho hombres.*"

"Smoke to the west and riders on our back trail," said Dutch. "Dent, Levan, Drago, and Tally, you'll ride with me. Hugh, pick two men and join us."

"Blackburn and Robb," said McCulloch.

Mounted on Whit Sanderson's horse, Dutch pointed to Pawnee and then to the east. The Indian led out at a fast gallop, Dutch and the seven other riders following. Riding for what Dutch considered ten miles, they reined up to rest the horses. Instead of mounting and riding on, Pawnee led his horse toward the crest of a ridge, drawing up behind some brush. Dutch and the rest of the men followed, and by then they could see the oncoming riders, half a mile distant.

"My God," said Tally Slaughter, "there must be thirty of 'em, and they're all leadin' pack mules."

"Yeah," Drago Peeler said. "A hombre don't have to be too smart to figure out their reason for trailin' us."

"By God," said Hugh McCulloch, "there's Emil Hankins, that varmint from Bonanza diggings."

"We're going to challenge them," Dutch said. "We'll all have our weapons ready, but no shooting unless they start it."

Waiting until the riders were not quite within rifle range, Dutch challenged them.

"That's far enough, Hankins. Unless you can come up with a damn good reason for hangin' on our back trail, the lot of you are going to turn around and ride back the way you came."

"We got all the reason we need," Hankins shouted back. "When you open up all them wagons at the Bitterroot diggings, we aim to be there with our gold and our pack mules, to claim as much as we can. We ain't breakin' no law, and you got no right to threaten us. Now you just turn around and hustle back the way you come. We'll be seein' you at the Bitterroot diggings."

Laughing uproariously, they slapped their thighs with their hats. Dutch's companions had fury in their eyes and fingers on their triggers, but Dutch shook his head. Silently he mounted his horse and rode west, the others following. Nobody spoke until they reached the waiting wagons. Explaining what had happened, Dutch was greeted with shouts of anger and disbelief.

"Damn it," said Brace Weaver, "I don't believe 'em. They aim to catch us off guard, bushwhack us, and take the wagons."

"I don't think so," Dutch said. "We know they're there, and we're not letting down our guard for a minute. In fact, we'll double—even triple—the guard, from here on to the Bitterroot."

"*Humo*," said Pawnee. Pointing west, he raised his left hand, spreading the fingers.

"Another five miles to water," said Dutch, "and Pawnee's discovered something. Let's get there while we have some daylight."

"I hope he ain't found another pile of bones," Tally Slaughter said. "Seein' too much of that can play hell with a man's nerves."

They pushed on, reaching the towering butte with more than enough time to see what Pawnee wished to show them. He pointed west and then to the top of the butte.

"He's seen smoke from the top of the butte," said Dutch. "I reckon some of us ought to climb up there and have a look."

"I'm game," Rusty Karnes said, "if the back ain't quite as steep as the front. Hell, it's straight up."

"The rest of you set up camp," said Dutch. "Rusty and me will go have a look at the smoke Pawnee saw from the top of this butte."

Pawnee rode out, followed by Dutch and Rusty. Dismounting, the three of them began the torturous climb to the top of the butte. There was no conversation, for they needed all their wind for the task at hand. A stone rolled under Rusty's boot, and he would have fallen had Pawnee not seized his arm. When they finally reached the top, the Indian looked upon Dutch and Rusty with some amusement, as they fought to catch their wind. With his hand, Pawnee shaded his eyes against the westering sun, but the smoke that had so excited him was no longer there. Dutch and Rusty grinned at the look of frustration on Pawnee's face.

"We'll just set here a while," Dutch said. "If Pawnee could see smoke, then we ought to be close enough to see some fire, once it begins to get dark."

"God, I wish I'd wore my coat," said Rusty, as the wind became chill. "I didn't need it on the way up, but I could use it now."

Pawnee said nothing, his eyes on the western sky. These men didn't doubt that he had seen smoke, and with the darkness there would be distant fire. Dutch allowed his eyes to roam the sky to the east. He had no doubt that Emil Hankins and his bunch were back there somewhere, and locating their supper fire would give him some idea as to just how far along the back trail they were. He wanted them no closer. The sun finally sank below the western horizon, and as though by magic, the first stars appeared. Suddenly Pawnee touched Dutch's arm, pointing toward the west. At first Dutch saw nothing, and when his eyes finally caught a tiny point of light, it immediately vanished.

"By God," Rusty Karnes shouted excitedly, "there it is. Somebody's fire."

It took Dutch a moment to find it, and then he lost it. Just as suddenly, it appeared again, brighter. He said nothing, his eyes searching the distant darkness, until he could see no less than half a dozen tiny points of light.

"That's got to be the diggings along the Bitterroot," said Rusty. "How far away, do you reckon?"

"A good thirty-five to forty miles," Dutch replied.

"Damn," said Rusty, "we should have brought Collins up here with us. He's been here before."

"He couldn't be any more sure of it than we are," said Dutch. "Now let's have a look along our back trail."

But try as they might, there was no telltale glow anywhere on the darkened prairie to the east.

"They're in some arroyo," Rusty said, "but the varmints are back there."

Once more, Pawnee touched Dutch's arm, pointing toward the west. There were many more points of light.

"*Bueno*," said Dutch. "*Bueno*."

"We'd better be gettin' back to camp," Rusty said. "They'll be thinkin' something's happened to us."

Stumbling down the hazardous slope, starlight less than adequate for their descent, Dutch slipped and fell. His head struck a stone, and for a few moments, he was unable to rise. Rusty helped him to his feet and they continued until they reached the bottom. There they mounted their horses and returned to camp. Sufficient firewood had been snaked in, and the supper fires had been started.

"We was startin' to wonder about you," Whit Sanderson said.

"We couldn't locate the smoke Pawnee had seen," said Dutch, "so we waited for dark. I'm confident that we saw the supper fires in the diggings along the Bitterroot."

"How far?" Haskel Collins asked.

"I figure thirty-five to forty miles," said Dutch.

There was shouting and laughter that almost spooked the horses and mules. It was Hugh McCulloch who asked a somber question.

"What about Emil Hankins and his bunch? Were you able to see their supper fire?"

"No," Dutch replied, "and we looked. I wanted to know how far behind us they are. I suspect they're holed up in an arroyo, so we can't see their fire."

"We know they're trailing us," said Brace Weaver. "Why would they care whether we can see their fire or not?"

"I don't know," Dutch replied. "That's why we'll be posting a double guard from here on to the Bitterroot."

CHAPTER 21

∿

*T*he night passed uneventfully, and there seemed to be no need for extra sentries. At dawn, Pawnee again rode west, and there was excitement among the outfit in anticipation of their nearing the Bitterroots. While there were some clouds far to the west, the wind was mild and the sun rose in a blue sky.

"My God," Whit Sanderson shouted, when they had stopped to rest the teams, "look over yonder."

The little patch of green proved to be shoots of grass, and after months of almost continuous snow, it could only be a sign of early spring.

"We could be drivin' south along the Bozeman over green grass," said Rusty Karnes.

Brace Weaver laughed. "Don't get too excited. This is the High Plains. There could be a foot of snow over that green grass."

Pawnee located water for the night's camp and rode back to meet the wagons. While there appeared to be nothing they could do about the many riders pursuing them, Pawnee was uneasy. The wagons reached water with daylight to spare, and when the teams had been unharnessed, the men began snaking in firewood. Christie had taken to helping Bonita with the meals, and supper was soon underway.

"Pawnee's gone," Bonita said.

"He'll be back," said Dutch. "He knows it's supper-time."

Pawnee had taken his horse and slipped away, seeking to learn how near were the many riders who pursued Siringo's outfit. Taking his time, he rode north, for he wouldn't be able to approach the camp until after dark. Sighting the glow from their distant fire, he dismounted and tied his horse, for they were downwind from him. There would be no moon until much later, and by starlight Pawnee made his way carefully. With the Henry at the ready, he had no plans for using the weapon unless he was discovered and forced to fight for his life. He heard their laughter before he was able to discover the reason for it. Big Bear had been stripped to the waist, his wrists bound to slender pines on either side of him. A man with a doubled lariat stood behind the Sioux, slashing his bare back. While Pawnee cared little what became of Big Bear, it rankled him to observe a man—any man—bound and beaten like a *perro*. Even a hated Sioux should be allowed to die with honor. It became a temptation not to raise the Henry and kill the man wielding the lariat, but such a foolish act wouldn't save Big Bear, and it might well cost Pawnee his life. Swiftly he made his way back to his horse. These men and their shameful act must not go unpunished. When Pawnee rode in at a fast gallop, Siringo and the rest of the outfit left their supper to hear what the Indian had to say.

"*Matar Grande Oso*," said Pawnee, pointing toward the east.

"Collins," Dutch said, "I need a horse. May I use yours?"

"Yes," said Collins.

"That bunch of varmints has killed or is about to kill Big Bear. There's a bunch of them, and I'll need some of you to ride with Pawnee and me."

"I'll go," Brace Weaver said.

"So will I," said Rusty Karnes.

In quick succession, Dent Wells, Levan Blade, Drago

Peeler, and Tally Slaughter joined the ranks, and led by Pawnee, the seven of them rode out.

"God," Jules Swenson said, "I hope they don't get themselves kilt over that Sioux."

"Anybody else, maybe," said Whit Sanderson, "but not Dutch Siringo. The rest of us would be ridin' with him, but we can't all leave camp."

"Mr. Siringo is a most remarkable man," Haskel Collins said. "Back in St. Louis, I've heard it is the destiny of every white man to kill Indians."

"Only if them Indians is tryin' to kill you," said Whit Sanderson. "You'd best take most of what you was told back in St. Louis and chunk it down a bog hole."

Christie Beckwith looked at Collins and laughed, and while he didn't respond, he didn't seem displeased.

Pawnee reined up far enough away that none of the horses were likely to nicker and reveal their presence. The Indian led the way to the point from which he had observed the camp. Big Bear slumped forward, obviously on his feet only because of the ropes binding his wrists. It seemed the men had grown tired of beating the Sioux, for they hunkered about the fire, smoking and drinking from tin cups. The moon had begun to rise, and with the starlight and the fire, most of the miners were visible.

"You in the camp," Dutch shouted, "you're covered. Cut the Indian loose."

"The Indian's dead," one of them shouted back. "He didn't have no sand at all."

"Emil Hankins," Dutch shouted, "this is Dutch Siringo, and I don't hold with murder."

"Murder, hell," Hankins shouted back, "he got what was comin' to him. We caught the varmint stealin' grub. Now you'd best ride back the way you come."

"Not until you cut the Indian loose," Dutch shouted.

"He's dead," Hankins shouted. "Ain't that so, Duckett?"

"If he wasn't, he is now," said Duckett. He fired twice,

the slugs slamming into the body of Big Bear.

Like an echo, Pawnee's Henry roared, and Duckett died on his feet. Hankins and his companions were taken by surprise, and before they could respond, Dutch spoke. "You're covered, Hankins. If just one more shot is fired, you're a dead man. Now all of you drop your guns. Drop them!"

Slowly they complied. Hankins spoke. "You ain't gettin' away with this, damn you. These hombres dug in along the Bitterroot is white men, and they won't take kindly to a bunch that guns down a white man over some no-account, thievin' Indian. I aim to see that they know all about you and the damn Indian that's ridin' with you. We'll be waitin' for you, and don't be surprised if we got us a vigilante bunch with some ropes, just waitin' to see justice done."

Dutch waited to hear no more. He mounted and rode west, his companions following in silence. Reaching camp, they found that Christie and Bonita had kept supper hot. There were no questions, for they knew Dutch would tell them after he and his companions had eaten. While he finished his coffee, he told them of Big Bear's fate and of Pawnee's angry response.

"That's exactly what Pawnee should have done," Bonita said. "It was a cruel thing they did to Big Bear, just because he was hungry."

"Do you suppose their word along the Bitterroot will harm us?" Collins asked.

"I doubt it," said Dutch. "They're going in with the intention of outbidding the bunch along the Bitterroot, and under those circumstances, I can't see them being welcome. Even if they do stir up trouble for us, I don't regret Pawnee gunning down the varmint that killed Big Bear. If he hadn't, then I would have. A man ceases to be a man when he compromises his principles."

"I'll stand behind you on that till hell freezes," said Hugh McCulloch.

There were shouts of agreement from his companions,

and when the excitement had died down, Dutch said, "We'll triple the guard from here on to the Bitterroot. While they may get there ahead of us and try to give us a bad name, I don't trust them not to come after us in the dark. This talk about turning the Bitterroot camp against us may be just to throw us off our guard. Don't any of you shuck anything but your hats, and keep your weapons ready."

During the night, while on watch, Dutch and Bonita talked.

"That was a fine thing you did, trying to rescue Big Bear."

"We were too late to help him, and we may have hurt our cause," Dutch replied, "but I don't hold with brutally murdering a man. Even a renegade Sioux. The time's coming when we're going to pay for senseless brutality toward the Indians, and it'll be hell for those of us hauling freight along the Bozeman."

"I believe even Haskel Collins can see that," said Bonita.

Come the dawn, Pawnee again rode west, and when he had found a suitable location for the night's camp, he rode on for another hour. Having observed the distant fires from the butte, he believed they were within a few miles of the Bitterroot. When he had ridden what he considered a second day's travel for the *carretas*, he reined up on a ridge. While it was late in the day for breakfast fires, in a camp of any size, there would be fire for other purposes. As repugnant as it was to him, where there were no squaws, men washed their own clothing and blankets. He waited, and his patience was eventually rewarded, for there was smoke from a single fire, and judging the distance, he decided he was not more than a few minutes from the Bitterroot diggings. It was something Siringo would want to know. He turned his horse, and at a fast gallop, rode back the way he had come.

"*Oro campamento,*" Pawnee said, when he reported to

Dutch. Pointing westward, he raised both hands, spreading his fingers. He then repeated the sign twice.

"Pawnee says we're thirty miles from the gold camp on the Bitterroot," said Dutch. "I reckon we can cover half that distance today. Tomorrow, after we've established our camp, some of us will ride in and spread the word that we're here."

"I'm not questioning your judgment," Collins said, "but as aggressive as these miners from the Bonanza have been, those from the Bitterroot diggings may be worse. They may ride out here immediately, without waiting for us to reach the diggings."

"I'm not sure that wouldn't be a good idea," said Dutch. "It would allow us to set up some kind of defense against any hell-raising. If Hankins and that bunch from Bonanza are as good as their threats, the Bitterroot miners will know we're coming. Unless you prefer to drive on to the diggings and take your chances, I recommend that when we establish our camp today, we plan on remaining there for as long as it takes to dispose of all your freight."

"I accept that proposal without question," said Collins. "I suspect there may be some violence, and if that be the case, then we will do as you have recommended in the past, meeting it at a time and place of our choosing."

"I applaud that decision," Hugh McCulloch said. "You have the makings of a frontiersman, Mr. Collins."

There were shouts of approval, and while Collins was modest enough not to respond, he was pleased. These were hard men, and winning them over meant a lot to him, but not nearly as much as the promise in Christie Beckwith's dark eyes.

"Let's be movin' out," Dutch said.

They again took the trail with the realization that they were nearing the end of it. The day was unseasonably warm, the sun shone from a clear blue sky, and there was promise of an early spring. Dutch noticed that Pawnee no longer rode ahead, and had his suspicions that the Indian

was observing their back trail. He was expecting retribution
from Hankins and his riders from the Bonanza diggings.
While Dutch shared his expectations, he doubted there
would be trouble until the wagons reached the camp on the
Bitterroot. Much would depend on how those miners along
the Bitterroot responded to the arrival of the men from Bonanza diggings. If Collins was right, and there was violence, Dutch could only hope that it was between the
miners from the competing camps. While he had sixteen
armed men, he could ill-afford to engage in a shooting fight
with the very men with whom Haskel Collins must trade.
Future trade in Montana Territory would depend upon their
reception here on the Bitterroot. They continued on, stopping only to rest the teams, cutting rest periods shy by a
few minutes. It was important that, after settling down for
the night, they had time to ride on to the Bitterroot for a
meeting with the miners. Long before they reached the end
of the day's journey, Pawnee again took the lead. Dutch
had no way of knowing whether Emil Hankins and his
bunch still rode their back trail, or if they had circled to
the north or south and were already on the Bitterroot, stir-
ring up trouble. Somehow he didn't believe they had made
good their threat, that Pawnee would have told him if the
miners no longer followed. It was a good sign, for if Hankins and his bunch hadn't ridden ahead to stir up trouble,
they weren't likely to be welcomed when they showed up
to compete for the goods in Collins's wagons. Pawnee
dropped back to within sight of the wagons, raising two
fingers. They were nearing the place they would settle
down for the night. It proved to be an arroyo that angled
off to the southwest, with a fast-running stream, probably
on its way to a confluence with the Bitterroot River. It was
a good location, with room to arrange the wagons as they
chose. Dutch reined up, jumped down from the box, and
began directing the other wagons into a single line beside
his own. It was a pattern that would allow Collins to work
from one wagon at a time, while each of the remaining

wagons could be secured by two men. When the teams had been unhitched, Dutch called all the outfit together, for it was time to decide who would ride in for an initial meeting with the miners.

"Collins," said Dutch, "we don't dare leave these wagons unprotected. I aim to take Pawnee and Tally Slaughter with me. Is there anyone in particular you'd like riding with you?"

"Yes," Collins said, surprising them all. "I'd like Hugh McCulloch and Christie Beckwith to ride with us."

"Then saddle the other buckboard horse for Christie," said Dutch. "Whit, I'll need to ride your horse."

"What about supper?" Bonita asked.

"Let it wait until we return," said Christie, "and I'll help."

"Yes," Dutch said, "do that, because we don't know how long we'll be gone."

Mounting up, the six of them rode out, Dutch and Collins in the lead. There was no conversation and no need for any, because they had no idea what kind of reception awaited them. It being near the supper hour, they drew the undivided attention of the camp. Half a hundred men came together, all of them armed. Dutch and his companions reined up, and Dutch spoke. "I'm Dutch Siringo, of Siringo Freight Lines. A few miles east of here, we have five wagonloads of trade goods. The owner of these goods is Haskel Collins, and he has something to say."

Collins stepped his horse forward, and Dutch admired the manner in which he was able to take control of the situation.

"Tomorrow," said Collins, "we will open up the wagons and auction off the contents to the highest bidders. There's hams, bacon, beans, coffee, dried apples, flour, sugar, and salt. There's hard candy, whiskey, coal oil, black powder, long handle underwear, shirts, Levi's, boots, and wool socks. There's buttons, blankets, matches, candles, sewing thread, needles, muslin, laudanum, cigars, Durham, and plug. There's a barrel of molasses for your flapjacks, and God knows what else that I've overlooked.''

There was a moment of silence, and somebody laughed. Suddenly they were all shouting and slapping their thighs with their hats. As the uproar subsided, one of the miners stepped forward and spoke. "I'm Virgil Pittman. Will you be bringin' the wagons in, or do you want us to ride out to 'em?''

"We'd like for you to ride out to them," said Collins. He looked at Siringo, and Dutch picked up the conversation.

"We have them positioned in a secure place," Dutch said, "because we're expecting some trouble from a group of men claiming to be from Bonanza.'' He quickly explained the situation, dwelling on the possibility that Emil Hankins and his bunch might seek to outbid the miners from the Bitterroot.

"It's our intention to defend ourselves and our goods," Collins added. "We don't take kindly to threats and intimidation.''

"By God," Pittman shouted, "we'll run them varmints out of the territory. Varner, you take a couple of men, ride around to the rest of the claims and tell every hombre in these diggings to drop what he's doin' and come a-runnin' with his gun.''

"Hold it," Dutch shouted. "We don't want shooting, if there's any other way. Some of you could die. If these varmints show up, there'll be twice as many of you as there will be of them. Put your dust together and outbid them.''

"That's it," said Collins. "We didn't tell you this because we want a fight, but so that you won't be surprised if they show up.''

"I have a suggestion," Dutch said, when they had quieted down. "A couple of you ride back with us, so you'll know where we are. Then, tomorrow at dawn, we'll open up the wagons for bids.''

Pittman and Varner rode out to the wagons, and after

satisfying themselves that all was as had been promised, returned to the Bitterroot.

"The worst of it should be over," Dutch said. "even if that bunch from the Bonanza shows up."

"Not necessarily," said Brace Weaver. "We're about to be blessed with another storm and more snow."

To the east there was a glow of a fire, evidence enough that the miners from Bonanza were there, waiting. While Dutch doubted that Hankins and his bunch would actually try to seize the wagons, he posted a double guard for the night. Far to the west, jagged fingers of golden lightning probed the darkened sky. Dutch, Collins, Hugh McCulloch, and Brace Weaver were standing watch.

"We're going to be so busy tomorrow, we won't have time to prepare for the storm," said Collins. "I'm wondering if we shouldn't wait until after the storm, before opening the wagons. What do you think, Siringo?"

"I think we should go ahead as planned," Dutch replied. "Open just one wagon at a time. I'll choose nine men, and we'll remain with you, while everybody else prepares for the storm. If Emil Hankins and his bunch become violent, we'll enlist the help of some of the Bitterroot miners. I aim to talk to them in the morning, before we do anything else."

"Good thinking, Dutch," said McCulloch. "I'd like to suggest that among those men assigned to the wagons include Pryor, Blackburn, Robb, Taylor, and me. We've worked the diggings ourselves, and we can relate to miners."

"I'm obliged," Dutch said. "Consider yourselves assigned. We want this sale conducted as fairly and with as much order as possible so that we'll be welcome when we return."

Not more than three miles east of Dutch Siringo's camp, the miners from the Bonanza diggings—their ranks swelled to more than a hundred men—had congregated. Hankins had sent several of the miners to watch the Siringo camp, and thus was aware that miners from the Bitterroot diggings had visited the wagons.

"In the mornin'," said Hankins, "we'll move in close enough to see what's goin' on, and when that bunch from the Bitterroot shows up, we'll be ready to move in. None of you pull a gun unless they start it. We're here because we're needin' supplies, not spoilin' for a fight."

But not all the Bonanza miners shared that sentiment. Lum Jarret and Os Borrum had been partners with Ike Duckett, whom Pawnee had shot after Duckett had killed Big Bear. Duckett, with a reputation for cruelty, hadn't been that well liked, and the rest of the miners—with the exception of Jarret and Borrum—had decided Duckett had gotten what he deserved. Now Jarret and Borrum were plotting a means of getting revenge for Duckett's death.

"We know them teamsters has got two women with 'em," said Jarret. "I been in this God-forsaken country fer nigh two years, an' I ain't even seen a woman, till now. I say we wait fer just the right time, an' snatch them two females. One fer you, one fer me."

"You're just beggin' fer a pair of nooses," Borrum said. "One fer you, one fer me."

"Not if it's done right," said Jarret. "Sure as hell, that storm will be rollin' in sometime late tomorrow night, and they'll be caught up in the sellin' of what's in them wagons until dark or after. I say we can grab them women and be in that cave in the foothills of the Absarokas before the storm blows in. After it's snowed fer an hour, they ain't a man alive that can track us. Now what are you scared of?"

"A thirteen-knot noose under my left ear," Borrum replied. "I've kilt a man or two, an' I got out of that, but I ain't never took a woman agin her will. That'll git a man hung, damn pronto."

"It never bothered Duckett none," said Jarret. "Ain't you as much a man as he was?"

"Duckett was a damn fool fer shootin' that Indian,"

Borrum said. "That's why they ain't nobody but you an' me cares a damn whether he gits avenged or not."

Jarret laughed. "Then think of it as fun fer you an' me. That claim's played out, and all the gold we're likely to git is in our saddlebags. The grass is already startin' to green, and when this comin' storm blows over, we got spring ahead of us. We can quit this territory."

"What do you aim to do with them women, after we've had our way with 'em?"

"We slit their throats," said Jarret, "an' leave 'em in that cave where they'll never be found. There's no way it can be proved agin us, an' after the snow starts, no way we can ever be trailed."

"I'll ride along," Borrum said, "but with or without you, when that storm passes, I'm quittin' the territory."

Dutch and his companions were having their breakfast while it was still dark, expecting the miners from the Bitterroot at first light.

"We'll need several more fires," said Collins. "I'm going to offer free coffee to any of the miners wanting it."

"There may be hundreds of them," Bonita said. "They'll have to drink out of their hats, because we don't have enough tin cups."

"I have plenty of them," said Collins. "For a price, of course. They'll need one for the whiskey, unless they have their own jugs or bottles."

That got Dutch Siringo's attention. "You aim to sell whiskey by the cup?"

"Why not?" Collins responded. "Unless, as Bonita suggested, they want to drink out of their hats. I figure five dollars per cupful."

"Then we're going to be operating a saloon from one of these wagons," said Dutch. "I thought we had agreed that everything goes to the highest bidder. Give me a good reason why that shouldn't include whiskey?"

"It can," Collins said smoothly, "as long as it's sold by

the barrel. That's fifty gallons and the bid starts at five hundred dollars. I believe most miners will be satisfied with just a cupful.''

"My God," said Whit Sanderson, "we could have five hundred men gathered here, and ever' damn one of 'em drunk as a coot.''

"I don't think so," Dutch said. "Collins, if you take to selling whiskey by the cupful, in two hours, it's going to be hell with the lid off. These men will lose all reason, overrun your wagons, and we'll be lucky to escape with our lives. The entire U.S. cavalry couldn't control them. Think, man.''

Every eye was on Haskel Collins. He swallowed hard before he spoke.

"Those are far-reaching consequences I haven't considered. Of course that would place us all in danger. How would you suggest I sell the whiskey?''

"By the barrel," said Dutch. "Raise your starting bid to seven hundred and fifty dollars. Several men can go in together and buy a barrel, and then resell it a cup at a time, after we're gone. How many barrels do you have?''

"Three," Collins replied. "A man without a wagon won't be moving one.''

"Then save the whiskey until last," said Dutch, "and we'll offer to haul it the rest of the way to the Bitterroot in one of our wagons. Is there anything else that might become a problem in the way that you intend to sell it?''

"Probably not," Collins said. "The flour, sugar, and molasses are in barrels. They can be bought by the barrel or portioned out in smaller amounts. I suppose I should speak to these men before we start, so that they can decide how many of them wish to bid together for what's to be sold in barrels.''

"By all means, do that," said Dutch. "Set a minimum bid on a barrel of flour, and let a dozen men pool their gold and bid on it. You lost the option of selling flour by the pound and whiskey by the cupful when you gave up the idea of building a trading post. I'd say it's going to push the hell out of us to empty these wagons before that building storm blows in here.''

"If I'm any judge," said Julius Blackburn, "it'll be snowin' like nobody's business well before first light tomorrow."

"That's what I'm expecting," Dutch replied. "Come dark, if we're still not finished, I'd say let's build as many fires as we need for light, and keep going. Now is there anything else we need to talk about before this medicine show begins?''

"Yes," said Hugh McCulloch. "You should tell them of all those human bones back yonder on the canyon rim and make your offer of grub and safe passage out of the territory for two hundred dollars per man."

"Damn right," Jules Swenson agreed. "We'll have plenty of room in the wagons for any belongings and gold. We won't be goin' nowhere until after this storm's done, and it'll give 'em time to make up their minds and get their things together."

"I'll tell them," said Dutch. "After I've done that, Collins, I want you to explain your starting bids and the need to sell barreled goods as they come—in barrels."

"Yonder comes that bunch from the Bonanza diggings," Tally Slaughter shouted, "and there's an almighty lot of 'em.''

His Henry rifle under his arm, Dutch walked toward the oncoming riders.

"Hello, the camp," Emil Hankins shouted. "We ain't lookin' for trouble. We're here to bid and buy. Are we welcome?''

"If you're willing to abide by the rules," said Dutch. "No hell-raising for any reason. If you lose to a higher bid, then you have no recourse. I'll shoot any hombre that pulls a gun. I aim to tell the bunch from the Bitterroot the same thing I'm tellin' you. Any of you allowin' your temper to override your better judgment will be told to vamoose. We won't accept your bid. Now is there anybody that don't understand, or don't think we're bein' fair?''

"That's fair," Hankins responded, "long as everybody gets the same treatment.''

"Here comes the bunch from the Bitterroot," Brace Weaver said.

Turning away from Hankins and the Bonanza miners, Dutch went to meet Pittman, Varner, and the men from the Bitterroot. He was astounded by their number. There had to be more than two hundred of them, and they seemed not to see Dutch. Every man was armed, and their eyes were on the miners from the Bonanza diggings.

CHAPTER 22

"*P*ut away the guns," Dutch shouted. "I'll shoot the first hombre that pulls iron. All of you that's here to bid and buy, you're welcome. The rest of you are welcome to ride back the way you came."

"Them varmints from Bonanza ain't welcome in our camp," a miner bawled.

"This ain't your damn camp," a Bonanza miner bawled back.

"This is neutral ground," Dutch shouted. "Keep it peaceful, and one of you is welcome as the next. We don't start the bidding until the lot of you pull in your horns and put the guns away."

Slowly, unwillingly, they complied. They crowded in as near the wagons as they could get, a dozen yards separating the two groups.

"Before we begin," said Dutch, "I have a proposition for you. Then Mr. Collins has a rule or two regarding some of the things you'll be bidding on."

Dutch waited until the grousing and grumbling died down and began by telling them of the human bones on the canyon rim.

"By God," a miner from the Bitterroot shouted, "that was Wilkierson an' McLean. They took their gold an' was quittin' the territory."

"They didn't make it," said Dutch, "and that's what the rest of you are facing. There's a way out of here, with your lives and your gold."

Quickly he told them of the proposal made by Hugh McCulloch, that a miner receive food and safe passage from the diggings for the sum of two hundred dollars. He asked Hugh McCulloch and his four companions to stand. McCulloch introduced himself and his four companions and told of their near-fatal experience with outlaws.

"That's why we come on to the Bitterroot with Siringo," said McCulloch. "We're paying two hundred a man for grub and passage to Kansas City. Any of you wantin' to leave the diggings alive and with your stake, this is your chance."

There was a roar of approval from the miners of both camps. Men waved their hats seeking to get attention, and Dutch waited until they were quiet. Then he spoke. "We'll be here until after the storm. Any of you who are interested in trailing with us will have time to make arrangements. We are seventeen strong, and we have an Indian scout. Whatever your feelings toward Indians, just remember that Pawnee is part of my outfit. He won't bother you if you don't bother him, and if you bother him, you'll answer to me. Now here's Haskel Collins to talk to you about the bidding."

Collins kept it brief, telling them of things which must be purchased in bulk, including the whiskey.

"A thousand in gold for a barrel of whiskey," somebody shouted.

"The whiskey goes last," said Collins. "That's to give us time to get out of the way before you all get snockered."

That drew some laughter, as the two camps got their minds off one another and began to focus on the event at hand. Collins had brought a scale to weigh the dust, and he began with the wagon containing many individual items of clothing and nonperishable food such as cured hams and sides of bacon.

"What am I bid for a ham?" Collins shouted.

"Twenty-five dollars!"

"Fifty!"

"A hundred."

Three hams quickly sold for a hundred dollars apiece to miners from the Bonanza, and not to be outdone, Bitterroot miners paid as much for three sides of bacon. Collins sold a hundred tin cups at five dollars apiece, and could have sold that many more. He had a huge galvanized washtub into which the gold dust was emptied, and he soon had to find a second container, for the tub had become so heavy it could hardly be lifted. Christie and Bonita had three fires going, with a coffeepot above each, for most of the miners who had bought a cup had done so to sample the coffee. Some of the miners—mostly those from the Bonanza diggings—didn't participate in the bidding. Two of these were Jarret and Borrum, and their eyes were on Christie and Bonita.

"By God," said Borrum, under his breath, "I'm startin' to like this idee more an' more. They sure ain't a pair of wore-out old squaws, but we can't take 'em while there's so many jaspers watchin' 'em."

"We wait till dark or near dark," Jarret said. "Best if they tap into a keg of that red-eye, an' ever'body gits a little drunk. We need some hell-raisin' goin' on, so's nobody's got time fer us. When it gits rough enough, they'll send them females out of harm's way, and that's when we take 'em."

Hugh McCulloch had a notebook and a stub of pencil, keeping a running total of the winning bids, and by the time the first wagon was empty, McCulloch whistled.

"How much?" Dutch asked.

"If I'm figurin' right," said McCulloch, "he's piled up more than eleven thousand, and there's four wagons to go."

"A dozen pair of wool socks, size twelve," Collins shouted. "What am I bid?"

"Five dollars a pair," came the response.

"Seven dollars."

"Ten dollars, and I want 'em all."

Dutch watched in amazement as the miners from Bonanza raised the bid on a barrel of molasses to twelve hundred dollars.

"My God," said Brace Weaver, shaking his head, "Collins won't have to bother makin' another drive. The varmint's gonna be rich when he leaves here."

Dent Wells, Levan Blade, Drago Peeler, and Tally Slaughter had spent the day snaking in firewood for the anticipated storm. By early afternoon, a chill wind had risen, and there was promise of worse to come. But nothing dampened the enthusiasm of the miners. While there had been no violence, there had been some hard words. And then Collins sold one of the barrels of whiskey for fifteen hundred dollars.

"Damn it," Dutch said, "you were supposed to hold the whiskey until last."

"This is the fourth wagon," said Collins, "and one of the three barrels of whiskey was in it. We're just one wagon away from being finished. Nothing can happen this late in the game."

But something could and did. The miners from the Bonanza diggings had bought the whiskey, and when they had manhandled it from the wagon, they tapped it on the spot. It was more than enough for them to get roaring drunk, which most of them promptly did. Next to whiskey, the most coveted item was tobacco, and while the Bonanza bunch was occupied with the newly acquired whiskey, the Bitterroot miners cleaned out Collins's supply of plug and Durham.

"That wasn't fair," one of the Bonanza crowd bawled, and he threw himself headlong into half a dozen Bitterroot men, who immediately clubbed him senseless. Had it not been for the effect of the whiskey, it might have ended there, but the miners from the Bonanza diggings were at the fighting stage on their way to an earth-shaking drunk.

They charged, a hundred strong, swinging fists and Colt revolvers.

"Christie, Bonita," Dutch shouted, "into the supply wagon."

The women wasted no time, as the fight escalated into a brawl such as nothing Dutch Siringo had ever seen. More than three hundred men struggled, cursed, kicked, and fought.

"What should we do?" Collins shouted.

"Stay the hell out of it," Dutch shouted back, "and hope nobody starts shooting."

But all the Bonanza miners hadn't thrown themselves into the fight. Lum Jarret and Os Borrum had taken refuge beyond the spring, where they could see what was going on, without being seen. Dutch had purposely moved the supply wagon well away from all the others. Jarret and Borrum had seen Christie and Bonita run toward the wagon, climbing into it. The front of the wagon faced the spring, and Jarret spoke. "By God, now's our chance. We kin git to 'em through that wagon, an' the horses is over yonder where we kin ride out without bein' seen."

"You're plumb crazy," Borrum grunted. "It won't be dark fer two hours. All one of them gals has to do is squall, an' that bunch will be on us like big red roosters after a pair of grasshoppers."

"Not if we wallop 'em upside the head with a pistol. Come on."

The two lit out for the supply wagon, on the run. The brawl between the miners from Bonanza diggings and those from the Bitterroot roared on. There was little that Dutch and his companions could do, except stay out of the way. Dutch had his hand on the butt of his Colt, tempted to fire into the air, but thought better of it. So far, there had been no shooting. A shot—from any quarter—might encourage gunplay among the brawlers themselves. Dead men from either faction would mean big trouble.

"My God," said Hugh McCulloch, "I've never seen

such a fight. How much longer can this continue?''

"I'm beginning to wonder," Dutch replied. "Even a damn drunk sobers up, if you slug him hard enough and often enough.''

Jarret and Borrum leaped to the wagon box and climbed over the provisions toward the women who leaned out through the wagon's rear pucker. Bonita was the first to notice the intruders, and before she could sound the alarm, Jarret had an arm around her throat. He hit her just above the right ear with the muzzle of his Colt and felt her go limp. But when Borrum got his hand over Christie's mouth, she bit him. He yelped in pain, and the girl was free of him, when Jarret slugged her with his Colt.

"Now git her on your shoulder an' let's go," Jarret growled.

Following his own advice, Jarret flung Bonita over his shoulder and lit out for the picketed horses. Shouldering the unconscious Christie, Borrum followed. But everybody's attention hadn't been focused upon the brawl. Pawnee's sharp eyes had caught Jarret and Borrum fleeing from the supply wagon. But the Indian had been watching from a distant rise, and the multitude of struggling men was between him and the pair who had stolen Bonita and Christie. Pawnee's horse was with the rest of the horses and mules, and Pawnee struck out on foot, gripping his Henry. There was no time to alert anyone else to what was taking place, and the Indian ran on, until he was within rifle range. But he dared not fire, lest he shoot one of the abducted women. He could see their picketed horses, and he paused, prepared to shoot when they released the women. But Jarret and Borrum did not lay down their burdens until they could use the horses for cover. Pawnee ran on, but from his saddle boot, Jarret drew his own Henry. Once, twice, three times, he fired across his saddle. The first slug tore through Pawnee's left thigh, while the second ripped into his right shoulder, slamming him backward to the ground. The third shot sang over his head. Hoisting the women to their saddles, Jarret and Borrum rode away to the southeast, toward northern Wyoming Territory and the Absarokas.

The ruckus had begun to subside, as some of the fallen miners failed to get up. The chill wind was still from the west, and it brought the sound of the three distant shots.

"Shots," said Dutch.

"Yeah," Tally Slaughter agreed. "From back yonder toward the Bitterroot."

"Get me a horse," said Dutch, "and then come with me. I reckon that's the trouble we've been expecting."

Slaughter caught up and saddled Whit Sanderson's bay, leading it back to Dutch. Dent Wells, Levan Blade, and Drago Peeler were already mounted.

"We'll ride along, if you want," Drago said.

"No," said Dutch, "not until we know what's happened."

They soon spotted Pawnee stumbling along, using the butt of his Henry for support. In an instant Dutch was beside the wounded Indian, who quickly told the story. Using his uninjured arm, he pointed southeast. He then spoke three words. "Squaws. *Dos* hombres."

"Tally," said Dutch, "help him up to the saddle with me."

Dutch mounted, and Slaughter lifted the wounded Indian up. Slaughter then mounted his own horse, and they rode back to the wagons. The battling miners battled no longer but glared at one another in confusion, those who were still on their feet. The rest of the outfit quickly turned their attention to Dutch, Slaughter, and the wounded Pawnee.

"Two men have taken Bonita and Christie," Dutch said. "Pawnee went after them, and he's been shot. Jules, I want you and Whit to see to him."

"Christie?" Collins shouted. "They took Christie?"

"Yes," said Dutch. "Tally and me are going after them."

"I'm going with you," Collins said.

"You'd better stay here," said Dutch. "You still have a

wagonload of freight and a fortune in gold."

"Damn the freight and the gold," Collins growled. "I'm going with you, whether you want me or not."

"Saddle up, then," said Dutch, "and fill your saddlebags with jerked beef. We don't have time for anything else. If we don't catch them before that storm hits, we never will."

"We'll dig in before the storm blows in," Hugh Mc-Culloch said, "and we'll see that nobody bothers the rest of the freight or the gold. Good luck."

Dutch and Tally stuffed their saddlebags with jerked beef, shrugged on their heavy coats, and with Collins following, rode back to where Jarret and Borrum had picketed their horses. The sun had vanished behind a band of gray clouds hovering on the horizon, while the wind had grown noticeably colder. Dutch studied the tracks of the horses for a moment and led out toward the south.

"We must catch up to them," said Collins desperately.

"This wasn't very well thought out," Dutch said. "The horses are carrying double, and they'll have to rest often. If the clouds will hold back for a while longer, we can follow them by moon and starlight."

They rode at a slow gallop, pausing only to rest the horses and be sure that they still followed the trail. The pair made no effort to conceal their tracks, obviously expecting the snow to do it for them.

"This is a damn fool thing to do," said Slaughter. "They must know there's a storm on its way, and they'll have to hole up. How far can they go, with just two horses?"

"After they've holed up from the storm and are ready to move on, I reckon they're not expectin' to need but two horses," Dutch said. "They'll kill Bonita and Christie."

"No," Collins shouted. "We must ride faster."

"Collins," said Dutch, "it's not going to help if we kill our horses or lose the trail. Now mount up and let's ride."

A few miles ahead, Jarret and Borrum had their hands full, for Christie and Bonita had regained consciousness. Their hands bound, the women sat in front of their captors and reviled them. Christie and Bonita struggled each time they were forced to mount, after resting the horses, buying a little time for the men they knew would be coming for them. After a particularly trying time, Jarret slapped Christie, and she laughed at him.

"Just you wait till we git where we're goin'," Jarret snarled. "Then we'll see just how much you feel like laughin'."

"When you take your britches off," said Christie savagely, "I look for that to be the biggest laugh of all."

She shrieked with laughter, and Bonita joined in. Jarret and Borrum rode on, silently cursing these women who didn't seem in the least afraid of them. The wind at their backs grew colder, and they turned their eyes toward the darkened heavens whence they knew the snow must soon fall.

Again Dutch and his companions had stopped to rest the horses, and as they looked toward the western horizon, a few frozen particles of snow stung their cheeks.

"These varmints must know of shelter somewhere in these parts," said Slaughter. "This is purely no time to go searchin' for it."

"I expect you'd be right," Dutch said. "As I recall, there was some mountains runnin' from northern Wyoming Territory into southern Montana."

"The Absarokas," said Collins.

"A man that's prospected these parts for a while might know of some caves," Dutch said. "He could likely find one of 'em in the dark, wait out the storm, and then quit the territory."

"My God," said Collins, "if we don't find them before snow falls, we'll never find them."

"Let's ride," Dutch said. "We don't have much more time."

Miles ahead, Jarret and Borrum were only too aware of the worsening weather, as the chill wind drove particles of snow under their hat brims and down the collars of their flannel shirts. When snow began to fall in earnest, all landmarks would disappear, and the world about them would become a sea of white.

"Yonder," Jarret shouted against the rising wind. "Ain't that the butte we're lookin' for?"

"God, I hope so," said Borrum, almost to himself.

They rode on until they passed the butte, riding across the high end of an arroyo. As they followed the east rim, they passed along the eastern face of the butte. Reaching the shallow end of the arroyo, they rode back along it until they reached the cavern beneath the butte. Suddenly they reined up, for the wind that whipped down the arroyo brought the distinctive smell of woodsmoke. Jarret and Borrum dismounted and drew their Colts. Rounding a pillar of stone, they came face-to-face with nine Indians.

"Don't shoot them," Bonita cried. "I know them. They're Crows."

The Indians looked at Bonita curiously, showing no sign of recognition, but it was the same nine who had spent three days in Siringo's camp, on the Little Missouri, eating everything they could get their hands on. They backed away, well beyond the fire, making no hostile moves.

"Stay over there, the lot of you," Jarret snarled. Holstering his Colt, he helped Bonita down from the horse.

"Now what'n hell are we goin' to do?" Borrum asked, after he had helped Christie to dismount. "How we goin' to have us a high old time, with these varmints watchin' us?"

"Shut up," said Jarret.

Christie laughed. "You two are *such* a disappointment. No man—or even an excuse for one—has ever had his way with me, while a bunch of Indians looked on. Can't you two do anything right?"

Borrum swung his fist at Christie, but she sidestepped it, kicking him in the groin. He doubled up, groaning, and some of the Indians laughed. Rattled, Jarret drew his Colt and stood there gritting his teeth in frustration.

"Untie my hands," said Bonita. "I want to sit by the fire."

Not knowing what else to do, Jarret freed her hands and then released Christie. The two women sat down by the fire, leaving Jarret and Borrum standing there facing the nine Indians.

"Now what?" Borrum asked, still breathing hard from Christie's well-directed blow.

"Hell," said Jarret, "set down with your back to the wall and wait. This storm's got to end sometime. When it does, these varmints will ride on. Then we'll have our fun."

"Like hell you will," Christie said angrily. "There's plenty more kicks where that one came from."

"You'll get some from me too," said Bonita. "When the storm lets up enough, the two of you had better ride out while you can. Dutch Siringo will kill you."

Jarret laughed, but it trailed off uneasily when Borrum failed to join him. Finally they all slept, not realizing that one of the Indians understood some English. It was he who had conversed as well as he could with Dutch Siringo, at the camp on the Little Missouri. The snow had already begun, but the Crow led one of the horses out into the arroyo. Mounting, he rode into the gathering storm, back toward the mining camp along the Bitterroot.

The snow had begun in earnest, and Dutch reined up, his companions alongside him. While they rested the horses, it was time for a decision.

"We've lost the trail," Dutch said, "and we don't stand a prayer of findin' our way back to the wagons. All we can do is look for a place to hole up and wait it out."

It was a hard decision, but Collins and Slaughter said nothing. Grimly, the three of them mounted and rode on, the storm growing in its fury.

The Crow Indian's name was Wolf Claw. He and the braves who accompanied him had only bows and arrows against the magic of the white men's weapons. The squaws had been bound, proof enough that they had been stolen away by their captors. Wolf Claw recalled the name, Siringo, from the camp on the Little Missouri. Would not Siringo and his men be riding in pursuit of their stolen squaws? But they would have lost the trail in the deepening snow, and without guidance they would never find the *malo hombres* who had taken their squaws. Surely Wolf Claw and his braves would be slaughtered, along with the squaws, unless Siringo found the cave. The Indian knew that the wagons were somewhere east of the Bitterroot, and it was in that direction that he rode. He reined up, thinking he had heard something over the roar of the wind, when his horse nickered. There came an answering nicker, seeming much closer than it was, because the wind carried it.

When his horse answered the faint nicker, Dutch Siringo reined up, with Slaughter and Collins beside him. Against the wind, the voice was faint.

"*Lobo Garra. Lobo Garra.*"

"*Amigos,*" Dutch shouted.

"Indian," said Slaughter. "Likely a Crow."

"We'll wait for him," Dutch said. "We have nothing to lose."

They saw the spotted pony first, for the Crow was swathed in blankets to protect him from the cold. He reined up, peering at them through the swirling snow. Then he spoke. "Sigh-reen-go? Sigh-reen-go?"

"I'm Siringo," said Dutch.

"*Lobo Garra,*" said the Indian. "*Malo hombres. Dos* squaw."

Dutch drew his Colt, pointing it into the darkness, the way Wolf Claw had come. The Crow understood. Turning his horse, he rode away, Dutch and his companions following. Wolf Claw reined up at the head of the arroyo. When he dismounted, Dutch, Slaughter, and Collins stepped down. Already out of the snow and howling wind, the Indian left his horse. Dutch and his companions left their mounts, and the four men proceeded on foot. The Indians, aware of what Wolf Claw had in mind, had distanced themselves from the fire. Haskel Collins was the first to enter the cavern, and Christie cried out. It was enough to alert Jarret and Borrum, and they went for their guns. Dutch shot Jarret, but Borrum rolled away, and the shot fired hastily by Collins missed. But Tally Slaughter didn't miss.

"We were afraid you'd never find us," said Bonita.

"We wouldn't have," Dutch said, "if Wolf Claw hadn't come looking for us."

"Wolf Claw, thank you," said Bonita. The Crow had his head down, embarrassed.

"This is the same bunch that went through two weeks' grub in three days," Slaughter said. "I reckon we can call it square."

"Wolf Claw," said Dutch, "the next time you and your braves are hungry, just come lookin' for us." He offered his hand, and gravely, Wolf Claw took it.

Haskel Collins took Christie's hands in his, and when she finally was able to speak, her voice trembled.

"You left your wagons and your gold, to come looking for me?"

"Yes," said Collins. "A man must see to the important things first."

Two days later, when the storm had blown itself out, Wolf Claw and his braves rode away. Shortly afterward, Dutch Siringo and his companions rode toward the Bitterroot, Bonita and Christie mounted on the horses that had belonged to their abductors. Reaching the camp, they found Pawnee well on his way to healing, the remainder of the freight intact, and the collected gold secure.

"We promised them you'd auction off that last wagonload of goods, once the storm was past," said McCulloch. "They took a head count and found it was a couple of those

miners from the Bonanza diggings that stole away Bonita
and Christie, and the rest of them were so ashamed, they
pulled out. So I reckon that last wagonload will go to the
men along the Bitterroot.''

"What about those wanting safe passage out of the territory?'' Dutch asked.

"About a dozen from the Bitterroot diggings,'' said
McCulloch, ''and maybe half that many from Bonanza.
They aim to join us when we pass near their diggings on
the way back.''

"You said when we reached the Bitterroot, you were
going to find a preacher,'' Bonita reminded Dutch. ''Have
you given up on that?''

"Yes,'' said Dutch. ''On my marryin' day, I don't want
to sleep on the ground, look at a mule's behind, fight Indians, shoot wolves, or chop firewood.''

"How do you feel about that?'' Christie asked, her eyes
on Haskel Collins.

"I have learned never to question Mr. Siringo's judgment,'' said Collins, and while he didn't smile, everybody
else laughed, Dutch Siringo the loudest of all.

On the Bitterroot. March 8, 1864.

Following the storm, the weather turned mild again. With
all but the supply wagon empty, preparations were made
for the return trip to Kansas City. A dozen miners preparing
to quit the Bitterroot diggings, all armed with Henry rifles,
had stashed their gold in one of the wagons. Haskel Collins
had decided to keep the buckboard, and with the horses
taken from Jarret and Borrum, Dutch Siringo and Rusty
Karnes had mounts again.

"Thanks to you, Collins,'' Dutch said, ''we'll have
plenty of grub to see us back to Kansas City. That is, if we
don't spend any time with Wolf Claw and his braves along
the way.''

"You've taught me a lot, Siringo," said Collins. "Especially about Indians. While gold is a powerful ally, it will never replace kindness. It's a damned shame that men of your caliber can't be sent to Washington and put in charge of Indian affairs."

Dutch laughed. "That would never work. I'd give the Indians back their lands and put everybody else on reservations."

Still healing, but able to ride, Pawnee took the lead, followed by Dutch in the first big wagon. In the third wagon, Brace Weaver stood up, waved his hat, and shouted the sentiments of them all: "I been over the mountain and seen the bear, but by God, there wasn't none of it the equal of ridin' the high box north to the Bitterroot!"

EPILOGUE

❦

*T*he Bozeman Trail was named for John M. Bozeman, an American pioneer. Bozeman went to the Colorado gold fields in 1861, and to those in Montana Territory in 1862. He was killed by Indians in 1867.

During the years 1865–66, the United States government built Fort Reno, Fort Phil Kearny, and Fort C. F. Smith for the protection of travelers along the Bozeman Trail. But following the Fetterman Massacre (December 21, 1866) all the forts were closed. They were immediately burned to the ground by the Sioux.

Henry Plummer, outlaw sheriff, was born in Connecticut in 1837, and hanged January 10, 1864, in Bannack, Montana. Plummer was convicted of several murders, managing to break jail, and in 1862, moved his operations to the rich gold fields of Bannack, Montana. Outwardly, he dealt faro for a living, but after running the city marshal out of town, he took the office for himself. Plummer's huge band of desperadoes called themselves ''The Innocents,'' and preyed on stagecoaches, payrolls, and miners who had struck it rich. The gang identified themselves with secret handshakes and neckerchief knots, and their password was ''I am innocent.'' During the first few weeks of 1864, vigilantes hanged more than twenty of ''The Innocents,'' including outlaw Sheriff Henry Plummer. Ironically,

Plummer was hanged on a gallows he had built himself. The vigilantes ignored his pleas for mercy, and when he begged for time to pray, he was told to "pray on the scaffold. . . ."

TERRY C. JOHNSTON
THE PLAINSMEN

THE BOLD WESTERN SERIES FROM
ST. MARTIN'S PAPERBACKS

COLLECT THE ENTIRE SERIES!

SIOUX DAWN (Book 1)
92732-0 _____ $5.99 U.S. _____ $6.99 CAN.

RED CLOUD'S REVENGE (Book 2)
92733-9 _____ $5.99 U.S. _____ $6.99 CAN.

THE STALKERS (Book 3)
92963-3 _____ $5.99 U.S. _____ $6.99 CAN.

BLACK SUN (Book 4)
92465-8 _____ $5.99 U.S. _____ $6.99 CAN.

DEVIL'S BACKBONE (Book 5)
92574-3 _____ $5.99 U.S. _____ $6.99 CAN.

SHADOW RIDERS (Book 6)
92597-2 _____ $5.99 U.S. _____ $6.99 CAN.

DYING THUNDER (Book 7)
92834-3 _____ $5.99 U.S. _____ $6.99 CAN.

BLOOD SONG (Book 8)
92921-8 _____ $5.99 U.S. _____ $6.99 CAN.

BEFORE THE LEGEND, THERE WAS THE MAN...

AND A POWERFUL DESTINY TO FULFILL.

On October 26, 1881, three outlaws lay dead in a dusty vacant lot in Tombstone, Arizona. Standing over them—Colts smoking—were Wyatt Earp, his two brothers Morgan and Virgil, and a gun-slinging gambler named Doc Holliday. The shootout at the O.K. Corral was over—but for Earp, the fight had just begun...

WYATT EARP

MATT BRAUN

WYATT EARP
Matt Braun
_____ 95325-9 $4.99 U.S./$5.99 CAN.